GLIMPSES OF PARADISE

NOVELS BY JAMES SCOTT BELL

Circumstantial Evidence
Final Witness
Blind Justice
The Nephilim Seed
The Darwin Conspiracy
Deadlock
Breach of Promise
Sins of the Fathers
Glimpses of Paradise

SHANNON SAGA*

City of Angels
Angels Flight
Angel of Mercy

THE TRIALS OF KIT SHANNON

A Greater Glory
A Higher Justice
A Certain Truth

NONFICTION

Write Great Fiction: Plot & Structure

*with Tracie Peterson

JAMES SCOTT BELL

A NOVEL

GLIMPSES OF
PARADISE

BETHANY HOUSE
MINNEAPOLIS, MINNESOTA

Glimpses of Paradise
Copyright © 2005
James Scott Bell

Cover design by David Carlson
Cover photo: Sasha, Getty Images

Unless otherwise identified, Scripture quotations are from the King James Version of the Bible.

Published by Bethany House Publishers
11400 Hampshire Avenue South
Bloomington, Minnesota 55438

Bethany House Publishers is a division of
Baker Publishing Group, Grand Rapids, Michigan.

Printed in the United States of America

Library of Congress Cataloging-in-Publication Data

Bell, James Scott.
    Glimpses of paradise / by James Scott Bell.
      p. cm.
    Summary: "This historical epic spins a story of war, murder, faith, romance, and drama from small-town Nebraska in the early 1900s to French battlefields of World War I to postwar Hollywood"—Provided by publisher.
    ISBN 0-7642-2648-7 (pbk.)
    1. Hollywood (Los Angeles, Calif.)—Fiction. 2. World War, 1914–1918—France—Fiction. 3. Nebraska—Fiction. I. Title.
    PS3552.E5158G58   2005
    813'.54—dc22   2004027881

To the memory of

ARTHUR AND DOROTHY BELL

"Padre" and "Mama Dot" were early residents
of Hollywood, hard workers, my loving grandparents.
Mama Dot taught me about God when I was young.
Padre's constant encouragement was "Go your best."
Padre had a favorite poem that he had framed
in the early 1920s. It now hangs in my office.

❦

THE VICTOR

A toast to the man who dares
No matter how dead his trade;
Who can win his luck
By his own good pluck
When the rest of the world is afraid.

Another to him who fights
When the trade is a whirlwind lure,
And who jumps right in
With a will to win,
Though rivals are plenty and sure.

So here's to the man who dares,
Though fortune blow low, blow high,
And who always knows
That the conquest goes
To the man who is ready to try.

—Author unknown

JAMES SCOTT BELL is the bestselling author of *The Trials of Kit Shannon* series as well as several contemporary thrillers. He is a winner of The Christy Award for excellence in Christian fiction and is currently fiction columnist for *Writer's Digest* magazine. He and his wife, Cindy, live in Los Angeles.

Visit the author's Web site at *www.jamesscottbell.com*.

PART I

AMERICAN DREAMERS

What a lot of things we have to add to make our comfort, to make our work easier, to give more pleasure in life: electricity, motor-cars, telephones, motion pictures, better, cleaner and finer foods. Sanitation may always have been known, but it wasn't much practiced. The open bin whence coffee was scooped did not improve the flavor nor retain the aroma. Folgers Golden Gate coffee in flavor-tight tins shows the progress of the age in its demand for better foods.

—*Newspaper ad, 1916*

The Germans have recently announced that the losses in the Prussian army since the war began amount to upward of 2,235,000. That means that the military forces of the German army have lost close to 4,000,000 out of the 8,500,000 troops they have put into the field. From this time on Germany's strength and resources are bound to diminish by comparison with those of the allies, unless the latter blunder even worse than they have already done.

National Editorial Service, January 4, 1916

‖ 1 ‖

"You are a wet blanket, Doyle Lawrence. A wet blanket and a fake and I won't stay here a moment longer."

"All I said was it is disreputable. I didn't mean anything else by it."

Doyle hated the pleading tone in his voice. But Zee Miller always seemed to play him to just this point. She was infuriating.

He fought for vocal control. "You can't argue with what I'm saying. It's irrefutable. It's logic."

"Oh, quit trying to sound like your father." Zee leaned her head back on the blanket, spread out on the green grass of Zenith Central Park. In the twilight Doyle saw the half smile of mockery on Zee's face—the smile that always both angered and captivated him.

At least she made no move to leave. That was a relief. Doyle never knew what Zee Miller was likely to do next. Which, he had to admit, was one reason he was smitten with her. Every other girl in town seemed ensnared in custom, like butterflies preserved in resin. They looked beautiful but no longer flew. Zee was the one girl who took wing. The only trouble was he never knew which direction she'd fly.

"You're not a lawyer yet," Zee said to the sky. Her burnished blond hair unfurled in a wild expanse. She wore it down whenever she was away from her father's gaze. "Why can't you just speak from the heart?"

Doyle waved his hand, the way he'd seen his father do it a million times. It was a Lawrence trademark, a physical dismissal. Being one of the richest families in town bestowed upon them, at least according to the Lawrences themselves, a certain position of social authority.

"Piffle. The heart is for dreamers, not men of the world."

"Piffle yourself." Zee sat up, her slender sixteen-year-old figure showing the first blossomings of young womanhood in a way Doyle could not ignore. Zee wore her co-ed cardigan sweater unbuttoned, with a white lace shirtwaist underneath. "I took first place in the dramatic readings last year, as a junior. And we competed with five other high schools. I will do it, I tell you, and if you try to talk me out of it again I won't speak to you anymore."

"But, Zee, moving pictures are frivolous things, a toy. A diversion. It's not anything that's going to contribute to society."

"And don't you think those are real people in them? Do you think Francis X. Bushman is a ghost? Mary Pickford? Lillian Gish?"

The smell of river birch trees wafted over them in the warm breeze. Nebraska was hot this time of year, especially in the southeast. The Zenith of 1916 was a growing metropolis situated smack-dab in the middle of a cluster of rural settlements representing various nationalities. To the south were the Germans, to the east the Hollanders, and the north was dominated by Swedes. The city was also in the rain belt of the Mississippi Valley, resulting in a moderately humid climate. But the June nights had been pleasant for the last week, prompting boys to ask girls out for strolls and picnics in the park by the river.

The band shell in the middle of the park stood sentry. Soon porch lamps would be lit and the town would put on its evening face. And Doyle Lawrence would still be mesmerized by Zenobia Miller.

"Haven't you heard of *Intolerance?*" Zee wrapped her arms around her knees.

"Yes," Doyle said. "I'm against it."

"You can be flippant if you want to, but it is a work of art. A motion picture is a work of art! Can you get that into your legal mind? The movies are only going to get better and better. I am going to be part of that."

"You just want to kiss Francis X. Bushman."

"And unlike you, I'll bet he knows how to kiss."

Mocking him again! She was so good at it. No one could get his goat like Zee.

She kept her eyes, indigo and luminescent, locked on his. She turned her head up slightly. He knew it then—she wanted him to kiss her. Take her in his arms, put his mouth on hers. For a second he thought he might. But a boy didn't kiss a girl unless he intended to marry her. And, having never kissed a girl, he was not sure how.

He'd seen it done in the movies, yet it left questions unanswered. Should he keep his lips soft or tense them up? How long should he stay? Who should break away first?

Doyle told himself to stay calm. He could easily feel like a bee in a jar when he was around Zee. With an insouciant cock of his head,

Doyle said, "Fast woman! Pretty soon you'll be cutting your hair and wearing rouge."

Zee did not back down. "Don't think I won't. As soon as I can I'm going to Hollywood, and you'll see what happens."

"I know what happens to girls who go to the big city. You'll be dressed in rags and selling flowers before too long."

The next thing Doyle Lawrence felt was a hard fist to his shoulder. Zee had quite a punch. Always had, ever since they were kids. She was tougher than most of the boys, could run faster and climb better than any dozen of them.

"You're not just a fake," Zee said. "You're hateful. Why don't you go and spread your applesauce somewhere else?"

"Zee, why must you be so difficult?"

"Why must you be so dull? Don't you ever just want to run away from this old town?"

"Sure. All the way to Omaha."

"That's just what I thought you'd say. That's what I'm going to call you from now on. Old Omaha. That's where you'll end up, you know. In some stuffy old office with a bunch of stuffy old lawyers."

"What's wrong with that? You against success or something?"

"Stupid! I'm against shutting yourself up to life." She got on her knees so she could spread her arms out wide. "There's a world out there way beyond Omaha."

"I can think of worse things than living in Omaha."

"What about your poetry?"

For some reason, he'd known she would bring that up. Zee had what his mother had derisively called an "artistic temperament." He didn't have it, his mother told him, but he'd never quite believed it as an absolute. There was a bit of the poet in him.

Which made him something of a curiosity around the high school campus—a star athlete who wrote the occasional lines of verse. In truth, it was the one thing he did that wasn't expected of him, which was why he liked it.

"There's no money in poetry, silly," Doyle said.

"Must everything be for money?"

"Yes, or else it is frivolous."

"Is frivolous so bad?"

"Of course it is."

"I hate you, Doyle!"

And suddenly Zee Miller was on her feet, flying across the grass, leaving her shoes behind.

"Zee!"

Her shadowy form darted, like a restless apparition, through the falling darkness. And for a moment Doyle Lawrence felt as if life itself were fleeing him, or a promise of life, and that if he didn't get it back it would be the saddest loss he'd ever suffer, even if he lived to be ninety.

He shot to his feet. "Zee!"

The shadow disappeared.

He ran, almost desperately, after her.

"Where are you?" Doyle stumbled over a tree root. The indignity, as much as the stagger, made his face hot. In his lace-up Oxfords he felt like a clod, not the terror of the gridiron. Lightning Lawrence, as the Zenith High School *Clarion* called him, was now reduced to tottering lapdog.

"Hey!"

Only silence, and the soft susurration of the river, returned. He circled the trunk of the tree that had ingloriously caused his stumble.

"This isn't funny!" Doyle shouted.

"Hark, I hear someone. Who could it be?"

The voice came from above.

Doyle looked up and saw two bare feet dangling from a tree limb. Even with Zee's athleticism, getting up in a tree that fast was an astonishment.

"Come on out of there, Zenobia Miller." He knew she hated being called by her full name.

"Sounds like the voice of a wet blanket. I didn't know wet blankets could talk."

Doyle removed his coat. "You want me to come up there and get you down?"

"Do wet blankets climb trees?"

"Just watch me." Kicking off his shoes, leaving only his socks, Doyle hoped she'd see he was in earnest and call him off.

Instead, she giggled, and he saw her reach her arm up toward the sky. It was a gesture of such verve and confidence it froze Doyle in place. The audacity of it! She had no fear of falling, no fear of anything it seemed. Least of all his pursuit.

Electricity rushed through Doyle and he began to climb.

Still laughing, Zee pulled herself up to the higher limbs.

And Doyle Lawrence thought, *I am climbing up a tree after a girl half the town thinks is crazy. What is wrong with me? If Father saw me now, he'd put me in a booby hatch!*

"Give up, Doyle. You'll never catch me. Never."

"When I do, I'll break your neck."

"Oh, the big strong man." Her voice was like a siren's. It drove Doyle into a sudden, crazed frenzy of clutching at branches and kicking out for footholds. No girl was going to make a monkey out of him. Yet here he was climbing like one.

He started laughing. Whatever the consternation she caused, it was fun being with Zee. Then the branch he thought was in front of him was not.

Down he fell, reaching out, grabbing at anything, clutching nothing, something sharp hitting him in the ribs. He lost breath. He got his hand around a limb for a second, breaking what might have been a fall on the head. Instead he righted himself and landed on his right ankle. Searing pain coursed through his leg.

He rolled on the ground, half hurting and half indignant that he'd fallen right under the nose of Zee Miller.

She dropped out of the tree next to him, landing softly, like a cat. "Doyle, are you hurt?"

"No."

"Liar."

"Thank you." He locked his jaw against the pain.

"That's what you get for calling me Zenobia. Come on, then." She reached down to help him up.

He smacked her hand away. "I don't need your help." He kept silent as he got to his feet. He almost fell back down as the pain exploded afresh in his ankle.

Zee took his arm. "You did get hurt!"

"I can walk." He pulled his arm away and went to fetch his coat and shoes. Each step was a new experience in agony. All those football games and never a broken bone. Now this! From chasing a girl who was mocking him!

"Just run along home," he said.

"No."

"Go on—"

"Button your mouth, Omaha," she said, taking his arm again. This time he didn't resist.

‖ 2 ‖

"I'm going to marry her, Rusty."

The Lawrence brothers shared a bedroom, even though there was no need. Two other rooms in the house would have done nicely for either of them, but Russell Lawrence had always wanted to be near Doyle, ever since he was a child. Three years younger than his brother, Rusty could sometimes be a nuisance. But Doyle liked having him around. Rusty was funny and smart beyond his years, almost like one of Doyle's own high school friends.

They often talked in the darkness, their hands laced behind their heads, gazing out the large second-story window that looked down on Cherry Street. Many a time they'd played ball in that street. Football, baseball, even basketball with a knotty oak limb substituting for the goal.

"C'mon," Rusty said. "Not that strudel."

"You shut up with that talk or I'll give you a knuckle shampoo."

"That's what they say about her."

"Who?"

"The fellas."

Doyle rolled over on his side and propped his head on his hand. "Listen to me, Rusty. People talk all the time, and most of the time they're stupid about it. They don't know Zee like I do. I'll admit she's a little different."

"She has a loose fitting." Rusty tapped his head with his index finger.

"She just sees things differently than most. That's not crazy."

"Seems like it."

"Some of the most famous people in the world were thought to be crazy. Old Tom Edison, they thought he was crazy. And look what we've got. Lights and phonographs and movies and all kinds of things. And Alexander Graham Bell. Nobody thought you could talk to somebody clear across the country through a wire. Now we can't keep quiet."

"So what's Zee Miller gonna invent?"

"It doesn't have to be an invention. It can just be the way you see things."

"I don't get it, Doyle."

"It's like this. You know those poems I write?"

"Sure. I like 'em."

"You and about two other people. But I don't write them for other people. I write them for me. It makes me feel like I've got something all to myself. I don't know if they're any good, but they're mine. Most folks would probably think I've got a loose fitting if they saw them. They're about oceans and places I haven't even seen yet."

"I like the ones that don't rhyme."

"You like those?"

"Yeah."

Doyle smiled, feeling good about that. He especially loved free verse. Like Walt Whitman. He had an edition of *Leaves of Grass* with Whitman's signature in it.

"Does Zee Miller write poetry?"

"Zee wants to be an actress," Doyle said.

"An actress! Dad's not going to be happy about that."

"Dad's got nothing to say about it."

"Hey, you can't be serious. You can't go against Dad on something like that." Rusty's voice was full of the respectful fear the two boys had for their father.

"I'm almost eighteen, Rusty, and I'm going off to college. I've got to start standing on my own two feet."

"Are you in love with her, then?"

Funny, but the idea of love—the love described by the poets and the dime novels—had not really crossed Doyle's mind. It was more like a compulsion. A feeling that he and Zee Miller had been created for each other, and there was just no getting around the fact.

"You're too young to be asking about love," Doyle said, ducking the question.

"Says you. But what's Betty gonna say?"

Betty was Elizabeth Warren, daughter of the most prominent doctor in town, and everyone sort of understood she and Doyle were going to get engaged. Everyone but Doyle. He liked Betty, all right. She was beautiful to be sure, the best-looking girl in Nebraska maybe. He had taken her to the school dance two years in a row, and that got the tongues wagging. But there was something missing in her. She didn't like poetry, for one thing.

"Betty's a good kid; she won't have any problems."

"Sid Cromwell says she told his sister that you as much as said you'd give her a ring this summer."

"The liar."

"So when are you going to do it?"

"Do what?"

"Ask Zee."

Doyle got gooseflesh at the prospect. Yes, he'd actually have to ask her if he wanted to marry her. She wasn't just going to waltz up to him and offer herself. But what if she should say no? He'd be humiliated. The whole town would probably find out that he'd made a fool of himself over Zee Miller.

But she couldn't say no. She wouldn't. Somehow, some way, they were meant to be together.

‖ 3 ‖

Zee finished feeding the chickens out back. It was her morning duty to keep up the modest fowl that brought in extra money. Even though her father had only her to care for now, his income at the church was barely enough to scrape by.

She came back into the house, kicking poultry dust off her worn lace-up shoes. The screen door, nearly coming off its hinges, slapped the doorjamb.

"Time for school," her father called out from the front room. "Mind you're not late again."

Zee grabbed her books, bound in a leather strap, and took a deep breath. She was going to ask him, and she'd have to play it very carefully if there was going to be any chance at all of his saying yes. She came to him at his desk, where he was hunched over an open Bible.

"When was the last time you got out for a little fun, Pop?"

His deep-set eyes looked more tired than usual. "Please don't call me that. You know I don't like it."

Since the death of her mother three years before, a curtain had fallen between father and daughter, where once there had been only a veil. And behind that curtain she sensed they were drifting further apart. Like an ice floe on a frozen river, she was breaking away from the solid assurance of her father's authority.

She did not want to hurt him, but nothing she did was right by him anymore, especially since she'd started high school. He wanted to keep an eye on her every move, and she was suffocating.

Zee kept her voice bright. "What say we go out for ice cream tonight? And then, I think—"

"We haven't got money for that type of indulgence."

"It's my treat! I've been working for Mrs. Mariner after school, remember? Dusting, cleaning. She likes me. I've got a little bit of money saved up."

"That money would go well toward household expenses."

She knelt by the chair and put her hand on his arm. "Pop, you've got to have some fun every now and then."

"If you call me that one more time, I shall get angry. And I do not want to get angry with you today. I've had enough anger for a month."

She wished he would never get angry with her; only that was a fairy tale. She loved him, but they were cast from different molds. Zee knew that despite his best intentions he would never understand her.

He had been in rather robust health most of his life. Then when Zee's mother died, something came out of him that had never been replaced. His hair had whitened considerably over the last three years. His large, muscular arms, which used to toss Zee up in the air when she was a little girl, seemed half the size they once were.

"Listen, Father. After dinner we can walk down to the ice cream parlor, have a dish, and then go see how a great American president saved the union."

"What are you talking about?"

She spoke quickly. "There's a two-reeler about Abraham Lincoln at the Palace. It's history! Mr. Battle was telling us about it in class. He didn't say we *had* to go see it, but he did say we might write about it if—"

"Out of the question." Reverend Lemuel Miller shook his head. "You know how I feel about the motion pictures."

"There's nothing wrong with going to the movies."

With a heavy sigh, her father took her hand. "Child, you still do not understand many things. I am a moral authority for my flock. What if someone should see me going into a picture house, eh? What if that sort of talk got around?"

Zee looked at the floor, knowing it would be of no use to talk further. What it all came down to, every time, was what *other* people might think. Especially about her. A minister's daughter couldn't be seen so much as sneezing wrong lest "talk got around."

Her father let go of her hand. "Where were you yesterday evening?" he asked.

"I was here with you eating supper."

"Before supper."

"At Mrs. Mariner's, working."

"Don't lie to me. I cannot abide your lying."

"But, Father, I was at Mrs. Mariner's. You can even ask her."

"I did. I called her on the telephone after you went to bed. She said you left around five o'clock. Since you did not come home until seven-thirty, there is some time unaccounted for. You only told me that you had been at Mrs. Mariner's. Where were you before you came home?"

"Oh, I was just talking with someone in the park. I didn't think it was important to mention."

"With whom were you talking?"

"Just a friend from school."

"Does this friend have a name?"

"Yes."

"Stop being difficult. Who was it?"

"Doyle Lawrence."

With a look of disappointment, Reverend Miller said, "You were alone in a park with a boy, and a Methodist at that."

"Pop . . . Father, he's a classmate."

"You're not to be out with boys alone, is that understood? In fact, it would be best if you did not go out by yourself at all."

"But—"

"You get off to school now. And you come right home after Mrs. Mariner's."

In a foul mood, Zee took her time walking to school. She didn't really care when she got there. She was tired of school, of looking like a girl from the other side of the tracks.

She was wearing, for the third time that week, a sailor middy dress. Her father got them out of the Sears catalog because they were a dollar eighty-nine each, made of practical cotton and easily washable. They also covered her up like a sack of potatoes.

She kicked a rock and it thudded against a telephone pole. She looked closer and saw that a handbill was tacked to the pole.

Summer Stock Auditions

All Types Needed
All Welcome
2 P.M. Saturday
Zenith Central Theater

A small spark of excitement ignited inside Zee. It was quickly put out by the chill of reality. *What good would that do me? Father would never allow it.*

She thought a moment. *If I do get a part in a summer production, at least I'll be out of the house. Pop might enjoy the peace.*

She ripped the handbill down, folded it, and put it in the pocket of her dress.

‖ 4 ‖

Doyle's father, Wallace Edgar Lawrence, slipped a cigar from his vest pocket and used a gold clipper to cut off the end. Doyle watched the familiar evening ritual. The supper dishes had been cleared after a particularly satisfying pot roast, courtesy of Cook, and now the family was gathered in the library to partake of Mr. Lawrence's favorite pastime—puffing and pontificating, setting up a colloquy through a haze of smoke.

His father's name was, as the *Zenith Herald* once put it, "written high on the keystone of Nebraska's legal arch." He had earned his Master of Laws degree from the University of Nebraska in 1895, and after settling in Zenith—and marrying the former Adelaide Faulkner of Polk County—began a rapid rise in the legal profession. His partnership with Arnott C. Ricketts, under the firm name of Lawrence and Ricketts, lasted until 1906 when by mutual agreement the partnership was dissolved.

Wallace Edgar Lawrence then opened his own office. He was admitted to practice before the United States Supreme Court in 1907, where he was counsel on the case that made his name, *Shirk v. Griggs*, a case that established the power of the state of Nebraska over the title to lands lying within its borders. He was urged to run for Congress after that, yet he was content to build a family as well as a fortune.

"Wilson is too smart to get us involved overseas," Mr. Lawrence said. "He has told us time and time again that we are going to remain strictly neutral. He's a smart man. He knows that under international law we may sell war materiel to anyone without taking sides. If we play this right, America will be much more prosperous as a result."

Doyle's mother sat, as usual, in deferential silence, knitting. Doyle's ten-year-old sister, Gertie, did the same. The female wing of the Lawrence clan would usually remain for the first half hour or so, ensconced on the walnut three-seat sofa under the portrait of Granddad Lawrence, then quietly leave the males to continue what Mr. Lawrence referred to as "meaningful discussions," which was what Mr. Lawrence called the mostly one-sided colloquies.

"What about doing what's right?" Doyle said. He realized this was the first time he'd stepped up to the rim of his father's ethics and questioned them.

"And what does right have to do with us?" Mr. Lawrence said. "We are not involved in this conflict."

Doyle was ready. "The French and the Belgians didn't invade themselves in fourteen. The *Lusitania* didn't sink itself. Those things are wrong."

"Therefore it follows that we should get involved in a foreign war?"

"The Germans killed a hundred twenty-eight Americans on the *Lusitania*. I would say that's a little bit of involvement."

Mr. Lawrence waved his cigar, creating a thin stream of smoke. "I'll remind you, Doyle, that a sarcastic tone won't get you very far in an argument."

"I'm only saying—"

"Do you understand? You talk like that in a court of law and the judge may issue a contempt citation. I don't know what's come over the young people in this town."

"Dad, I don't think a strongly held opinion is wrong. And if I want to say it in a convincing way—"

Mr. Lawrence held up his hand for silence. "You will speak in a respectful tone, young man. You must learn to defend a position without rancor."

"Give me a chance and I will."

Peering at him through a gray haze, Mr. Lawrence seemed on the verge of one of his bouts of anger. Doyle had seen that look many a time, had felt the sting of his rebuke often. But then, in what was a small victory for Doyle's emergence as a man, Mr. Lawrence nodded his approval to continue.

Doyle took a deep breath. "The Huns are violating all manner of civilized conduct. They bomb civilian locales. They used poison gas at Yepres. Poison gas, Dad!"

"The fact remains they are not at war with us. We are not at war with them. This happens all the time in world affairs. We can't go running off overseas every time there's some war going on."

"But how can we stand back when atrocities are committed? If we are to be the beacon of freedom for the world, as Teddy Roosevelt says, we cannot allow such things to happen to innocent people. It's not right."

Mr. Lawrence looked at his wife. "Our son has become a philosopher."

Mrs. Lawrence tried to smile.

"Pray tell," Doyle's father continued, "where does this notion of right and wrong come from?"

Doyle was taken aback. "Everyone knows what is right and wrong."

"Suppose the Germans feel that what they are doing is right?"

"It can't be."

"Why not?"

"Because they are killing innocent people."

"So?"

"So! It's . . . *wrong*." Doyle felt backed into a logical corner. His father had done it to him again.

"You see, son, what we are left with is very simple self-interest. That is all countries and people have. That means neutrality is the way we should go, in our role as a supplier. We can sell to the combatants. And, after the war is over, we'll still have commercial connections to all the parties. There is no reason to bother with vague notions of right and wrong."

Doyle shook his head, trying to jostle reason into his brain. "But that is putting money before principle."

"That, my boy, is a time-honored stratagem, the way of the world."

"If that's the way of the world, then I don't know if I want any part of it."

"Oh?" Mr. Lawrence put on his cross-examination face. Doyle had seen him do that in court on many occasions. It was a narrowing of the eyebrows coupled with a skeptical look—one that told the witness he was about to be skewered. "Then what part of the world do you expect to end up in? You can't write poetry and make a living."

Doyle felt his cheeks start to burn. His poetry was something private, a chance to reach down into his soul when he felt moved to. He was embarrassed that his father would bring it up now. Doyle folded his arms to keep his fists from banging on the chair arms.

His mother cleared her throat. "I think it might be time for checkers. Father, you and Rusty haven't played in—"

"I want to settle something," Mr. Lawrence snapped. "Doyle, I want to know if you were with the Miller girl yesterday."

Doyle swallowed. "Who told you?"

Mr. Lawrence's look was as hard as Pittsburgh steel. "I am going to overlook your disrespectful tone this time. This time, but not again. Is that clear?"

"Yes, sir." Doyle *had* been disrespectful. That he was avoiding his father's wrath was a momentary relief.

"As I said, I don't know what is happening to the youth of this country, and this town. When you go off to Princeton next year, you'll be away from all this and will learn to be a gentleman. You will learn how to behave and how to speak, and this will prepare you for a career in the law."

Yes, Doyle thought, *the career that has been picked for me, carved in stone since my birth.*

"Now, you have but a few months until that training begins," Mr. Lawrence continued. "You are not going to do anything that will reflect ill on you until you leave. And that means no more of this nonsense with the Miller girl."

Doyle began to speak, but his father indicated he was not finished. "You are a young man and entitled to a little fun. But when it comes to keeping company with young ladies, you must be discriminating. And the Miller girl is not someone you should be seen with."

"But, Dad, I've known her since—"

"It does not matter that you go to school with her. She does not have a good reputation."

"People are idiots."

"No, people are good judges of character, by and large. After years of living in Zenith one develops a good name or a bad name."

"You have never spoken to her, Dad."

"I don't need to. Everyone knows she is a sorrow to her father, a man I respect, even if he is a Baptist. I don't want you seeing her again, Doyle."

"Dad, I can—"

"Is that clear, Doyle?"

All too clear. All too familiar. "Dad, I'm seventeen—"

"And you have the good name of Lawrence. I am not going to have you ruin it."

"Seeing Zee Miller is not going to ruin anything."

Mr. Lawrence stood up, looming over his son. "You are not to see her, and that's final."

‖ 5 ‖

Sunday was church day for the Lawrence family. More of a procession, Doyle always thought. The morning's preparations—bathing, dressing, Mother making sure everyone was presentable—were all in the service of looking prosperous and well-groomed.

Then all of them piled into his father's pride and joy, his 1915 Rolls-Royce Silver Ghost, for the half-mile ride to Zenith First Methodist Church. Mr. Lawrence took three miles to get there, however, by driving the long way around Elm and Pike streets, then down First, so that plenty in the town could see them all, sitting there like potentates behind the Spirit of Ecstasy hood ornament.

Doyle felt less like a potentate than an exhibition. Getting to church was in part a relief, in part a burden. For it meant another hour-long oration from Dr. Philander M. Mahler.

Zenith was sometimes called, by its boosters, a city of churches. One could find within a square mile Congregational, German Congregational, Presbyterian, First Baptist, Church of Christ, Lutheran, and German Evangelical Lutheran. Zenith also had a Seventh-day Adventist Church and even a Reorganized Church of Jesus Christ of Latter Day Saints with its membership of about thirty-five.

Arriving at church, the Lawrence family would be greeted by a cavalcade of familiar faces. Horace Wolvin, the druggist; Axel Morgan, the peat farmer who had two of the most obnoxious children Doyle had ever known (Priscilla, the eight-year-old crier, and Nathan, the ten-year-old liar); James Martin Cain, editor of the *Zenith Herald*, a man whose literary skills did not quite match his ambition to become the next Greeley; William Cherry, the fireman; Harlow Ballard, the sign maker and house painter; and of course the Warrens—Augustus and Eliza, along with son Zachary and daughter Elizabeth, called Betty by all.

Betty waited for Doyle to greet her, as she always did on Sunday mornings. Doyle had to admit she was a thing of beauty on the Lord's Day, and today was no exception. She was wearing a dress of royal blue, pleated in clusters with silk-covered buttons. Adorning her head was a wide-brimmed hat with ribbons, tasteful and elegant. And never did she seem to wear the same dress to church twice.

"Hi, Betty," he said.

"I'm not speaking to you." Betty Warren raised her head a degree above normal, a roost from which to look down her nose.

"Oh? And why not, pray tell?"

"A girl only talks to those from whom attention is paid."

"I said hello, didn't I?"

"How long has it been since you've come to have a lemonade?"

"I haven't been counting."

"Too long, for a boy who teases girls."

"Who teases?" Doyle started feeling hot under the collar.

"I forgive you."

"Forgive me for *what?*"

"Look, it's time to go inside. You may call on me this afternoon."

She swept by him, her elegant dress swishing like the soft hiss of spring leaves. Doyle thought Betty Warren the near opposite of Zenobia Miller, and he understood neither. Women were a mystery, as inscrutable as God.

It was warmer than normal in church, and Doyle did not look forward to the service. He had been up late again, reading Browning and Blake. His eyelids were heavy from the moment he sat on the hard wooden pew.

The singing of the hymns proved a chore, though Doyle liked the way Charles Wesley could string words together. The reading of the Scriptures, by Deacon Jeptha Osterhout, was interminable. The selection was from Isaiah, and Deacon Osterhout, a tanner rumored to be a frustrated actor, rolled every word on his tongue as if it were a precious marble, ending with a stentorian crescendo about the wolf and the lamb feeding together, the lion eating straw like a bullock, and dust being the serpent's meat.

Doyle nearly visited the land of Nod, saved from his father's wrath only by Rusty's discerning elbow. "If I have to take it, so do you," Rusty whispered to his brother.

But that was only the warm-up act, so to speak. The main event, Dr. Philander M. Mahler, followed shortly thereafter.

Once again, Doyle found himself wondering why he did not respond to Dr. Mahler's preaching. In every way, to Doyle's way of thinking, the man was the model of the Christian minister. Tall, angular, with a resonant voice, Dr. Mahler cut an authoritative figure in his purple robe and Geneva tabs. Doyle's studies in rhetoric taught him that the minister's sermons were exemplars of the homiletic enterprise. No word was carelessly chosen, and the point, though often a long time in coming, was clear by the end.

In fact, in those fanciful moments when Doyle imagined himself standing before a jury or perhaps someday on the floor of the Senate, he heard himself sounding much like Dr. Mahler.

So what was it that was missing each and every time Doyle heard one of his sermons? He couldn't quite figure it.

"My friends," Dr. Mahler began, "we have come to a time in the history of our sphere when nation has risen once more against nation, and man takes arms against man. Oh, wisdom is better than weapons of war! And 'one sinner destroyeth much good'! Today we must consider how to treat our fellowman so that such folly may be avoided. If it is not, we are lost indeed."

Doyle was starting to feel a little lost himself—lost to the world of the wakeful. He heard words intermittently, but nothing was making sense to him.

Then, suddenly, he was in the park again, with Zee Miller in the tree. It was sunny, and the leaves rustled languidly in the soft wind. Zee smiled at him and then reached for the sky. Doyle gaped, entranced. She smiled at him and he liked it, but wondered why she wasn't in church, why they both weren't in church, and then the tree came crashing to the ground—

"—up! Wake up!"

It was Rusty's insistent voice. Doyle jolted awake. Everyone was standing.

Back in church. It was Sunday and hot and they weren't even out of the service yet.

But the vision of Zee in the tree filled Doyle with something he hadn't experienced all day. Happiness.

‖ 6 ‖

Sunday morning in the First Baptist Church of Zenith, Nebraska, was for Zee Miller akin to being a mouse in a cage. No way out, with people staring at her as if wondering what she would do next.

For Zee was Pastor Miller's wild daughter, when wild meant not wearing her hair up all the time and daring to speak back to a teacher who was treating her unfairly. A number of whispered complaints had been uttered by the observers outside her cage.

There was one other resident of the enclosure, a Mrs. Hallie

Winchester, who had taken it upon herself to be Zee's keeper in church. Somehow, without Zee's knowing it, Mrs. Winchester was *assigned* to her, to sit next to her during services, the better to keep an eye on her. It wouldn't do, no, to have the preacher's daughter squirming or fidgeting or trying to escape.

But more than that, Mrs. Winchester had it in her mind to train up Zee in the "way that she should go." She let Zee know this, in a way which made it seem an inevitability, much like the snows of winter.

This particular Sunday morning, Mrs. Winchester sat her prodigious frame next to Zee with a stern and beefy-faced, "Good morning, Zenobia."

The chill of it set Zee on edge. Not that she wasn't there already. She was itching in her Sunday dress, wool serge in a plaid pattern. She had only three dresses, donated by the local dressmaker, Henrietta Greer, also a member of First Baptist. This one was tighter now, as her body was taking on a new shape. It felt even more constricting in the muggy atmosphere of the church.

In the pew in front sat the Grubb family—the father Harrison A., a banker, along with his wife, two sons and daughter, Amelia, who went to school with Zee. Not that she was a friend. Amelia Grubb was part of Betty Warren's circle, the royalty of Zenith High. Only a select few were allowed in, and Zee had never received an invitation. She wouldn't have taken it anyway.

They all sang, listened to offered prayer, sang again. Zee held a hymnal open and moved her mouth so Mrs. Winchester would think she was singing.

Then it was time for the sermon. The worst part of all. For she would have to sit for forty minutes to an hour, pretending to listen.

She never thought of her father as her father when he preached. He was a different man in the pulpit, as if assuming some aspect of a long-ago prophet. At home, even in the bad times—of which there were more lately—she could at least look into his eyes and see the man who had taken care of her all these years.

When he preached, though, his eyes took on a fixed gaze, an impenetrable stare. They burned holes in the wooden floor and set the rafters aflame. His voice matched his eyes.

"Before it is too late," he intoned, "for hell is a real fire. It is not a figure but a place. A place for those on whom that awful sentence will be pronounced: 'Depart from me.'"

Oh no, Zee thought. *Another of his hell sermons. And in this heat!* There would be wailing and gnashing of teeth, all right. Hers.

Even worse, as the sermon wore on, Zee noticed something. Every time her father emphasized the punishment due the wicked, Amelia Grubb would turn her head slightly to the right and cluck.

Yes, that was it, a little cluck of the tongue behind her teeth, and a look seeping out of the corner of her jaundiced eye. *Are you listening, Zenobia?* it said.

"Let us look back and shudder at the thoughts of that dreadful precipice, along which we have so long wandered. Let us fly for refuge to the hope that is set before us, and give a thousand thanks to the divine mercy, that we are not plunged into this perdition."

Amelia Grubb clucked.

Something had to be done. The wrath of God was a long way off, but the wrath of Zee Miller could not wait.

Surreptitiously, Zee removed an offering envelope from the hymnal rack and placed it at her right side. Her father's voice was rising at the moment, and that comported with her tearing of the envelope into halves, then fourths.

As her father came to a particularly grueling point, Zee slipped a quarter of the envelope into her mouth and let the natural wonder of saliva take its course.

On "burning sulphur" she shoved in another quarter, keeping her jaw as steadfast as possible lest Mrs. Winchester detect her incipient deed.

By "smoke of their torment" Zee had the entire paper product down to a wet pulp in the right side of her cheek.

Amelia Grubb clucked twice more.

Finally, the perdition of the wicked was over and all stood for the singing of "Come Ye Sinners, Poor and Needy." It was then that the true genius of her plan revealed itself.

Zee had once seen a magician at a carnival (without her father's knowledge, of course) who had stunned some hapless rubes by making a buttermilk biscuit disappear before their very eyes. Not her eyes, which had been trained on the magician's *off hand.* Zee had found a beginner's magic book at the Zenith library one summer and had read the chapter on Misdirection. She knew that was what the carny prestidigitator was up to, and so she followed the hand which did not purport to hold the biscuit, but really did. As the magician pretended to toss the biscuit in the air with his left hand, he turned his body slightly and dropped it in his coat pocket with his right hand.

It was all in the misdirection.

For her feat, Zee held her hymnal open and forward so it hovered over the space where Amelia would soon return her backside. And she held it in such a way as to obscure the gaze of Mrs. Winchester should she bother to look down.

The final verse being sung, Zee gently released from her right hand, below the hymnal's back cover, her sodden surprise.

Then all the congregation sat down. Amelia squirmed a bit, though apparently without any sense of realization.

"What on earth are you smirking at?" Mrs. Winchester whispered.

"Oh," Zee replied, "I am just happy that I am counted as one of the elect and so shall avoid hell's flames."

"Do not count your chickens," the old woman said sternly.

Chickens indeed. It was a glorious, sodden egg that Amelia Grubb would be hatching.

‖ 7 ‖

"I noticed you were less than interested in the sermon today, son." Mr. Lawrence cut into his slice of Sunday roast, a family ritual after church.

Doyle shrugged. "Dr. Mahler does all right."

"That was not what I said. I said *you* did not seem interested. In fact, you kept nodding off. Don't think I didn't notice."

"It was hot, Dad. I was a little tired." He still was. But he was also bursting with the desire to speak to his father alone. He simply had to get matters clear regarding Zee Miller. His father's pronouncement on the subject was meant to be the final word. Regardless, Doyle was no longer a child and he wasn't going to acquiesce like one.

"You can stay alert by turning your attentions to the speaker. What if you are in court one day, feeling tired, and it's hot in the courtroom? The judge, the jury, your client—they will not be sympathetic."

"Papa?" The voice was Gertie's, which surprised Doyle in a pleasant way. His little sister was usually the silent one.

"What is it?" Mr. Lawrence said.

"I don't understand Dr. Mahler."

Doyle's father stuck his fork into a large square of beef. "You are a child; of course you won't understand all of what he says."

"I don't get him either," Rusty said.

Mr. Lawrence had barely placed the beef in his cheek. Now that cheek was flushing. He chewed in silence as everyone at the table watched for his reaction.

He finished his bite with a consternated swallow. "*Get* him? What sort of talk is that?"

"What Rusty means," Doyle said, "is that—"

"Let Rusty speak for himself."

"I wanna speak," Gertie protested.

Doyle saw his mother hide a smile at the youngest Lawrence's amusing impertinence. Doyle wasn't smiling. He was near to bursting out of his chair. How long was this meal going to take? How long before he could get his father alone and speak his mind clearly and unequivocally?

"Let's not everyone speak at once." Mr. Lawrence placed his fork down on his plate, firmly, like a gavel. "Gertie, you go first. What is it that you don't understand about our minister?"

"He uses too many words," she said.

"Is that all?"

Sheepishly, Gertie nodded her head.

"All right, Miss Gertrude Lawrence has a point. As the great Justice Story said, *'Be brief, be pointed, let your matter stand lucid, in order, solid and at hand.'* That's how you win a case."

"Father," Doyle began, using the more formal appellation, "I wish to make a case."

His father raised his eyebrows. "That is always permissible in this house."

"Privately."

"Very well. When we are finished here you may—"

"Now, if you please." Doyle got up from the table and walked immediately to the library. He had not asked to be excused, a violation of Lawrence protocol. His father would be upset, but he did not care. He had to speak now.

His father entered the library silently, closing the doors behind him. He gestured for Doyle to sit in one of the leather chairs and then sat in the other. What a relief that his father did not rebuke him. Now came the hard part.

"Dad," Doyle began, "I'm nearly eighteen and I'll be going off to Princeton in the fall. I want to ask that this summer I be treated like an adult."

His father's silence was a signal that he had yet to offer any compelling reasons. The case remained to be made.

"I've always done well in school. I've always done what you and Mother have asked me to do. And I believe that demonstrates that I am ready to make decisions on my own."

"What sorts of decisions?"

"What my field of study should be at Princeton, for one."

"I thought we had already discussed that."

"It was never really discussed."

"You will take the training that will prepare you for a career in the law. We certainly discussed that, did we not?"

"Suppose I wanted to take more classes in the field of literature?"

"There is nothing wrong with literature in moderation. However, it is not to be your major field of study."

"Suppose I—"

"There is no supposing to be done. If you want to make decisions for yourself, you must prove to be wise. It is not wise to ignore the path that has been chosen for you. You come from a prominent legal family. You have your future settled in a way that most boys your age would give their eyeteeth for."

"I want to feel that I am free to explore other areas of interest."

"Explore, perhaps. Briefly. Now is there anything else? I'd like to go back to my dinner."

Doyle did not like the feeling of being dismissed once again. "I want to be free to see whomever I please, and . . ."

"Go on."

"And whom I will marry."

His father scowled. "Aren't you a little young to be thinking about that?"

"Not to get engaged."

"And you've someone in mind?"

"Yes."

"Is it Elizabeth Warren?"

"No."

"I certainly hope you are not thinking of that Miller girl."

"What if I am?"

Mr. Lawrence drew a thoughtful breath. "Son, listen to me. I've worked too long and hard to let you foolishly throw away your chance at success. Years from now, you'll thank me." He stood up. "I'm hungry. Let's go back and—"

"I'm not hungry, Father."

"Come on along—"

"No," Doyle said. "I can decide that I'm not hungry, can't I?"

Thankfully, his father left it at that.

Later, in the grip of a rotten mood, Doyle walked through town. He kept his hands in his pockets, looked at the ground, only grunted when people greeted him by name.

He took a left at the dry-goods store and walked toward the train depot. The smell of coal dust grew heavy in the air. He kept on walking past the tracks into the lower section of Zenith. Here was Scheffel & Sons Monument Works and the L.M. Carlson Mattress and Auto Top factory. Not too far away were the stockyards with a smell all their own.

This was also where the one-story homes had been built—the ramshackle shelters of early Zenith residents, which sat like old men on wooden chairs, long past caring about themselves and the world around them.

And then he was on Flat Street, where Zee Miller lived.

Maybe I'll go over there right now, he thought. *I'll ask her to marry me, and we'll just go away together, over to Julian maybe, find a justice of the peace. We'll get married and then there's nothing anybody can say about it. It'll be done and it'll be one thing I've done for myself.*

He wondered what she'd say if he asked.

"Hey, Doyle!"

It was the Livingston kid, Andrew. He was ten years old and liked to show up at the Zenith High football games. His father was a drunkard and worked at the radiator factory.

"What have you got there, Andy?" Doyle asked, knowing that it was a football in the boy's arms. He must have seen Doyle through the window and come running into the dusty street.

"Can you show me how to dropkick?"

"Dropkick, huh. You want to play football?"

"If my pa lets me."

"Give me the pigskin." Doyle held the ball in two hands, the ends pointed up and down. "You hold it like this, see?"

Andrew Livingston nodded. He had unruly blond hair and a sunny disposition, despite having to live with an old man who hit both Andrew and his mother.

"You hold it out, take a step with your right foot, then your left"— Doyle demonstrated—"then you drop it, and when the ball hits the ground you put the foot to it. Watch."

Doyle repeated the steps, dropped the ball, and kicked a perfect thirty-yarder, right down the middle of Flat Street.

"Wow!" Andrew Livingston said. "That's as good as Jim Thorpe!"

"Not quite, kid. Thorpe can kick it sixty, they say."

"You could if you tried."

Doyle gave Andrew a clip on the shoulder. "Maybe."

An angry voice growled from a window of the Livingston house. "Boy! Get in here!"

Andrew stiffened.

"Hello, Mr. Livingston," Doyle said, waving toward the window.

"Huh? Who is that?"

"Doyle Lawrence, sir. I was just showing Andrew the dropkick."

"Eh? Kick?"

"Yes, sir. Football, you know."

There was a pause. Doyle could only see a dark form, featureless, in the window.

"No time for games!" Mr. Livingston said. "Boy's got chores to do."

"You better get," Doyle said to Andrew. "I'll fetch the football and toss it in your yard."

Andrew didn't move.

"Go on." Doyle gave Andrew a little push. "You have to do what your father says." The words dropped bitterly from his tongue.

"Come back again, will ya?" the boy said.

"Sure."

"Andrew!"

The boy ran to the house.

Doyle waited until the door slammed shut, then walked down the street toward the football. Sadness washed over him suddenly, like a huge wave. What chance did a kid like Andrew Livingston have in the world? He'd probably grow up to be just like his father, working long days and drinking at night.

As he picked up the football he wondered what chance anyone had in life. Your place was picked for you. Maybe his father was right after all, and he should just follow the path that was set for him.

He wondered if Zee was home. He wondered whether he should just forget all about her.

‖ 8 ‖

"Now Lillian Gish. Now Dorothy. Now Lillian."

Zee smiled with exaggerated sweetness. "Now Billie Burke."

She began to change her facial expressions, one after another, displaying emotions like fear, anger, fright, delight. "Florence Lawrence, the Biograph Girl!"

Zee twirled in the clearing, pretending her cotton dress was a grand gown in a period picture, about the French Revolution maybe. This spot by the river, in a cluster of trees, was her favorite place to be alone. She often came here to swim, think, and dream.

"And now, Zee Miller, the greatest of them all." She paused, bowed. "Yes, Zee Miller brought the audience to its feet in her latest picture. All of Hollywood is singing her praises. They're saying—"

"She's nerts, is what they're saying."

Zee yelped and turned toward the voice. Timothy Logan was leering at her. His red hair, as usual, was unkempt. The Logans were a church family, but Timothy was about as devout as she was. He also picked his nose in public and cheated on tests at school.

"You oughtn't sneak up on people that way," Zee said. Timothy was about her height, covered with freckles, and smelled like the cheeses of his father's trade.

"I got a right to take a walk," Logan said. But Zee was sure this was no casual stroll. He must have followed her after church.

"Then why don't you turn and walk back to town?" Zee said.

"You think you own the place or something? Go on with your actin'. I'll be the audience."

"I'll do nothing of the kind."

"Come on, you're gonna have to perform in front of people if you want to be an actress."

"People, yes. You, no."

"You makin' small of me?"

"Run along now. Your mother is calling."

"Don't you make small of me, because you'll regret it."

"Oh pooh. I'm not scared of you."

"You better be."

"Now go on and leave me alone."

"You think you can look down on us, don't you?" He took a step toward her. "Just because your old man is a preacher don't make you special."

"I don't look down on anybody, unless they come out from under a rock." She glared at him, willing him to go away.

"You're no better than any of us," Logan said.

Zee saw that he was balling his hands into fists. What was wrong with him? Timothy Logan had always been an ornery, disagreeable sort. But he never threatened people.

Her instincts told her to turn and walk away, get back to the road. Instead, she stood her ground.

Even when Logan took another two steps toward her, she didn't move.

"You and your old man are so high and mighty," he said.

"Scram, Timothy."

"Your old man's bugs, too, and everybody says so."

Irritation rippled her insides. "You be quiet."

"Why don't he quit his yapping? He just makes everybody mad."

"Shut up!" Her words exploded.

Timothy Logan's mouth dropped open. Then he smiled. "Yeah, he's crazy, that's what he is, and a codger."

Screaming, Zee ran at him, jumped and grabbed two fists full of red hair.

Logan shrieked and fell to the ground, Zee landing on top of him.

"Shut up shut up shut up!" Zee jerked his head up and down.

Logan cried out, tears bursting through his closed eyes.

Zee didn't stop. She wanted to pull his hair out and make him sorry, make them all sorry.

Timothy Logan grabbed her arms, pulling at them. He was strong with desperation.

"You say you're sorry," Zee demanded. "Say you're sorry and I'll let you up."

Logan said nothing. His nose was running and his cheeks were flushed. His freckles stood out like brown pebbles on a pink tablecloth.

"Say it!"

He did not say it. He pulled at her arms harder. He then sank his teeth into Zee's left wrist. The pain was excruciating. Zee let go of his hair and with her right hand hit him in the ear with all the force she could muster. His jaw opened and he squealed. Zee rolled off him, her wrist throbbing. She saw teeth marks and blood.

Timothy Logan scrambled to his feet, puffing and snorting. He started to run. "You're gonna be sorry!"

She was already sorry. Not for him, but for living in this stinking town in a stupid old house with chickens in the backyard.

‖ 9 ‖

"I don't know what I'm going to do about you."

Zee's father sighed, as if bearing unseen burdens. Zee quite understood his feeling and found little blame. What, indeed, could he do about her? She had a flame inside her that she could not extinguish.

She sat quietly in the *rebuking chair*, which was what she secretly called the wooden chair her father made her sit on when castigating her. As usual, her father stood so he could look down on her.

"I was told by Mrs. Grubb what happened in church. What you did was filthy and disgusting."

"Don't you want to hear my side, Papa?"

"You have no side."

"But I do, Papa. Amelia Grubb was making fun of me, right in the middle of your sermon!"

"Is that all? Making fun? Haven't you learned yet that Christ was mocked and did not retaliate? Let alone make a disgusting ball of paper and spittle."

"He made mud out of spit, though."

"Do not be frivolous with me."

"I was . . ." She stopped herself. What was the use?

"That's not all I want to talk to you about. Where did you go after church?"

"Walking, like I sometimes do."

"Where?"

"By the river."

"What were you doing there?"

"Just walking, Father."

"Did you meet anyone?"

He knew. Somehow he knew. "Did Timothy Logan tattle on me?"

"His mother spoke with me. How could you do it?"

"He was saying bad things about you, about us."

"Haven't you heard a word I've been saying?"

"He bit me!"

"And why did he bite you?"

Zee looked at the floor. "Because I was whipping the tar out of him."

"I thought so."

"I went out there to be by myself. I was practicing."

"Practicing what?"

"Oh, Father, please. There is an audition for an acting troupe. I want to try. If you will only see me, if you will only let me, you will see that it is—"

"You will not go there. You will not be part of the theater."

"But it's the one thing I want to do."

"You are only sixteen. You have no idea what you want to do."

"I don't want to get married to some stuffy old person, I know that."

"Marriage is what every young woman should want. Marriage to a fine Christian man. Someone who can take care of you."

"Maybe I want to take care of myself for a time. Father, please—"

"What is this?" He reached behind him and pulled something off his desk. He showed it to her, and Zee felt her face flush.

It was a copy of *Picture Progress*, the magazine published by Paramount Studios. It talked all about their stars, like Pickford, John Barrymore, Blanche Sweet, and Hazel Dawn.

"Where did you get that?" she asked.

"Where did *you* get it?"

"The drugstore."

"I forbid you to read this material."

"Father—"

"Do you understand me?"

"No!" she said, too loudly.

Her father reacted as if a sharp pain gripped his heart. He sat down heavily in his chair.

Zee went to him, kneeled, put her hands on his arm. "Father, I'm sorry."

"No," he said, "I am sorry. I am sorry that I have been so remiss with you. I have done you no good."

"But you have—"

"No. I must take a harder stand with you, child. Hence, you will not be allowed to leave this house unless I am with you."

She looked at him. "What about school?"

"You will no longer walk to school. I will take you there, and you will wait until I come to fetch you."

A chill touched Zee's neck. "But everyone will know."

"What everyone knows does not concern me."

"How long will this last?"

"Indefinitely. I simply must do this. Please go up to bed."

Fighting back tears, Zee trudged up the stairs. Bed? Not tonight.

She waited until she heard the clock toll half past seven. Then she went to the stairs and saw that the light from the study was still on. Her father's routine on Sunday evening was to turn in around eight. He would shuffle to his room, past her door. He never looked in on her.

Still, she took no chances. She stuffed her bed with old clothes, making the crude outline of a body and then slipped out the window, shimmied down latticework, ran through the backyards of several neighbors, over to Elm Street where Victoria waited for her in a flivver.

They drove over to Julian, where there was a late show. Tonight it was a one-reeler Stroud-General comedy with Happy Sanders, and then the feature, *Joan the Woman*, starring Geraldine Farrar and Wallace Reid, directed by Cecil B. DeMille.

When Joan of Arc was tied to the stake, Zee saw herself in the role. Not only that, she saw herself as Joan of Zenith. She would burn up here into ashes.

‖ 10 ‖

The end of the year dance at Zenith High School was a tradition stretching back to 1891, when Miss Rose Danner had taken the helm as principal. She brought with her from the East a commitment to good breeding and manners, to social grace and the "inestimable value of the proper gesture." For her, the dances were as much a part of the education of the young as mathematics or geography.

And, at seventy-four, she still fancied she could turn a feathered waltz, though her girth suggested to the eye that this was more fancy than fact. Nevertheless, near the end of the dance, one of the senior boys, in homage to her stature and influence, and selected according to long-standing tradition, would ask her to take the floor with him.

This dubious honor was dispensed by the assistant principal, Mr. Wiley Broad. His selection was held a secret until the night of the dance itself, lest word got out to the school community and the honoree was forced to endure an onslaught of verbal barbs and practical jokes.

So it was with some trepidation that Doyle Lawrence, dressed in the new Brooks Brothers suit his mother had received from New York, entered the gymnasium of Zenith High School on the night of June 9, 1916. Zenith High had cost $500,000 to build in 1912, and the money showed through. With a capacity for twelve hundred pupils, it boasted thirty-six classrooms, a gymnasium, swimming pool, a large auditorium, music and art and lecture rooms. It was four stories high, built of cream-colored pressed brick.

Doyle entered the gym slowly, cautiously. As captain of both the football squad and the debating team, and with his acceptance at

Princeton, Doyle knew he was the logical choice for the dance with Miss Danner. Though he had a decent respect for her, he knew if his shoulder were to be the one tapped by Mr. Broad it would mean at least a month of snickers coming from his friends. Last June he had been one of the chief tormentors of Evan Walsh, whose face was prone to redness anyway, when Walsh became, in the argot of the school, the "Dunce of the Danner Dance."

Unfortunately, Doyle reflected upon his entrance, justice would probably demand his pound of flesh. He was prepared for the worst.

As unpleasant as that eventuality was, it was not the foremost concern on his mind.

Zee Miller was.

He had not seen her in a week, since the night at the park. He wondered if she were sick, or hurt. Maybe in a fall from a tree. With Zee you never knew.

He had resisted calling on her. Pride had played a part, Doyle would himself admit. He did not want to appear too anxious in his pursuit. According to an article he'd read in *Liberty*, women did not want their potential life partners to appear overly enthusiastic.

One thing for certain, he wouldn't be seeing Zee at the dance. Her father spoke fire and brimstone about dancing. Doyle decided to grin and bear her absence, try to have a good time. Dance with a few of the fair maidens. His ankle had finally healed enough to allow it. He was ready to give it a workout.

The familiar faces of his classmates were a sea of decked-out evening wear. The girls wore silk crepe de Chine or taffeta, the boys distinguished in dark serge suits and their fathers' silk neckties. An orchestra made up of woodwinds and strings took up a corner of the gymnasium, which was a shimmer of red, white, and blue bunting, crepe, and strings of electric lights.

"Better watch yourself, Old Man."

Doyle turned to his right and met the ruddy, smiling face of Cornelius Pugh. Corny was the center on the football squad and had pitched many a ball to Doyle over the years. He'd also pitched his share of pranks, being the biggest joker in the school.

"Watch what, Old Sport?" The two had taken to calling each other "Old Man" or "Old Sport," depending on which expression had not been used last. It was part of their preparation for the Ivy League.

Corny was matriculating to Dartmouth in the fall.

"Broad has been asking if anyone's seen you," Corny explained, his voice in a low, conspiratorial register. "My guess is this year's Dunce is a certain prospective law student."

"Bats! He hasn't fingered anyone else?"

Corny shook his head, hardly able to contain his smirk. "If you want me to, I can try to block. Just like I do out on the field."

"Won't that look jim-dandy, me following you around all night like I'm waiting for the pigskin."

"There is no way out, Old Man. My suggestion is that you get over to Betty Warren and commence hiding behind her."

Doyle followed Corny's eyes across the gym floor, to a trio of girls standing under the basketball hoop. Betty Warren, as usual, stuck out from the others like a rose emerging from the leaves on the stem.

She was the town beauty, no doubt about it. With raven hair and glistening blue eyes, she was the admiration not only of Doyle but any of the boys with romance on their minds. But for Doyle, admiration was where his heart stopped. Betty Warren did not stir him in the way Zee Miller did, a phenomenon that never ceased to amaze him.

"Oh, look," Corny said, "she's got you in her sights."

Betty Warren, homing in on him, smiled at Doyle. And suddenly she was gliding across the dance floor, graceful as a swan, ignoring the greetings of others as she made her way forward.

"You're on your own," Corny said. "I'll go watch for Broad."

Doyle cleared his throat and straightened his tie. He wondered if it wouldn't be right after all to marry Betty. It made so much sense. They were from the same monied class. They had breeding and bright futures. Why not?

"Why, Doyle Lawrence, you naughty thing." Betty held up her hand, encased in a delicate lace glove, and wagged a rebuking finger at him. "I should not even be talking to you."

"What did I do?" Doyle tried to keep his voice light, in response to her genial mocking.

"Not calling me, not offering to be my escort. All the other girls have boys on their arms."

That was a lie, of course, but a coquettish one. Few of the girls came with escorts, and most of the boys came stag.

"You'll have your pick, Bets."

"Well then, I pick you." She tapped his arm with the fan she held in her left hand. "So you may ask me to dance."

Doyle tugged at his collar and before he could answer caught something out of the corner of his eye. He turned and saw the approaching figure of Wiley Broad and, behind him, the grinning countenance of Corny Pugh. Some friend!

"Let's go." Doyle took Betty's arm and whisked her toward the dance floor.

"My heavens, such robust action," Betty said. "I like that."

And then they were engaged in a waltz, Doyle deftly leading Betty away from the presence of Mr. Broad.

Betty Warren was a great dancer, as light as a feather to lead. She had a hint of perfume in her hair, not enough to appear the strumpet but just enough to entice.

"You have the feet of winged Mercury," Betty said. "Why don't we do this more often?"

"Because you have the hearts of all the boys. There's no room for mine."

"Goose, you know yours is the only one I give a care about."

Doyle spun the two of them around, keeping his eye on the periphery lest Broad try to cut in. So far so good.

"Down here," Betty said with moderate rebuke.

"Sorry."

"Doyle?"

"Hm?"

"You will be going off to college soon."

"Yes."

"You are going to be a grand success, Doyle. Everybody knows it."

"Sure," Doyle said, feeling the bitter taste of the word on his tongue. Everybody didn't just know it. They expected it. Especially his father.

"I bet you'll forget about this old town."

"Hardly."

"Will you forget the people?"

"There are some I'd like to forget." Doyle forced a laugh. "Like old man Broad. Say, Betty, do you see him?"

Betty did not turn her head. "Will you forget about me, Doyle?"

"Do you see him?"

"Don't make me pinch you. Isn't it about time you made plans for something more?"

"More?"

"You know what I mean. A man has to plan for his future. The choices he makes will have far-reaching consequences."

Doyle felt the skin under his collar start to chafe. This is what it must be like to be a cornered rabbit, he mused. Old Broad looking for him on one side, and Betty Warren clutching him from the front.

What was the way out?

She came closer to him then, and with her left hand she pushed his right elbow, guiding his right hand to the small of her back. The delicate lace of her evening gown tickled his palm. Doyle left his hand there and knew immediately that Betty Warren was not wearing a corset.

"Why, Doyle Lawrence, you're blushing."

Yes, and now his cheeks began to burn. First Zee, now Betty. Both seemed to love to make him squirm. He knew Betty read Mencken in *The Smart Set*, and delighted in being called a "new woman." She bobbed her hair, unlike Zee, whose father didn't allow it. And she had an aggressive way about her that was disconcerting. He wished all the girls would just calm down about it.

"Could it be that you care for me after all?" Betty said.

"I care enough to give you one dance," he said.

"Oh, you. Don't be so dim. You know I am the woman you must marry."

"Betty—"

"And if you make a fuss about it I'll scream."

"Betty—"

"But if you will propose this evening, I shall be happy to give you my answer."

The music came to a sudden and, in Doyle's mind, very convenient end.

"Thanks for the dance, kid," Doyle said.

Betty Warren's eyes burned new holes in his head. "Doyle Lawrence, if I were a man I would thrash you."

"Hell hath no fury like a woman scorned." He heard his father's voice on that one. Now he got to see it. "If you were a man, you'd look awfully funny in that dress."

At that her eyes dropped their smoldering virulence and, inexplicably to Doyle, filled with tears. She whirled quickly and hurried away from him, her dress swishing behind her like a comet's tail.

I don't know if I will ever understand women, Doyle thought. *Too many complexities! Why didn't God make them simple? Why, if I ever—*

A hard tap on the shoulder brought him out of his reverie. Doyle knew before he turned around who it was.

‖ 11 ‖

"Mr. Lawrence."

Old Broad's voice was unmistakable. It had an oily sound, a forced smoothness. Doyle always thought Broad would have made a good Uriah Heep.

"Oh, hi, Mr. Broad."

"I have a wonderful piece—"

"Great dance, sir." Doyle spoke quickly, attempting to delay the inevitable. He imagined he was a condemned man before the firing squad, taking his sweet time with that last cigarette.

Broad smiled, showing yellow teeth. "Mr. Lawrence, I—"

"Say, have you seen Betty Warren tonight?"

"Betty . . . weren't you just dancing with her?"

"Oh, was that Betty?"

Broad's eyelids twitched. "Mr. Lawrence, I find the tenor of this conversation quite confu—"

"Look." This time Doyle was in earnest. For over Old Broad's shoulder he saw the person he'd least expected to show up at a Zenith dance function.

But sure enough, it was Zee Miller entering the gym.

She had a dark, drab coat around her. Her eyes were bright, though her face appeared to carry signs of trouble.

Old Broad had turned around at Doyle's "Look," and that was all the break he needed. As he did on the football field, Doyle saw the opportunity and dashed through it. Before Broad could say another word, Doyle was past him and on his way to greet Zee.

She laughed when she saw him charging toward her. "Whoa there, mule!"

"Zee. What are you doing here?"

"My coat, please." She turned around so Doyle could remove it. Underneath was a dress that was not formal evening wear, not of the sort someone like Betty Warren would wear. It was more like a Sunday go-to-church dress, but Doyle figured this was all Zee had in the way of stylish clothing.

"Say, Zee, what about your father?"

"Piffle," Zee said. "Don't let's talk about silly things. Check my coat and ask me to dance."

Doyle bowed, moved quickly to the coatrack and got a check. He turned around and found Old Broad's nose practically touching his own.

"Mr. Lawrence, you are to dance with Miss Danner. I do believe you've been anxious to hear that."

With a sigh Doyle said, "You have made my night, sir. Thank you."

"Nothing of it. It's a great honor, you know."

"Oh, how I know."

"I will give you notice, so keep alert."

So it was done. He would do his duty, be the Dunce of the Danner Dance, and take his medicine. He decided to shrug it off and concentrate on having a good time with Zee Miller, who had shown up out of the blue.

But before he could take a step, Old Broad had him by the arm. "Lawrence, you need to listen to me."

Resisting the urge to yank his arm away, Doyle waited.

"The young lady, Miss Miller?"

"Yes?"

"She is not allowed to dance."

"Sir, this is a dance, isn't it?"

Broad's eyes narrowed. "You know what I mean. Her father is well-known to me. He has entrusted his daughter to our school. Are you aware of the doctrine of *in loco parentis*?"

"I am sufficiently up on my Latin to know it means in place of a parent."

"Precisely. We are guardians of those in our care, as if we were the parents ourselves. I cannot allow Miss Miller to dance. It would result in, how shall I put it, a scene."

Doyle glanced toward the dance floor, looking for Zee, but she was not in view at the moment.

"Mr. Broad, why can't you cut her some slack? She's going to be in real dutch just for showing up."

"Mr. Lawrence," Broad replied in a replica of Doyle's tone, "we are not paid to cut anyone slack. We are here to mold character, and I know I can count on you to do the right thing."

The menace in Broad's voice was irritating. And he still had hold of Doyle's arm.

"You know," Broad said, "you have not yet officially graduated. We would not want anything disrupting your plans for college, would we?"

Old Broad must have seen Doyle's look of realization, for he let him go at that point and smiled.

Doyle's hand trembled into a fist. If he was going to defy Old Broad, why not go all the way and give the man what he deserved?

Yes, and bring dishonor to the Lawrence name. Wouldn't that be wonderful.

He stormed through the crowd, looking for Zee. He found her surrounded by Betty Warren and two of her friends.

"What a *lovely* outfit," Betty was saying. "Is there a horse without a blanket tonight?"

The other girls laughed.

"No," Zee said, "but there might be a girl without teeth in a minute."

"Yes, how in keeping with your reputation."

Doyle stepped into the middle of the feminine conclave. "Why isn't anybody dancing?" he said.

Betty threw back her head. "Horses don't dance, do they?"

As if he knew what was going to happen before it did, Doyle reached out and caught Zee's wrist as her arm made an arc toward Betty Warren's cheek. "I do believe we have this dance," he said.

He spun Zee around, but not before catching a glimpse of the most shocked and angry look he'd ever seen on a woman—or anyone else for that matter. Betty Warren looked as if she wanted both a gun and a place to hide.

"Hey, that hurts!" Zee twisted in Doyle's grasp.

"Let's dance." Doyle brought Zee to him. Her body was tense, her muscles firm for a girl. She let Doyle lead her but looked away from him. He finally nudged her chin toward him with his index finger.

Her eyes were full of tears.

"Hey," he whispered.

"Be quiet," Zee said.

"Don't let them—"

"I'm getting out of here."

"Now?"

"I mean out of this town."

Doyle saw Old Broad on the other side of the dance floor, scowling at him. Good. He didn't care.

"What are you talking about?" Doyle said, keeping Zee moving with the other dancers as best he could. But she was stiff.

"Running away," Zee said. "Don't you tell."

"Running . . ." He stopped when Zee pulled away from him, staring past him as if seeing a ghost. Doyle turned and immediately understood.

At the gymnasium doorway, filling it with a mixture of rage and energy, stood Reverend Miller.

Doyle felt Zee behind him, hiding. "Oh no," she said.

Old Broad was already at Reverend Miller's side. The men spoke, then Broad turned around and looked across the dance floor until his eyes locked on Doyle's.

"Come on," Doyle said, turning, grabbing Zee's wrist again.

"Where we going?"

"Just come on."

Ignoring the looks of Betty and her friends, not caring what Old Broad and Reverend Miller were doing, Doyle ran with Zee toward the back of the gym and the exit. He knew Broad and Zee's father would not be able to catch up through the crowd. Not for half a minute or so.

That was all he needed. Outside the gym it was dark, save for shafts of light from the windows. Doyle had left his roadster by the back path, its top down.

"What are we doing?" Zee said.

"Escaping. You want to?"

Zee's laughter filled the night. "My hero!"

‖ 12 ‖

"Doyle."

He looked at Zee. Moonlight reflected in her eyes. Doyle wanted to take her in his arms and kiss her then. But he still wasn't sure how to do it. Better to wait until she said yes to his question—if he ever got up the nerve to ask it.

They were sitting in his roadster—a gift from his father—just off the woods of the old Menger place. They'd played here as kids, catching bullfrogs in the creek and throwing berries at each other.

"You didn't have to do all that back there," Zee said. "Getting me away from that awful Betty Warren, and then my father and Broad. You're going to be in dutch."

"I'll get out of it somehow."

"You're wonderful."

Wonderful. Now is the time. "That's me," Doyle said.

"I mean it. That was brave, in front of all those people."

"I don't care about those people. Most of 'em are phonies."

Zee smiled. "You're about the best friend I ever had, Doyle."

Doyle's throat tightened. "Is that all I am? A friend?"

"We've been friends a long time, haven't we?"

"I want to say something."

"So say it."

An owl gave a haunting hoot from some dark tree. Was it urging him on, or warning him?

He tried to swallow. His tongue felt like a leather strap, but he had to speak now.

"You know I'm supposed to go off to Princeton."

"Of course, Old Omaha."

"Don't call me that."

"Are you cross with me?"

"I was in the middle of saying something."

"Sorry, Doyle. Go ahead."

"New Jersey's a pretty state, so they say."

"The Garden State."

"What if I didn't go there alone? What if you came with me?"

"Huh?"

"As my wife."

There was no hooting from the owl now. No sound at all, so it seemed. The only noise Doyle heard was the pounding of his pulse in his ears.

"Doyle Lawrence. Did you just ask me to marry you?"

"I did. That's for sure. That's what I did, all right." And then he thought, *Quit chattering, you fool!*

"I never thought . . . Doyle, do you . . . love me?"

"Of course I do. Do you . . . love me?"

"I always have."

His heart soared. "Then what's stopping us?"

Zee folded her hands on her lap and looked down at them. "Love isn't enough. A girl who wants to get somewhere, well, she can't stop just because of love."

"You're talking nonsense. You said you love me, and I love you. That's it."

"You see? We would fight all the time. You see the world one way and I see it another."

"So you don't really love me."

"I do, I do, Doyle. Don't say that. But you are going to be a great success. I would only hinder you. Besides that, your father hates me."

"I can talk to him, Zee—"

She shook her head. The night sky seemed to close in on Doyle, like it was watching.

"There's something inside me I cannot get rid of," Zee said. "My father thinks it is a bad seed. Doyle, that's what I am. I'm not for you."

"Suppose I decide what's right for me. And what's right is marrying you."

"I am going to be in motion pictures, Doyle. If I marry you, I shall have to give that up, won't I?"

Doyle sighed. "That's childish fancy, Zee. Motion pictures!"

"We're fighting already."

She was wrapping him up in knots again. Maybe she had a point. Maybe she saw into the future much more clearly than he did. Was she some sort of bad seed? No. He knew her too well to believe that. But a restless seed, perhaps. Someone for whom being tied down, in domesticity, would be like a death sentence.

A sudden, deep sense of loss spilled over him. It felt like a death. Of innocence perhaps. On the cusp of grown-up life, it suddenly seemed to Doyle that it was going to be a lot darker out there, away from this town that had been his home. Things weren't going to be certain. And that was disconcerting. He wanted Zee with him. Needed her.

"Hang it, Zee. What if I go out to Hollywood with you?"

Her eyes began to glisten. Doyle didn't know what to make of it. Why were women such a mystery?

"No," Zee said. "I'd never be happy knowing I took you away from your own destiny."

"What if my destiny is to be with you?"

"Some destiny! No, Doyle, it won't work. I know it. I've made a mess of my life so far, at least according to my father. Well, I've got to see it through now. I've got to know if I can do what I set out to do. I can't have a home and family. I'm no good, Doyle. Not for you, not for anybody."

She jumped out of the car.

"Zee!"

Doyle heard her sobbing as she ran into the dark woods.

"Zee, come back!"

She didn't come back. Doyle made an attempt to find her, shouting her name, but she never answered.

Figuring she had made her way back to town, Doyle gave up the search in anger. He'd made a fool of himself. It wouldn't happen again.

‖ 13 ‖

"Papa, please don't say that."

"You are shaming this family, Zenobia. You are shaming the name of God."

Hot tears filled Zee's eyes. She willed them not to fall, but knew she could not hold them for long.

Shaming the name of God? It was the worst thing he could possibly say. She knew it was a sign he was at the end of his rope with her. Yet this instant understanding and even empathy for her father still did not dull the harsh sting of the words.

"I have allowed you to continue in your rebellion," he said.

She was curled in the chair by the fireplace, legs up under her, the way she used to sit on her father's lap long ago. The Reverend Miller stood and paced slowly in front of the fire, his large arms and hands folded across his chest.

"But it's not rebellion, Papa," she argued, though she had a hard time believing it herself.

"What do you call it when you lie to me?"

"I did not lie."

"You deceived me, then. You went to this, this dance party. You have been seen sneaking into movies. I have forbidden these things, and you do not obey me."

She could not argue with him. "I can't help it, Papa. I can't help who I am."

"You are a troubled soul and it's my fault."

"What are you going to do?"

"I am going to remove you from school and seek a position for you."

The room seemed to grow dark around her. "I don't want a position."

"What you want does not matter now. You are too young, too rebellious, too much caught up in fantasies. Hard work is likely to clear your mind."

"What if I refuse to work?"

"You will not."

"You can't treat me like one of the chickens, Papa."

"I can treat you as I see fit. You are my daughter."

She stood to face him. "And you are embarrassed to have me for a daughter, aren't you? You hate what people say about me!"

"Do not raise your voice—"

"You hate me!"

Reverend Miller slapped Zee across the face.

Zee put her hand on her cheek. The shock was worse than the slap. She could not hold back her tears. Never before had he struck her.

His eyes widened. "Oh, Zenobia, I'm sorry . . ." He reached for her but she stepped away from him.

"Zenobia—"

"No!" She ran from the room, out the back door, past the chicken coop. She kept on running into the night.

14

August was miserable. It seemed the perfect month to shake the dust of the old town off his feet.

His feet, in this instance, were shod in brand new Oxfords, to go with the fresh coat and trousers personally selected by his father. The straw skimmer was Doyle's idea, borne of his vision of what a Princeton man ought to look like.

Standing here on the platform of the depot, the train hissing its impatience, Doyle felt a sense of relief. Only at this moment did he realize how much he wanted to get away.

From Zee Miller, whom he had not spoken to since the night of the dance. (Had not seen her, in fact, though from time to time he looked for her in the middle of town.) From Betty Warren, whose eyes seemed in a state of permanent batting whenever he was around. From his mother's insistence that he conform his behavior to societal expectations, and his father's unspoken yet unambiguous expectations. The only one he'd really miss was Rusty. It was time to move on.

His mother was starting to weep now. "You be sure to write us, and often," she said.

"I promise, Ma," Doyle said.

"The boy will be busy with his studies," his father said. "Write when you can, son."

"Yes, I will."

"But above all," Wallace Edgar Lawrence said, "use this time to prepare for your place in the world. This will be a precious time for you, and set you on a trajectory. Make friends judiciously, work hard, please your professors. Beware of early romantic entanglements."

"Don't worry, Dad. That's the furthest thing from my mind."

Rusty gave his brother a knowing look.

"Boaaarrrrd," the conductor announced.

"Well, good-bye, then," Doyle said.

His mother threw her arms around his neck. He felt the wetness of her tears on his cheek. "Stay warm this winter," she said.

"I will."

He shook Rusty's hand. "I'll keep the room neat in case you come back," he said.

Then it was his father's turn. The old man held Doyle's hand hard. "I'm counting on you, son. I'll need a partner in a few years."

"All right, Dad."

At his seat Doyle lowered the window to wave a final good-bye. His stomach began to churn, a mixture of butterflies and bricks. He had never left his hometown before, not in the way he was leaving it now. He was out on a limb, out over a gorge, letting go, trusting that the water below was deep enough to receive him, calm enough so he could swim. And though he had waited for this moment, this moment of leaving, finally, now that it was here, a sadness swept over him.

It was the sadness of a child who had known only security, who knew the way home from school, who could depend on an evening meal overseen by his mother, who knew where his bed was and who his friends were; this child now in an unfamiliar place, all security blown away like prairie dust in a windstorm.

The train whistle blew. And the train began to chug forward.

Doyle's mother, holding a kerchief to her eyes with one hand, waved with the other. His father stood stoically and nodded once. Rusty waved his hand with vigor and smiled. He was the adventurous one in the family and probably thought this was all a wonderful jaunt. Gertie blew Doyle a kiss.

Doyle gave a wave of his hand, kept his eyes on his family as they started to grow distant. Several other people on the platform were waving and shouting good-byes. Most of them Doyle knew by sight, if not by name. In a strange way they were his family, too.

As the train cleared the depot, Doyle looked out the window and gave one last wave back. But he could not tell if his family saw him.

Just before he brought his head back in the window, Doyle glanced at the town sign, which jutted above the roof of the station house. It had yellow letters on a brown background, which read, simply, *ZENITH*.

Someone was behind the sign. Yes, on the roof, watching the train go.

He saw who it was. Zee, her face just above the yellow letters.

PART II

GATHERING STORM

✦

Over there, over there
Send the word, send the word,
Over there,
That the Yanks are coming,
The Yanks are coming,
The drums rum-tumming everywhere!
So prepare,
Say a prayer
Send the word, send the word
To beware.
We'll be over, we're coming over
And we won't come back till it's over over there!

—*"Over There," music and lyrics*
by George M. Cohan (1917)

✦

Eat More Corn!

When you eat corn instead of wheat you are saving for the boys in France.

Corn is an admirable cool weather food.

Whether or not you like corn bread, corn muffins, "Johnny Cake," or corn pone, you are sure to like POST TOASTIES.

The newest wrinkle in corn foods—crisp, bubbled flakes of white corn—a substantial food dish with an alluring smack—and costs but a trifle.

MAKE POST TOASTIES YOUR WAR CEREAL!

—*Newspaper ad, 1917*

‖ 1 ‖

Doyle lay in a field of wheat, sun on his face, the sky clear blue. A gentle wind rustled through the stalks, creating a pleasant whispering sound. Though he did not know where he was, he felt safe here. Nothing could harm him in this field. He knew this to be true, the way people know things in dreams.

He felt like a child again, when the world was full of wonder and promise and all good things. He had nothing to fear, for his father and mother were near. He could not see them in the wheat field, but he could feel their presence.

He did not want to leave this place. He could stay here forever, soaking up the sun.

Then he heard a rumbling sound. Far away, yet insistent. Thunder? The sky suddenly darkened. A rumble again, this time sounding like a voice. *Moo oww, moo oww.*

The voice was in the sky. Was it the voice of God? He heard it again, and this time the words were distinct. "Move out. Move out."

"Move out!"

Doyle jerked awake. No, not the voice of God. The voice of Sergeant Halliday. "Up, ladies! Boarding in one hour!"

What time was it? It was pitch-black outside the makeshift barracks that had once housed livestock. Inside, lanterns began blazing an imitation of day.

"Next stop, France," Sarge yelled. "We don't want to keep them Fritzies waiting."

So they were shipping out at last. He and the men he had come to know in a flurry of training over the last month were actually setting out across the sea to fight a war.

The Stars and Stripes division had been formed from National Guard organizations in twenty-six states and the District of Columbia. Doyle had joined twenty-seven thousand other men who came together at Camp Mills on Long Island, New York, to be shaped into a fighting force.

Why did he do it? He chewed on that quite a bit, especially during those first, grueling days at camp. To defy his father? Perhaps. It was the first major decision he had made without his father's counsel. He was doing something on his own at last.

And truth be told he had not taken to Princeton. Oh, his grades were solid and his reputation impeccable. But inside him there was a gnawing sense that he was insulated from something—something big and important. The war in Europe was a struggle between the forces of good and evil, and good had to prevail. America was good, and Doyle was American. It all added up to his enlistment, even though more than one of his professors at Princeton told him that he was crazy.

To his surprise, Doyle had no difficulty ignoring their characterizations. He felt as though some inner magnet drew him, that he was destined for the army, for something greater than mere academic success.

Was it dangerous folly? When he reached Camp Mills and was issued his olive drab uniform, he started to think so. The uniforms were stiff and heavy and scratched like the dickens.

And it was in those uniforms they drilled all day, under the harsh yet nurturing tongue lashings of the drill sergeants. They did not have long to become a force worthy of fighting for their country. Running around with rifles and bayonets in uniforms that felt like wool blankets was supposed to do the trick.

Somehow, they made it, and boys slowly came closer to being men.

Which was a wonder to Doyle—how such a disparate group of young men from all corners of the States could come together with such zeal and unified purpose. There were machine gunners from Pennsylvania and Wisconsin, signal troops from Missouri, trench mortar battery men from Maryland and New Jersey. Tennesseans and Oklahomans were trained in the driving of ambulances. It was a force forged from all walks of life, all stations of society.

Now, on October 18, 1917, a little over a month since the men had arrived at Mills, at two o'clock in the morning, the Stars and Stripes began boarding a convoy of ships at the docks at Hoboken.

Doyle's ship, the *Abraham Lincoln*, smelled of rust and sea and sweat. He was surprised at how small everything was, how many hammocks could be crammed inside a single space. That was all they got.

As Doyle laid claim to an upper hammock, a voice thick with

Tennessee hill country said, "Mind if I take the under?"

It was the marksman, Alvin Beaker. Doyle had marveled at Beaker on the shooting range at Camp Mills. A skinny, sinewy fellow, Beaker kept hitting bull's-eye after bull's-eye. Only once did he miss when Doyle was watching. Beaker looked upset, then smiled with his crooked teeth and said, "The wind come up. Threw me off!" Beaker then hit three bull's-eyes, shooting with only one arm.

"Sure, take the lower," Doyle said, positioning himself in his hammock so he wouldn't fall out. "I feel safer having you around. You can shoot better with one arm than any of us can with two."

Beaker laughed. "But when God handed out the handsome faces, you was in front of the line. I was at the end, and He ran out, I guess."

A deep voice said, "Move aside."

The big Kansan, Thorn Fleming, the one bad apple Doyle had come across at Mills, glowered down at Beaker. No doubt Fleming was a good fighting man—he was twice as wide as Doyle and had hands the size of hams—but that did not make him a pleasant human being.

"Sorry, friend," Beaker said. "I got claim to this hammock."

"I need a lower," Fleming said. "You're skinny, you can fit anywhere."

"I can fit here is what I can do."

Doyle marveled at Beaker's moxie. Fleming looked as if he could grab the marksman with one hand and squeeze him like a tube of shaving cream.

"I'm tired," Fleming said. "I ain't in the mood for arguing."

"Then don't," Beaker said.

Fleming's body twitched. Doyle, in his hammock, was eye level with Fleming. "Listen, friend, we're just getting started here, so don't make trouble."

"No trouble, *friend*," Fleming said. "You just mind your own business."

"Who bunks under me is my business," Doyle said.

For a moment Doyle thought Fleming was going to reach up and pull him down. But then another voice, that of Sergeant Halliday, popped in. "Let's get situated here."

Fleming looked at the sergeant. Beaker took the opportunity to slide into the lower hammock, like a lizard into his favorite hole.

"All set here, Sarge," Beaker said.

The fury on Fleming's face sent a shiver down Doyle's back.

"Come on, then," Halliday said to Fleming. "Move along."

The big man shot Beaker and Doyle one last glare, then was gone.

"We better keep our eye on that one," Doyle said.

Beaker waved his hand. "Back home, there was a twenty-foot bear"—Beaker pronounced it *bahr*—"and he was comin' fer me. I didn't have my rifle, neither. All I had was a little ol' hard biscuit I was carryin' around in my pants for days, on account of I forgot to eat it. So I took it out, and took out my slingshot, and I shot that bear in the head. He fell over dead."

"Uh-huh," Doyle said, smiling.

"Now the moral to the story is this. The bigger the bear, the bigger the rug."

"Inspiring," Doyle said. "You have any biscuits with you?"

"I guess I'll have to get me some."

Doyle put his hands behind his head. "Until then, you watch my back and I'll watch yours."

Two hours later the *Abraham Lincoln*, along with a full contingent of American troops, was on its way to France.

2

"Stop that girl!"

The man's voice rang out like a rifle shot, ricocheted around the theater, and hit Zee between the eyes. She was an easy target.

A thick rope covered with burgundy velvet hung down from the rail of the balcony. Zee jumped up and grabbed hold of it, scampering upward. It was just like rope climbing in high school. She used the wall for her foothold as she climbed the rope, having no idea what she was going to do once she reached the balcony. But there was no time for thinking. She got to the top and pulled herself over the rail.

What a pickle! What a way to be introduced to Omaha theater society!

Someone shouted, "She's in the balcony!"

Another voice said, "I'll block off the stairs."

Zee saw there was a window, sort of like a skylight, at the far end of the balcony. She ran for it, knowing that if it was locked there would be no way out.

She heard the heavy thud of footsteps clambering up the stairs.

Why was she so afraid? She'd only wanted to see a bit of the rehearsal. According to the marquee outside the theater, the play was *Daddy Long Legs*, a big New York hit. So what if she saw a little of what went on in a real theater? How else was she going to learn? She had little money. She hadn't thought that far ahead.

Now they had seen her, caught her behind the scenery when she knocked over a prop plant as she was trying to get a closer look at the beautiful actress playing the lead. That was when the director, the man who had shouted "Stop that girl," told her to come to see him. But she had panicked and started to run instead, down the steps and toward the theater doors.

But a man was coming in that way to see what the commotion was, so she'd picked the rope to the balcony. Fool!

She got to the window and found that it was indeed locked. Now what?

A large man appeared at the balcony entrance. "Come on, girl. We're not going to hurt you."

No, she thought, *but they will take me to the police and the police will take me back to Zenith, where my father will beat the devil out of me. And there's plenty of devil in me. There must be. Running away from Papa like that. He's better off without me.*

The big man advanced faster than his gentle invitation would have indicated. Zee backed up against the wall. When the man smiled and showed his crooked teeth, she got even more suspicious. Then when he was only a few feet away, she grabbed one of the wooden chairs and hurled it at him, striking him in the stomach. He doubled over. She raced by him and saw two other men coming at her from the same direction.

There was nothing else to do but go down the way she came. She jumped over the rail and was suspended in the air for a split second before reaching out with one hand and grabbing the velvet rope. She slid down, burning her hands in the process.

Her feet never hit the floor.

She landed in the arms of the director.

"Let me go!" Zee struggled, but he held her fast.

He laughed. "Hold on there, young thing. I'm not going to tell the cops you're here."

That got her to stop. She looked at his face. He had friendly blue eyes and a dark complexion, a striking contrast.

"That's right," he said. "Even though you have all the characteristics of a thieving street urchin."

"I am not a thief."

"What are you, then?"

"An actress."

The look of astonishment on his face almost made Zee angry. Why should he not believe her? But then she realized her actions were not exactly those of a lady of the theater.

He gently put her down and looked at her with his hands on his hips. "If you are an actress, pray tell, what have you appeared in?"

"We did a Clyde Fitch play at school last year," Zee said. That much was true. And then she lied. "I was the ingénue."

The director smiled. "Well now, that's something. Clyde Fitch! My name is Desmond Nichols."

He shook her hand. He was lean and well-proportioned. Zee thought his face the most intelligent she had ever seen.

"I am Zee Miller."

Nichols pondered that for a moment. "Where are you from, Zee Miller?"

"Zenith."

"Nice little town, Zenith. There's a small theater there."

"Cheap vaudeville mostly."

"Don't knock cheap vaudeville. Our own Mrs. Bosworth started as a chorus girl."

Zee smiled. "Truly?"

"So you see, anything is possible."

His statement filled her with a warmth like the summer sun. The light was breathtaking to her, opening vistas in her imagination.

"Do you think I might be an actress?"

"Now, I don't know," Nichols said. "But any girl who can climb a rope and toss a chair at a stagehand the size of a moose, and get away with it, might be able to do anything at all."

"So I may have what it takes?" The question sounded like the most important she had ever asked.

"Young Miss Miller," Nichols said, "I have looked into the eyes of many actors and actresses over the years. I've gotten so I can tell if someone's going to have that certain something that reaches across footlights and into the audience. Duse had it. So did Bernhardt. In the movies, it's Pickford and Nazimova. It's not something you can teach in an acting class. It has to be there."

Zee listened as if poised over a cliff. Desmond was holding her and could let go. She was nearly breathless.

"Miss Miller," he said, "you have it. I believe, with the right training, you can be an actress."

Up! He had pulled her up and more. She was soaring in the clouds.

And from there she could look down on Zenith, on everybody there who thought she was just crazy and didn't belong, and Papa who didn't understand. She was going to show them all, and they'd see her in the clouds, among the stars in the sky, and nothing was going to stop her now.

‖ 3 ‖

The Stars and Stripes debarked the *Abraham Lincoln* in the little port town of St. Nazaire. In the rain. The town seemed little more than a mudhole with nondescript buildings plopped down, filled with curious but rather unfriendly people.

The rain did not let up the first couple of days. The mud became ankle-deep. The stores and cafés in town showed their gratitude for the arriving Americans by charging exorbitant prices. With the collapse of Russia and of Italy, it seemed to Doyle that the American boys would be here, a thousand miles from home, for four or five years. That was the rumor, anyway. The mood was not a happy one.

Yet when the training schedule began, the boys had no time to think of complaining.

Doyle and Alvin were put through daily drills under the eyes of French and American instructors—drills in artillery, machine guns, rifles, pistols, trench mortars, and 37-millimeter guns; bayonet and gas drills, digging trenches, building shelters and wire entanglements, roads and bridges; visual and mechanical signaling and the art and science of liaison; grenade throwing and marches, and various terrain problems.

Now they were in the midst of a one-hundred-kilometer hike toward the Germans. Alvin was marching alongside Doyle on the dusty road halfway to an area called Rolampont. This was where the Stars and Stripes were going to set up camp before the actual orders to move into battle.

"Doyle, you got yourself a girl?"

"I guess I've got me a whole town full of girls." Doyle winked. "Got one for every day of the week, and two on Sundays."

Alvin's mouth fell open. "You're funnin' me, aren't you?"

"Why should I fun you, Alvin?"

"Because that's all you city folk do to hillbillies like me."

"You mean that story about you shooting a twenty-foot-tall bear— I mean, *bahr*—with a hard biscuit hurled from a slingshot, that wasn't *funnin'* me?"

"Aw, now you went ahead and found me out." Alvin spit some tobacco juice on the hardpan of France. "What say we call it even?"

"Deal."

"So you gonna tell me if'n you got a girl or not?"

Doyle's mind immediately brought up a picture—of Zee sitting in a tree in the middle of town as night was drawing near. Zee reaching toward the sky. Funny, but in the last few weeks he had almost managed to keep himself from thinking of her. What he wanted to appear in his mind was a portrait of Betty. That was who he would end up marrying after all. It was fated, like some tide in the affairs of the world that could not be turned back.

But try as he might, it was Zee who dangled her feet in his memory. And then her face that night at Menger woods, when she had told him she could not marry him. That picture punctured him most of all.

He had ignored her the rest of the summer, knowing it hurt her feelings, but thinking that might bring her around. He wanted her to realize the error of her ways and come to him and beg him to take her back.

But she did not. She seemed to withdraw into her own little world. Since then Doyle tried to let her go. But she had a persistence in him, even though he wanted her gone from his mind.

He wondered if he would ever see Zee Miller again. Maybe she was part of the reason he enlisted. Wasn't it the tradition to join the French Foreign Legion to forget about girls who broke your heart? On the battlefields of France he wouldn't have time to regret the refusal of Zee Miller.

Or so he hoped.

"I got a girl," Doyle said to Alvin.

"What's her name?"

"Betty."

"Pretty?"

"Sure. What about you, Alvin? You got a girl back home?"

Alvin issued a little chuckle. "I guess I do."

"You guess?"

"Her name is Minerva. She's just about the prettiest thing in five counties."

"What are her intentions toward you?"

"She's gonna marry me, of course."

"Well, congratulations. Did you give her a ring?"

"Oh, she don't know it yet. I got a bit of convincing to do. I'm gonna write her love letters while I'm over here. You know, a girl can't for certain say no to a man who knows how to put pretty words together."

Doyle wiped the sweat from his forehead. " 'How do I love thee? Let me count the ways.' "

Alvin almost howled. "Hooee, that's pert near the prettiest words I ever heard. You write 'em?"

"No. A poet named Browning."

"Got to get me some of them words. I was fixin' to tell Minerva she's about as golden as the corn on a summer day. I dunno, something about that—"

"Hey, put a sock in it, will ya?" The voice, low and grunting, came from behind.

Turning, Doyle laid eyes on Thorn Fleming. Alvin issued another tobacco stream into the dirt. "Just passin' the time."

"Well, don't pass it so I can hear you." Fleming's face was flushed, though whether it was the heat or anger, Doyle was not sure.

"No harm in a little friendly chat," Doyle said.

Fleming glared at him. "I don't want to hear your voice neither, college high-hat."

Bristling, Doyle turned back to the march. He hated anyone calling him *high-hat*, or any other name implying social superiority. He'd never pulled elite rank on anyone.

"You hear me, boy?" Thorn Fleming's voice was not only insistent; it was full of bile.

Doyle ignored him.

"I'm talking to you!"

"Don't push it, Fleming," Doyle said.

"Suppose I do?"

Indeed, suppose. Fleming would not be an easy opponent to take down. Doyle had fought as a middleweight on the Princeton team. The one time he'd gone in against a heavy he'd almost gotten his block knocked off. That the judges awarded a draw was a minor miracle.

Before Doyle could fashion a retort, Alvin Beaker jumped in. "You got the brain of a idiot, Fleming."

"What!"

"And you oughta give it back. You ain't usin' it much."

Doyle couldn't help laughing. Alvin Beaker could come up with some good ones, all right.

The humor was lost on Thorn Fleming. "You little people shouldn't mouth off like that. Not healthy."

"Why don't you just march on?" Doyle said.

"I'll march," said Fleming, "and maybe we'll have ourselves a little chat later."

Doyle had no doubt that he meant to keep to that "little chat." He felt an odd sensation. He was about to go to war. He was about to shoot at real people, and be shot at. But there was a greater dread at the uncouth and unmerited enmity of this Fleming. Doyle had been raised his entire life in gentility and the art of civil behavior. That there were such as Thorn Fleming in the world was not so much a surprise as a frustration. There could be no rational discourse with such a man. Sooner or later, he was going to snap.

‖ 4 ‖

Desmond Nichols was unlike any man Zee had ever known. Omaha was the moon and Nichols some sort of moon man, advanced beyond mere humans, a super-intelligent creature who knew things people back in Zenith could hardly even imagine. He'd lived in New York and seen some of the greatest actresses of the day. He had seen Laurette Taylor in *Peg o' My Heart*, spoken to Nazimova! And had two lines in George M. Cohan's *Seven Years to Baldpate*. He'd been on Broadway!

He'd seen Mary Pickford and Lillian Gish in *The Good Little Devil*. Now, only four years later, Mary Pickford was in the motion picture *Rebecca of Sunnybrook Farm* and had just signed a million-dollar contract with Adolph Zukor.

And Desmond Nichols was knowledgeable about it all. He even spoke French! He had *je ne sais quoi*, as her high school French teacher taught her to say.

But best of all he was passionately committed to the theater. He also had an expansive knowledge of the motion picture. It was on this basis that Zee began to wonder if she was in love with this man.

After only two meetings? Why not? It happened in the magazine stories, and those were written by people who lived in New York. They knew. It could happen in real life. In fact, Zee was certain real life could in every way be just like the magazines. If she could not hope that it was, what point would there be in living at all?

They were walking down Farnham Street the day after her infamous entrance into the theater. They made their way past the huge courthouse with its incredible stonework and the J.L. Brandeis and Sons store. Desmond Nichols told her this walk and talk was to be part of her audition.

Audition! Yes, he was considering her for the company! He had even let her sleep in a room at the theater. This was the doorway to a dream.

"So you see, the theater exists for the soul of man," Desmond was saying. He'd been talking for nearly half an hour straight, and Zee was drinking it in like a Bedouin at his well. His gestures were like the motions of a conductor leading an orchestra. His hands floated through the air. They did not jab, as her father's hands did when he stood behind his pulpit.

"The soul of man is artistic," said Desmond Nichols. "It craves art and craves to express itself. That's what I want in my actresses, Miss Miller."

She was about to tell him to call her Zee, but stopped because she thought it might not be socially acceptable. He knew all the right things to do and say, and she did not want him to think her a mere rube—which was what she felt like in his presence. If she didn't speak, it couldn't hurt her. She didn't speak.

"I have a vision for you." Desmond stopped and put one hand on her shoulder. Zee felt a jolt of electricity course through her body. Once, in a class on the physical sciences at Zenith High, Mr. Bramblett let the students feel a small electrical charge. Most of the kids said they did not want to, and so they were not made to do it. But Zee wanted to. She wanted to know the feeling. And Desmond Nichols's hand on her was very much like that feeling.

"What I see in you is a young woman who has grown beautiful, whose gaze is beyond the horizon, and who stands aboard a ship, a ship that is about to suffer a terrible fate."

Zee cocked her head. This was an odd vision! But when he spoke, it was as if he was caught up into a different realm.

"You stand there not knowing that, in just a few hours, the ship will hit an iceberg, and a sentence of death will be pronounced on over a thousand doomed souls."

Now it was beginning to sound familiar.

"Yes, Miss Miller. Someday I am going to go to Hollywood and I am going to film the story of the *Titanic*. But not merely of the ship. It will be a love story, two star-crossed lovers aboard the vessel, and what happens to them on that fateful night."

What was he telling her? That he wanted her to be in his motion picture? Her, Zee Miller of Zenith, Nebraska, in the story of the *Titanic*!

"All dreams are angels' wings. I want you to feel that you can reach the height I just described. It will take work. It will take sacrifice. It will take more heartache than you can know at your tender age." His blue eyes flashed in the Omaha afternoon. "But if you stick to it, if you make that commitment to the theater, I see in you the chance to make angels' wings into your own."

She was feeling faint. At that moment she knew she would do whatever he told her. If he opined that she was the queen of Sheba, she would have believed him.

"Do you want that, Miss Miller?"

All breath left her. She tried to open her mouth to speak but nothing came out. It took a long moment to get her words.

"I want that," she said. "More than anything."

Desmond Nichols looked at her long and hard. "I believe you, Miss Miller. I do. But you are young—"

"I'm nearly eighteen!"

"Yes, and full of the hope and sparkle of idealistic youth. Do not ever lose that. It is your greatest quality. It is what seeps out of your very pores! I'm going to have you read something."

Zee swallowed. "Yes?"

"Don't worry. I won't put you on Shakespeare. Not yet. Something from Clyde Fitch, say. Or Cohan. And you will fill the theater with your voice, Miss Miller."

She believed that she would.

Her feet hardly touched the ground all the way back to the theater. She was looking at Desmond Nichols's face as they turned the final corner. He was telling her about the time he saw a production of *Othello* when—

He stopped, concern etched on his face.

She looked. At the front of the theater stood two policemen. One of them pointed at her.

‖ 5 ‖

Dear Father and Mother:
I hope this letter finds you well. I have but a few moments to set pen to paper, to let you know that I am in good spirits, even though we have tasted battle at last. I must tell you how it hap-

pened, and let you know I made it through fine.

Two days ago we arrived at some town by train, and then started marching. Twenty-two miles in one day. This first day's march constituted a strong test of endurance in light of our softness and lack of training, especially as, in addition to a heavy rifle, bayonet, ammunition, and spade, each of us lugged a knapsack containing emergency provisions—tinned meats, coffee extract, sugar, salt, rice, and biscuits, and various tin cooking and eating utensils. Stuffed in there also were a second pair of shoes, overcoat, slicker, changes of underwear—but you need not know all the details. We had parts of tents, too, and the entire weight of our sacks was in the neighborhood of fifty pounds.

Too bad I'm not back at Princeton on the boxing team now! I think I shall end in better health than ever, so long as I stay away from the cooties. (Do not worry, Mother. I'm told they know how to burn these vermin out of us with a hot liquid concoction from the pit of . . . you know.)

At sunset we reached a small wood, and there tucked in the middle of it was a monastery, seemingly oblivious to the touch of war. It was odd, yet serene. I thought of good old Zenith, of Central Park and the summertime.

Camp was made, tents put up, fires lit, and coffee brewed. I must report that I have become a caffeine fiend. Don't worry, though. I have not lost any sleep. We have a saying around here: If you can't sleep at night, it isn't the coffee, it's the bunk. Har har.

It was a wonderful picture under the stars at night. The boys sat around the campfires softly singing in chorus, while behind us the shadowy figures of the monks in and out of camp as they brought refreshments to the troops. In the red glow of the campfire I could see the eager and enthusiastic faces of the young officers, and I wondered what they were thinking. Even if it was thoughts of war, the beauty of the surroundings was intoxicating.

I stretched out, using my cape as a blanket, and even though I know we are at war, I felt like I might write a poem. Did you hear that, Dad? Indulge me!

The next day we marched again, heading toward the front. We were to start our experience in actual war, but we began with the dismal, drab work of digging new gun pits and erecting dugouts under camouflage in a fresh spot of a sector as yet unknown to the Fritzies.

To get to the new location, we crossed fields pitted with shell holes. The place looks like a land afflicted with smallpox. In places the shell holes were filled with water, and their regularity of form and location on the ground suggested your muffin dish, Mom, just before it is to pass into the oven.

We made camp, but the next day began to hear the noise of war. Far away, the repeated rumblings which sounded like distant thunder, the rat-a-tat-tat of machine guns. My stomach started to churn then, let me tell you.

Presently, a mounted supply officer came rushing with a message to our colonel. We were summoned to the colonel, who addressed us in an almost businesslike way. "Gentlemen," he said, "accept my congratulations. I have good news for you. We may meet the enemy today, and I sincerely hope to lead you to the fight before evening."

We went on the march, coming ever closer to the cannonading, and in the midst of a dense forest we again came to a short halt. Orders were given to load rifles, and upon emerging from the woods we fell into open formation, the men marching abreast, the companies at a distance of three hundred yards, with the battalions at a distance of about a thousand yards.

"Drivers and cannoneers prepare to mount," the battery commander shouted. "Right by sections!"

Doyle gave Alvin Beaker a pat. "Here we go."

"Right with you," the shooter said.

All around, the activity was intensifying. The cracking of the guns ahead mixed with the rumble of caissons and wagons, and the swish of flying water as the eight-horse hitches splashed along the winding, rain-soaked road.

The drivers rode as if nailed to their seats. They drove with one hand, holding the reins snug in their left fingers and controlling the off horses with their short artillery whips.

Doyle estimated that the entire battery filled a mile of roadway. There were perhaps ten caissons, a couple of ammunition wagons, one rolling kitchen, three supply wagons, and other vehicles of various sorts. Three junior lieutenants rode up and down the line, making sure the orders bugled from up front were being carried out by the section chiefs.

We kept to the right of the road, leaving the left side free. We passed many ox teams drawing primitive wagons and now and then a big French army truck or automobile containing officers. If the auto had a general in it, there were two stars stuck on the windshield.

They marched on, for perhaps a quarter mile. The sound of gunfire grew louder, though Doyle estimated they were still at a safe distance.

"Down!"

The command came from the rear. Doyle and Alvin, along with all the men around, hit the muddy road. Facedown, heart racing, Doyle heard the whizzing of a motor overhead and looked up. A German aeroplane!

And then an explosion close behind.

"They found us!" someone yelled. Doyle figured the German plane had signaled their approach and now was probably directing Gerrie fire and closely watching its effect. A chain of hills was hiding the squad from the view of the enemy, who had to fire indirectly.

The plane hovered above their heads. One soldier fired his rifle at it.

"No firing!" came the sharp order.

"Why not?" Alvin said to Doyle. "I want to try for it."

"It's too high," Doyle said. "And what if the bullets come back down on us?"

"This is war, boy," Alvin said.

Then a volley of rifle fire came up from the rear—a section chief must have ordered his men to fire anyway. Amazingly, it did the trick, and the aeroplane rose and disappeared into the clouds.

> *It was about to get rough, but then a section of our own artillery came thundering on, occupied a little hill that gave them the chance to fire on the enemy. What a sound! The thundering of our own artillery was thrilling, and most of the boys thought we had never heard any more welcoming sound. It got rid of the jitters in us, the nerves on edge as we thought we were going into battle. It gave us back our confidence. We were ordered to take up positions and dig trenches, any further advance being out of the question, as the Hun artillery overlooked and commanded the entire plain stretching in front of us.*
>
> *But for some reason, as yet not discovered, the enemy retreated. We were ready and willing to fight. We still are.*

So your boy is safe and sound, but ever ready to meet the Fritzies wherever they may be engaged.

In another letter, I will tell you about my new friend, Alvin Beaker, of Tennessee. He is not like anyone you ever knew in Zenith, Nebraska! But boy, can he shoot a rifle.

I must go now, wishing you all my love. Tell Rusty to keep his nose clean and his powder dry. Give Gertie a kiss for me.

Your loving son,
Doyle

6

The preacher took up the periodical and read the editorial he'd penned.

Which Side Is God On?

Each of the nations claims God as its own. It is one thing to claim Him; it is another and a different thing to have Him as an ally. He moves in a mysterious way His wonders to perform, and a thousand years is as a day in the working of His will.

Now it happens that certain scoffers, mockers of the sacred things within the hearts of men, have jeeringly asked which side God is on in this greatest of all wars that the earth has known. It is said bandied about among the infidels that God is waiting to see which side is more likely to win before declaring himself—and such irreverent witticism is in itself a contemptible mockery of the great passionate faith which has steered the nations as they grimly lay their precious sacrifices of blood and bone upon the battlefields.

Pausing, the preacher remembered how these words, when written, had been so heavy upon him. As the editor of *The King's Business,* the official publication of the Bible Institute of Los Angeles, every editorial he wrote carried great weight with Christian and lay readers alike.

At sixty-two, he had dealt with many controversies over the years, but never one so perplexing as this terrible war.

The Kaiser went to war declaring that God had given the

sword into his hand. Equally does our president declare a divine mission. This has become a religious war. No matter how it started, what racial enmities, what economic irritations, what scheming of corrupt interests may have given rise to its origin, it has become a religious war. The very intensity of faith of the striving nations has made it a religious war. "God is with us!" say the Germans; "God help us!" say the Allies with no less confidence, but with more humbleness of spirit.

It will be made plain in the results of this world war which side God is on.

We reject, however, the doctrine currently being tossed about in some quarters that the sacrificing of one's life in this war guaranties eternity in Heaven. No man will be saved by dying for his country.

True patriotism demands that we repent of our sins, that we get right with God, that we accept the Lord Jesus as our Saviour, and surrender absolutely to Him as our Lord. Only then can any soldier, indeed any man or woman on earth, march forth into any conflict with confidence.

The preacher put down the periodical, closed his eyes and, in the morning light of his office, prayed that his words would find true purchase in the hearts of men and women.

Then the preacher, Dr. Reuben Archer Torrey, whispered, "And have mercy upon our nation, O Lord. Thy name be lifted up."

‖ 7 ‖

Doyle and Alvin reclined on cots inside the heavy canvas tent at rest camp. The fading orange sun gave a firelike sheen to the place. Earlier that day, up near the front lines, fifty of the Stars and Stripes engaged in the glamorous work of making latrines, filling sandbags for the night, thickening the parapet, and building dugouts. Doyle never worked so hard in his life. Every joint and muscle in his body groaned. So did his stomach. They got only thin rations and one mess tin of water for a whole day. That was why Alvin taught Doyle the fine art of sucking a pebble to defeat thirst. It worked surprisingly well.

Doyle propped himself up on one elbow and looked at the

Tennessee shooter. "You believe in God, Alvin?"

"'Course I do, Doyle. You got to be crazy not to believe in God."

"Then why do you suppose He lets this happen, this war? Aren't there just as many Christians on the German side as on our side?"

He wondered if Alvin, being from the hills, unsullied by city life or college training—where you could slice any idea into a thousand pieces and never put it together again—had some sort of basic insight into the mysteries of the universe.

Alvin's brow creased. "That's a good'un, all right. Don't rightly know the answer. But I always figured God knew things we warn't suppose to know, lessen we got to be like them folk who built up the Tower of Babel. The Good Book says they wanted to be just like God, and I don't suppose that's what we're all here to be."

"I guess I need to know more than that," Doyle said.

"The Good Book's got the answers."

"That's just one book."

"No, Doyle! It's the Word o' God. It says what you ought to do and what you oughtn't. And if you do what you ought, God's gonna bless you. And if you do what you oughtn't, God's gonna rebuke you. And I always try to do what I ought."

"Sounds too simple."

"Don't you have no Bible learnin' where you're from?"

"We have churches."

"Now, just 'cause you sit in a nest don't make you a bird."

"You've got yourself a point there, Alvin."

"You miss home, Doyle?"

"Sure."

"What's it like where you live?"

A flood of images came at once. Home. Cars and dances. Ice cream. He saw himself on the track and the football field, the spectators cheering. Zee.

"I guess it's like any old place," Doyle said.

"What would you be doin' right about now, if'n you were back home?"

"I wonder. Maybe I'd be writing a poem."

The little Tennessean sat up on his cot. "You write poems?"

"Well, don't get bugs about it, I—"

"I got a poem!"

"Really?"

"You think we ain't got poetry in Tennessee?"

"I never thought about it."

"We got lotsa poetry."

"And you wrote one?"

"Want to hear it?"

"Sure I do."

Alvin smiled, his lips curving up the left side of his face. It looked to Doyle as if he may even have blushed a little.

"Okay, here goes. My daddy liked it real good." Alvin cleared his throat and recited:

"The sky is a big blanket
And them stars
Is made by angels,
Pokin' holes in it
With their cigars."

The silence was heavy between them. Alvin Beaker looked expectantly at Doyle.

"That's . . . beautiful," Doyle said.

"You like it?"

"How could a lover of fine poetry not like it?"

Alvin beamed. "It rhymes and everything."

"Among its many virtues."

"Now you."

"Me what?"

"Tell me one a your poems."

Now it was Doyle who felt a sudden shyness. "Nah."

"Come on there, Doyle. It's only fair." And then, like a lawyer sealing his case, Alvin added, "Ain't it?"

Doyle sighed and swung his legs over the edge of the cot. "Okay. But I don't write poems for anybody to read. They're just for me."

"I won't tell nobody."

"All right." Doyle leaned his head back, searching his memory.

"Like a harvest abandoned in a field
The variable aspects of you
Are waiting to be known.
Like a wave

That knows no peace
Only another shore
Restless, but more—
Open, unbidden, pure."

Doyle was aware that Alvin was staring at him, mouth agape.
"Doyle?"
"Yes?"
"I don't know what you just said."
Doyle sighed.
Then Alvin added, "But it sounded real pretty."
"It's about a girl I used to know."
"The one you were tellin' me about? Betty or somethin'?"
"No. Another girl."
"What happened to her?"
"I don't know," Doyle said. "But sometimes I wonder."

‖ 8 ‖

Zee thought about jumping off the train and hitchhiking a ride back to Omaha. But she knew it would be fruitless. Her father would only alert the cops again, and now they knew she was connected to the theater company.

The policeman beside her had no humor, no mirth. "Just doing my job" was all he said to her the whole time. He didn't even tell her what she already knew—that her father had arranged for her "arrest" and forced return.

Desmond told her not to fight it. He told her to go on back, but that he'd work it out somehow. She hadn't seen the last of him.

Or were those mere words?

She thought about Doyle then. Good old Doyle, Old Omaha. Maybe she should have married him. What would life be like now? She'd know what her future would be. Home and family, and a man she could trust to provide.

And she'd make life miserable for him. No, wedded bliss was not for her, unless it was to a man who shared her passion for living.

Desmond Nichols maybe? ·

She allowed herself a moment's fantasy, then waved it off. *Don't be a naïve little girl, not anymore. You're going to be an actress, a famous one.* Desmond had said so.

The countryside swept past her—farmhouses and dirt roads, trees and meadows. Not a theater in sight. Little dirt-water towns.

This was not going to be her lot, no matter what her father said.

Her father. She dreaded seeing him. He would try to put the fear of God in her once again. She was not going to have any of it. She did not fear God, because God was not really there.

She shuddered a little at the thought. But she did not back away from it. She did not believe in God. At least not the God she had grown up hearing about. Maybe there was some power in the sky somewhere, maybe not.

But people were all alone on earth and had to make their own way. She realized she was clenching her fists. Yes, that was what she would do—fight through all this and get to the top.

No matter the cost.

‖ 9 ‖

The platoon ended the day's march at the outskirts of a courtyard with a modest house right in the middle. The house looked abandoned, like so many others they'd passed along the road. The Boche, as the French called the Germans, were getting close. Most Frenchies chose to leave while the leaving was good.

Doyle and Alvin kept guns at the ready. You never knew if snipers were inside. Alvin set his Springfield on the top of a wall, taking aim just in case. Blake and Sanders, Nottingham and Ellsworth, took it upon themselves to check the house from both sides. When they gave the all clear, the men, issuing what seemed like a collective sigh of relief, entered the quaint courtyard, which didn't hold much but an abandoned vegetable garden and some old tools—a hoe, a rack, a scythe.

And a woodpile by a window.

A woodpile that moved. A healthy chunk fell down the pile with a loud clatter. Thorn Fleming happened to be the nearest soldier to the woodpile. When he heard the noise he spun around, spooked, and at once had his rifle aimed at the heart of the pile.

Fahey, a shooter from Texas, laughed. "That's it, Thornie, you teach that woodpile a lesson!" This brought a small chorus of chuckles from a bored and tired group.

More wood moved.

Fleming, issuing a grunt, kicked at the pile.

The wood screamed.

In a flash Thorn Fleming reached his big hand into the pile and pulled something out. It was a boy. Fleming had him by the hair.

The boy, who was only ten or eleven, screamed again, this time in pain more than fear. He wore a plain brown shirt, short brown pants, and no shoes.

"Well, look what we got here!" As if he were holding up a bagged bobcat, Fleming jerked the boy forward.

"It's a kid!" It was Fahey again. "Let him go."

"Maybe he's a spy!" Fleming made no move to release the lad, whose face was squinched in pain. "I'll wait till Sarge gets here. Meantime, maybe we can get a story out of 'im."

Fleming jerked the boy's head back and forth.

"Leave him be," Fahey said. "Maybe he lives here."

"Then where's his ma and pa?" Fleming turned the boy's head toward him. "Where are they, huh?"

The boy screamed pitifully.

"He's a Frenchie," Fahey said. "He's on our side."

"I'm not takin' any chances."

Doyle saw tears streaming down the boy's face. "Let him go, Fleming."

The big man fixed his eyes on Doyle. "What did you say, college boy?"

"I said let him go."

Silence seemed to descend on the whole countryside. For once the snap of distant artillery was stilled, as was the *clink-clank* of canteens against Sam Brownes.

Fleming smiled and jerked the boy's head again.

Doyle unshouldered his rifle and held it butt-end toward Fleming's face. With a quick move he thrust it, coming within one inch of the big man's nose.

The feint served its purpose. Fleming flinched, released the boy's hair, put his hand up in a defensive position. The boy took the opportunity to scramble away.

Thorn Fleming's hand went down to the handle of his trench knife. Doyle watched the sausage-sized fingers clench the weapon, and had no doubt that if this had been a secluded alley in a dark city, Thorn Fleming would have drawn it with murderous intent.

Doyle's pulse quickened as he kept the rifle in his hands like a club.

"Here, what's going on?" Sergeant Halliday was striding toward them. He did not look pleased.

"Nothing, sir," Doyle said.

"Put down your rifle."

Doyle did so, keeping his eye on Fleming.

Halliday looked at Fleming. "Anything wrong with you?"

Looking at the ground, Fleming mumbled something that sounded like "No."

"Then let's keep it that way," Halliday said. "Now get some rest. We're here until tomorrow morning."

But that left early evening. When Halliday and a patrol went up the road to check trenches and make contact with the advance unit, Fleming told Doyle to meet him in the woods to settle accounts.

They met there, inside an anxious group of men surrounding them like a human ring. Doyle was not under any illusions that the Marquis of Queensbury rules would be followed by Thorn Fleming. This fight was going to have to be conducted with all the cleverness Doyle could muster. He certainly would not win it on strength alone.

Doyle, shirtless like the big Kansan in front of him, took the boxer's position, as it had been drilled into him by Coach Cleary of the Princeton team. Right fist under the chin. Left out lazily but ready to strike like a cobra. Elbows in. Look for your spot.

This was not the kind of fighting Doyle thought he'd be seeing in the farmlands of France.

Thorn Fleming spit into his huge hands, rubbed them together, then formed the giant paws into fists. They were bricks on the ends of his arms. Bricks with knuckles—huge lumps like walnuts under the skin. His round shoulders and full, muscular arms made him as solid as a tree. Only this tree could move, circling to the left, eyeing Doyle as the bricklike fists made lazy circles in front of the big man's chest.

"I'm gonna enjoy teaching a lesson to the college boy." Thorn Fleming smiled. One of his front teeth was missing. Doyle looked into the black hole where the tooth should have been, and it was an abyss where good men fell.

Fleming motioned to Doyle. "What're ya waitin' for?"

A low rumbling began to arise from the gathered men. It didn't matter that the Fritzies were down the road waiting for a real battle. This was an all-American event, two men with fists and a grudge. And one of them would fall for certain.

Doyle heard Alvin Beaker's voice. "Remember, the bigger the bear, the bigger the rug!"

"Come on, little man," Fleming taunted.

Doyle didn't move. He wanted the big man to come to him.

He didn't have long to wait. Fleming lunged, throwing a right at Doyle's head. Doyle ducked, turned left, jabbed with his left fist. It caught Fleming on the jaw, snapping the big man's head back.

The soldiers roared.

Fleming looked stunned. But only momentarily. His snarling grin returned as he started toward Doyle again. "That was a lucky one. Your last."

Doyle decided not to wait. Mixing up the tactics would be the name of the game with Fleming. So this time it was Doyle who lunged forward, bending at the waist, and throwing a full right into Fleming's midsection. Doyle's fist impacted a layer of fat and muscle. It hardly fazed Fleming.

It would take a lot more body shots to bring him down. Work both, Doyle told himself. Keep him guessing.

Fleming made a sudden feint. Doyle stepped back, but as he did his foot slipped on a patch of wet French soil. Fleming charged, threw a roundhouse right. It caught Doyle flush on the side of the head.

Flame erupted behind Doyle's eyes. As he fell to the ground he thought he would lose consciousness. He hit hard, his nose filling with the smell of dirt and wet leaves. The left side of his face felt caved in. He was vaguely aware of the voices shouting, and heard Alvin calling to him to get up. He did not know if he could.

He willed himself up. He shook his head to try to get his focus back. As soon as he did he saw Fleming lunge toward him. Pure instinct made Doyle duck and jump left, and the big man missed with a left hook that surely would have finished Doyle.

Fleming stumbled into the crowd, falling to one knee. Doyle backed up quickly, gaining better perception by the second, and with that a realization.

As soon as Fleming turned around Doyle shouted, "Open your fists. You're holding something."

Fleming stopped short and quickly looked around at the faces. And that was when Doyle knew he had him.

"Open your fists, Fleming."

Fleming fairly growled. "I don't have to do nothin'. Come on, coward."

"Open up so everybody can see."

Fleming didn't bother to say another word. He flew at Doyle in a rage. Doyle forgot all about the Marquis of Queensberry. He felt for the first time in his life the primal desire to kill.

When Fleming was three paces away, Doyle lowered his shoulder and charged. He had led his football squad in tackling every year. He'd practiced in his yard by hitting heavy bags hung from an oak tree. When his shoulder rammed Fleming's chest, Doyle drove hard with his legs. He felt a heavy blow on his back, but that did not stop him. He continued to drive with his legs and reached down and pulled at Fleming's knees. The big man fell backward, Doyle on top of him.

Fleming was momentarily stunned. Doyle rose on one knee and brought his full weight down behind his elbow, jamming it into Fleming's face.

He heard the crunch of cartilage and a grunt from the big man. Doyle, blinded by inner fire, began pummeling Fleming's face with his fists.

He would have continued until Fleming's face was raw meat, but he was pulled off by a couple of soldiers.

"Open up his hands!" Doyle screamed, feeling more animal than man. "Open them up!"

It was Alvin Beaker who put a boot on Fleming's right wrist and ground it. Fleming, his face bloody, gurgled and opened his hand.

A round piece of iron rolled out.

Doyle flew at the downed man again, screaming. This time four men had to restrain him.

‖ 10 ‖

"The theater is depraved," Zee's father said. "It is a place where young women become corrupted. You are too young to understand that. But I know what happens to young girls who go to the theater or become enamored with the motion picture. And as long as I am looking out for you, I must forbid you from doing this to yourself."

It had been three days since her return home, and in that time he had hardly said ten words to her. She had the sense that he was working up to this moment and that he had prepared to speak to her with as much care as he prepared a sermon.

"Don't you believe that I can look out for these terrible things?" she said. "After all, you have taught me—"

"It is too much. You would be like a lamb among wolves. You must run from these things, not try to withstand them, for that you cannot do."

"But, Papa—"

He put his hand up, then put his finger on his worn Bible. "'Ye adulterers and adulteresses, know ye not that the friendship of the world is enmity with God? Whosoever therefore will be a friend of the world is the enemy of God.'"

"But we live in the world, Papa! How can it be so bad? Didn't God create it?"

"Creation fell, through sin. This world is in the hands of the devil. Don't you see that?"

Zee shook her head.

"I want to save you from that, Zenobia. You are so young. You don't know what can happen."

"I only want to be an actress."

"I forbid it."

"Father, I am nearly eighteen. I have decided—"

"You may decide nothing. Do you realize I could have you committed to an asylum?"

A chill blew across her soul. "Father, you would not do that."

She saw his eyes begin to brim with tears. "If I thought your soul was going to the devil, I would do everything—"

"It is *my* soul, Father."

"Your soul belongs to God."

"It is *mine*."

Her father sat down heavily, looking defeated. Zee had never seen this in him before. She had seen him angry and frustrated and disappointed. But not this. Yet wasn't this what she had wanted all along?

"Father, I don't mean to bring you trouble. I truly don't."

He said nothing.

There was a knock at the door. It was so loud it startled Zee. Her father gave her a glowering look and pointed at her. "You stay right there," he said.

Zee listened as she heard her father open the door and say, "What is it?"

"May I speak to you, sir?"

It was Desmond's voice! Ignoring her father's admonition, Zee rushed to the front door.

"Who are you?" her father said.

"My name is Desmond Nichols, and I've come all the way from Omaha just to speak with you. May I come in?"

"Are you the theater man?"

"I am."

"Then I have nothing to say to you."

Zee tugged on her father's arm. "Oh, let him come in, Papa, please."

"There's nothing he can say that will change the situation."

"That is what I've come about," Desmond said. "If you'll let me say my piece, I will only say it once. And then whatever decision you make, I will abide by it. I will go back to Omaha and that will be that."

Her father thought about this for a long moment. Zee marveled at that. Desmond had a way of getting people to listen, even those who were dead set against him. She expected her father to slam the door, but instead he nodded and said, "I will give you five minutes, sir."

Her father let him inside but left the door open.

"Reverend Miller, you may not realize it, but your daughter has an extraordinary gift. She has what it takes to become a truly fine actress."

Her father's iron face did not move, even to twitch. "You can tell all this from a few moments with her?"

"We spent more than a few moments together," Desmond said, then quickly added, "You must understand, sir, that everything was perfectly proper in every respect. I assure you."

"I do not know you from Adam, sir, so your assurances hold no weight with me."

"He's not lying, Father!"

Rebuking her with a look, her father turned back to Desmond. "The clock is ticking."

"Sir, the theater has very few stars. Many come to try, but only a handful are blessed with that certain quality your daughter has."

"Did you come all the way from Omaha just to tell me that?"

"I did, yes."

"You have nothing else in mind regarding my daughter?"

Desmond Nichols stiffened. "Certainly not."

"Why should I believe you? You are from a world that is known for its moral degeneracy."

"Papa!"

"Quiet, girl. You are too young to know of these things. I believe that Mr. Nichols knows exactly what I am talking about."

"What assurances can I give you?" Desmond said.

"None."

"Papa, please—"

"Quiet!"

"Mr. Nichols has been a perfect gentleman, he came all the way from Omaha—"

"Zenobia!"

She fell silent, and knew nothing she could say would move him. Nothing Desmond Nichols could say, either.

"I am quite sorry that you made the trip," Reverend Miller said, "but I must ask you to leave my home."

Desmond bowed slightly. "Thank you for your time. Good-bye, Zenobia. You must listen to your father."

Then he was gone.

Zee tried to keep the tears from her eyes.

"Believe me, child, when I tell you that this is for the best," her father said.

She no longer believed him. She ran up to her room and slammed the door shut, then threw herself on the floor.

Oh, how had it come to this? From dreams of stardom to a prisoner again in this house? What autocratic God was taking such pleasure in her unhappiness?

‖ 11 ‖

Major Horace Rennert brooked no nonsense when it came to discipline. All the boys knew it. So Doyle was sure he was about to be busted out of the army.

Standing like a schoolboy in the major's tent quarters, Doyle waited for the inevitable. Rennert finished scribbling something on a sheet of paper and then looked up.

"You almost killed a man yesterday."

Doyle couldn't deny it. His rage against Thorn Fleming had been total, overwhelming. "Yes, sir."

"Problem was, he was one of ours. Usually we try to kill the enemy."

"Yes, sir."

"Tell me, Lawrence, why you wanted to hurt this man."

"I have no excuse."

"I'm not asking for an excuse. I'm asking why you wanted to kill him."

"It was just something . . ."

"Inside you?"

"Yes, sir."

Rennert nodded. "Hate?"

"I suppose that's one word for it. I wasn't really thinking of words. I lost control, sir."

"That much is evident." Rennert tapped his fingers together. "But don't for one minute think that hate is a bad thing. It's in the nature of war to hate. The Hun hates us. It's part of his makeup. Your Fritz soldier is not happy unless he hates something. We hate them right back. Because of what they're doing. Without hate, it becomes difficult to kill. Do you follow?"

"I think so."

"The Huns are dangerous because of their hate, and they have something else. The courage of despair. They know Germany can't win the war, but they hope that the Allies will fight amongst themselves, and the folks back home will grow weary of war and force their governments to make peace. To fight against this requires a certain ruthlessness on our part."

"Yes, sir."

"You demonstrated that you have that. If turned in the right direction, it can be a great asset. You think you can channel that rage against the Huns, Lawrence?"

"I think so, sir."

"Forget thinking. Can you do it or not?"

He could. He knew that now. "Yes, sir."

Rennert stood up, grabbed a pipe from his small desk. He lit it and took several puffs. "From the report I received on yesterday's incident, I don't believe you were in the wrong. You may have carried it a bit far, but you were on the right side of the fight. Besides, I've gotten reports on this fellow Fleming for some time. We're dealing with him."

"Dealing?"

"He won't be bothering this division anymore. And I trust I'm not going to have further trouble from you."

"No, sir."

"There may come a time, Lawrence, when I have to select a few men for something beyond the call of duty. It may require ruthlessness, no hesitation in the field. Do you think you're up to it?"

"I will certainly try," Doyle said. A weak answer, but all he could come up with at the moment. He had no idea what the major was asking of him. Except that the request turned his stomach into a churning mass.

"All right, then. That'll be all. Reserve your fighting for the enemy. Tomorrow you'll be . . ."

‖ 12 ‖

. . . crawling. In the early morning mist they crawled. A platoon of the Stars and Stripes—128 men—making their way toward a little clearing in a wood. Doyle would learn later that they called this place La Croix Rouge. In peacetime it must have been a quaint and pastoral location. A place for lovers and picnics, for outings with the family dog.

Now it was full of Germans with big guns.

Yesterday, with the platoon a mile away from this spot, Doyle could hear the *puppety-pup* of the Germans' best and deadliest weapon of this war—the machine gun. Sarge had told them that the woods would be full of the Hun, but that the hills beyond would be the place where the battle would be decided. For up there under cover of tall grass were the machine-gun nests that could mow down dozens of soldiers at a time.

Add to that the desperation of the veteran Army of Imperial Germany, fighting at the tail end of four years of almost superhuman effort against a fresh foe—the upstart Americans—and you had a dangerous recipe. "All bets are off," Sarge said. "Kill the men in gray or take them prisoner. Just don't let them keep on firing."

Doyle and Alvin took positions behind a couple of stumps as the rest of the boys fanned out in a rough semicircle near the clearing. Soon would come the order to attack.

"About time," Alvin said. "We need to show the Gerries who the big dogs are, and it ain't them."

"Simply and elegantly put," Doyle said.

"Elle gant?"

"It's a good thing."

The sun was breaking in through the mist now, causing shafts of smoky light to appear. *Like in a church*, Doyle thought. Some church. On the altar of the god of war there would soon be sacrifice. *Make them German*, he told himself.

What was it like back home now, he wondered. Was Rusty off with some of his friends, playing war games? Or taking a soda down at the

Candy Emporium? Maybe he was at Sims Drug Store, looking for a new comb or pomade. Maybe he was thinking about a girl for the first time in his life.

Zee. What would she be doing about now?

A sharp snap, like a twig breaking. Doyle turned. Someone coming? Then he heard a scream. One of the men was rolling on the ground grabbing at his head. Doyle saw red through the man's fingers.

Doyle's body clenched. Alvin yelped like a hunting dog. The battle was on.

The first part lasted an hour. It was not a rush from the woods but a slow, painful advance. It was almost like what Doyle pictured Indian warfare to have been in George Washington's time. From behind trees the men would look for gray targets to shoot with their rifles. And back would come the answer from deep within the woods where the enemy could barely be seen.

But advance they did, this unit of the Stars and Stripes, until the shooting stopped for a time. The Germans had retreated—or at least stopped firing. There was cheering from some of the boys when the news was passed along, but Sarge put a stop to that. "This is only the beginning. We are going to dig in."

The only tools the men had with which to dig shelter trenches were little short-handled shovels. They reminded Doyle of the little spade he used as a child to dig pirate caves on the sandy shores of Lake Menger. Now with these shovels, along with mess kits, helmets, and bare hands the men dug their concealed positions.

Late in the day, Sarge crawled to the shelter Doyle and Alvin had managed to fashion.

"I need you two to reconnoiter up ahead. Major Rennert says you're the guys. We need to know what we're looking at. I want Beaker to go because he's the best shot in the company. Lawrence, I want you to be the eyes and ears. You think you can manage without getting shot?"

‖ 13 ‖

"Hurry!" Desmond Nichols's insistent voice rose up above the hum and murmur of the Pierce Arrow engine. Zee had scurried through Mrs. Skyler's garden toward the back road where the car was idling. Even though it was late and her house was well behind her, Zee thought her father's strong hand would grab her neck at any moment.

"Are you sure about this?" Desmond said as Zee threw her tiny suitcase in the back of the runabout and jumped into the passenger seat.

She threw her arms around his neck and kissed his cheek. She felt him tense, then suddenly he put his hands behind her head and pulled her mouth to his.

A kiss! His lips were soft yet insistent. A seal of their new life together. Man and wife!

He had made his proposal so cleverly, so romantically. Hand-delivered his letter to her as she came out of school. In theatrical makeup! He wore a bushy white mustache and large-brimmed hat, very much like a Southern gentleman.

"I cannot live without you," he whispered, and she knew it was him. "Read this."

It was the first love letter she had ever received, and a proposal of marriage as well! It was just like in a movie. Together, he said, they would take theater and movies by storm. Together, no one could stop them. He ended the letter by telling her where and when he would be waiting, if she accepted his proposal.

Her body vibrated with longing for three days, until the night came. She wrote a note to her father:

> *Papa, by the time you read this I shall be a long way off. I do not want you to be troubled about me any longer. I will be a married woman, and that should ease your mind. I have begun a new life, with Desmond Nichols. Please do not attempt to interfere. Perhaps someday you will soften toward me and accept us both. You will see, Papa. It is all for the best. Z*

"Let's go!" Nichols gunned the car. It lurched forward.

Toward freedom.

"Scared?" Desmond said.

"A little," Zee said, even though it was much. "Are you?"

"Why?"

"You could get in an awful lot of trouble for this, couldn't you?"

"Not if we are married, which we shall be presently."

"When we get to Omaha?"

"We are not going to Omaha."

"No?"

"I do not want us to be found, not yet. I have a plan."

A plan. The very thing she needed. Everything had happened so fast.

"Where shall we live?" Zee asked anxiously.

"Where would you like to live?"

"Shall we begin in New York? I would love to see New York."

"It's the greatest city in the world."

"Should we conquer Broadway before Hollywood?"

Desmond laughed into the wind, and she loved him wildly. It was intoxicating, this feeling, this longing that was as wide and deep as any ocean. *This is what real love is like,* she thought. Not puppy-dog love, like the kind she once fancied between her and Doyle. That was for kids. Not this. It was indescribably more.

"I say we go straight to Hollywood," Desmond said. "All the excitement is shifting there. Sure, they will always have Broadway. But imagine going back to New York as a major movie star. You could write your own ticket. Have your pick of plays—"

"With you directing, of course."

"Of course! You would insist, wouldn't you, dearest?"

"I should throw a fit of insistence!"

"That's my girl."

His girl. Forever. A man and wife team that would be the talk of the movie and theater worlds!

They journeyed a bit in silence. Zee put her head back against the seat and looked at the stars. They were shining like diamonds, and she thought of a diamond bracelet. One that she would wear on her wrist one day as a great movie star. Maybe the greatest ever.

Sleep well, Papa. Don't ever worry about me. We are both better off. You'll see. You'll see. . . .

‖ 14 ‖

Up in the hills behind a veil of grass were the Germans. How many there were Doyle could not say. Every so often the sound of the machine guns blasted, and Doyle figured they were shooting at the forward positions. He wondered how many of his comrades were going down, how many could be saved if he could get to the guns.

Alvin said, "I'm good at shootin' but not so good at thinkin'. What do you think we should do?"

Doyle surveyed the ground around him and the wide open space between the trees and the plateau. "You know, if we could get to the side of that machine-gun nest without being seen, I don't think they'd be able to turn the guns on us. If we find the right spot, we can pick them off. Only problem is we don't know how many Germans are between us and them."

"Don't matter to me."

"I say we go off to the right there, step by step, tree by tree, and be sure no one is behind us. Then we make for the hill, and the nest."

Alvin squinted in a manner that suggested he was mulling it over. "I'm thinkin' that's why we came here."

Doyle clapped him on the shoulder. Then, slowly, like frogs bouncing from one lily pad to another, Doyle and Alvin made their way around the right-hand side of the clearing where most of the fighting was taking place. They stopped each time they reached a new location and listened. Doyle heard a slight wind in the trees between volleys of machine-gun fire.

Then Doyle thought he saw something move about fifty yards away, in a wheat field. Was it the flash of a German uniform?

He saw it again. Yes. A soldier of the Kaiser's army, ducking. Doyle nudged Alvin and pointed. The two lifted their Springfield rifles and took aim in the general direction.

For a long moment they listened. Doyle could only see the swaying gold of wheat, and nothing else.

Alvin Beaker's rifle cracked. Doyle almost jumped out of his tunic. There was nothing to shoot at out there. Doyle waited, crouching for the return fire.

Alvin started forward. Doyle grabbed him by the pant leg and pulled him back. "Don't! He'll see you."

"Who?"

"The Hun soldier out there."

Alvin showed his gap-toothed smile. "Nah. I got him."

"How do you know that?"

"Because I shot, son. I don't shoot lessen I aim to hit something. Come on."

"Be careful. Go slow."

But like a hound dog covering a coon trail, Alvin Beaker made a line directly to the spot where Doyle had last seen the German soldier. Doyle kept his rifle up in the crook of his shoulder, expecting to be fired upon at any second.

No shots came. Alvin led Doyle confidently to the patch of wheat where the German soldier had last been seen. Using his rifle to point through the stalks, Alvin showed Doyle the dead man.

A small pool of blood colored the ground around the soldier's head. Alvin's shot had caught him in the back of the neck, just under the flared helmet. It was, at once, the most remarkable and most horrifying thing Doyle had ever seen.

That Alvin could have sensed this man's position from where they had been, and shot him, was the remarkable part, a feat of marksmanship that was beyond Doyle's imagination.

But Doyle felt sick. The German soldier lying lifeless on the ground looked frighteningly like his brother Rusty. The hair was light and sandy, the skin fair, and his eyes were open, blue, like his brother's.

For a second he thought he was in some nightmare and wanted to scream so he could wake up.

Alvin yanked him back to awareness. "Come on, Doyle. There's gotta be more."

Suddenly the machine guns started up again, furious this time. There was only the slightest pause between bursts.

"What're they shootin' at?" Alvin said.

"Our boys," Doyle said.

"What do we do?"

"We hurry."

‖ 15 ‖

"Where are we?" Zee said when Desmond cut the motor.

"A little cabin that belongs to my partner. We'll be safe here for the night."

"It is so dark here." No light from the moon or stars came through the thick canopy of trees.

"Scared?" Desmond said, then he took her hand. "Of course you are, my dear. I've snatched you away from the only home, the only town you've ever known. But let me remind you that a life in the arts is a risk. That is what makes it so exhilarating. You will find that your greatest art comes from that place inside you where fear lives."

Zee wished she had a book of all his sayings. Desmond Nichols knew things she wanted to remember forever. Even his offhand conversation was full of nuggets of gold, sparkling stones and music.

The cabin was dank but, in its way, quaint. Desmond lit a lamp, and the muted light matched the illumination of her heart. She was on a journey now; it was really true. But it was a journey toward light and freedom and she had the right guide.

Suddenly she heard her father's voice. It was not the angry voice, but one of warning. She tried to ignore it. It was all just part of this risk Desmond had spoken of. But the words were there just the same. *Protect your virtue.*

"Where shall I . . . we . . ." Zee let her voice drop off in girlish embarrassment.

"Sleep?" Desmond said.

He could read her thoughts. He was amazing.

"My dear, you shall have the soft feather bed in the other room. I shall be comfortable on the cushions out here. There are plenty of blankets, and lots of crisp, clean air."

She almost said, "I love you." She would have meant it, but it was so inadequate to express what she was actually feeling. Soon enough, she would show him just how much she could love.

"But let us talk for a few moments more," Desmond Nichols said. "Let us wrap ourselves in blankets and I will make a fire and we will talk of the theater, of the motion picture, of stardom, and of great women—with whom you will take your place one day."

He built a fire that flamed and crackled and threw warmth into the cabin. With a blanket around her, and sitting on a large pillow, Zee felt at long last free and protected. She had seen cocoons and the butterflies that emerged. She was growing wings. They would be beautiful one day.

"Tell me something," Desmond said. "Did you have any boys hovering around you in Zenith? I would imagine you had to beat them off with a sharp stick."

"Oh no. I rather think I am not considered the height of womanhood."

"No?"

"Not when I could beat most of them in running and climbing."

"So no beau?"

"Not really. Oh, there was one boy . . ."

"Tell me."

"A good boy. He came from a well-to-do family. His father is a lawyer. He liked me very much. I liked him, too."

"Very much?"

"Yes."

"Did you think you might marry him?"

"He wanted to."

"You turned him down?"

"I think that he and I are on different paths of life. We would not have been right for each other. He is a thinker and is going to be a great lawyer someday. He needs a wife who will be at home for him and help to make him a success. That cannot be me."

Desmond's face was reflected in the fire. *Like the face of Perseus in Athena's shield,* she thought. A more handsome face she had never seen, and eyes with depths unknown.

"You are wise beyond your years," Desmond said. "You know that your soul is that of an artist. We are peculiar people."

"And what about you, Desmond? So long as we are talking about our pasts. Have you ever been married?"

He nodded wistfully. "To a beautiful actress. Her name was Nora.

We met in New York and fell in love immediately. I was about to go on tour with a repertory company, playing Mercutio in *Romeo and Juliet*. She was in a New York company, as the understudy for the lead in *The Easiest Way*, the Eugene Walter play. We faced the prospect of being torn apart. We were, at the time, in a room in an apartment in Greenwich Village."

"Desmond!"

"Scandalized?" He smiled. "I wanted to make an honest woman of her, as the tired old saying goes. But I was willing to let her stay. She did not want to stay. She wanted to come with me. I tried to talk her out of it, halfheartedly, of course."

He laughed softly, and Zee felt an inner heat that was not from fire or blanket.

"So off we went. We found a justice of the peace and exchanged our vows. And spent the next week of our life in Schenectady. Soon it was time for rehearsals, and she auditioned for a position in the company. She was accepted, of course. She was a dazzling actress."

"I can see that in your eyes."

"Yes. She lives in me still. There will always be part of her in me." He sighed. "Unfortunately, the realities of the theater life intruded upon us in an almost supernatural way."

"Supernatural?"

"First of all, the actress whom Nora understudied in *The Easiest Way* fell off a trolley and was out of the play. The actress who took over, Miss Frances Starr, won great acclaim from the critics. Nora tried to hide her disappointment, but it was evident she held something against me."

"But you couldn't have known—"

"Ah, hell hath no fury like an actress losing a career part."

"And so she left you?"

"No. We were together in repertory. But then there was the decision to do the Scottish play."

"Scottish play?"

Desmond put his finger to his lips. "One never speaks the title when in production. Too many things happen that cannot be explained."

Zee shook her head, perplexed.

"*Macbeth*, my dear. The Scottish play. And Nora won the role of

Lady Macbeth, from another more established actress. It caused some fireworks, I can tell you. But I was proud of Nora, and for a few days we were happy again. Nothing makes an actor happier than winning a plum role! And nothing casts him into the depths of despair like losing the same.''

"What happened?"

"The spirits of the Scottish play dropped a curtain bag on her. Put her in the hospital. Well, that turned out to be one event too many. She held it against me that she had no career in New York and no leading role in Shakespeare. She began to drink a little.''

"Oh dear."

"Yes, and that is never good for an actress. Remember that. No booze. Eh?"

Zee nodded and looked into the fire. She saw dreams dancing in the flames.

"We were divorced later that year," Desmond Nichols said. "It's been seven years since."

Suddenly, Zee's cheeks flushed. She felt the schoolgirl and a woman at the same time. "And why have you not remarried?"

He threw up his hands. "Until now, I would have said that theater life is not the soil for matrimony. Too demanding, a jealous mistress. But now . . ."

He looked at her, but with the fire behind him his face was nearly a silhouette. She could not tell what his eyes were saying.

"Well now," he said softly. "We'd best turn in. Tomorrow we will have miles to go. Once we do, there's no turning back. Zee Miller, do you want to call off this mad adventure and return to your father's house?"

"No, Desmond. I have made my break."

He nodded. "That's what I wanted to hear. You are going to make it, my dear. You are going to be a glittering star."

‖ 16 ‖

Doyle could see maybe half a dozen men in the trench, about twenty yards short of the German wire, pinned there by the constant barrage of the machine guns on the hill.

Then the firing stopped for a time, and Doyle heard the awful screams of the wounded. Bodies writhed on the ground. Men were crawling back to the trenches, falling in like rocks rolling over a cliff.

Then the firing started up again, this time around a shell hole between the trench and the wire. Doyle saw why. Three men were trapped there. The German gunners had seen them and were not going to let them out. Bullets fell like hail.

Doyle fixed his bayonet to his rifle. "Alvin, you see that rock?" Doyle nodded toward a small boulder, not much bigger than a wash-tub.

Alvin looked. "I see it."

"Can you get a position there to fire up at the nest?"

"'Course I can."

"And cover me?"

"Where you goin'?"

"To flank the nest. I want you to keep 'em busy."

Alvin grabbed his sleeve. "I'm goin' with you."

"No, I need you down here. I need somebody to give 'em trouble, and you can fire better and faster than any of us."

"But, Doyle—"

"Do it, Alvin."

Another flurry of shots. Doyle looked out at the shell hole and saw someone running toward it. Spence, the kid from Maryland. What was he doing? Maybe the men in the hole were wounded and he was bring-ing help. He had a satchel strapped to his back. It bobbed up and down as he ran.

Spence was fast, though, and he cut back and forth like Red Grange dodging tacklers on the gridiron. He was going to make it.

At the rim of the shell hole he was hit. His body jerked backward, then fell, a spatter of blood issuing from his body before it collapsed to the ground.

Doyle's own body seemed to explode with rage and desperation. He hit Alvin on the shoulder and cried, "Now!"

Alvin Beaker, low and slinky, headed for the boulder. Doyle ran into the woods. He was nearly blind with his drive to get to the nest.

He was in a grove of apple trees now. They were bereft of fruit and leaves, haggard-looking branches up in the air like soldiers surrendering. Doyle kept going, keeping the hill to his left. He started to think he would make it without being seen.

Then, seemingly out of nowhere, a German soldier appeared in front of him. He was young, like Doyle, boyish with blond hair. He looked as shocked as Doyle.

Doyle raised his rifle and, at the same time, realized he had not put in a magazine.

For a few beats of a heart they looked at each other. Then the German dropped his hand to his side, slapping for his revolver.

Screaming, Doyle charged.

The report of the German's gun sounded like a firecracker. Doyle's left shoulder jerked back.

He was hit, figuring himself for dead, but the German did not fire another shot, though he tried.

Jammed? The words of Major Rennet burst through Doyle's mind. "... *ruthlessness, no hesitation* ..."

The soldier's eyes expanded, round and blue and fearful.

Doyle drove his bayonet up, under the German's chin. A guttural chuffing sound issued from the soldier just before he fell backward. Blood spurted from the gash in the German's throat.

With blind rage Doyle thrust the bayonet into the soldier's chest. The young body quivered. Doyle thrust again, crying out with a sound that came from a cave deep inside his chest. His bayonet broke through skin and bone. The German's body was still.

For a long minute Doyle was still as well. His body hardened, refused to move. He had killed a man face-to-face. He had not hesitated. And with that realization, any innocence he may have harbored as a tie to his boyhood melted away.

He felt wet blood on his chest, just above the heart. A bullet wound?

The renewed sound of the machine guns shook him back to the moment.

Doyle ignored the blood and the pain and shoved a new clip into his Springfield's magazine.

Hurry up, he told himself. *Hurry up*.

From his vantage point on the side of the hill, he could look up but could not see the German position. He heard the guns, knew where they were. But he also knew the second he came out from behind the tree he would be spotted. He had fifty feet of hill to climb, with nothing between him and the Gerries but dirt and rock.

Because of the terrain, there was no need for the enemy to position sentries. It would be enough for one of them to give an occasional glance down from the perch. It was the perfect position to hold. And no one would be fool enough to try and take the hill from this side.

But Doyle had come this far. Something had to be done. Eventually the Stars and Stripes would break through down below, yet at a terrible cost. Unless the guns up top could be stilled.

If he got near the top, he could toss a grenade and follow immediately after, perhaps reaching a position to clean out the nest. He'd have to make sure the grenade found its way home. And he was still unsure what the exact position was.

He saw a German head look down from the hill, give a quick glance, then disappear.

Now! He charged up the hill with all the strength he had left.

He made for a leafless tree on the ridge, about twenty yards from where he'd seen the German soldier. If he could get there, it wouldn't be a permanent hiding place but could afford him precious time in which to unleash a grenade or rifle volley. He was probably dead, but he would take as many Germans with him as he could.

He ran on.

All the way across the terrain he heard the hot sound of machine-gun fire.

Stop them! Stop them, whatever else happens to you.

Keeping his eyes up at the ridge, Doyle got closer to the tree, his lungs burning. He was moving as fast as he could, but against the steep ridge and in full regalia, he felt as if he were running through mud.

He was sure he would be seen now. He was ready in his mind's eye to stop and fire at the first sign of a German helmet. He'd have one shot, one chance to take him out, then get to the top where he would decide what to do.

His boot hit a loose rock, and down he went. The smell of dirt and death burst into his nostrils.

He rolled, feeling like a prize fool, and scrambled to his feet again. Still no German. He had only thirty yards to go.

Thirty. He used to do that in seconds on the football field. Now he wondered if he'd live even to see another football game.

Machine-gun fire kept him moving upward.

Twenty yards to go.

A flash in the sunlight.

The Huns.

Doyle was close enough to see his eyes, and the eyes widened with shock.

Just as he'd rehearsed it in his mind, Doyle whipped his rifle into firing position. So did the Gerrie, his Mauser rifle at his shoulder.

Doyle heard a rifle shot, but he wasn't hit. Instead, the German's head disappeared.

What?

Then Doyle heard a voice behind him. "Come on, boy!"

Alvin grabbed Doyle's tunic and pulled him up. Doyle didn't say anything as the two made it up to the small tree that couldn't protect them.

From that vantage point they could see the dead German soldier, lying alone in the small trench. The trench continued on about five feet, then cut right. That was where the rest of them would be.

Doyle said, "What are you doing?"

"Figured you'd be in trouble by now," Alvin said.

"How many you figure are up here?"

"Maybe twenty. From what I seen. Four machine guns, I think."

"I'll lead," Doyle said. "I'll toss a grenade at the crook. You be ready to shoot anything that moves."

Alvin winked. "Gimme a hard one next time."

Doyle jumped into the trench and lurched forward, bounding over the corpse of the German sentry. At the same time he took a grenade off his belt and pulled the pin with his mouth. Holding the lever down with his fingers, he made the turn.

And saw the nest. Four machine guns. Gunners and belt feeders at each.

Behind them, and down the line, over a dozen Germans.

Doyle threw the grenade.

Several German heads looked up, then at Doyle. Three heads dropped in rapid succession. Alvin had shot them.

The grenade exploded.

And then everything seemed to happen at once. Doyle was aware of a machine gunner trying to swing around. He shot the gunner with his rifle. The other guns had been stilled from the grenade explosion. German soldiers ran for cover behind a small ridge. Alvin hit two or three as they did. Doyle readied another grenade to throw behind the scattering Huns. He threw, heard the explosion, then saw a belt feeder, bloodied at the chest, moving—a revolver in his hand. Doyle shot him.

The nest was now littered with dead Germans. Doyle had no idea how many were left, or how many were waiting for him and Alvin behind the ridge.

There was no giving up now.

Doyle waved Alvin forward.

The marksman took two steps past Doyle. Doyle saw his face—determined and wide-eyed, young and heroic.

Doyle saw something flying through the air toward him. Instantly he thought, *German grenade.* He opened his mouth to warn Alvin. The moment he did, the explosion came. The force was two hammers hitting the sides of his head.

Dead.

Alvi . . .

All thought was swallowed up in black soundlessness.

‖ 17 ‖

She could not sleep. Too excited. A strong wind outside the cabin made her think of storms and ships and adventures. What a wonderful sound! A wind like this whipped up oceans and toppled trees and filled sails. It was like the wind of her artistic soul. She'd give herself over to it, utterly.

This is what it feels like to be a woman.

One of the magazines she'd managed to sneak a look at in Palmer's Drug Store—when she was sure no one was looking—had a story about Theda Bara and her power over men. It had used the term "sex appeal," and it nearly frightened Zee to see that in print. But when the story described how one man had shot himself outside Theda Bara's gated home, Zee thought she understood. A woman like that had power.

The door to her bedroom creaked open. A shaft of yellow light poured in. Zee sat up quickly, startled. "Desmond?"

His shadowy form moved into the room. "Are you still awake?"

"Yes. I haven't been able to sleep."

"I came to check on you, that's all." He left the door open and walked toward the bed.

"I'll be all right," Zee said, holding the covers up to her neck. She had not realized until now how cold it had become.

"I know you will be all right," Desmond said. "I want you to remember that."

That was an odd turn of phrase. It almost sounded as if he did not expect to see her again. Had he changed his mind about her, about them?

The wooden floor squeaked slightly as Desmond reached the foot of the bed. And stopped. "I have not been able to sleep, either. I have been out by the fire thinking of you and the limitless possibilities of your womanhood. I want to be a part of that. I want to be your guide. If you listen to me and trust me . . ."

The strange, dual reaction arose in Zee. The words should have thrilled her, been more of the wind that lifted her into the skies of a glorious future. And part of her mind told her that was what he meant.

But just alongside those wonderful thoughts was an undercurrent of disquiet. For Desmond seemed at that moment like an actor. He was trying too hard. And that confused her.

"Do you trust me?" he said.

"Of course, dearest."

"I knew you would say that." He stepped around now closer to her, and his hands went to his shirt. Zee thought he was touching his chest out of some form of gratitude, but then saw his fingers moving downward. He was unbuttoning his shirt, ever more rapidly, and before she could think anything else he had removed it and thrown it to the floor.

"I want to be close to you," he said. "I want to impart something of me to you." He went to his belt now, and Zee pushed herself back against the headboard. "I want you to impart something to me."

She had to think. "Please, Desmond, not until we are married."

He slowed his undressing but did not stop it. "Time is short. The world moves."

"Not now, please. Let me—"

"Shh." He began to lift the covers.

She brought her legs to her chest. "No . . ."

He was beside her. Instinctively she pushed outward with her legs, hitting Desmond on his naked hip.

He fell off the bed and hit the floor with a grunt.

"Desmond, I'm so sorry, please . . ."

The next sound that came from him was something animalistic.

And then he was upon her, one hand at her throat, the other tearing at her nightshirt.

‖ 18 ‖

The smell of something rotting hit him first, yanked Doyle back to his senses. Moans around him bespoke human suffering. A flash of white and a red cross. Women in uniforms.

Field hospital. He was on his back.

Could he move? Yes. His arms moved. His left shoulder was encased in bandages. His legs had a dull ache, but he felt them, wiggled his toes. He'd had a dream that he was only half a body. Now he felt a wave of relief.

It started coming back to him. German gunners. Something had exploded. A Gerrie grenade. And he'd gone out.

But he was alive.

Alvin. What had happened to Alvin? Doyle looked at the cot next to him, expecting Alvin to be there. It was somebody else. Doyle didn't recognize him.

He waved at a nurse. She was young and had a nice smile. She did not belong here.

"Can you help me?"

"I will try." She had a thick French accent. In better times it would have been endearing. Now it only seemed like a hindrance.

"I had a friend—"

"Yes?"

"Beaker. Alvin Beaker. Can you tell me what happened to him?"

"I am so sorry. Name I do not."

"Can you find out? Is there someone in command?"

"*Com and?*"

"Yeah, somebody—" A sharp pain in his legs stopped his voice.

"No talk, eh?"

"Talk, *yes*. Alvin Beaker. Find out."

She looked troubled, but nodded and hurried off. She did not return. Time crawled. Doyle stared at the ceiling.

Finally he fell into a fitful sleep.

When he awoke, the nurse was standing over him. She told him in her fractured English that she had the information he had requested.

She hurried out of the room, and a moment later returned with an American field doctor, who introduced himself as Clark.

"How you getting along, son? We took a lot of shrapnel out of your leg."

"Do you know about Alvin Beaker?"

Clark removed a folded piece of paper from the pocket of his shirt. "Your friend died in the field, I'm sorry to say."

The fire in Doyle's leg raged upward, filling his chest and head.

"Let me read the report." The doctor unfolded the paper. "It says that Private Beaker was wounded in the chest, arms, face, and neck as a result of a grenade blast. Your name is in the report. Your wound came from the same blast. But because of what you did, stopping the machine guns, your company was able to charge up the hill. When the company reached the two of you, they found Beaker propped on one arm, firing his weapon with the other. He took out ten of the enemy before help arrived."

Doyle saw it in his mind. The Tennessee hillbilly picking off the Germans with his one-armed shot. Just like he used to do back home.

"Private Beaker died shortly after the end of the battle. According to the report his last words were about you."

"Me?"

Clark read from the paper in his hand. "I don't really understand it, but this is what was recorded. Private Beaker apparently wanted the message to Doyle Lawrence to be not to worry about him, that he'd be poking holes in a blanket." Clark looked at Doyle. "Does that mean anything to you?"

Doyle put his hand over his eyes.

"Just one more thing," Clark said. "I thought you might like to know. You and Private Beaker are going to be recommended for the Congressional Medal of Honor."

PART III

INTERMEZZO

The vast majority of men who seek happiness do not find it. You may say what you please, but for the majority of men this is an unhappy world. I go down into the houses of the poor, I do not find many happy people there. I go into the homes of the rich, I do not find many happy people even there. Study the faces of the people you meet on the street, at places of entertainment, or anywhere else, how many really radiant faces do you see? When you do see one it is so exceptional that you note it at once. But there is a way, and a very simple way, a very sure way, and a way that is open to all, not only to find happiness, but to be unspeakably happy. Listen, "Whom having not seen, ye love; in whom, though now ye see him not, yet believing, ye rejoice with joy unspeakable and full of glory."

—R. A. Torrey

Doyle stowed his duffel in a lockbox at the station and decided to walk back through town. No one was there to meet him.

That was not strange in the least, for he had not told anyone he was coming.

The dusty smell of Zenith's oak trees and streets was the same. The way the sun played off the copper-topped dome of the courthouse was another recognizable sight. Yet the comfort of it barely registered with him; in some ways, it was like landing on foreign soil.

As he walked out of the depot he saw old Mrs. Evans from the Methodist church. She had known the Lawrence family for years, though not intimately. Enough that she should have recognized Doyle. But she merely nodded at him and he her. Doyle thought that with his hat and mustache, he did not look anything like the fresh-faced young Princeton freshman who had left town nearly eighteen months before.

He liked the fact that he might be somewhat anonymous. The last thing he wanted was people rushing up to welcome him home like some conquering hero. In fact, if invisibility had been a reality instead of a speculation by the likes of imaginative writers, he would have gladly assumed a ghostly aspect.

In many ways the town had not changed. From the depot, looking down Main Street, Doyle saw the familiar outline of the town's various establishments. On the left like a stodgy soldier on watch was Miller's Emporium, the largest store in Zenith. Made of brick and stone and a large plate-glass window, the store always looked to Doyle like a fort with a soda fountain inside. Not to mention various sundries like combs, shaving kits, needles, and thread. People would be shopping there, as if nothing had ever happened in the world to make them stop and wonder at the evil that men do.

Across the street from Miller's was the competition for the second largest store in town, Kendicott's Hardware, where one could buy everything from guns to nails to small carriages. But the market for carriages was fast drying up under the relentless tide of the automobile. Doyle was aware of the sounds now in Zenith, the sputter and rattle of autos even more pronounced than when he left.

Up and down Main Street, Doyle saw past and present in a suspicious dance, an antagonistic promenade between horse and auto. Farmers looking like stubborn elves drove their horse teams to market, while goggled gentlemen in Model T's honked at the animals and their owners, not to mention the people trying to cross the street.

At Hapwood's Drug Store, Doyle paused to look at the window advertisements, which had always changed like seasonal leaves. On one large card a handsome man with a cigarette winked at the passersby; the phrase *I'd walk a mile for a Camel* was emblazoned over his head.

Two boys, about twelve years old, stumbled out of the drugstore, laughing, half wrestling each other over a peppermint stick. One of them bumped flush into Doyle. The boy stepped backward and, with an insouciant grin, said, "Sorry, pops," and then he ran on to join his friend.

Pops. Doyle didn't know whether to laugh or moan. Did he look that old? He felt it. He had several lifetimes in him now, packed in by abundant deaths.

Continuing on, Doyle passed the State Bank with its odor of money, the pool hall with its stench of tobacco, and the tobacco shop itself, which smelled like old, dry wood. The four-story Zenith Hotel stood up as testimony to the insatiable enthusiasm of the city's boosters. Doyle always thought its yellow exterior was a bit gaudy. Now it seemed merely mundane.

Not once during his walk home did a single person stop to say hello. Loneliness opened its mouth inside him, swallowing him. In his own hometown, he was alone. In the world he was alone. He knew that now, and best get used to it.

On a wooden fence he saw a large, colorful poster of the bald-pated William Jennings Bryan. Bryan was coming to town to deliver a lecture on the "Aftermath of the War." What did Bryan know about it? *I don't recall seeing him in France with mud on his shoes.*

Doyle stepped to the fence and ripped the poster, leaving half a head of Bryan flapping on the wood.

He stood there with the paper in his hand. Now, why had he done that? He was doing things now, thinking things that were shocking in their unfamiliarity. Things that came upon him suddenly, like jungle cats.

"Nervous out of the service," he said to himself, walking on.

A few blocks past C Street he saw the schoolhouse where he had been a student before going on to high school. Some children were running around in the yard of the school, playing tag and throwing balls. It was in that very yard that Doyle first learned to play football. The memory seemed distant now, part of another person's past. It brought no joy to him to remember.

All at once he noticed a ball rolling toward him. A boy of perhaps ten ran up to the split-rail fence that surrounded the school yard and shouted, "Hey, mister, can you get our ball?"

Doyle leaned over and, with one hand, effortlessly scooped up the ball.

"Kick it," the boy said excitedly. Suddenly several other of his fellows saw what was going on and ran over to the fence. "Kick it! Kick it!" they started shouting, as if this would be a grand event to witness.

Kick it, Doyle thought. Just like he used to. He could make the pigskin really fly at one time. What would it be like to do it again?

"Kick it! Kick it!"

Why? Why do anything anymore? What did one action have to do with any other, and what difference would it make to anyone, truly?

Doyle rolled the ball toward the fence. The kids issued a huge, disappointed groan.

Doyle turned his back and sat down on the curb next to a telephone pole. A cool wind blew across his cheeks. The voices of the children behind him were sharp in his ears.

And then, quite suddenly and unexpectedly, he began to cry.

‖ 2 ‖

Five days later Doyle sat on the front porch of the Lawrence home, in the old porch swing that creaked with rusty capitulation, wrapped in a blanket. He watched the last of the leaves falling from the spreading shingle oak tree in the front yard. He found himself fixated on one brown leaf clinging to a branch. It looked stubborn, alone, like a solitary prayer unheard. Doyle wanted to see the moment it fell.

He heard the front door open. His mother came out with a mug in her hand. "Thought you'd like some coffee."

"Thanks." Doyle took the mug. His mother stood there as if looking for approval. He sipped the coffee and smiled. "Good," he said.

His mother smoothed her apron. And again.

"What is it, Mother?" He knew what it was and didn't want to talk about it again, but this was his mother and she wasn't going to move without saying it.

"You know how much your father and I think of you, don't you?"

"Sure."

"You know how good it is to have you home."

"Sure."

"We want you to feel that you can rest here."

Doyle filled his mouth with coffee. It was bitter, but sweet compared to the sludge he'd grown used to in France.

"And when you're all rested, we'll get you ready to go back to school. Your father's—"

"I don't know if I'm going back to school, Ma. Not just yet."

As though prepared for this moment, Mrs. Lawrence cleared her throat and spoke quickly. "Now, we won't have any more of that sort of talk," she said in a voice halfway between plea and rebuke. "Your future is too important to—"

"My future is—"

"—us, all of us, including Rusty."

Rusty? So that was what this was about. For the last five days they'd been at him. First his father, in a conversation that ended with Doyle shouting and leaving the house. That must have shocked Wallace Edgar Lawrence, for he withdrew in his interactions with Doyle after that. And unleashed his mother. *"You talk to the boy,"* Doyle imagined his father saying. *"I don't know what to do with him anymore."*

His mother had been unleashed, all right, with her fumbling attempts at persuasion embarrassing them both. Now, desperately, she was going to use his brother against him.

"Leave Rusty out of this," Doyle said.

"But he looks up to you so. You should have heard the way he bragged to his friends about his brother the soldier."

"I don't want him to brag."

"And about how you were going to come back a hero and become a famous lawyer and all of that."

"Ma, please—"

"For his sake, Doyle, for Rusty's sake. Can't you at least make a decision about returning to Princeton? Just a decision like that would give Rusty confidence again."

Doyle looked up and closed his eyes. "Mother, please don't talk about this right now."

"If not now, when?"

"I don't know."

"Will you talk to Rusty? Will you spend some time with him?"

"That's not going to change anything."

"It might. Will you—"

"Perhaps, Ma. Now, if—"

"There's one more thing, Doyle." Mrs. Lawrence looked at her hands, her fingers entwined and flexing.

"Yes?"

"It's your birthday on Saturday."

His birthday. He'd forgotten all about it. "It's not anything to make a fuss over," he said.

"We thought, that is, your father and I thought, that it would be nice to host a small dinner party for you. We've invited—"

"No, Mother."

"—a few of our closest friends, and some of your old friends, too, Doyle. So many people have been asking—"

Doyle jumped up off the swing. "I said no, Ma. I don't want to see anybody for my birthday."

"But it was to be a surprise—"

"I said *no*. Do you hear me? No!"

His mother's delicate resistance crumbled. She burst into tears and ran back into the house.

‖ 3 ‖

A city of concrete and crowds, a teeming sea of hot humanity and cold, predaceous skyscrapers.

And she, the girl off the train, with a simple leather bag in her hand and a secondhand hat on her head, was just another of the faceless and frenetic.

Yet this was where all things would become new.

This was where she belonged. Los Angeles was the city of angels and dreams, glitter and light.

She put her hand on her stomach and felt nauseated again. One thing she did not have here in this adopted city was a doctor, a family doctor like the one who had known her most of her life. But that was another world, another time.

She wondered if she would have to find someplace to be sick.

She stood firm on the corner, where one sign said *Broadway* and another *Fourth*. The electric trolleys clanged down the center of the street. Two rivers of automobiles, at crosscurrents with each other, roiled and flowed, creating the noise of the city.

Around her people moved with closemouthed purpose. Jaws clenched, little talk, a circus of motion.

City of dreams.

"You lost?" a man's voice said.

She turned, and the man leered at her. A burning of hate erupted inside her.

The man backed up, turned and walked away.

She felt a dizzying wave of nausea then and thought she'd better find a drugstore, get some dyspepsia pills, anything. If she was to make her mark, she would have to be the picture of health, the new American sweetheart.

Even though any sweetness she might have felt had been torn away from her in a cabin in Nebraska.

For one fleeting moment she thought about turning back, but she fought it away with anger and determination.

This is, she said to herself, *what you wanted. And this is where you'll stay.*

‖ 4 ‖

Doyle woke up screaming.

The dream had been about Alvin Beaker. Another kid, too—a soldier whose face was obscured by blood. They were running through a forest of silver trees in a black night. Doyle was in front of them, urging them to hurry, but they were slow, knee-deep in mud.

Hurry, hurry, you idiots, the Huns will be here any minute and we've got to get back—back to camp, back to where there will be warmth and food and—

The silver trees began to move, but Alvin and the blood-faced soldier didn't see what was happening. The trees turned into giant Hun soldiers, spindly German soldiers with limbs that became bayonets.

Look out, don't you see it?

Then they saw the trees, yet the mud was too deep and they couldn't run.

The blood-face screamed as ten bayonets skewered his body.

Alvin cried, *Doyle! Help me!*

Doyle couldn't move. His legs had sunk into the ground so that he was as fixed as a post.

When Alvin was sliced by the bayonets, Doyle screamed, and that was how he woke up.

His body heaved, heavy panting, in the darkness of the room.

Had he awakened the whole house? The town?

A light in the hallway, spilling under the door. The door opened slowly, pouring illumination into the room.

"Doyle?"

"It's all right, Dad." He wished it weren't his father who had heard him scream.

"Trouble sleeping?"

"It's all right. I'll be fine."

William Edgar Lawrence, silhouetted in the doorway, said, "Why don't you come on downstairs. I'd like to talk to you."

"Now?"

"There's some chicken in the icebox. Let's have some and a glass of milk." His father used his authoritative voice, his take-charge tone. There would be a fight if Doyle resisted.

Doyle got his robe.

His father did it all, putting out the chicken which had been their dinner the night before. They sat at the kitchen table, as normal as could be.

"We're sure glad to have you back, son."

"Thanks."

"Recovering from your wounds and all. We know what you went through over there."

Doyle said nothing.

"I know you'd like to be back fighting with your comrades, but you've done your duty, and done it admirably."

Silence.

"Ed Pepper's boy. You remember Ed Pepper, don't you?"

"Yes, Dad."

"Ed's boy, Sonny, came back with one leg. Now he's working with his dad at the big auto garage on Main. Sonny always had a way with machines. Still does. Now he works on automobiles with his father."

"You said that already."

"Said what?"

"That he works with his father."

"The wonder of it is that he does it all on one leg. Sonny's got one of those wooden legs the army gave him. But he is as hard a worker as he ever was."

Doyle took one bite of cold chicken leg. It was dry in his mouth.

"What I was thinking, Doyle, was that you could come and work for me for a while."

"Work?"

"As a clerk. You could do that for a few months, get your sense of how a real law office works, then re-enroll at Princeton. I think a lot of the boys will take some well-deserved time off."

Putting the chicken leg down, Doyle said, "Time off is a good idea."

"For a few months. And then you'll be ready."

"Dad, I don't know—"

"And you'll learn how to find case law, prepare a brief. It will be invaluable."

"I don't know if that's exactly what I want."

His father placed both his hands flat on the table as if trying to push something down. "Son, in this world it is not always what we want that is what we get. You have been given an opportunity to take your place in society, to make a success of yourself. Your schooling is a gift."

Doyle shook his head. "I've tried to remember that, Dad. Honest. But I can't. I try to see myself back at Princeton, but I can't."

"You've been through a long trial—"

"It's not just that." Doyle tensed, wanting his father to know, needing him to understand. For the first time in his life, Doyle felt that he was talking directly to him, man to man. "I was never really comfortable at Princeton."

"You never told us that."

"I didn't want to disappoint you. Or Mother. But all the time I was there I had this feeling that there was something I was missing, or not seeing. One day I stopped in the middle of the campus, students moving all around me, and I thought of us as mice in a large cage. We moved, but where were we really going?"

His father looked at his hands, still on the table as if to hold him steady.

"I thought then maybe that's why I like to write poetry sometimes. When I do that, I'm trying to capture something with words. I'm trying to . . . make real the thing that is just out of my grasp. I feel that if I rush back to Princeton, I'll miss that thing."

There was a long silence between them. Then his father slowly shook his head. "I think it would be best for you to come to work for me. What you need to find, what you are missing, is a place to work, to contribute. That's what I will give you."

"Dad, I need—"

"On Monday you can begin."

Doyle suddenly felt like a child again, his father commanding, he about to obey.

"There is one more thing, son." His father reached into the pocket of his robe and pulled out a letter. It was in a brown envelope. "Your mother and I received this from the War Department. Why didn't you tell us?"

"Tell you what?"

"About the Congressional Medal of Honor."

"How long have you had that?"

"I was waiting for a good time to bring it up. They want to have all of us come to the ceremony."

"I told them I don't want it."

His father shook his head slowly. "That's ludicrous, son. You are being awarded the nation's highest military honor."

Doyle's chest tightened. "Dad, I just . . . I just want you to understand. I'm sorry I didn't tell you about it."

"But this is an honor for all of us."

"Is that really it? That it's an honor for the Lawrence family?"

"What's wrong with—"

Doyle stood up. "Throw the letter away, Dad. Pretend you never got it. Please."

"Doyle—"

But Doyle was already at the kitchen door, opening it, charging out into the night where he could breathe.

Down the familiar streets he walked, in no particular direction. The smell of the night air brought back a memory from his childhood, the time he and Corny Pugh sneaked off to the carnival and paid two bits for the sideshow. They wanted to see the freaks, thought it would be a big laugh and something they should do to become "men of the world" at ten years old. They'd heard about dwarfs and skeleton-boned men and ladies with beards. That would be a lark.

But they weren't prepared for the geek.

Even now, Doyle could see the pathetic man's face, a bearded contortion of human misery, and hear his shrieks as he threw his arms around in the air, beat the ground in the crude pit, and his desperate lunge for the live chicken they tossed in with him.

Doyle would never forget the horrific sight of a man putting the head of the chicken in his mouth and biting down, the blood spurting and the ripping of the head from the feathered body.

For weeks the geek haunted Doyle's dreams. How could a human being become such a freak, such an outcast? What could be going on inside his tortured soul?

Tonight Doyle thought about the geek and that maybe he could at last understand.

The wind off the river blew cold. Doyle folded his arms over his chest. He would not return home for a coat. He was an outcast now, he knew that, and such did not have homes.

‖ 5 ‖

Dr. Reuben Archer Torrey hurried up the walk to his Pasadena home.

Though he'd taught two classes at the Bible Institute, and led a short chapel at 4:00 P.M., he was in the grip of energy. At age sixty-two he could still do prodigious intellectual work, especially when he felt called upon to defend the faith.

As he did now.

Clara, his wife of nearly thirty-nine years, appeared at the sound of the door slamming.

"What on earth?"

Torrey was already taking off his coat. He kissed his wife on the cheek. "I'll need my dinner in the study. I'll be working tonight."

"What's happened, Archie?"

He loosened his tie. It was something of a joke, he knew, around the institute, this matter of his formal dress. But he always thought that a man professing the Gospel ought to look his best, to honor the Lord.

"Another lecture on the New Theology is being advertised," Torrey said. "To take place at one of our largest churches! I must scrap my Sunday sermon and answer."

As he went into his study, Torrey reflected on the wave of opposition that was rising in the wake of *The Fundamentals*. This enterprise, which Torrey had helped to edit, was a stand against the watering down of Christian theology by fanciful ideas imported from Europe. Funded primarily by Lyman Stewart, the oil magnate who was also the moving force behind the Bible Institute of Los Angeles, *The Fundamentals* was a series of articles by Christian scholars on such subjects as the accuracy and authority of the Bible, sin, judgment, and salvation by grace. *The Fundamentals* had been sent, free of charge, to pastors all across America. And had created a firestorm of controversy.

Some prominent churchmen came out in opposition to this project, arguing that the age of believing in a divinely inspired book was past.

If that was so, Torrey firmly believed, then Christianity could not long survive.

He practically threw himself into his desk chair. He opened a drawer, took out fresh paper, then picked up his pen.

At the top of the paper he wrote, *Will the Bible Survive Its Critics?* And then, in a furious rush, he scrawled the opening.

If the Bible is the Word of God, the only trustworthy revelation from God himself, of himself, His purposes and His will, of man's beauty and destiny, of spiritual and eternal realities, then we have a starting point from which we can proceed to the conquest of the whole domain of religious truth.

But if the Bible is not the Word of God, if it is the mere product of man's thinking, speculating, and guessing, not altogether trustworthy in regard to religious and eternal proof, then we are all "at sea," not knowing whither we are drifting, but we may be sure that we are not drifting toward any safe port.

He paused, closed his eyes and prayed. Torrey's sermons were often printed and distributed as brochures or booklets. He bathed them, always, in much prayer. He sensed now that this would be one of the most important, and far-reaching, of his addresses. He prayed fervently.

Lord, may these words reach far and wide, and draw many nigh unto thee.

And then, once more, he began to write.

I believe the Bible to be the Word of God first of all because of the testimony of Jesus Christ. . . .

‖ 6 ‖

"How do you like Mother's new pop-up toaster?" Rusty said. "Can you beat that?"

They were in Central Park on Thursday afternoon, two days after Doyle had charged out of the house after talking with his father. Mrs. Lawrence, always sensitive to the crosscurrents of emotion under her roof, had finally persuaded Doyle to spend time with Rusty. She had packed them a picnic lunch for the occasion.

Rusty unpacked the meatloaf sandwiches and apples and slices of peach pie. Good thick slices, the kind Doyle always liked. His mother knew what the heavy artillery was, all right. Rusty and peach pie.

Doyle's stomach turned.

"Frankie's brother," Rusty said. "You remember Frankie Frisch, right?"

"Yeah."

"His brother was in the war and brought back all sorts of souvenirs."

"Good for Frankie's brother."

"Maybe you should go see him."

"Who?"

"Frankie's brother."

"Why?"

"Because you were in the war together."

"Yeah. Sure."

Rusty picked up one of the sandwiches and gave it a bite. Doyle looked at the band shell in the middle of the park. And beyond that the tree that Zee had climbed one evening a thousand years ago.

Where was she? The story he'd been told by his mother was that there had been this big scandal. That she had run off with a man, a theater director of some sort, and was now gone for good, probably using an assumed name.

Her father had gone (his mother whispered the words) "a little crazy."

What a world. What a crazy, ugly, mixed-up world we are left with. Zee, I hope you find your way, I hope you do, and if you would've said yes that night, maybe both of us would be happy now . . .

" . . . scared? Were you?"

Doyle picked up Rusty's voice again. "Pardon?"

"Were you scared, Doyle? Being in battle and all?"

"You can read about it."

"Did you kill many Gerries?"

Doyle looked at his sandwich, which sat on a plate on the picnic table. An ant was making its way toward the plate.

"Did you, Doyle? How close were they?"

"Why don't you just read a book or something?"

"But were you scared?"

Doyle squashed the ant with his thumb. "Listen to me, Rusty." He looked at his little brother. Rusty's face was still so young and fresh. Freckles like tiny mud splatters across milky white skin. Red hair. A regular Huck Finn. "You need to do all the stuff Dad wants me to do. You need to go to college and make something good out of your life. You need to hang on and keep believing in yourself."

"But what about you, Doyle? Aren't you going to go back to Princeton? You have to."

"Did Mom tell you to say that?"

Rusty looked at the ground.

"Don't worry about it," Doyle said. "You did your duty. You can tell Mom you tried."

"She also wanted me to talk to you about—"

"About what?"

"The medal." And then Rusty unleashed a torrent of words. "You're a hero, Doyle, and everybody in town knows it and you're getting the Congressional Medal of Honor, Doyle, and Mom and Dad and me and even Gertie, we're all—"

"Rusty—"

"—proud of you, Doyle, and everybody's gonna know about—"

"Rusty!"

His brother bit back the last words.

Doyle put his hands on Rusty's shoulders. "Listen to me, will you? You're too young to know what you're talking about. Just drop it, the whole thing. Okay? Don't talk to me about it again."

"But, Doyle, tonight's your party, and it's all anybody's gonna be talking about."

Suddenly Doyle's hand was in a fist, and the fist was in front of Rusty's jaw. "If you don't . . ."

Rusty's eyes went wide.

Doyle looked at his fist, a foreign thing on the end of his arm.

"Get out of here, Rusty."

"Doyle—"

"Go home!" Doyle pushed the picnic basket at his brother, got up, and walked toward the river.

‖ 7 ‖

"After the war, what will our obligations be to France and Belgium? The Huns are throwing the world back a thousand years. Cities like chalk."

Doyle recognized the voice of Dr. Paige, one of Zenith's most prominent citizens. He was, in fact, the doctor who had delivered Doyle into the world. Doyle was beginning to wonder if that had been a good decision after all.

He sat on the staircase in the family home, seeking a respite from the party his parents were throwing. There were too many people in the house, too much prodding and poking going on. If he'd had any sense, he would bolt right now and never come back.

But he didn't want to hurt his mother any further. Just this one night, he could endure it.

In response to Dr. Paige's voice, Doyle's father came back with his familiar argumentative style. "I say give them some food and supplies, and then let them build themselves up again. Get Germany to pay reparations."

"With what, William? The Gerries have nothing."

"Loans, then. Anything we give should be paid back, with interest."

"That will not do," Dr. Paige said. "The Europeans haven't the spirit of the Americans. We can bounce back from calamity at a smart pace, while they are the peasant class for the most part. They lack the initiative of the Western Hemisphere. As we helped drive the despoilers from their land, we must help them to regain their homes."

"And when they are all built up again, what's to stop the next war?"

"Common, human sense, man. What do you think of the idea of an organization of nations, after all this is settled, to hash out peaceful resolutions?"

"A pipe dream."

"Let us remember that all free peoples of the earth have existed and operated under a law far stronger and more binding on them than the rule of force. It is the moral law."

"Poppycock. Man is an animal who loves to fight."

"Then you are against even the attempt at such an organization? After all we have been through? That is rank pessimism."

"Realism, Doctor."

Both of you are fiddling while the world burns, Doyle thought. Talk talk talk, that was all anyone ever did, and nothing changed. Men got blown up. Children starved to death.

"Doyle Lawrence, you are a naughty man."

Betty Warren had found him.

"Why are you avoiding everybody?"

Betty was still the prettiest girl in town, and was dressed in a stunning blue gown made of some sort of silk with beaded embroidery, no doubt the latest fashion. Betty always knew about the latest fashions. She swept up to the stair below him and sat like a queen joining the common folk.

"You look very nice tonight," Doyle said.

"Oh, you charmer. That's the sort of thing a girl likes to hear. 'You look very nice.'" She nudged his leg with her elbow. "Come on, where's the poet?"

When Doyle didn't answer immediately, Betty jumped in to fill the awkward silence. "You remember Chap Wilson?"

"Sure." Chap had been on the football team with Doyle.

"He's the captain of the varsity debating squad at Yale. Doesn't that just beat all?"

"Sure."

"I got a letter from him just the other day. You know he's writing me quite a bit lately. A girl might get the idea a boy likes her that way."

"Chap's a good fellow."

Betty slapped Doyle's knee with the closed fan she held in her gloved hands. "I am telling you that to make you jealous, Doyle Lawrence."

"That's very direct of you."

"Come, come, goose. Times are different now. Girls are not as shy and reticent as they used to be. What would you say if I told you I have a flask in my garter?"

Doyle conjured up the image. "I would say that's a thigh of relief."

Betty laughed, a bit too loudly. "That was the berries, Doyle! The absolute berries!" She giggled some more.

"Let's get berried," he said.

Betty stopped laughing. She looked at her hands, her face suddenly serious. "What did you just say?" she asked. "Did you say *married*?"

Doyle wished he hadn't tried to be so clever. "I'm sorry, Betty."

"You know, I don't really have a flask on my leg. I was just trying to . . . I wanted you to think of me in a new way."

"Why?"

"Because maybe then you'd want to . . . oh, hang it all."

Doyle thought for a moment she was going to cry. He couldn't take that. He reached for her hand. "Betty, you've always been a good kid. You deserve to be happy."

"You don't love me. That's all there is to it."

"Love is as strange a thing as there is in the world."

"Everyone falls in love."

"That's hooey. That's for the women's magazines."

"Oh, Doyle," Betty sighed, "it's the war, isn't it? It's made such a mess of things."

"Maybe it's life's way of clearing weeds."

She looked at him uncomprehendingly.

"It's the way nature, in this case human nature, destroys part of itself."

"But why?"

"I don't know."

Betty opened her fan and waved it in front of her face. "I love you, Doyle."

Doyle's mother appeared suddenly, like waking light in a dream. "There you two are. Is anything the matter?"

"No, Mrs. Lawrence," Betty said. "We're having a grand time, Doyle and I."

"Well, then you won't mind if I take Doyle for a moment? His father wishes to see him."

Actually, Doyle was relieved at the timing and followed his mother to the study. His father was waiting there with a man in a crisp army uniform.

"This is Major Rowan from the War Department," Mr. Lawrence said.

Doyle stiffened and almost didn't take the man's hand.

"Funny thing," his father said. "The major's father and my father were acquaintances sometime back, did a little mutual business in Chicago. Isn't that ironic."

"Very," Doyle said.

"Well, there's no use beating about the bush, with a party going on and all. I asked the major to come over and speak with you personally, Doyle."

"Didn't think to speak with me first?" Doyle said.

"That was partly my doing," Major Rowan said. "I felt it would be better to spring it on you like this. Sometimes a young man caught in his thoughts will, shall we say, think too much."

"It's no use," Doyle said. "You've wasted your time."

His father quickly said, "Now, Doyle, that's not fair to the major. The least you can do is hear him out."

Doyle looked at Major Rowan and waited.

"The Congressional Medal of Honor is not something to treat with disdain," the major said. "It is an honor that goes to a very few men, and it is incumbent upon those men to return the honor. Your letter of refusal has been denied. I'm sure that upon reflection you will reconsider."

"And if I don't?"

"I would rather not consider the unpleasantness this might cause your future. Your family's happiness needs to be taken into account, don't you think?"

Doyle looked at his father, who was staring at him with barely concealed disappointment.

"I can't take it, don't you understand? It's all a big mistake."

The major said, "I assure you it is no mistake. A full report was issued—"

"What about my report?"

"Yours as well."

"Not everything was in it."

Major Rowan looked at Doyle quizzically.

"All right," Doyle said. "Here it is. I'm sorry, Father. I'd hoped to spare you and Mother."

He thought he saw his father tremble slightly. The major stood nearly at attention, like a good soldier.

"A grenade exploded in that nest. It killed Alvin and wounded me. Alvin stayed alive long enough to save me. But I didn't save him."

"You had no control over that grenade blast," Major Rowan said.

"Who cares? He trusted me."

"You didn't do anything wrong."

"You weren't there! I waved him forward, don't you see that?" Tears were stinging his eyes now, and he turned so his father wouldn't see them.

"What do you mean, Mr. Lawrence?"

It was no use. They would both see he was crying. He looked at them again and let the words pour out. "I don't want your lousy medal. I don't want to hear about you or the war or the army or anything else again, you hear me?"

His cheeks were wet, and he felt ashamed. He ran out of the parlor, past a confused Betty Warren, and up the stairs to his room.

‖ 8 ‖

Los Angeles Times
August 9, 1918

AROUND THE COUNTRY
by Merle Case

Shopping for Beauty

Outside of the large laboratories in which various cosmetics are produced as a side line, there are in our otherwise orderly country a total of nearly 500 face foundries, the output of which is valued according to industrial census reports at exceeding $26,000,000.

These are the beauty shop preparations. They are not health foods or medicinal agents. They are merely for use in dolling up a dame's face in a way in which she imagines it is being beautified. They include hair dyes, complexion powders, face enamels, toilet waters, grease paints, creams, skin bleaches, beauty washes and other make-ups.

What is it all about anyhow?

Women do not kalaomine for the purpose of entertaining one another. They know that they cannot deceive or hoodwink their own sex. The fact is that they think a man likes a highly colored, highly spiced woman. If she looks a little bit devilish, she is presumed to be irresistibly attractive.

It used to be that a woman's career of deception began when she first took to rubbing henna in her graying locks. Now the high schools are full of baby-faced flappers who carmine their lips and pencil their eyebrows every day!

The beauty shops are not monopolized by dumpy dowagers having their mushes ironed out. The crowd is more likely to be made up of movie-going maids of 17 who know more about colors than Rubens or Titian ever did. There are dinky little girls of 15 whose kisses leave a crimson mark. If this thing keeps up, the mother of the future will begin painting Mabel when she is in the cradle.

Heaven help her and the rest of us when she grows up.

The New Vagabonds

Conditions and problems arising from the present war, for which no preparation has been made, and with present difficulties that must be met promptly and efficiently, must soon begin to develop. One of the most vital and immediate needs is provision for the men now returning to this country maimed, disabled, or "shell shocked."

These men are entitled to and must receive from the government compensation and insurance which will enable them, at least, to remain self-respecting citizens. But the machinery of the departments handling the claims of discharged soldiers is slow, and many months may elapse before the man draws any money from the source.

Men who have offered their lives for their country, and paid the penalty of their self-sacrifice, must not be permitted to suffer, or even to lack for comforts, during this time of waiting. It will be an everlasting shame to all Americans who remain at home, if such men should be compelled to appeal to charity, or to borrow money at exorbitant rates, at this time. Men who are convalescing from wounds, or recovering from the effects of shell shock or gassing, should not be worried or hampered by lack of the income which is due them.

The number of men discharged for disabilities continues to increase, and many cases of deprivation and discouragement are already coming to light. Some of these men have become part of a new class of rootless vagabonds, and we have ourselves partly to blame.

‖ 9 ‖

The rail-yard bull turned his back, swung his big stick like a baton, and strutted off toward the depot. Doyle watched, crouched behind a snatch of scrub brush. The smell of coal and cattle filled the air, distracting Doyle from his own scent—a mix of dirt and sweat, along with a hint of desperation.

No money. Doyle had never worried about money in his life. Now he realized he was a full-fledged member of the underclass.

Funny, but he did not care. He thought, before hopping the freights, that he would have. But now he knew that was just a childish fear. It was better not to care.

The sun was heading down, a burnt orange ball behind the veil of smoke that came from factory and train together. A good sign. Soon it would be too dark for the bulls, and then he'd make his move.

He'd caught the first train out of Zenith with an actual ticket, paid for with the last of his army money. Sure, he could have counted on some scratch from his mother. Rusty, too, would have gladly given what he had.

That was why Doyle left at night without a word. Slipped out the window with only a small satchel and whatever he had in his pocket. Took the night train to Casper, Wyoming, then hitched rides into Idaho. One good thing about Mr. Henry Ford. He had put the country on wheels, and those wheels were moving Doyle.

Movement was what he craved. As long as he moved, the past could not catch up with him.

I'll write when I can, he'd written in the note he left. *Try not to worry. I know what I'm doing, even if I don't know yet why I'm doing it. I'll be thinking about you, and about the whys and wherefores, and I won't get into trouble of my own making, that's for sure. This is something I have to do. Love, D.*

He hadn't written a card home yet, and thought he ought to. His mother would be worried. And Rusty. His father? Ready to wash his hands of his firstborn son? Perhaps.

Cool night air started to gust. Doyle pulled his coat close around him. He'd ripped a hole in one arm, and an icy finger stuck through it, making him shiver. He opened his satchel and took out the extra shirt, a woolen, and put it around his shoulders like a shawl. *Some tough monkey,* he thought.

He hadn't figured on being a hobo, but that was just what he was now. Riding the rails, heading in whatever direction whatever train he caught happened to be going.

He was hungry, too. The carrots he'd pulled from an anonymous garden in town were running out. Besides, he was beginning to hate carrots, which he'd had his fill of. A thick steak would be good about now.

But he knew it would be a long time before he tasted meat again.

Finally it was time to move, so he could get to the train before the bull came back.

Doyle crunched his way across the gravel apron toward the rear of a train that had been the center of a lot of activity earlier in the day. One car in particular, slatted wood, seemed promising. That was what Doyle went for.

He jumped up on the side ladder but found he couldn't manipulate the latch of the heavy sliding door. Stuck or something. He didn't have enough leverage where he was in order to give it his full weight.

And then the train started to move.

He had to make a choice. Jump off now and try another car or scurry to the coupler and try to stand between two cars until he could figure out what to do.

If he stayed where he was, he risked being seen as the train pulled up to the lights before heading out into the countryside. If he tried to get between cars in the dark, he could very well slip and kill himself.

Or he could climb.

He didn't trust top riding, feeling that it had to be the most precarious place of all. But right now, with the train picking up speed, it seemed a pretty good option.

Carefully climbing up the ladder, he could see the bright lights of the checkpoint up ahead, some men standing on a platform watching.

His right foot slipped on a rung. He had to hurry.

He made it to the top of the car. Clouds like ghost ships filled the sky, moonlight behind them. He was going to make it.

Then a face appeared in front of him, suddenly, an apparition. Doyle stifled a yelp.

"I was wondering when you'd get here," the face said.

The face belonged to a man with a graying beard and floppy hat. And a line of patter that would not stop. Doyle listened to the man chatter away about the fine art of rail riding, even as he showed Doyle how to get inside a boxcar from the top.

Once inside a hay car, settled in among the bales, the man's lecture continued. It went on through twilight and dusk. It was a mix of everyday observations: "Nervousness has nothing to do with the nerves. It comes from an outraging of the stomach. Too much protein and sugar, for two"; one-line axioms: "A man's reach should exceed his grasp, unless free food is at stake"; and pontifications on universal themes: "In a world gone mad it is the mad who will rule. Cities will become waste and then the mad will kill each other off." Doyle didn't ask his name, and the old man didn't offer it. Doyle just started thinking of him as *The Philosopher*.

Finally, taking a pause in his discourse, the man addressed Doyle directly. "Your first tour as a hobo, I take it?"

Hobo. His mother and father would be horrified.

"I never thought I'd be called that," Doyle said.

"You're lucky. Nothing better than a hobo's life."

"Nothing?"

"Look at me! I am free. How many men can say that? I am free as the north wind and twice the blowhard. I can say what I want and do what I want, and no one is there to nag at me. You know, the secret of life is to get out of the nag-osphere."

Doyle, reclining on the pile of hay he'd fashioned, said, "Nag o what?"

"Nag-osphere, that layer of noise and insistence that pounds your ears. Everywhere you look, there's another nag, another one to tell you what to do and what not to do. There's the nag on the corner who wears a badge, and tells ya to get out of the way there! Get out of the way because the mayor's comin' through in a fancy parade. And he's another nag, a politician with his reforms and his high-hat ways."

"Is that all?"

"All? I have hardly begun the list, my friend." The Philosopher took a pipe from his pocket and began to fill it with tobacco from a worn leather pouch. "Those who are subject to the ring have another class of nag. The wife! No sooner is the man captured and tamed than the wife begins with the whip of marital cords. 'Get a job, why don't you, you good for nothing! My mother was right about you.'"

"Sounds like you've had experience in that area."

"I was under the lash for two score years, but I will tell you, my friend, I was true. True to the woman." He paused to light his pipe, a glimmer of remembrance reflected in his eyes from the match flame. "I will admit that there were times I loved her, but I was not meant to be a husband."

"What became of her?"

"She ran off with a whiskey drummer from Kansas City. I can't say as I blame her, but I would have stayed true myself. Though she nagged me, I would have been true. Now I am free, and will not again return to the yoke."

He puffed, a swirl of smoke rising from his shadowy head, silvery against the moonlight outside the train car.

"That's a rather cynical view of marriage for a philosopher," Doyle said.

"You speak, but you do not understand. You want philosophy?"

"Sure."

"Then learn. Men and women in love get married, do they not?"

"Sometimes."

"And what is marriage? It is an institution, is it not?"

"Yes."

"Now then, love is blind. Ergo, my friend, marriage is an institution for the blind."

He puffed away on his pipe as if he had delivered the wisdom of the ages. Doyle couldn't help laughing.

But The Philosopher kept his serious tone. "And then there are the nags in the pulpit. The worst of the lot."

"The clergy?"

"Clergy! A dignified name for them. Do you know the poet Blake?"

Doyle was somewhat surprised this hobo was bringing William Blake into the conversation. But then again, The Philosopher spoke like an educated man.

"Blake," said Doyle. "I'm familiar with some of his work."

" 'And priests in black gowns were walking their rounds, and binding with briars my joys and desires.' "

"You are an atheist, then?"

"Sir, you wound me. Far from it. I am a believer in God. How else does one find meaning in such a universe?"

"But you just said—"

"It is the self-proclaimed mouthpieces I object to. The pretenders. Those who saw the air with their hands and equate the volume of their voices with the conviction of their message. Bah! Give me a man who is certain, but who does not beat you over the head with it. Let him convince me with reason, and I will be his friend."

Doyle shook his head. "There is no reason." He was thinking of Alvin Beaker. Of war. Of death.

Would he ever truly be free, like this old man? Or would the memory of Alvin haunt him forever? Just when it seemed that he might get over it, a fresh picture of Alvin would come roaring back to his mind, triggered by a chance phrase or sight or smell.

It was almost as if some devilish presence had been assigned to keep Doyle from finding respite from the memories. He'd heard of guys who'd come back from the war with what they called "shell shock." Guys damaged in the head. Sometimes they went berserk; sometimes they got put in sanitariums. Sometimes they committed suicide.

Was one of those to be his lot? Certainly Doyle didn't feel right in the head anymore. Why else should he have cast away all of the comforts of hearth and home? All of the honors waiting to be bestowed on him by the War Department?

Because he was not who he was, and wherever he ended up, it would probably be a disaster. For the only hope now was in the yammering of this strange old goat he'd ended up with on a train.

Some hope.

With The Philosopher expounding away, Doyle gradually fell asleep, and dreamed of absolutely nothing.

10

"Now here are the rules," The Philosopher said, "if you want to stay breathing."

Doyle nodded. It was the following evening, and the two had jumped off outside the town limits because The Philosopher knew where all the town limits were. He may have seemed a little too advanced in age for such activity, but his body was wiry and he knew how to hit the ground.

They were dusting themselves off as they walked. The old man had said they would make camp with other "men of no current position" at a place he knew.

"The first rule is you don't ask anybody his name. If they volunteer it, that's one thing. If they don't, it's their business. Understand?"

"Understood," Doyle said.

"The next rule is you don't ask about a man's goods. What he has is his, and that's that. If he offers you something, that's between the two of you."

"All right."

"Next is this. It's every man for himself. Sleep with one eye open."

"That would be a neat trick."

"But if we catch wind of the bulls or the cops, we spill the news so everybody gets a chance to get out with their stores intact and their heads uncracked."

"Got it."

"And the biggest rule of all is simple. Do what it takes to survive. We're not out on some camping trip. This is Darwinism, and if it comes down to you or me, I have to take me. I expect you to do the same."

"It won't come to that," Doyle said.

"Ah, my young, naïve friend."

They came to a marshy place full of reeds and weeds and tall grasses. Doyle heard the trickling of water before he saw the small stream.

"Almost there," The Philosopher said.

"One question."

"What is it?"

"If this is every man for himself, why are you showing me all this? Why are you giving me the rules?"

The old man showed his teeth—what was left of them, anyway—through a smile. "I just got a soft spot for you, I guess. But don't let that fool you. If I'm running, and you're in my way, I'm gonna knock you down."

They entered a wooded area where Doyle smelled smoke. The Philosopher led on to a clearing, and that was where they met the other men of the tracks.

Four or five were seated on the ground around a fire, holding potatoes on sticks over the flames. Beyond that, in various stages of rest or indolence or desperation, were men on blankets on the bare ground, some sleeping, some staring at the sky.

"Greetings, gents," The Philosopher said. "We're just off the train and hope to pitch camp here."

One of the men at the fire, the largest one, nodded. "You're welcome. My name's Joe, and I'm big, so I'm called Big Joe."

"I thank you for offering your name, friend," The Philosopher said.

"Just so you know," Big Joe added, "I rule this roost. You clear on that?"

"As crystal," said The Philosopher.

Big Joe looked at Doyle. The man's face was square as a brick with a flattened nose plastered on the surface. "You?"

Doyle nodded.

Through a squint Big Joe said, "I don't know why, but I feel like you're gonna be a problem, mister."

"Mind your business," Doyle said, "and I'll mind mine."

A moment of electric tension passed between them. Doyle clenched his right fist behind his back and felt a fury surge within him. It was like another him, inside, and for a moment he marveled at it, wondering where it came from, wondering what he might do if it were to take him over completely.

Then Big Joe gave a quick nod. "That's fair. You two can take a spot over there, on the other side of the tree line. Feel free to grab a spud from the fire. One each. It's the last you'll get from us."

"Much obliged, Mr. Joe." The Philosopher looked around, picked up a stick, and went to the fire, where he expertly speared a potato and placed it in his outer coat pocket. He did the same with a second spud for Doyle.

"Ah, that warms the body and soul. Good night, gents."

As they laid out their bedding, The Philosopher said, "You've got a linchpin loose up there, friend. You don't talk to a man like that in his own bailiwick."

"Didn't see any ownership papers on him."

"Ownership ain't just about papers. It's about who can crush your noggin if you get on his bad side."

Doyle lay down on his blanket, looking up at the night sky. "I'm tired of worrying about bad sides and good sides. I'm going to worry about my side for a while."

The Philosopher flopped back on his blanket. "Ain't no one side. We are not alone in this cockeyed caravan. Look at those stars."

Doyle looked. An emptiness opened inside him, and the words of Alvin's poem shot into his mind. *Them stars is made by angels, pokin' holes in it with their cigars.*

"Makes you appreciate the Chief," The Philosopher said.

"Chief?"

"The Creator, my friend."

Doyle grunted. "If there is one, He didn't see fit to stick around."

"You don't think so?"

"Live in the world long enough and you find out."

"I've lived a little longer than you have, and I found the opposite to be true."

"Bully for you," Doyle said. "Now I want to get some sleep."

"A man's got to live for something bigger than himself." The Philosopher had his hands behind his head.

"Why?" Doyle countered. "Why must we have something *bigger*?"

"Because there isn't anything lasting any other way. 'No man is an island,' Donne said. We are participants in a grand scheme."

"Seems to me the scheme is just people shuffling other people around. Politicians, businessmen, preachers, bootleggers, even hobos. The only meaning they have is what suits their ends. It's every island for himself."

"I think the Big Chief is looking down on us. If we didn't have that, there wouldn't be any need to behave decent."

"I don't follow."

"If there is no immortality, anything we do on this earth is permissible. We'd be accidents of nature."

"Accidents?"

"The descendants of animals that swing in the trees. And before that, swam in the water. If we buy that evil-ution, that's where we'd be."

"You sound like William Jennings Bryan."

"Voted for that man three times, but I suppose it wasn't in the Big Chief's plans."

"Was it in the Big Chief's plans to kill and maim young men in France? How do you figure that?"

The old man sighed. "You hit on the one great mystery of life. It is the question of the ages."

"Maybe we're all just fools to think there's an answer."

"How did one so young get to be so hopeless?"

"When I was growing up, I heard ministers preaching the gospel of peace. They said the world was becoming a better place, that Christian principles were bringing us together like nothing else before or since. Then the war . . ."

German gunners. Alvin. Blood.

" . . . what good did it do us?"

The Philosopher paused before answering. "If I didn't think there was some plan, I'd probably want to cash in my chips right now."

Why not? Doyle wondered. *What reason, really, was there for going on? Hamlet said it was the "dread of something after death, the undiscovered country from whose bourn no traveler returns, puzzles the will."*

Hamlet! What did he know?

Shakespeare, what did he know?

What did this old man know? Or anyone? Who knew anything worth knowing, really?

"You were fighting the war not so very long ago," The Philosopher said. "Don't you think America is worth the fighting?"

"For who? It's politicians who make war, and then sends boys to die in them."

" 'The purpose of all war is peace,' wrote St. Augustine."

"What war did he ever fight in?"

"He fought a war for his soul, and lost to God."

"Sap."

"Ah, but all men must someday—"

"Why don't you put a cork in it? I want to get some sleep." Doyle turned on his side, and for once, The Philosopher was silent.

But Doyle couldn't sleep. He kept staring at the stars and thinking of Alvin Beaker. He was not poking holes in any blanket. He was gone, just like Doyle would be someday. Like they all would. Worm food. And no fool philosophy could replace the despair of being alone in a cold, purposeless universe.

‖ 11 ‖

Los Angeles Times
November 12, 1918

ARMISTICE!
BEDLAM IS THE KAISER'S DIRGE AS ALL
LOS ANGELES CELEBRATES PEACE

Los Angeles has had many great days. Yesterday was her greatest day. The war is over. Nothing else matters. The Prince of Peace has resumed His throne; the crown of thorns blossoms into a Crown of glory. The war is over. The long night is past. Soon our soldiers will be coming back to us. Praise God from whom all blessings flow.

The war is over. And so Los Angeles celebrated. There were no plans; no marshal of the day had ordered that the citizens should march up Hill Street. It wasn't that kind of a celebration. That will come later. This day belonged to the people and they claimed it for their own.

By eight o'clock in the morning the downtown streets were jammed and flags were being placed. Everywhere the Stars and Stripes were flying; apparently they had risen with the sun.

All afternoon the crowds grew and grew until the marvel was that the streets could hold them. The heart of Los Angeles was bared yesterday, and back of all the noise and cheering and fiesta could be sensed the mighty undertone of feeling, best expressed by a group of sidewalk singers who formed a tiny swirl in the mighty swirl in the mighty eddy of the day. Snatches of their song rose even above the din:

"For mine eyes have seen the glory of the coming of the Lord . . ."

And finally above it all:

"Glory, Glory, Hallelujah."

‖ 12 ‖

Sister Mary Monica of the Benedictine Sisters convent in San Fernando was deep in prayer when the first knock came. This was strange, for it was the dead of night and no one came to that door at such an hour.

But the knock was insistent and somehow ominous.

Sister Mary crossed herself and rose from the kneeling rail in front of the statue of the Blessed Mother.

Another knock on the heavy oak door of the chapel. It clearly was not one of the sisters. The chapel doors were never locked.

Sister Mary's walk was as insistent as the knock. It could be one of the *obreros*, working on the vestry, but why would they be seeking someone at night?

One more knock and then Sister Mary opened the door.

A hooded figure stood there, barely visible by the muted candlelight coming from inside the chapel.

"*Como?*" Sister Mary said. The face under the hood was *blanca*. "How may I be of service?"

The voice was a whisper but clearly a young woman's voice. "Can you help me?"

"What is the matter? Come in."

"No," the figure said.

"You have nothing to be frightened of, my child. Come, sit. I am Sister Mary—"

"I cannot come into a church."

The tone of desperation in her voice was as evident as the dark hoverings of the convent's pepper trees, which spread their shadowy forms behind the girl.

"Anyone can come into God's house," Sister Mary said.

"No." The voice was insistent and, to Sister Mary's thinking, insolent. Had this come from one of the girls in her classes, a swift rebuke would have been appropriate.

"Then how may we help you?" Sister Mary said.

"You have an orphanage?"

"We do. For girls."

"With a school?"

"Yes, with schooling."

"And adoption?"

"Do you wish to seek a child?"

"No. I am going to have a child."

So that was it. Another of the young ones who had fallen into temptation. Sister Mary had first come to the convent in Southern California thirty years ago. But in that time she had witnessed Los Angeles and its outlying areas become more crowded and "citified" and with disastrous moral results. In the last ten years, with the growth of the immoral motion picture industry, more young women it seemed had fallen from standards that should have been ironclad and inviolable. Here, no doubt, was another product of that devilish system.

"The father of the child," Sister Mary said, "does he know?"

"No."

"He must be told."

"Impossible."

There was the impudent voice again. A stubborn girl, this one.

"Can you help me to deliver my baby, and can you take it in?"

"Tell me your name, child."

The form in the darkness said, "That's not important."

"Of course it is. You are a child of God."

"Do not call me that."

"What may I call you?"

"Nothing."

"But—"

"Nothing," the form repeated. "I have no name."

PART IV

❧

THE GLITTER FACTORY

◆

The parking problem is one that bobs up in some form almost every day. If a man parks his wife in a downtown tea room, he is liable to find her smoking perfumed cigarettes and talking Yogi stuff with a copper-colored Mahatma.

—Los Angeles Times, *1921*

◆

My candle burns at both ends;
It will not last the night;
But ah, my foes, and oh, my friends—
It gives a lovely light!

—*Edna St. Vincent Millay*

Zee Miller stopped by the light post and pretended to look in her handbag. She poked at the meager insides with her hand, feeling around as if in search of an item, but in reality keeping watch out of the corner of her eye.

The grocer was finishing up his sidewalk display for the morning, whistling as he worked. Zee watched and listened. Her gaze from time to time fell upon the two oranges that sat especially succulent in the morning sun, atop a pile of freshly unloaded citrus.

There were some window signs on the front of the grocery—*Carnation Milk, 11¢ per can; Roasted Coffee, 2-lb. pkg., 40¢; Ben-Hur Soap, 5¢ per bar*. She couldn't afford any of it. Luxury items all. But oh, did the coffee sound nice.

Zee made a pretense of looking ever more carefully in her bag, as if a loose dime had fallen to the bottom. In truth she had not even a dime. But she made it seem so, telling herself that this was the way Mary Pickford would look for a dime were she a young wife with a bit of trouble at home. Wide eyes, furrowed brow, increasing the appearance of concern.

The market on Ninth Street near Flower was, Zee had come to know, one of the busiest in the downtown district. A crossroads for the shopping traffic that would include a large sampling of the female population of Los Angeles—the upper crust from Angeleno Heights and Elysian Park; hardworking housewives from east of the Los Angeles River; domestic help from the mansions on Adams Street; unmarried women from Glendale and Hawthorne who trollied in to their jobs at the phone company or stenographic pool.

Even the occasional down-and-outer, the ones who defied classification because each had her own sad story, her tale of woe, one that occasionally turned up in the crime sheet of the paper when the inevitable happened—caught stealing or skipping the rent, or occasionally rousted from a prostitutes' den.

Or a girl who'd left a child, born out of wedlock, at a convent orphanage over two years ago, then ran away, back to the city, the concrete jungle of obscurity.

At least she had survived. Doing domestic work where she could get it—the *Times* had constant listings in the classifieds—garnered enough that she could put up half the rent for the little Bunker Hill apartment she shared with one Molly Pritchard. They'd met at a job hunt and hit it off, both full of dreams of acting careers. Even though they seemed to live on the cutting edge of oblivion, they were somehow making it as two single women in a sea of domestic idealism. How often had she seen yet another column in the Sunday papers on "How to Land a Husband"? "Wedded Bliss Made Simple"? "A Happy Home Makes a Happy Husband"?

Why did the papers never expound on "How to Survive As a Young Woman in the City"? Learning the fine art of avoiding the landlord was a skill she could have told them about, as was the subtle deception she was about to unfurl.

Zee was Mary Pickford as she feigned frustration and forgetfulness. She wore a plain brown walking dress and brown leather shoes with fraying laces and a missing eyelet. Her brown shirtwaist had a hole just under the left arm, which necessitated turning her right side toward the grocer. She did not wish to arouse suspicion.

Turning now to a crate of apples, the grocer began whistling another tune entirely. This Zee recognized as "Ain't We Got Fun," a ubiquitous melody these days.

Los Angeles was song crazy, crazy for the new jazz, and crazy for anything that *moved*. That explained the streets heavy with automobiles and trolley cars and people hoofing it from one end of downtown to the other.

And as foot traffic increased this morning, so did Zee's chance to bag the oranges.

She was sure the grocer's suspicions were just about to coalesce around her when a well-appointed woman wearing a shepherd-check suit and wide-brimmed silk hat, and carrying a parasol, engaged the grocer in conversation.

"Good morning, Mrs. Cotter," the grocer said. He was a friendly, corpulent man in a long white apron.

"Mr. Cotter will be wanting his eggs tomorrow morning. I am afraid he was not pleased with the Quaker Oats."

Zee began to look over the oranges. She was now a shopper, the way Norma Talmadge might play her—patrician, yet somewhat innocent.

When the grocer turned into the store, Zee dropped the first orange into her bag. She looked quickly to her left and then to her right. No one, it appeared, was watching.

The grocer was still inside. Zee picked the other orange and into her bag it went.

This was when the real acting began. For she knew from numerous motion pictures depicting the lives of the poor and downtrodden that boys and girls who stole immediately tried to run away, casting suspicion upon themselves. Invariably they were apprehended by large policemen, who took them home to be scolded by parents.

Zee did not, therefore, run. She resumed her shopping, scanning the other fruit stands. She put on a slightly bored face, like a housewife from Vermont Avenue.

But then the grocer appeared out of nowhere. "I know what you're doing," he said.

Her heart jumping to her throat, Zee stayed in character. "I beg your pardon?"

"Looking for the peaches," the grocer said with a smile. "Cute little thing like you can bake a honey of a peach pie, I'll wager."

Blush and smile, Zee told herself. She looked down shyly. "Why, I do like to bake, that is for certain."

"For a hungry husband?"

"Oh dear!"

The grocer leaned back. "What is it?"

"My husband! I almost forgot we are to meet." She curtsied. "Thank you, sir. I shall return."

"See that you do," he called after her. "I'll have those peaches in later this morning!"

‖ 2 ‖

"Two soups, my good man," Zee said.

Tommy squinted at her. "No more credit, Miss Layne. Boss man says I can't."

Miss Layne. She was getting used to it now, the new name she had chosen for herself. Soon to be on movie posters across the land—*Taylor Layne, America's New Sweetheart.*

Zee and Molly Pritchard were planted on two stools at the lunch counter of the Owl Drug store. This was their usual spot for a cheap meal. While living together in a flimsy Bunker Hill apartment cut their expenses in half, they weren't exactly living like queens on the dimes they made doing domestic chores.

Tommy was a good kid, willing to cut them a break from time to time. Zee flirted with him for credit, and usually that was enough. Not today apparently.

"Haven't I been good for it?" Zee said, batting her eyelids.

"No."

Zee pouted a little. "Aw, Tommy. I thought we were friends."

"My boss says business is business, that I've got a good head on my shoulders and that I'm going places. But I've got to watch the cash register, that's what I've got to do. And you ain't paid in weeks."

"True enough, but I've got a good possibility at Universal. The nephew of the fella who delivers lumber to the set design building is a friend of the boy two doors down from Molly and me. Right, Molly?"

With a sheepish smile, Molly nodded. She was the quiet one of the two, which suited Zee just fine. She provided a certain steadiness to the tandem. She was not the glamorous type, though she was, in the right lighting, rather pretty. They had met when applying for jobs at Overell's Department Store. Neither one of them got the job, but at least a friendship was born.

"And he's promised he'll talk to him and get me an audition for the new Lillian Keane picture."

Tommy folded his arms. "No soap."

Zee put her face fetchingly in her hands and leaned forward on her elbows. "Why, darling, you wound me."

Tommy snorted. "That's Pearl White in *Know Your Men.* You should at least write your own lines."

Zee put her right hand over her heart, and her left on top of her head, then looked at Tommy sideways. "Me?"

"That's the same look Louise Townsend gave Fritz Leiber in *The Red Queen*."

With a defeated sigh Zee fell back on her stool. "Serves me right for trying to con a picture fan."

Molly patted Zee's arm. "Your acting was superb, even *better* than Louise Townsend!"

"I'd say you was worth at least a one-reeler," Tommy said. "All right, even though I could get in real dutch, two soups on the house. But this is the last time."

"You're an angel," Zee said. "And that's from the heart."

Tommy grunted and went to get the soup.

"Thank the good Lord you can act," Molly said. "I'm starving."

"And I've got a treat for us. Two of the best-looking oranges in California."

"Oranges?"

Zee pointed to her handbag.

"But how?" Molly said.

"What you don't know won't hurt you."

"You didn't steal again."

"It's not stealing. How many times must I tell you, it's on credit."

Molly looked at her reprovingly. "It's credit when the store knows about it."

"I'm good for it. You know that. I keep a record right here." Zee tapped her head. "I'll pay the man when my ship comes in."

"Oh, Taylor," Molly said, "do you think it will? Do you really think it will?"

"Piece of angel cake," Zee said. "Now, what picture shall we see tonight?" She took out the few pages of the *Los Angeles Times* that had been discarded on the counter. It held the motion picture ads.

"How can we afford a picture?" Molly said.

"Leave that to me."

Tommy set down two bowls of soup.

"Extra crackers please," Zee said. "For old times' sake."

Tommy reached under the counter and came up with a bowl of crackers.

Zee and Molly quickly crumbled several Saltines in their chicken soup. Zee grabbed the bottle of ketchup on the counter and *splooched* out a healthy dose for each.

Molly folded her hands in front of her. "May I return thanks for us?"

Zee's whole body went cold. A picture of her father jumped into her mind.

"Do what you want," Zee said.

As Molly said grace, Zee looked at the newspaper on the counter.

When Molly was finished, Zee said, "What do you say about going to see *The Four Horsemen of the Apocalypse*? Says it's *the* movie of 1921!"

"That Rudolph Valentino is a dream," Molly said.

"He was a bit player, too—before becoming a star. You see, it can happen."

"What's at Grauman's Million Dollar?"

"Let's see. Colleen Moore and John Barrymore—"

"Another dreamboat!"

"I prefer Doug Fairbanks. What say to *The Three Musketeers*?"

The two sipped soup and pored over the ads. Zee loved doing this. She dreamed as she did. She saw her picture there in the newspaper—Taylor Layne, the Great New Star, in Cecil B. DeMille's epic of old Russia, *Catherine the Great*.

It was in the midst of that fantasy that Zee saw the man at the other end of the counter, watching her.

Or so it seemed.

He was dark-haired and sharply dressed. About thirty, with deep-set eyes. Zee held his gaze a second too long, knowing it appeared that she noticed him.

She quickly tried to recover, but it wasn't one of her better acting jobs.

"What is it?" Molly said.

"Don't look now," Zee said quietly, "but there's a creepy man giving us the eye."

"Really?"

"He looks like Wallace Reid."

"Maybe it is Wallace Reid."

"In a greasy spoon?"

"I have to look."

"No!"

"Maybe it's your ship."

"Huh?"

"Maybe he's one of those scouts, you know, always looking for the next new face?"

Zee allowed herself to entertain the possibility. But only for a moment. She was too accustomed to life kicking her in the teeth.

Suddenly Zee smelled the wonderful warm scent of a thick, juicy hamburger. Tommy set two fine examples of this culinary delight in front of the girls.

"Compliments of the gent at the end," Tommy said. "Did you give him the wink-wink or something?"

"Who is he?" Zee whispered.

"Never seen him before." Tommy leaned close. "But he's got a pinky ring with a rock that'll knock you silly."

Zee took a breath and then looked at the man. His eyes were locked on hers.

"Take 'em back, Tommy," Zee said.

"But, Taylor!" Molly protested, her eyes wide on the burgers.

"Who does he think we are?"

"A couple of charity cases," Tommy said. "And he's right."

"Now, you hold on there—"

"Take it easy." The man was suddenly behind them. Zee whirled around on the spinning stool.

He was even more mysterious up close, with a hint of danger emanating from him as palpable as the smell of onions on the grill.

"Sir, we are not in the habit—" Zee started to say.

The man put his hand up. He wore immaculate white gloves like some uptown swell, though his face was anything but dandy. "You don't need to explain. I can tell by looking at you that you're not out to pinch anybody. I just thought I might offer this repast as a way to introduce myself, and see if we might find some common ground."

Molly quickly said, "Thank you, mister. If you don't mind?" She indicated the hamburger.

Zee kicked her underneath the counter. Molly ignored her and picked up the burger.

"Be my guest, Miss . . ."

"I don't see as our names matter," Zee said.

A knowing glint flashed from the man's eyes. Zee shifted uncomfortably.

"No," he said, "I suppose not. After all, what's in a name? Besides, what the cops don't know won't hurt anything."

Cops? What was he talking about?

"There's been a rash of orange thefts lately," the man said. "A regular crime wave."

Now the look in his eye made sense! He knew. Somehow he knew. He must have seen her and followed her from the grocer. Was he police himself? Would he arrest her? Zee's face got hot and she had to look away, all acting ability gone. She felt *Guilty* flashing through her like a neon sign.

"I'm not here to dwell on the more unpleasant aspects of civic life," the man said. "I am looking, instead, for talent."

Talent! Zee tried to keep calm, but it was no use. A scout!

Molly froze with a mouthful of hamburger. She looked like a scared chipmunk.

"What sort of talent?" Zee asked.

"A fresh look, a willingness to learn, and a desire to make good money."

Zee cleared her throat and said, "If we hear of anyone, perhaps we can contact you."

Molly kicked her, hard.

The man smiled. "If you do," he said, "send them this very night to 243 East Ninth Street. Tell them Jess sent you . . . I mean, them."

A man in a black overcoat and bowler hat opened the door of the diner and immediately approached the talent scout. "It's time," he said.

The scout nodded at him. "Enjoy your meals, ladies." He turned quickly and walked out ahead of the other man.

"What do you suppose?" Molly said.

"I suppose we'll have to go show off our talent," Zee said.

3

Eight hours later, Zee was ready to do just that. She knocked on the heavy black door that was off the alley on Ninth Street. One dim bulb above the door broke the darkness.

"I'm scared," Molly whispered.

"Don't be." Zee took her hand, gave it a squeeze. "I'm right here. I will kick and scream at anybody who tries to hurt us and we can run away, how is that?"

Molly laughed. "I wish I could be more like you. You're not scared of anything."

"I'll tell you a secret," Zee said. "I get butterflies in my tummy all the time. The secret is not to get rid of the butterflies. It's to make them fly in formation. Now, come on, you and I are going to fly into fame and fortune."

Molly nodded. "Okay, kiddo."

A moment later the small window in the door opened, and a face like a great ape stared out at them.

"Yeah?" the ape said.

"Jess said we were to come here to meet him."

"Get lost."

He started to close the window. "Hey, you tell him it's Taylor Layne, if you know what's good for you."

That stopped the hulking primate. His face furrowed and he said, "What's your name again?"

"Taylor Layne, the actress."

"You wait here." He slammed the window shut.

Molly said, "You shouldn't have antagonized that man."

"That was no man," Zee said. "That was Mr. Darwin's missing link!"

The night was dark, and the automobiles moving along Ninth Street, honking and sputtering, sounded like the roar of animals in the jungle. Los Angeles was sort of like an urban jungle, Zee mused. And as Mr. Darwin had suggested, it was survival of the fittest. That much she knew by now. Survive and thrive.

Several minutes passed. Finally the big door opened, and Zee saw the great ape, dressed in evening clothes, scowling at her.

"This way," he said.

She entered, holding Molly's hand.

They were in a narrow corridor. Dull, yellow walls stretched out before them. The faint sound of a ragtime tune filled the air.

At the end of the corridor was another huge door, this one made of steel. The ape gave three quick knocks on the door with his substantial fist. The door opened.

Inside was a smoke-filled room crammed with people sitting at tables and having a grand old time. Zee knew at once this was what the papers called a bootleg joint, or speakeasy. The people were dressed as if going to a nightclub but were throwing back glasses of amber liquid or lifting crystal flutes filled with champagne. A small orchestra added the background music, jazzing the place up.

"Follow me," the ape ordered.

Zee felt Molly's hand trembling in her own and squeezed it. She looked at her friend and gave her a wink. Nothing to it, she wanted to say. If this was where the talent scout wanted to meet with them, then this was where they would meet.

They were led across the room to a booth on the opposite side. In the booths sat four people, one of whom Zee recognized as the man from the greasy spoon. He had the same hard look on his face, and the same white gloves.

Next to him sat a woman dressed all in white, including white beads in her hair, as if her hair itself were made up of strings of pearls. Next to the man from the greasy spoon was a very large fellow, larger even than the ape who had let them in. This one's face was scarier, too. Zee thought this the sort of man who could do evil things without so much as a blink.

The other gentleman at the table was a smaller, grayish man who could have been somebody's grandfather. He had a worried look on his face.

"This is the one, Mr. Norton," the ape said to the man in the middle.

"Thank you, Max," Norton said. "You may go now." Like an obedient circus animal, the ape turned and sauntered off.

"Welcome to the Angel Club," Norton said. "I have not had the pleasure of meeting your friend."

"Her name is Molly," Zee said, "and she is every bit as talented as I am."

The lady in white laughed. She held a cigarette in a long black holder between her fingers and took a leisurely puff. That was when Zee recognized her.

"You are Louise Townsend," Zee said.

"Guilty," Norton said.

"Miss Townsend, I just want to say, that is, I would like to say, that you are the best actress working in the motion pictures today. I have seen every one of your films, and it is a privilege to meet you."

The woman in white gave Zee a long, lingering look. "Charming," she said. "Tell me, dear, where are you from?"

"Nebraska."

"I've heard of it. Somewhere east of here, isn't it?"

The other men at the table laughed.

"Well, my dear, why have you come all the way from Nebraska to little old Los Angeles?"

"I have come to become an actress."

"Really? How dreamlike of you. Have you had experience?"

"Some," Zee said.

"What productions have you appeared in? They do have theaters in Nebraska, don't they?"

Zee's face flushed. "I . . . I was in a theater company in Omaha." *For about two seconds, before a snake named Desmond Nichols had his way—*

"Oh, Omaha! Quite a theater town." Louise Townsend forced a laugh through her teeth. "I understand the cows there often have speaking roles."

The large man at the table made a *har har har* noise.

Jess Norton elbowed the man, who immediately stopped his noise-making. "Just a little fun, Miss Layne. Louise here is a big star, you know, and sometimes stars are so far off in heaven they forget what's down here on earth."

"Really, Jess, you *are* a flat tire sometimes." Louise Townsend placed the cigarette holder between her lips.

"Can you dance?" Norton asked Zee.

"Dance?"

"Yes, dance. Move your legs and torso in rhythm with music. It's the latest thing."

Zee felt herself blush even more. "Of course I can."

"She's a good little liar," Louise Townsend said.

Norton said, "I'm going to be having a chorus. You and your friend here look like you might be able to hoof it. What do you say?"

"Don't waste your money, Jess," Louise said.

Zee was about to say something sharp to one of the biggest stars in Hollywood when she felt a tug at her sleeve. Molly.

"Excuse me." Zee turned around. "Well?"

"I don't want to," Molly whispered.

"Why not?"

With wide eyes, Molly looked around. "I don't like this place."

"Come on, it's a job."

"I can't dance, and neither can you."

"Sez you." Zee was beginning to get annoyed. "Take a chance for once in your life, Molly."

"I don't want to move around in front of all these—"

"Well?" The impatient voice of Jess Norton interrupted her.

"No dice," Louise Townsend laughed.

Zee spun back and looked into the icy eyes of the great star. She thought, for a brief instant, that Louise was afraid of her.

"I'll do it, Mr. Norton," Zee said. "Tell the orchestra to give me 'Baby Face.'"

Norton smiled. "Now? You propose to audition now?"

"And tell them to make it jazzy, will you?" Zee turned around to encourage Molly to join, only there was no sign of her.

Norton himself spoke to the bandleader, then addressed the crowd like a carnival barker. "Ladies and gentlemen, I trust you're all having a fine time tonight."

Zee heard the grunts and cheers of affirmation, and the first slithery tendrils of fear began to whip inside her. *Easy girl. You wanted this. Now go and take it.*

"Then it is my pleasure to introduce you to a young lady who has come all the way from Nebraska just to be with us tonight. A dancer who would like very much to perform for you."

Now the cheers were wilder, whipped up to a frenzy by bootleg booze. What were they expecting? Zee was suddenly aware of the plainness of her dress. She kicked off her shoes and undid the top two buttons of her blouse.

"Then let's bring her on, folks. I give you, for the first time in the city of Los Angeles, from the great stages of Omaha . . . Miss Taylor Layne!"

Zee trembled as she made her way toward the bandstand. *Don't quit on me now,* she told her legs. Jess Norton waited for her with one arm outstretched. He looked down at her feet and shook his head.

"Where's her dancin' shoes?" a man shouted.

Another voice cried, "She's a hick!"

Norton put his arm around her. "That's not the way to make an artist feel welcome. Or maybe you yokels don't know that barefoot dancing is all the rage in Paris."

Zee rather doubted if that were true, but it quieted the crowd.

"Miss Layne, the night is yours."

And then she was alone.

She almost jumped when the band started up.

Now what?

Move!

She put one foot out, pulled it back. Tried to keep time with the music. It was jazzy, all right. She tried to move the way she'd seen them do it in the movies. She felt like she was in a barrel of tar. The band made it through the song in what seemed like seconds. And then, suddenly, there was no sound. A dead silence swept over the smoky room, which was then broken by jeers.

"That's nothin'!"

"What kind of horseradish is this?"

"Send the tomato back to the patch!"

Frozen, Zee looked around until she landed on the hard visage of Louise Townsend. She was laughing uproariously.

Do something!

"Say, folks, where were you?" Zee put her arms out in mock confusion. "I was waiting."

At a front table a well-dressed bald man, with the look of a condescending souse, fairly screamed, "We want our money back!"

His companions, two women and another man, seemed only the slightest bit embarrassed.

Zee marched to the table, hands on hips. "You want your money back, or your money's *worth*?"

"Wussa diff'rence?"

"You're about to find out." Zee stepped back and addressed the crowd, "Come on! You all know 'Baby Face.' You want some dancing; I want to hear some singing!"

She looked at the bandleader. "Don't hold anything back this time. And keep it going until I tell you to stop!"

With a shrug, he turned to his orchestra and started up again.

"Let's hear it!" Zee shouted.

Tentatively, a few in the crowd sang out.

"Baby face . . .
You've got the cutest little baby face . . ."

More voices joined.

"There's not another one could
Take your place,
Baby face.
My poor heart is jumpin'
You sure have started somethin' . . ."

Zee began to dance, or rather move her body like a madwoman. She tried to let the music pulse through her and let arms and legs flail and kick to the beat. She was going to overpower them with movement.

"Baby face!
I'm up in heaven
When I'm in your fond embrace . . ."

She kicked high with her left leg, then her right. Her dress made a tearing sound. She kicked again, jumped, spun.

"I didn't need a shove
'Cause I just fell in love
With your pretty baby face . . ."

"You're doing fine!" Zee cried. "Again!"

The song started once more, and now everyone it seemed was joining in the fun. Except the bald man at the front table. Something came over Zee then and she was caught up, acting and not thinking, inside the music and swept away by it.

She jumped onto the bald man's table.

Glasses shook and fell. Zee kicked one away. It crashed to the floor. And Zee danced.

The crowd sang and cheered, whooped and hollered.

"Baby face!
I'm up in heaven
When I'm in your fond embrace . . ."

She kicked and whirled and leaped.

"I didn't need a shove
'Cause I just fell in love . . ."

Zee fell—not knowing if she meant to do it or not—into the lap of the bald man.

"With your pretty baby face!"

When the music stopped the whole place was on its feet. Cheers and applause and whistles fell around her like audible confetti. She was breathing hard and looking up at the bald man's perplexed face.

"Want your money back now?" she said.

‖ 4 ‖

Reuben Archer Torrey sighed and slumped back in his chair. The letter lay on the neat desk in front of him. He could not remember having felt so tired.

He was now sixty-five, and even though he'd always had a good constitution, he could feel himself slowing noticeably.

"What is it, Archie?" Clara said, entering the study with some afternoon tea for her husband.

Torrey said, "Do I look tired to you?"

"Do you want the truth?"

The preacher smiled wryly. "When have I ever been interested in anything else?"

She patted his cheek. "Then, yes, you do look tired. But more than that. Discouraged?"

"You know me well, my dear. What would I do without you?"

"Have you a reason for feeling this way?"

Torrey picked up the letter and shook his head in bewilderment. "Let me read this to you. It comes from a prominent minister in town, someone I know of but have not met. He is from a rather large congregation, and is also high in the ruling council of his denomination. This is what he writes.

"'Dear Dr. Torrey:

It is not without much regret that I write this to you, knowing of your many years of labor on behalf of your beliefs. However, I feel I must, for not to do so would be the greater sin.

It has been nearly six years now since completion and distribution of your Fundamentals project. Surely, in that time, you must have become aware that this is a project doomed to failure. Everything in life is a matter of progress or decline. By continuing to align yourself, your church and your Bible institute with these ancient beliefs, you are joining forces, wittingly or unwittingly, with the party in decline.

In other parts of the church, progress in theology is taking place at a rapid pace. Your fundamentalism, so called, is a roadblock. Not that it is a permanent obstacle. It will simply take us a little longer to bring the whole church up to the new positions because of the prejudice awakened by such belated matter as is set forth in *The Fundamentals*.

It is inevitable that these tracts will become mere theological curiosities in the not distant future. I am amazed that some of the men whose names appear in this series have lent themselves to such reactionary methods. The only way, absolutely, to save the things they really love is to go forward to the very positions they here antagonize. For this reason I am sorry for these publications. They will only retard the progress of the modern theories by a generation or two.

My fervent hope, Dr. Torrey, is that you will allow yourself the time to assess the situation anew. Our world faces many challenges. The memory of the Great War is fresh in our minds. Mankind is on the brink. What we need is more than a simple faith in ancient creeds, or a childlike reliance on an ancient Book. She is a Good Book, we all agree, but she is also human. And humanity must progress or die.

Progress will not cease, but it can be slowed. My appeal is that you will step aside from the warlike positions of your camp and seek to slay our common enemies, as Dickens once put it, ignorance and want. Do you recall? Most of all beware ignorance, the ghost cautioned Scrooge.

I am certain that you will receive this letter in the spirit it was intended. With that certainty I remain,

your servant,
Robert Jonathan Smith'"

Mrs. Torrey paused, her face a study in concern. Torrey loved her for it. For all these years of labor in the fields of the Lord, she had been his support and companion. She had raised their children and provided comfort for the family in time of need.

Never before had he felt such a need for her support now.

"Do you remember the crowds in Melbourne and London?" he said. "The revivals? I was so sure that it would happen here, that God would use Los Angeles as a flame that would ignite the country."

Mrs. Torrey nodded. "That is just it, isn't it, Archie?"

"Just what, my dear?"

"It is what *you* were sure about. Don't you see God may have lit the flame in an entirely different way?"

"How so?"

"How many young men have you taught at the Institute? How many young women have been trained there? How many leaders will go from this place to establish great works of the Lord out there? Who is that young man you spoke to me about the other day?"

"You mean Charles Fuller?"

"Yes. You see great potential in him. The way you talk about him reminds me of so many others. I recall that dynamo several years ago—Barnhouse."

"Donald Barnhouse, yes."

"Young men who have grown to love the Word as you do, and are even now sowing seeds that will bring a great harvest in years to come."

"But there are tares in the field, like this man." Torrey waved the letter.

"As there will always be in the fields of the Lord. You know that as well as I. Now let us not grow weary in well-doing."

Weary. That was how he was starting to feel in the field in which the Lord had planted him. Los Angeles seemed jaded all of a sudden. It had happened quickly, though he had seen the signs. The popularity of the movie business, the citizens' thirst for liquor, and the prospects of getting rich quick had brought all sorts of questionable characters to prominence. Young people were flooding into the city from farms and small towns, eager to grab the glitter and the dream.

"Let us seek the Lord's counsel together," he said to Clara. "On our knees."

She nodded and knelt by his chair. He joined her.

And together they sought the Lord.

‖ 5 ‖

Doyle Lawrence, tired and hungry, jumped off the boxcar half a mile outside the Los Angeles city limits in a perfect, unseen move even the old Philosopher would have approved of. He'd gotten the move down pat, but was hoping this would be the last time he'd have to use it.

For two years Doyle had been a vagabond in the earth, a Cain without a mark. He'd bummed with The Philosopher into south Texas, where they'd both spent some time cutting heavy ranch grass for meals and a bunk. When the old man decided to try his luck down Mexico way, Doyle bid him farewell. Though it didn't matter where he ended up, Doyle still felt something for America, a vague sense of adhesion. Not that he expected the country would do anything for him, or he for it. He was a resident, nothing else, with no permanent address.

In his occasional postcards home he tried to put a hopeful face on things, for the sake of his family. In Yuma he got spot work on a farm for a time and made it seem that he'd found gainful employment. Up in Utah he scaled freshwater fish and was in "food services." When he shoveled dirt and pounded rocks in the Florida panhandle, he was "participating with industry." He tried to make each enterprise seem like a temporary stop on a journey toward . . . something. But he was quite sure his father wasn't buying any of it.

The only constant in all of these places, besides the trains he hopped, was the *presence* inside him, the boiling rage that sometimes came out of its own accord. It got him fired from a couple of jobs, the last one resulting in injuries to a foreman that necessitated Doyle's quick run out of town.

Which was what landed him here, in Los Angeles, the terminus of the Pacific line of the Santa Fe.

What manner of place was this city? They said it was a place that dripped sunshine, and certainly that was true this winter morning. In Nebraska, Rusty was probably shoveling snow! Here, Doyle could take his shirt off and not be uncomfortable in the slightest.

He walked toward what he supposed was the center of town, com-ing first to a plaza and active marketplace that reminded him of Mexico after all. Most of the people were brown-skinned. A street sign announced that Doyle was on Olvera Street.

He walked farther on, then seemed to pass through a curtain into a completely different realm.

Streetcars and automobiles clanged and chugged down busy thor-oughfares. A thick river of people ebbed and flowed on the sidewalks—men in suits and straw skimmers, women in walking dresses and wide-brimmed hats. Signs attached to every building announced businesses and amusements—*Boos Bros. Cafeteria, Loews State Theatre, Nerney's Grocery and Meat Market, Woolworth's 5¢ and 10¢ Store, the National Hotel, Moline's Auto & Supplies, F. W. Pierce Furniture,* and the tow-ering edifice of the U.S. Post Office.

Doyle stopped at a corner and fished a crumpled newspaper out of a trash basket. It was a few pages from the *Los Angeles Times.* Some listings about real estate in a place called Lankershim. *Many lots at $1,450! A wonderland to come! Gateway to the beautiful San Fernando Valley!* Then there was a caricature of a man calling himself Saving Sam, who sold automobile tires. He had a little mustache, this cartoon character, which made him look like one of those snake-oil salesmen from the Old West dime novels. Doyle supposed Los Angeles was where the new hucksters were flooding. It was wide open and there were plenty of sheep ready for fleecing.

And what was he now? Sheep or shearer? Or in some other cate-gory that defied description? The new faceless man, unknown in the city and staying that way. Los Angeles seemed like a place he could disappear into.

Doyle walked half a block and sat down on the stool of a little outdoor diner—no more than a counter and seats for eight, and a grid-dle behind. Two pots of coffee gurgled on a burner to the side.

Doyle sat back to read the newspaper and take a load off his bark-ing dogs.

The next section in his hands was titled *Churches.* It was the Sat-urday edition, and the churches were taking out ads for their Sunday services. There were several dozen listed, everything from Methodist to Congregationalist. Titles of sermons were given in the little box ads, such as "The Great War, the World and Christianity," delivered by Will

A. Betts, D.D. of the First Methodist Church on Jefferson Street, and "May a Christian Frequent the Motion Pictures?" by a Reverend O. T. Griggs of the Zion Baptist Church on Grand.

The largest ad had a picture of a church building on it. This was the Church of the Open Door. Doyle nodded in half approval of the name. It always seemed to him as crazy to have so many denominations, and many of those denominations specialized in keeping people out. A church with an open door? Now there was an idea. The preacher there was a man named R. A. Torrey, and the copy said he was a *World Famous Evangelist.*

Further down the page were other ads for churches, but these were of a distinctly different type.

There was something called the United Lodge of Theosophists. The title of the address was simply, "Apparitions." Down below it said, "Theosophists and others who are seeking a philosophy of life that really explains matters are invited to attend. Expand your mind."

How far does a mind expand, Doyle wondered, *before it snaps?*

A group called the Vedanta Society was hosting an informal reception for a guy called Swami Abhedananda. Doyle imagined a fellow in a turban. Would there be rope climbing or snake charming?

Two churches had women as ministers. The Central Spiritualist Church featured the Reverend Elizabeth R. Courtney speaking on "A New Spirit for a New Year." Then there was the Home of Truth Church on Flower Street with the Reverend Annie Rix Militz. She was going to talk about "The Purpose of Life." Would she be able to explain it in thirty minutes?

Finally there was Universal New Thought, featuring a man named Frederick L. Rawson, who was billed as "lecturer and healer." The subject of his lecture was "The Inevitability of Wealth." *Well,* Doyle thought, *if it is inevitable that I get wealthy, maybe all I have to do is sit back and think new thoughts.* He shook his head.

"Hey, you." The man behind the counter was looking at Doyle. He wore a stained white apron and a dark scowl. If the Los Angeles boosters were looking for a goodwill ambassador, Doyle mused, they would want this man's opposite.

"You sittin' or eatin'?"

Doyle scratched his stubbly chin. "Maybe I need to think about it for a bit."

The counter man shook his head. "Order something or give up the stool."

"Well now, I can always order something. I could order a cup of coffee. That sounds good about now."

The counter man leaned in closer. "I know you can order it," he said, "but can you pay for it?"

"I will tell you about that. I may not be able to pay for it at exactly this moment, but I expect to find work soon and I will surely return with the money."

"I thought so." The counter man folded his arms. He looked at Doyle for a long moment, then jerked one thumb toward the street. "Blow."

A light flickered in Doyle's head, one he had come to know well, the first flames of anger. Like the lighting of a gas stove, it could ignite at any time. But before the flame erupted, Doyle heard a voice.

"Give man Adam and Eve."

Doyle and the cook looked to the side. A small Chinese man had appeared on the stool at the far end of the counter. He wore the traditional Chinese queue under a black silk hat. His plain coat with wide sleeves was typical of the Chinese laborer.

The cook glared at him. "What'd you say?"

"Give this man Adam and Eve! I pay!"

Doyle's anger subsided in a gentle wave of mirth. The man's use of American slang was sweet-natured, as was his face. He smiled at Doyle.

The cook sighed. "Well, you heard the man. How do you want 'em?"

Two eggs sounded very good to Doyle. Being a charity case did not seem like such a bad thing at the moment. "Wreck 'em."

The cook gave a curt nod and went to prepare the scrambled eggs.

The little Chinese man got off his stool and shuffled to the one next to Doyle.

Before he sat down he bowed and said, "I am Wong Lun."

"Doyle Lawrence."

"You are new to city?"

"You might say. Just rolled in."

"What is work?"

"I haven't quite figured that out yet."

"World move fast. Men need work. Rush, rush."

"I don't know what men need, really. Besides three squares a day."

"Labor make for good citizen."

"You sound like a politician."

Wong Lun shook his head vigorously. "No politician, no good, no good."

"I'm with you on that," Doyle said. "What's your labor, Mr. Lun?"

"Laundry."

"There's a surprise," the cook said over his shoulder.

Doyle shot him a glare.

"Work here many year," Wong Lun said. "Come from China, twenty year now. Good place to live, Los Angeles."

"But these Chinks breed like rabbits," the cook said.

"Just cook the eggs," said Doyle.

"My place, my rules. People want to have a conversation, I'm in."

Doyle looked at the man. He reminded him of someone, and for a moment he couldn't quite place it. Then he remembered. Thorn Fleming, the brute from France's battlefield. No wonder Doyle was taking an immediate dislike to him.

Ignoring the cook, Doyle said to Lun, "Where is your establishment?"

"Other side town."

"Business good?"

"Always dirty clothes. I make clean, press. Like no other place. Starch not too much."

The cook put a plate of eggs in front of Doyle.

"Potatoes," Wong Lun said. "And coffee."

"Let's see your money," the cook said.

"I have money! Yes!"

"Let's see it first, rice belly."

Doyle snapped his eyes to the cook. "What did you call him?"

"You heard me."

"He's a customer. Treat him right."

"I treat him the same as all rice bellies."

White light exploded behind Doyle's eyes. His hands shot out of their own accord. It was happening again, the rage, and Doyle reflected on it only a moment, even as he pulled the man halfway across the counter.

The cook shook his head as if trying to clear it. Then his own large hands clamped on Doyle's wrists. A moment later both men were on the cement in front of the counter. Doyle heard himself grunting in rage.

And then they were rolling on the sidewalk amidst a swirl of feet and voices. People shouted. Doyle made out Mr. Lun's voice crying, "Stop now! Stop now!"

No one moved between the fighting men.

Doyle's hand found the cook's throat and squeezed. His nails dug into the man's flesh.

With a kick of the leg Doyle rolled on top of the cook. His hand felt windpipe; his eyes saw only the cook's face flushing. Everything else was faded and blurry like vague impressions around a photograph. He heard sounds in his head, and they were guns. Big guns, like in France. Machine guns. A nest of Germans . . .

It wasn't the cook's face looking back at him. It wasn't a face at all. It was an adumbration, a shadow, a thing to be hated and killed.

Doyle put all of his weight on the man and his throat. Explosions, sounds of guns, noise and fire. The cook's eyes were starting to bug out, his face growing purple. Doyle could not pull his hands away. They stayed.

"Stop now!" Lun's voice again, pleading. It made Doyle look up and that was when he saw the cop. He was rushing toward them, his nightstick in his hand. Doyle saw him and still Doyle did not let go.

Explosions, sounds of guns . . .

And then another explosion, his head bursting, pain in every atom of his skull. For a split second he thought it was a grenade and in the next split second thought he was going to die. Then all thought ceased.

‖ 6 ‖

Zee fought wakefulness, while the gentle yet firm voice of Molly Pritchard fought back.

"I made you coffee," Molly was saying. "It's late."

Zee rolled to the other side of the bed. "Let me alone."

"We have to go to the office, remember?"

Hanging on to the last pleasant vestiges of sleep, Zee moaned, "What office?"

"The stenographic office. We begin our training today."

Oh yes. Molly's plan to get jobs as working stiffs.

"You go on," Zee said, digging deeper into her pillow. "I have a job, remember? And you could have had one, too, if you'd stayed."

"That's not the place for us."

Alertness came like an unwelcome guest. Zee sighed and sat up. "You didn't see me. I had them on their feet, Molly."

"But you said you'd come with me to the training."

"What does it matter what I said?" Zee felt a little woozy all of a sudden. She put her hand on her forehead.

"What's the matter?" Molly said.

"Nothing."

Molly sat next to her on the bed. "Did you have anything to drink last night?"

"Who are you, my mother?"

"You did, didn't you?"

Zee tossed off the covers, put her feet on the cold wooden floor. The steam heater was out, and the landlord had shown no particular interest in fixing it.

"Come on along." Molly was fully dressed in the one good outfit she possessed, a woolen dress with matching coat and a white cotton blouse. Plain and functional, for her first day of work.

"I told you, I'm not interested. Where is that coffee?" Zee rose and shivered in her cotton nightshirt. She snatched the top blanket from her bed and threw it around her shoulders.

Morning sunlight was fighting through the yellowed window shade. Zee squinted her way into the small kitchen, where the only heat in the apartment emanated from the old wood-burning stove. At least Molly had done something useful that morning by making a fire.

Molly followed. "A speakeasy's not going to get you anywhere. Besides, it's against the law."

"Silly girl," Zee laughed. She took a chipped cup from the

cupboard, poured coffee, and sat on one of the two chairs in the kitchenette.

"What is so silly about obeying the law?" Molly sat in the other chair.

Zee took a sip of hot coffee, savored it, then looked at Molly. "Mr. Norton explained all that. The law is the least of his worries."

"I don't trust him."

"Of course not. You rushed out of there like he was made of Limburger cheese."

"He is a criminal."

"You don't know what you're talking about."

"I read the papers."

"You read too much."

"Please, Taylor, come with me."

Zee put her cup firmly on the table. "Let it go, Molly. Don't you understand? This is show business. I'm going to be dancing in a show. And Mr. Norton knows a lot of people. That was Louise Townsend at his table, the witch. I'll be at the table soon. He can do us a lot of good. I think I can talk him into giving you a second chance—"

"I don't want any part of it."

"You don't want to be an actress? What about our dreams?"

"I do want to be an actress," Molly said with little conviction, "but I want to do it right."

"Who is to say what's right? What's right is what works."

Molly shook her head. "That's just foolish talk."

"What's so foolish about it? Look around at this town, Molly. Who is getting ahead?"

"That Mr. Norton, what does he want from you? Have you thought of that?"

Zee narrowed her eyes. "Do you think I'm stupid? I know just what Mr. Norton wants. I know what all men want. And if I can get what I want out of them, why shouldn't I offer a little here and there?"

"Taylor!"

"Oh, be quiet! Go on, get to work. You're starting to drive me bughouse."

Molly's chin quivered. Then she stood and walked toward the door. She looked pitiful in her old clothes, like a well-dressed beggar.

When the door closed Zee let out a huge sigh.

Oh, Molly, to make it in this city, this world, you have to be tougher than that. Maybe you're not meant for this. Go off and get married and have a bunch of children and—

Zee put a hand to her chest. *Children . . .*

She poured herself more coffee and, putting her hands around the warm cup, willed herself not to think of children. She closed her eyes, battled back memories. The past was an enemy. She would not let it hurt her, ever. She would not let it slow her. She would not look back because that way was death to dreams.

‖ 7 ‖

"How do you like the stink down here?"

Doyle heard the voice through the haze behind his eyes and the ringing in his ears. His head felt as if it had cracked in two and some-one had pasted it hastily back together.

"Stinks, don't it?"

Who was talking? Where was he?

On a hard surface of some kind, on his back.

The battle. Yes, the battle . . . Where was Alvin? Where—

"Somethin' wrong with your head?"

Yes, wrong. Shot. He must have been shot. He was holding his head in his hands.

Wait. Doyle's eyes began to focus. There were slats. No, bars. Iron bars. "Where am I?" His voice sounded removed, a distant echo.

"You're with me, pally. You're a public enemy, you know."

Doyle forced himself up. A sledgehammer pounded inside his tem-ples.

The cop. That was what it was. There'd been a cop there at the stand. The Chinese man. The cook. The fight.

He'd been knocked unconscious by the cop's billy club.

"I'm in jail?" Doyle said to his unknown companion.

"You just figurin' that out? They must've got you good, rotten louses."

Doyle looked across from his cell to the one on the other side of a thin strip of flooring. A man with two days' growth of white beard and a shock of white hair leaned against the bars of his own home away from home.

"Welcome to the pit, lad. I know why I'm here. Because I'm innocent, that's why, innocent of everything but telling the truth. They don't want to hear it, do they?"

Doyle shook his head, trying to get the words to fall into some sort of coherent pattern. "Truth? They?"

"I'm an anarchist, son. They say that's a crime, but I don't see it on the books. They're scared, scared that Comrade Lenin is going to walk up to city hall and shoot the louses."

"Is this the county jail?"

"That much I know." The man rubbed his stubble with a wrinkled hand. "But I know a lot of other things, too. What did they say you did?"

"I don't know. I got hit."

"Cossacks! Here in Los Angeles! Don't that beat all?" The old man suddenly laughed. "Yeah, that's what they do. They beat all!" He laughed again, a crazy hysterical guffaw.

Loony bin, Doyle thought.

"Only revolution is gonna help us now, son," the anarchist said. "The institutions, you see, are corrupt at the core. Mr. Volstead has seen to that. They call it Prohibition, but all it prohibits is the law-abiding folks. Yes, sir, now we got a trade in hooch that everybody's got a piece of. The mayor, the chief of police, the cop on the beat— the one that beat you, I'll wager—all in a boat on a sea of illegal booze. Capitalism! What's it get you?"

All Doyle wanted at this point was four aspirin. Maybe a doctor.

"And they don't even give us prisoners a place that don't stink to high heaven! Rats are treated better than we are, son. What say we break out of here, huh?"

"Sure," Doyle said, rubbing his head. It wouldn't stop pounding.

"And we'll start ourselves a revolution. The working man won't take this anymore. I'll scream for the guard—you grab 'im as he walks by."

"Keep quiet, will you? That's crazy talk."

The old coot laughed again and shook his head violently at the same time. "You poor young slob, you don't even know what crazy is. You're just another dirt clod on the road of life, and they're gonna kick you right off'n it. Fools always make me laugh." And then he shouted, "Guard! Get in here!"

The man's voice went through Doyle's head like an ice pick. He winced and covered his ears.

The anarchist screamed again. Then a new sound pecked Doyle's brain like the beaks of mad birds. The anarchist was banging his tin drinking cup on the bars of his cell.

That brought a guard in right quick. "Cut that racket!" he said. He carried a billy club and pointed it at the troublemaker.

"We demand justice!" the anarchist shouted. "Bring us a lawyer!"

"Shut up, you, or I'll open your cell and brain you."

"Yeah, that's just your way, isn't it? I have a witness!"

The guard turned and scowled at Doyle. "You making trouble, too?"

"I want no part of this," Doyle told him.

"Traitor!" the anarchist shouted.

"What am I being held for?" Doyle said.

"You'll find out when we're good and ready for you to find out. Now I don't want any more out of the two of you or I'll lay down the law." He slapped the billy club in his hand as a warning and then he was gone.

"You see that?" the anarchist said. "And you want to stay silent? Rise up!"

Doyle closed his eyes.

"Rise up, I say."

"Why don't you shut your big mouth?"

"Fool! You'll see. You'll see!"

Doyle fell back on his cot, trying to see some kind of future.

An hour later the jailer walked in and slipped a big key into the lock on his cell.

"Come along, Lawrence."

"Where?"

"Shut up. Just go where you're told."

Doyle shut up.

The guard put Doyle's hands in shackles.

When Doyle was led into an upstairs courtroom, he saw that the gallery was filled with an assortment of derelicts and weeping women he took to be long-suffering mothers, a few men who looked ashamed to be here, and three women of the sort who would not have been invited to church picnics back in Zenith.

Doyle sat in one of the wooden chairs where the guard had pointed him.

There was a man in a well-tailored suit walking in and out of the swinging gate separating the gallery from the well of the court. Doyle took this to be a lawyer who was being retained by some of the people here. The lawyer spoke to a weeping mother who had her arm around a trembling young man. The lawyer conferred, walked back to his table, and scribbled notes.

Doyle wondered if that was the sort of man he would have become had he finished Princeton and gone into law. What sort was this? Did he think about anything besides his work? Did he ever think about death? Did he wonder what would happen if the world came to an end? And since the answer was nothing, what was his motivation to go on? He imagined this lawyer, this man, just like most people, as operating in a dream world.

The door of the courtroom opened and in walked a most curious sight. It was a woman, but she walked with a purpose that Doyle would have associated with someone of the male gender. She wore a fashionable and professional cream-colored dress, but nothing ostentatious. She appeared to be around forty, and her hair was a stunning shade of auburn. She wore a wide-brimmed hat. Her eyes were fiercely intelligent. Most curious of all, she carried a leather briefcase in one hand.

She moved directly through the swinging gate and plopped her briefcase on the same table being utilized by the lawyer.

The two of them conversed as if they knew each other.

Doyle wondered if this woman was some sort of assistant. Perhaps the lawyer's secretary had come to deliver a forgotten file. But the two of them separated, and the woman opened the briefcase and took out a sheet of paper.

She looked out into the courtroom and said, "Doyle Lawrence?"

Stunned by the reading of his name, Doyle stood up. "Over here."

"Step into the jury box, please," the woman said.

Confused, Doyle put his hands out and shrugged. The woman motioned to him. "If you please, into the jury box."

Doyle stepped through the gate, went into the jury box and sat on one of the wooden chairs. The woman took a chair next to him.

"My name is Kathleen Shannon Fox. I understand you need a lawyer."

"Yes, but—"

"I will represent you."

"You?" For some reason he had never imagined a woman in a lawyer's role. He had known that such existed, though there were very few in Nebraska. His father had once commented that there were two women in partnership in Omaha, in a way that manifested disapproval. But there had never been a picture in Doyle's mind of a woman practicing law, especially inside a courtroom.

This woman, however, seemed to have a knowledge and competence that was palpable. Her expression was discerning, also compassionate. But within that compassion there was a toughness.

"Your friend, Mr. Lun, came to see me."

"Mr. Lun?"

"You do recall Mr. Lun, don't you?"

"Oh. Yeah. Sorry. My head." Doyle touched the lump tenderly.

"He told me what happened. He asked me to see you."

"Miss Fox, I have to tell you I don't have any money to retain a lawyer."

"It's Mrs. Fox. And suppose you let me worry about the money."

"But—"

"Go on and tell me your version of the events."

"Well, I'm not really sure. My head has been scrambled like the eggs the guy was cooking for me."

"You had ordered some eggs, is that right?"

"Mr. Lun had ordered them for me. He was being nice to me. But then this cook, this guy started in on Mr. Lun. About the Chinese and all, you know?"

"And you decided to do something about it?"

"I don't remember thinking about it. All of a sudden I grabbed the man's shirt and all I wanted to do was . . ." Doyle paused, his breath growing labored.

"Yes?"

"I don't know what I wanted."

"You were enraged."

"I guess you could say that."

"What else do you remember?"

Doyle sifted through the memory, foggy as it was now. "There was a cop. I think he knocked me out. I came to in jail."

Mrs. Fox nodded. "They take good care of their indigent clientele, don't they?"

Indigent. Poor. The bottom of the heap. Yes, that was him, all right. A far cry from being the royalty of Zenith.

"We haven't much time, Mr. Lawrence. The judge will be coming in and he'll want a plea. I won't know what the charge will be until I talk to the deputy district attorney. So, in the few minutes we have left, I want you to tell me as much as you can about your background and what you are doing in Los Angeles."

"In a few minutes?"

"Talk fast," she said.

‖ 8 ‖

"Just kick with me, honey," the peroxide blonde said to Zee. "Left, right, left, right. Think you can do that?"

"Sure," Zee said. She wasn't sure. Sitting in the little dressing room—-nothing more than two tables, two mirrors, and a closet to hang the clothes—the five dancing girls were in various states of undress.

Zee had just put on the beaded dress with a hem that came to just above her knees. Good thing her father wasn't here for this! It would have stopped his heart on the spot.

Gilda, the blonde, was the ostensible leader of the dancing girls. In two days of rehearsals Zee had been expected to absorb all four of the routines they'd be doing each night. Jazzy steps with traditional chorus line moves, line kicks, and struts. At least Zee was a quick enough study that she felt she could fake it the first few nights.

"Will Mr. Norton be watching?" Zee asked.

"Of course he will." Gilda paused to light a cigarette, then went back to rouging her cheeks. "He always comes to give the once-over to the new girls." She turned to Zee. "Play your aces right and you'll be in the lettuce."

"Aces? Lettuce?"

"Don't be a dumb Dora. You know what I mean."

Zee swallowed. "Sure I do."

Gilda laughed. "You really don't, do you? You came in on the Nebraska turnip truck." She took a drag on her cigarette and crossed her legs. Zee thought she looked older than she really was. There was a tiredness behind her eyes.

"It's this way, see? Mr. Norton likes to sample the merchandise. As long as you know he's just window shopping and you don't make a stink, you'll be in the chips."

"So that's it," Zee said bitterly.

"That's it. Welcome to show business."

"And what if the merchandise doesn't want to be sampled?"

Gilda shook her head. "There's always more to be found. Just like he found you."

Zee said nothing. Part of her wanted to bolt right now. Maybe Molly was right and this was a bad idea from the start. But the other part was ready to dive out into unknown waters of glamour, where people became stars.

"Maybe Mr. Norton saw something in me he really likes," Zee said.

"Oh, brother." Gilda stubbed her cigarette out in an ashtray. "Don't start believing in fairy tales. I did once, and believe me, it wasn't worth it."

"You and Mr. Norton?"

"For a couple of weeks," Gilda said. "He made me believe he had picked me out of the line, out of all the girls in Los Angeles. But I should have known I couldn't play in the same ballpark as . . ."

"Who?"

"Louise Townsend, that's who. Best stay out of her way, if you know what's good for you."

"Let's go!" The voice of Bienstock, the stage manager, shot through the door. "First number up!"

Gilda crossed her fingers and held them up to Zee. "Luck, kid."

For her first official stage-show appearance in Los Angeles—even though there was no stage and this was not exactly a theater—Zee felt strangely calm. The sea of faces in the smoky parlor, alcohol sodden and full of convivial laughter, seemed to accept her. The hoots and hollers from the men energized her dancing.

She smiled at the faces individually, making eye contact with the men. She felt their hungry glances in return, and the power of that was more intoxicating than liquor.

She wondered which of the men was the chief of police. Gilda told her that he was a frequent visitor to the place. Or who were the politicians, the city fathers, who also came and went nightly.

But there was no Jess Norton. He didn't arrive until the second number.

When the girls came out, Zee saw that Norton was at the table nearest the dance floor. Louise Townsend, in sequins and pearls, held his arm.

Both looked directly at her.

Zee smiled her dancer's smile and continued the routine. She didn't have to wonder what Norton and Louise Townsend were thinking. It was evident from their faces. Norton was looking at the merchandise. Louise was looking for trouble.

9

The judge was a sour persimmon of a man. He reminded Doyle of old Mr. Swenson, back in Zenith. He was the city dogcatcher, and rumor had it among the boys that he had been bitten so many times he lacked the proper amount of blood in his veins. His face fell inward, forming a permanent scowl. His disposition was in perfect keeping with his looks.

This judge, the night-court magistrate, wore a dull gray suit and severely knotted tie. No regal black robe for him. He looked as though he hated his job.

And after he had dispensed with the first few accused, Doyle was sure the only thing he loved was visiting his wrath upon the unlucky.

The boy with the weeping mother was accused by the district attorney of vagrancy. The fancy Dan lawyer attempted to convince the judge that the boy was a misunderstood lad who had trouble with his father. And that his mother would vouch for him and see to it that he never wandered the streets again.

The mother tried to address the judge directly, but he silenced her with the pounding of his gavel.

"Ten days," the judge said. "Next."

The woman wailed. The judge ordered the fancy lawyer to remove her from the courtroom. A deputy sheriff walked over to the young man and ordered him to move out the side door.

Frontier justice, Doyle thought. *And I've got a woman lawyer.*

The judge sentenced a plain drunk to days in the county jail, then faced the three ladies with painted faces. He gave them a ten-minute lecture on the evils of loose morals.

And then, incredibly, he let them go.

Before Doyle could think anything further, he heard the judge bark out his name. Mrs. Fox motioned to him to join her at the counsel table.

"Charge of assault and battery," the judge intoned. "How do you plead?"

"We would like a reading of the complaint," Mrs. Fox said.

Both judge and prosecutor turned toward her at the same time.

"What was that?" the judge said.

"Under the code of procedure, Your Honor, as you well know, the accused is entitled to a reading of the complaint before entry of a plea."

"But . . . that's not how we do things here. You know—"

"I know the code section, yes."

Doyle marveled at what he was seeing. A moment ago a tyrannical judge and somewhat bored prosecutor had mowed down one case after another. Suddenly, with only a few words, this woman lawyer had them both flummoxed.

The judge made a noise that sounded like *harrumph.* "Mrs. Fox, your legal acumen is well known to this court. But surely you are aware that we are a bit more informal here. It helps things to move along."

"I quite understand that, Your Honor. In this case, however, we would like to move under the full light of the law. Of course, if the prosecutor does not have a complaint drafted, he can always move the court to dismiss the charge."

The prosecutor swayed backward.

"What have you got for me, Mr. Vale?"

Vale looked at the judge with pleading eyes. "I did not know this was going to be asked of me."

"Frankly, neither did I. How long will it take you to draft a complaint?"

"I don't know, a day?"

"Are you telling me or asking me?"

"A day."

"Then I will allow you twenty-four hours to draft a complaint. The accused will return to jail and—"

"Excuse me, Your Honor," Mrs. Fox said. "Mr. Lawrence has been incarcerated for forty-eight hours, and under the law he has the right to be formally charged. As there is no formal charge, he cannot be incarcerated further."

The judge's face hardened. "Are you telling me what I can and cannot do in my own courtroom?"

"The People of the State of California's courtroom, Your Honor. And, no, I am not telling you what to do. I am certain that it is the desire of this court, and of the district attorney's office, to see that justice is done. I would never presume to question that. I would only say further, on behalf of Mr. Lawrence, that he is one of our boys who served honorably on the battlefields of France, fighting for the rule of law we all revere."

The judge smiled. "A doughboy? Why didn't you say so, Mrs. Fox? I believe the D.A.'s office would join me in saying that there has been some misunderstanding here. Would you say that, Mr. Vale?"

"I . . . I . . ."

"Thank you." The judge leaned over. "Mrs. Fox, I do not want to see your client in here again, is that clear?"

"Quite clear, Your Honor."

He peered down at Doyle. "And you, young man, go make something of yourself. The case is dismissed."

Outside the courthouse the air was cool and misty. The lights of downtown Los Angeles glowed like a port in a storm.

"What just happened?" Doyle asked his lawyer.

"You are a free man. But do not take that for granted. You heard what the judge said."

"Why did he just let me go?"

Mrs. Fox whispered conspiratorially, "Ex-Marine. One of the secrets of practicing law in this town is knowing your judges."

Doyle shook his head in grateful wonder.

"Now, Mr. Lun has said you are welcome to stay with him if you so desire. Do you have a place to sleep?"

"No."

"Then come along and I'll call you a cab to take you to Mr. Lun's."

She started down the steps.

"But I don't have any money," he said. "I told you."

"And I told you not to worry, didn't I? Come now."

‖ 10 ‖

Zee swallowed a lump the size of Nebraska as she was let into Jess Norton's office at the speakeasy called the Angel Club. What time was it, anyway? Well past midnight, to be sure. She was exhausted from the night's performance and wanted only to get home to bed.

But the boss had called.

As Jess Norton was speaking on the telephone, the big man, the one always around to protect his boss, gave her a twisted smile.

Norton kept talking into the phone, then waved dismissively at the big man. The man grunted and left the office, closing the door behind him.

Norton motioned with one of his white-gloved hands for Zee to sit.

"And another thing," he barked into the mouthpiece, "I don't want to have any more of your deputies sniffing around, making a big show. They want to get ahead, let 'em prosecute the bunco artists. I run a business here."

He slapped the phone back in its cradle and looked at Zee. She shivered even though the office was stuffy.

"You're going to find out," he said, "that when you make it big in this town there's dogs yipping at your keester. And you, my dear, have a fine keester."

Zee swallowed again. The lump was growing.

"How'd you like your first night in the spotlight?"

"Oh, it was fine, Mr. Norton. Just fine."

"I've seen many come and go, but you have got what it takes. My good customers, they couldn't get enough of you."

He moved from around his desk, and for the first time Zee noticed how he moved with a smooth swagger. And his hair. *Rudolph Valentino has nothing on you, Mr. Norton, when it comes to lustrous hair! You ought to be in pictures.*

"I appreciate your giving me the chance, Mr. Norton."

"Not at all. It's what gives me pleasure in life. Have a drink with me."

"I don't think—"

"Champagne. I'll have some brought in. To celebrate your first night."

He picked up a phone and waited a moment. "I want a bottle of champagne, and it better be properly chilled. And two glasses."

He put the phone down and smiled. "Like I was saying, dreams come true. Yours has just begun."

A thrill bubbled up in her. But it was immediately tempered by the memory of similar words flowing from the mouth of Desmond Nichols.

"You don't look convinced," Norton said.

Idiot! Don't let your guard down. She smiled. "Why shouldn't I be convinced?"

"Because maybe you think I'm handing you a line."

"Are you?"

He looked her dead in the eye as she held her ground and kept herself from shuddering.

Then he laughed. "Maybe I am, Miss Taylor Layne. You know, something tells me you didn't just arrive in our fair city on a pumpkin wagon."

He put his finger out, just under her chin. His touch was light, with a slight upward pressure. For a moment Zee thought he was going to kiss her. She had no idea if she would let him. Then just as quickly he dropped his hand.

"You interest me, Miss Layne. Do you know about me?"

"A little."

"Only what you've heard, right?"

"I suppose."

"It's all true. I came to this town after a stretch in the pen. I was a little younger than you are now, I would guess. Didn't have a thing but the clothes I was wearing and the blarney my own sweet mother passed down to me from her forefathers."

"You're Irish?"

"On my mother's side. My father was a mongrel, a mean one, too. I guess I've got a little of him in me. I needed it in those days. This town has grown up quite a bit. Back then, back when the McNamara brothers blew up the *Times* building, you could get yourself killed if you didn't watch it. So I watched. And waited. And when my chance came, I took it."

The look on his face made Zee think of death. Of murder. She did not doubt now that he was capable of it. Or had been at one time.

"Now the question before the jury is whether you'll be ready to take it, Miss Layne. Take that chance."

"Oh, I'll be ready."

He leaned in, close enough so she could see his whiskers and smell his cologne. "Fine words, but easier out of the mouth than put into practice."

"Whatever do you mean, Mr. Norton? No one is going to work harder at being a dancer for you, and pleasing your customers."

"There's only one customer you need to please, Miss Layne. And that's me. You do that and you are going to be—"

There was a sharp rap at the door. Norton opened it and took a silver tray from the waiter standing there. On the tray were two champagne flutes, a silver bucket filled with chipped ice, and a bottle stuck in the middle.

With practiced ease he popped the cork and poured the champagne. Zee watched the bubbles rising in the flutes and thought of her father. How many times had he warned his congregation of the perils of drink? She was dismayed to hear his voice again, but more, to give heed to it. She had not shied away from liquor the last time she'd been in Norton's place, the night of her dance on the table. Why should she do it now?

Norton was holding out the glass for her to take and she thought, at all costs, she mustn't.

"What's the matter?" he said.

"Nothing." She took the glass, shaking aside all thoughts of her father.

Norton clinked his glass against hers and drank. Zee drank, too, the bubbles burning her throat as they flowed over her tongue.

"Sip it," Norton said. "Savor it."

Zee nodded and tried to play the sophisticate, the way Louise Townsend did in her pictures. She took a delicate sip of champagne and smiled coquettishly at Norton.

"As I was saying, Taylor, you need only please me to get ahead in this town."

"I hope to do that."

"I know that you will." With his free hand he reached into his coat pocket and pulled out a necklace made entirely of diamonds.

Zee nearly choked. Norton held it up in his fingers, saying nothing, twirling it ever so slightly, the diamonds sparkling in the light.

"Like it?" he said.

"What's not to like?"

"Would you like to have it?"

She nearly dropped her glass. "I don't know what to say, Mr. Norton."

"I'll do the talking. I take care of my girls. I like to see them happy. I make them happy. It's a very simple arrangement, really. Do you want to make me happy, too?"

The air was suddenly stifling, and Zee knew exactly what he meant. All men were the same after all. They were Desmond Nichols, they were . . . she thought of Doyle, in a flash, and wondered if he was just the same as all the rest.

Zee put her champagne glass down. "I sincerely hope that my dancing will indeed make you happy, Mr. Norton, and I—"

"Don't play the innocent, Taylor. It's not the right role for you." He put the necklace back in his pocket and took a step toward her.

She fought the urge to run. That was not the way to make exits, not the way Taylor Layne would, anyway.

"What about Miss Townsend?"

Norton shrugged. "We have an understanding. And now I want the two of us to have an understanding."

"And if I refuse to understand?"

"You know, I once had the opportunity to buy a horse. But I had to choose between two. One horse was a winner, tested over a season. Proven. The other was an unknown. I really liked the looks of the unknown. I thought it had a chance to do great things. I'm a businessman. I don't usually take long shots. In this case, I did. And you know what? That horse started to do great things."

Zee wanted to leave. Now.

"But this horse had a little too much spirit. Fought with the trainer more than he ought. One day on a practice run he tried to jump a fence and broke his leg. I shot it myself. I thought that was only right."

Zee's heart started pounding.

"All I'm saying is that too much of the wrong spirit can lead to disaster. Stick with someone who knows how to win, and the sky's the limit. What do you say?"

He took another step toward her, close enough to slip his arm around her waist. She was sure then that he would pull her into a kiss, and from there into something else.

She put her hand on his chest and pushed. "I don't eat oats, Mr. Norton."

He looked a little surprised, then nodded.

"Pity," he said. "You could have been big."

‖ 11 ‖

Mr. Lun opened the door to his tiny hovel as if it were a castle. Doyle felt as if he had to bend over to fit inside. The place smelled of linen and cooked rice. The walls were brown, with the wallpaper peeling from them in various places. A paper lantern hung from a hook in the middle of the ceiling with a black wire running from it across the ceiling, held with nails, and down one wall where it was attached to a socket.

"My home," Mr. Lun said proudly.

"Very nice," Doyle said.

A woman shuffled into the room. She was petite and had close-cropped black hair. She wore a plain gray Chinese blouse over black pants. Doyle was not used to seeing a woman in pants. Her small feet were encased in tight black slippers. The Chinese woman smiled, her face lighting up with its own interior warmth. She bowed several times toward Doyle.

"This my wife," Mr. Lun said. "Yu-i."

"How do you do?" Doyle said.

"Am well," Mrs. Lun said in a soft, squeaky voice. "Thank you for knowing me."

"She not so good with language yet," Mr. Lun said, laughing.

"She sounds like she's doing very well," Doyle said. "Thank you for having me in your home, Mrs. Lun."

She puzzled over his words for a moment, then bowed again and said, "I am mad?"

Doyle squinted and eked out a meaning. "Glad?"

"Yes, yes. Glad. You stay dinner."

Compared to what Doyle had been used to, the meal was sumptuous fare. Mrs. Lun prepared heaps of rice and noodles, vegetables and chicken, barley soup, and something Mr. Lun called "congee." Whatever it was, it tasted like heaven. They all drank tea as they ate, and the conversation turned out to be an adventure in guessing. Eventually, however, Doyle was able to express his appreciation for the Luns' hospitality and get some of their story.

Mr. Lun had come over in 1902 to work as a fisherman in San Francisco. He worked his way to Los Angeles, landing in the middle of a *tong* war, and almost died for refusing to take sides. "This America," he said to Doyle. "Everybody same."

Lun survived the war and was able to establish his laundry, which quickly became a favorite. He made enough money to marry the woman who had been pledged to him in childhood. Yu-i came from the Baoshan District outside Shanghai in the fall of 1911, and she and Wong Lun were wed. They had no children, something Mr. Lun saw as part of the cosmic order.

Doyle continued to eat to a pleasant satiety. Every time his plate was close to empty, Mrs. Lun would scoop something else onto it.

"You have work?" Mr. Lun asked at one point.

Doyle shook his head. "Just arrived."

"What work you like?"

With a shrug Doyle said, "Haven't figured that out yet."

"Figure?" Mrs. Lun said, her face squinching in confusion.

Doyle pointed to his head. "I don't know."

"You have place stay?" Mr. Lun asked.

"No."

"You stay here."

Doyle looked around at the apartment, which was smaller than half the first floor of his parents' home. "I can't impose."

"Impose?" Mrs. Lun pronounced.

"You've been too kind to me already. You even hired a lawyer for me."

"No hire. Ask. Mrs. Fox, she help poor. And is best lawyer in town!"

"At this point, I can't argue with that." Doyle thought of how to express the next thought. "I just take up too much space." He put his arms out to indicate his span.

That caused Mrs. Lun to break into laughter. She put her hand up to her face and rocked back and forth in her chair.

"Big joke," Mr. Lun said to Doyle, shaking his head.

"Joke?"

"Wife think big people funny. Like man in picture."

"Man?"

"Happy man, you know?"

Doyle thought a moment. "Happy Sanders?" He'd seen the name plastered in movie ads.

"Yes! Funny."

"If I were that funny," Doyle said, "maybe I'd be in pictures, too."

"We want you stay," Mr. Lun said. "Bed for you. You help me. Now I help you with feet."

Doyle puzzled that one, and got nowhere.

"Up," Mr. Lun said. "Feet."

"Ah, help me get back on my feet."

Lun nodded vigorously.

"Thank you," Doyle said. "Thank you both. But I am not going to stay around here. I've got to keep moving."

"Why move?"

How to explain? Not only to the Luns, but to himself. Los Angeles was clearly not inviting him with open arms. A cop's billy was not what he'd call a welcome. Yet it was more than that; it was the feeling that unless he kept going, somewhere, anywhere, kept on the move, that something behind him would catch up. Something he did not want to think about.

"You stay night," Mr. Lun said firmly. "Stay night. Tomorrow, we talk."

True, he didn't have any place to stay the night. He could have found a church with a mission and wangled a bed for one night. But that would take at least a couple of hours, and he was tired. Not to mention the headache that still plagued him, courtesy of the cop.

"Tomorrow," Doyle said, "I go."

‖ 12 ‖

In her dream, Zee screamed.

She could not wake up, and the screams did not keep the devil from reaching into her body and wrapping his fingers around her heart, and pulling. Pulling, and it was coming loose.

Then the devil had his hands on her shoulders. He shook her.

She screamed again. The devil shook harder. The devil had a voice, a woman's voice.

"Taylor . . . Taylor . . ."

Zee sat up, her face drenched in sweat. Molly was on the bed, her hands still on her shoulders, now gently squeezing. "Taylor, wake up."

Relief and fear poured through her. Zee threw her arms around Molly and held her close.

"You had another nightmare," Molly said softly, stroking Zee's hair. "What is it? What do you dream about?"

Zee had never told her. She never told Molly about the loss of her heart, the baby she had given up, and her fear of hell. She did not want to mention those things out loud, ever.

"You can tell me," Molly said.

"It's nothing," Zee said.

"It must be something. Don't they say that dreams tell us about our childhoods?"

Zee leaned back on her pillow. *Childhood. Zenith. Zee of Zenith. No*

cares. Boys can't catch me. Climbing trees in the summer sun. Doyle.
Doyle Lawrence. Papa . . .

"I don't know what dreams say, one way or the other. Come now,
tell me about your first day of work. You were asleep when I got home.
Here"—Zee patted the bed next to her—"come and tell me."

Molly looked down.

"What is it, Mol?"

"I didn't . . . they didn't want me." She sat heavily on the bed.

Zee slid next to her, put an arm around her shoulder. "Didn't want
you? How could that be?"

"That's what they said. Said they were full."

"But they told you. They gave you a spot."

"They took it away. They said there were too many girls. I showed
them the letter, but they said that wasn't a binding . . ." Suddenly
Molly Pritchard was crying, hard.

"No." Zee pulled her close, like the sister she never had. "Don't
do that."

"I can't stay here. We need money. I was stupid to come here."

"Shush."

"What am I going to do? You at least have a job."

Zee threw back her head and laughed. "Oh, that's too rich! Not
being rich! We're not rich; we're a couple of begging fools!"

That stopped Molly's crying. She rocked back and looked at Zee.
"What are you saying?"

"I walked out on him."

"Mr. Norton?"

"Don't call him 'mister.' He doesn't deserve it. Him and that
python in pearls, Louise Townsend."

Molly smiled, her cheeks still wet.

"Yeah, the whole lot of 'em." Zee stood up on the bed. "What are
we doing, Molly? You and I, we're just letting 'em tell us what to do.
The fellows at the steno school, the bootleggers and phonies. Why are
we taking it?"

Molly shrugged. "What else can we do? They're the bosses."

Zee started jumping up and down on the bed. Molly squealed at
the fun. Good. She was starting to forget all about the bad things.

"Come up here," Zee said. "Jump with me."

"Oh, Taylor . . ."

"Come on!" Zee pulled Molly up, and the two of them started jumping on the old bed. They giggled and held hands and jumped.

"Tomorrow!" Zee shouted.

"Yes?"

"Tomorrow we'll go and take it to 'em!"

Molly nodded eagerly.

Zee stopped, looked Molly square in the eye. "We're going to Stroud-General Studios tomorrow, you and I, and we're going to march right up to the gate and we're going to get in and tell somebody to put us in pictures."

Now Molly looked stunned. "But you can't just walk up."

Zee squeezed her hands. "Why not? We can and we will. And just let 'em try to stop us."

She then started jumping again, up and down, faster and faster, beating back the dreams until they faded into puffs of breath.

‖ 13 ‖

On a beautiful Sunday afternoon in 1887, a wealthy man named Horace Wilcox took a carriage ride with his wife, Daeida, along a stretch of road through what was known as the Cahuenga Valley. It was a pleasant getaway from the bustle of downtown Los Angeles.

On this particular day, driving behind a team of two prize Arabian horses, the Wilcoxes enjoyed the smell of orange groves and the gentle colors of peach and apricot orchards, the easy pace of the small farms that had been leased by absentee owners to mainly Chinese fruit growers. They had been here before, but today Mrs. Wilcox commented on the charm of the unhurried life. Horace Wilcox grunted. As a land speculator his comment to his wife was, "This would be a nice place for a lot of people to buy homes."

He pulled his horses off to the side of the road, into an orchard of figs and apricots. Ahead were the Santa Monica foothills, gateway to the San Fernando Valley. He turned to his wife and said, "Why not?"

In no time at all, Wilcox purchased the orchard and 160 acres around it. He intended to subdivide and modestly name his new city "Wilcox," but Daeida had another idea. She loved her English holly bushes at their home in Los Angeles.

"We shall call this city 'Hollywood,'" she told her husband one day. Horace Wilcox approved.

By 1899 Hollywood had some five hundred residents. An electric trolley line connected the young municipality to its older neighbor to the east. The residents voted to incorporate in 1903, and by 1904 a long, dusty road dubbed Sunset Boulevard linked Hollywood and Los Angeles directly. For the next ten years Hollywood developed and grew like many other suburbs around the city of Los Angeles. Orchards faded into house-lined streets. Protestant churches—Methodist, Episcopal, Presbyterian—sprouted like bougainvillea. By 1914 Hollywood had its own bank, high school, and concert hall. It also had something else, something that was to change its face in a way Horace and Daeida Wilcox could not, in their wildest imaginings, have ever visualized.

It had the attention of a small group of businessmen who thought that movies would become a highly profitable enterprise.

Sy Stroud was one of these men. A Russian Jew, he had escaped the persecution of the czar as a teenage boy. He arrived at Ellis Island in 1898, at the age of twenty. The officials there changed his name from Seriohza Strydlanov to Syrus Stroud.

He had no family and no prospects. What he had was a dream of a better life and an awesome capacity for work. Starting at the bottom in the garment industry in New York's Lower West Side, Sy Stroud was soon running his own haberdashery on Seventh Avenue, two doors down from a motion picture house he thought was a mere novelty.

And then one day Stroud noticed a crowd of people moving rapidly past his store without even a glance at his window display. At first he thought they were fleeing a fire and went outside to see where the smoke was. But he discovered in the faces of the crowd not fear but anticipation and glee. Children laughed as they went. They were going into the movie house. On the marquee was a new sign that must have been erected that morning while Stroud was busily starting his day.

The sign read: *The Great Train Robbery! Sensational!*

"Ach," Stroud said out loud. "A moving picture! Some dumb, eh?"

But as the crowd grew, and a line of people snaked past his door,

Stroud grew curious. He turned the store over to his assistant, Arnie Goldman, a young kid with much potential if not very good business sense, and joined the line of people.

Sy Stroud had never seen a moving picture in his life.

But there in a seat in the Seventh Avenue Majestic, Sy Stroud was transformed. He watched along with the stunned crowd as a dangerous train robbery took place right before their very eyes. With background music provided by a man at a piano, up on a white sheet guns went off and people fell. A train rushed through the countryside as the villains took over. When the robbers rode off on horses into the forest, several people around him shouted, "No!"

The posse came in and surrounded the bandits. A great gunfight ensued. Justice prevailed!

For a long moment no other sounds issued from the crowd. And then the lights went on in the small theater and everyone burst into applause. Everyone except Sy Stroud. Instead, he was calculating just how much money a man could make if people filled many movie houses just like this one, every day, for multiple shows. If someone were clever enough to make these moving pictures and own the movie houses as well, that man could make a whole lot more money than a haberdasher stuck in a single store.

Sy Stroud and Arnie Goldman went into the motion picture business together. Beginning with five-minute "movies" about city life in New York, Stroud was soon producing one-reelers featuring Yiddish comics. His comedies became so popular that Stroud was able to begin buying movie houses in several eastern locations.

In 1911 he formally incorporated as Stroud-General Studios. In 1912 he sent Arnie Goldman to a place called Hollywood where another maker of quick comedies, Mack Sennett, had set up shop. Almost as soon as Goldman arrived he wired back to Stroud: FUTURE HERE STOP COME NOW STOP.

Investing all the money they had, Stroud and Goldman bought ten acres on Gower Street in Hollywood and set about making Krazy Komedies. They also made several stars. Happy Sanders was the biggest, rivaling Sennett's Fatty Arbuckle in audience appeal. And while no one reached the heights of the English comedian Charles Chaplin, Sanders was not far behind.

By 1916 Stroud-General had filmed hundreds of one- and two-reel comedies around the environs of Los Angeles. The streets themselves became his set, and often his film crews grabbed whatever they could from actual crime scenes and fires and whatever else was going on.

In 1917 Stroud-General began turning out feature films, even dramas. The studio grew steadily until 1919. That year the studio shot to the top when it turned an obscure Chicago dancer into one of the biggest stars in Hollywood.

Her name was Louise Townsend.

‖ 14 ‖

"Where do you think you're going, missy?"

"Inside, to speak to Mr. Stroud."

Zee stood up to her full height and stuck out her chin. She and Molly were on the street side of the iron gates that separated the kingdom of Stroud-General Studios from mere passersby.

"Mr. Stroud? Oh, my mistake. And why don't we get you in to speak to the President of these United States while we're at it?"

"You don't understand, sir. We are serious actresses. Mr. Stroud will want to know that."

"I'll be sure and pass along those sentiments to him. Who shall I say called on him? Mary Pickford and Lillian Gish?"

"No. You can tell him Taylor Layne and Molly Pritchard, the next sensations."

"Well, thank you very much for calling. Now, why don't you two run along and get yourselves husbands?"

Just then a large automobile blared its horn from Gower Street. The big guard looked up at a white Rolls-Royce about to pull into the large gate. He smiled and waved it on.

Zee looked closely into the car and thought she saw a familiar face.

"Was that Happy Sanders?" she said.

"Now listen, that's none o' your business. You look like a nice little girl, you and your friend. This ain't the place for you."

"Don't you know how much trouble you'll get in when Mr. Stroud finds out?"

"I'll take my chances, missy."

The iron gates to the studios were swinging open for the Rolls.

"Go away," the guard said.

Zee turned to Molly. "Come on!" And with that she dashed past the befuddled guard toward the gates.

"Hey!" the guard shouted as the auto started to pull through the gates. Zee ran through alongside the car, aware of another guard at the gate who was making some sort of alarming sound.

Zee kept pace with the car and then jumped up on the running board.

She was nose to nose with a most famous face.

Happy Sanders opened his mouth, and the large cigar that had been planted there fell from his lips. He screamed—an odd sound to Zee, coming from a man she had only seen in pictures—and slammed his foot on the brake. The car screeched to a stop.

Zee flew forward, hit the pavement, and rolled. She felt as if she went half a block in a ball, then rotated up on her feet again, just the way she used to do it rolling down a hill in Zenith. It always astonished the boys, who were afraid to do the same.

She hovered there for a moment, dizzy, the studio buildings around her spinning. Zee was half aware of people running, guards in dark uniforms, voices shouting.

Next she was on her rear end, her legs splayed in front of her, her mind a blank, white screen.

She was only vaguely aware of the commotion around her. There may have been stars on the lot, but the stars circling around her head were more prominent. She felt herself being lifted to her feet and thought she was in for it now. They would throw her in jail, perhaps cover her with tar and feathers, and put her on the next train back to Nebraska.

But then she heard a voice full of laughter. "That was sensational! Can you do it again?"

She looked toward the voice and saw the big moon face of Happy Sanders. "What?"

"If you can do that sort of thing when a director tells you," Sanders said, "then I want you in my pictures. Are you under contract here?"

A gruff voice in a uniform said, "No, Mr. Sanders. She tried to sneak on. I'll take care of her."

A hand grabbed her arm. She yanked it away as she got to her feet.

"Never mind," Sanders said. "I'll take it from here."

"But she hasn't got a pass," the guard said.

"She's got Happy Sanders! What more does she need?"

The guard scowled, turned and went back to his kiosk by the gates.

"Are you quite all right, my dear?" Sanders said.

"I think so." Zee shook her legs a couple of times. No pain.

"Splendid! Come along, you and I are going to talk some turkey. And I don't mean drumsticks." He opened the passenger door to his Rolls.

"I have a friend." Zee looked back at the gate, saw Molly standing there with a sheepish look. "She comes, too."

"A team?"

"You might say that."

"I've scored a double! Let her in, Magruder!"

The disgruntled guard allowed Molly to pass. In short order the two were in the back of Happy Sanders's car and being driven through the back lot of Stroud-General Studios. It was like a crazy dream where nothing stayed the same for very long. They passed Roman soldiers and cowboys and women from the French Revolution. There were horses and even an alligator, walked by a wrangler with a floppy hat and nervous smile.

Presently Happy Sanders pulled his car to a stop in front of a large bungalow, painted robin's-egg blue with a huge moon on the wall. The moon had eyes and a smile, fitting for the comedian the press called "The Great Moon Face."

Inside, the bungalow was done up in satin and silk and golden ropes, like the palace of a crazy caliph. Happy Sanders was known for rather eccentric tastes. That was what the gossip columns said.

A large mirror sat atop a long dressing table, which held a variety of jars, brushes, face paints, and . . . bottles. Zee recognized them immediately as the same sort of bottles Jess Norton had in his speakeasy.

"Now, my two darlings, as we'll be working together, let's get to know each other. How about a drink?"

Zee looked at Molly. Molly closed her eyes and shook her head.

"It's a bit early," Zee said.

"Is the sun up?" said Sanders. He paused. "I thought so." He poured himself a drink, took off his coat and sat in the large wing chair that resembled a throne.

"Sit," he commanded, motioning to smaller chairs covered with blue satin. "I am a supreme judge of talent, most especially my own." He laughed. It was a peculiar, high-pitched *ack ack* that was at once childish and infectious. Zee immediately liked him. He seemed to be a man full of life and fun.

"I have judged that you should be in my next picture. But we will start you off slowly. Extra work. You must prove yourselves in the crucible of the working film location. And then—" he paused and took a long drink—"you will become part of the Hollywood firmament. How does that sound?"

Zee cleared her throat. "So long as it is understood that Molly and I go together, like—"

"Like scotch and soda. I agree. I will go see Mr. Stroud this very morning. I want his imprimatur upon our little venture."

Zee stood up. "It is also clear that we are professionals . . . nothing more."

Happy Sanders paused mid-sip, and his eyes widened into perfectly round shapes—the look that made millions of people laugh in movie houses around the world.

"I'm glad you see it our way, Mr. Sanders." Zee took Molly's arm. "Where shall we report?"

‖ 15 ‖

"You help now. You press."

Mr. Lun took hold of the steam press and pushed down. It hissed and spat a puff of hot air. Doyle felt the hot, moist cloud engulf the room.

Lun smiled. "See? Easy. But must be very careful. Too hot, no good. Not hot enough, no good."

Last night Doyle and Lun had reached an agreement. Doyle would stay on one week and work for Lun in his laundry. Lun offered pay, but Doyle said the lodging, and Mrs. Lun's cooking, would be enough.

Today was his first lesson in the laundry business.

Wong Lun approached his work with a seriousness Doyle had seldom seen in his own countrymen. He proudly showed off the tiny establishment on Sixth Street that he had worked so hard to lease. There were two rooms—a small outer room that faced the street, and a much larger inner room for just about everything associated with the business.

Shelves were lined with water, soap, alkali, bleach, starch, paper, boxes, and shirt boards. Two large hand-cranked washing tanks took up the middle of the floor, next to a flatwork ironer with heavily padded steam flats.

"Now you ready," Mr. Lun said. "Any question?"

"No."

"Then what we talking for?"

Doyle spent the next two hours pressing, hanging, folding, and sorting. He listened from the back room as Mr. Lun dealt with customers, most of whom were not Chinese, which made for some intriguing conversations.

About two o'clock Doyle heard Mr. Lun talking rapidly, differently. His voice rose and his words fell over themselves.

Another voice, a man's, told him to "Shut your maw."

More words from Lun, all in Chinese. Doyle went to the door and looked out. The man Lun was talking to was dressed in a suit, tie, and fedora, and looked steamed himself.

"That's the way it is, Lun," the man said. "You got two hours. That's all I got to say."

Doyle stepped through the door. "What is it, Mr. Lun?"

The stranger glared at Doyle.

Clearly upset, Lun said something indecipherable. He turned to Doyle with hands flailing like a man about to drown.

To the stranger Doyle said, "Something wrong here?"

"Who are you?" the man said.

"I work for Mr. Lun. What do you want?"

The man snorted a derisive laugh. He was about Doyle's height and age, only slighter. He looked like a man trying to dress to look more important than he really was. Doyle had seen that look a lot his first year at Princeton.

"You work for Lun? Shouldn't he be workin' for you?"

"What's your business here?" Doyle said.

"There something wrong with your head? Workin' for a China-man?"

Doyle went to the other side of the small counter, where the man stood. The man took a short step back but jutted his chin. "Stay out of this."

"Looks like I'm already in it," Doyle said. "You and Mr. Lun appear to be having trouble talking to each other. Maybe I can help."

"No trouble," the man said. "Mr. Lun understands. Ask him."

"Is that true?" Doyle asked Mr. Lun.

"I know what he say." Lun looked at the floor.

"Suppose you tell me," Doyle said.

"It's business," the man said. "I don't deal with the cheap labor."

Doyle heard a small snap in his brain, like the report of a distant gun. He grabbed the man's coat.

"You're dealing with me. I want to know what's going on."

Mr. Lun ran around the counter. "No, Doyle!"

Doyle didn't let go. The man's face changed color, deepening to red. He tried to break from Doyle's hold, but he wasn't strong enough. Doyle pulled the man's face to his. Then he felt Wong Lun's hands on his back, pulling him.

"No no no. You let go."

It was Mr. Lun's call. His place.

With a push, Doyle let the man go.

The man brushed his coat, shook his head. "You're gonna be sorry you did that."

"Get out," Doyle said.

The man looked at Wong Lun. "And you, too." Then he was out the door.

"Oh, very bad, very bad," said Lun.

"What's this all about, Mr. Lun?"

"Business! My business! You just work here!" He turned and walked toward the back, shaking his head and muttering, "Very bad. Very bad."

Yes, Doyle thought, *very bad. That's the way things are all over. That's the way things will always be. So press the clothes, boy, and keep your mouth shut.*

‖ 16 ‖

Zee and Molly sat on the curved concrete bench in Pershing Square, listening to the fountain talk to itself. A clump of bamboo by the bench rustled in the wind. Passing by were men and women hurrying to and from work—stenographers in their ankle-length skirts and men in their business suits.

"Working stiffs of the new metropolis," Zee said. "Not like us. We're movie stars now."

Molly laughed and shook her head. "I think we have a little way to go yet."

"Not far. Watch and see. First thing we'll do is get new digs, as befits us."

"Why don't we wait until we get paid actual money first? That would seem more prudent."

"Always the prudent one, aren't you?"

"I just don't want to end up living down here."

Indeed, Pershing Square was a gathering place for the down-and-outers. Zee had figured this out the moment she'd arrived in Los Angeles. Penniless herself, she'd walked nervously around one entire night, listening to the odd sounds and staying away from the odd people as best she could. It was a carnival of crazies.

"Don't worry so much. We'll get ourselves a big house in the hills and look down on all this." Zee waved her hand like a queen indicating a kingdom.

They were interrupted by a loud voice behind them. Turning, Zee saw a young man in a suit, holding a Bible in one hand and gesturing with the other. "Do you know the certainty of salvation today?" he said.

"I guess it's church down here today," Zee said. Street-corner preachers were another fixture in downtown Los Angeles.

The young man, in earnest tones, shouted, "Oh, friends, what a joy it is to know that there is not one single tiny cloud between you and the Holy God, whom we call Father and who rules this universe.

That joy can be yours right now if you will only turn to Jesus and believe on Him.'"

"I haven't been to church in a long time," Molly said.

"Grauman's Million Dollar Theatre," Zee said. "That's our church."

The preacher was getting warmed up, gathering a small crowd. "Suppose that you had offended the laws of the nation and had been sent to prison on a life sentence, and a pardon were brought to you, do you not think you would be happy? But that is nothing compared with the joy of knowing that your every sin is blotted out."

Zee stood. "Come on, Mol. Let's get an ice cream."

Just then a well-dressed woman, looking like the secretary in a professional office, approached them, holding some sort of cards in her hand. "Good afternoon."

Zee wondered if she was going to ask for money or try to sell them something.

The woman held out a card. "May I invite you to church?"

Selling something. "No, thank you," Zee said, moving past. Molly, lagging behind, took the card from the woman.

When she and Molly reached the corner, Zee said, "Toss it away, why don't you?"

"I'd like to at least look at it."

"Why?" Zee made no attempt to hide the harshness in her voice, and this surprised even her.

"I just thought—"

"Forget about it, kid." Zee put her arm around her, noting that Molly slipped the card into her pocket. "Where you and I are going, no one can stop us."

Zee felt a little rumble of fear then, as if in acknowledgment that there was something out there just waiting to stop her. Was it just a residual fear of walking out on Norton? Was it a lingering disquiet about Louise Townsend?

Or was it something more, something deeper than that?

‖ 17 ‖

The orange ball of the afternoon sun was still hot when Doyle walked out of Lun's Laundry and headed up Sixth Street, which was alive with people and cars and paperboys shouting.

A strange place indeed, Doyle thought. The City of Angels seemed, on the surface, a place of unlimited potential, set to bloom in this semitropical piece of earth. That was why people were flooding in, flush with postwar money to spend on land and food and business ventures.

That meant there was plenty of room for bunco men and con artists of various stripes. The criminal element, too, punting down a river of bootleg booze just ahead of the law.

And what about you, Doyle Lawrence, presser of clothes? You have been dumped in this city of dreams and knocked on the head and now you walk the streets like any other bum—without prospects, without desire, not feeling hopeful or sad, just . . . not feeling.

If you had any guts you'd take a gun to yourself, or swim out to sea as far as you could and drop—

He heard the squealing of rubber on asphalt at the corner. A large auto stopped and nearly jumped up on the sidewalk. A large man with a face set to intimidate stepped from the car. He wore a black overcoat, even in the heat, and had his hands in his pockets.

"Don't try to run," the man said, "or it'll be the last thing you ever do."

A holdup? "Don't bother, friend. All I have is lint."

"Get in the car."

Doyle felt something behind him. He turned and saw the man he'd scuffled with at the laundry. The man now had a wicked smile on his face. So this was all about that business with Lun.

Doyle said, "Not interested in any rides today, thank you."

The man's jaw clenched. "I'm holding a gun on you, just so you know. I can finish you off and drive away."

"Then why don't you do it?"

That brought a look of confusion to the man's face.

Doyle nearly laughed. "That's right, put a slug in me."

"Don't think I won't." But the man's voice was anything but firm.

"Do it, I said. You'd be doing me a favor."

"You're asking for it."

"I'm begging for it."

"I'll do it, I tell you. Then I'll finish off your Chink boss."

Doyle almost sprang at the man. "You stay away from him! You and that rummy behind me."

"Come along then, pally. Somebody wants to talk things over with you. If you don't, I have to tell him, and that will make him upset and wouldn't be good for you or the Chink."

They had him. Doyle had to find out what sort of trouble Lun was in and help him if he could. Before he left the world, that would be one good thing he could do for the only man to show him a little decency in this city.

"Lead on," Doyle said.

❧

"So you're the guy." Jess Norton sat behind an ornate mahogany desk. Doyle had heard the name, or read it in the newspapers. Bootlegger.

"What is it that interests you in giving my boys the runaround?"

Doyle folded his arms. "What's your interest in pushing around an old man who's just trying to make a living?"

Norton looked Doyle up and down. He motioned for him to sit down. Doyle hesitated, but then the big hand of the overcoat man forced him into the leather chair.

"You're new to our fair city, eh?" Norton said.

"What of it?"

"Take the chip off your shoulder, son." Norton waved two fingers at the big man, who immediately opened the humidor sitting on Norton's desk. He took out a large cigar, clipped off the end with a gold cutter, handed the cigar to Norton and then lit it for him.

Doyle thought of his father then, of his evening cigar and talks.

"Cigar?" he said to Doyle.

"No thanks."

Norton blew a thick puff of smoke into the air. "You know my name. Now I'd like to know yours."

"Doyle Lawrence."

"Where do you hail from, Mr. Lawrence?"

"Nebraska, by way of France."

"Doughboy?"

"I did my tour."

"And a fine thing you did, too." Norton nodded approvingly. "You put the Gerries in their place, and the world's a better place for it."

"Where do you come from, Norton?"

Doyle saw the big man move toward him, from the side. He stopped immediately at Norton's raised hand.

"You're what they call a hothead," Norton said. "If you're going to make it as part of our community, you're going to need to watch that mouth of yours. It's not a machine gun. You understand?"

Doyle said nothing.

"Good." Norton leaned back in his leather chair, took another puff on his cigar. "I love this country, that's where I come from. I paid my dues in Chicago, San Francisco. But I like Los Angeles most of all. A man can stretch his legs here. There's room enough for everybody. And there's no reason everybody can't get along, if"—Norton pointed his cigar at Doyle—"everybody minds their own business."

"Just what is your business, Mr. Norton? And what does it have to do with a old man just trying to make a living?"

"You think I'm against folks making a living? I'm trying to make life better for guys like Lee."

"Lun. His name is Mr. Lun. You still haven't answered my question."

Norton's expression darkened. "Remember something, Mr. Lawrence. You're in my office at my request. I'm doing the asking."

"Request? Some ugly goon threatens me at gunpoint to get me here?"

The ugly goon grunted next to him.

"Would you have come otherwise?" Norton asked.

"No."

With a wave of the hand, Norton said, "And so here we are. So if you'll calm yourself down, I'll give you all the information you require.

I'm a man of business, and I'm sure everything can be handled in a peaceful manner."

Doyle folded his arms. There was, no doubt about it, a certain charm to this Norton fellow. Doyle had no illusions that this was some solid citizen. Law-abiding residents of Los Angeles did not surround themselves with gunslingers in overcoats. On the other hand, if you left them alone, like the wolves, they'd go about their business.

The problem, though, was that one of the wolves was snapping at Mr. Lun. That had to be settled, here and now.

"I'm listening," Doyle said.

"It's like this. I believe in what you boys were fighting for over there. Freedom. Am I right? Freedom to choose, to live in a country where we can do what we want."

"Sure. Freedom."

"But the boys in Washington, they don't believe in freedom. That monkey suit, Harding, he's worse than useless. And he drinks like a fish."

"So I've heard."

"But now they want us all to go without a little social liquor. Why? Because enough of those Bible-thumping temperance troublemakers have raised a stink to high heaven, you'll pardon the expression. They want to tell us all what to do. I say the Volstead Act is only the beginning. Pretty soon, the patients will be running the whole asylum."

"So you're a bootlegger."

Norton shook his head. "Why such an insult, huh? I provide a service. People want my service, and I'm not just talking about your average working stiff. I mean your cops and your politicians, your movie stars and millionaires. What harm are they doing at my places? They come there to socialize and have a good time."

"But what's that got to do with Mr. Lun?"

"How did you end up working for a Chinaman?"

"Leave that. Tell me what your business is with him."

"There's that chip again." Jess Norton narrowed his eyes. "That's going to get you in trouble if you don't watch it."

Doyle knew the man meant it.

"Now listen," Norton said. "Your boss has a long-term lease on a place that I can use. I'm planning to put up a flower shop next door."

"Flower shop?"

"In a manner of speaking."

"Speaking of a speakeasy."

"You're with me. I need Lun's place, too. But he doesn't want to move."

"He's been there for years."

"There are other places. I've offered to take over his lease; I've offered him more money than he'll make there in a year. But the old man refuses to budge."

"Did it ever occur to you that he might not be interested in the money?"

"Everybody's interested in the money, Mr. Lawrence. Eventually, that's what it all comes down to. And I'm hoping, as an American, you can talk some sense into your boss."

"Mr. Lun is an American, too."

"He have papers?"

"I don't know. He has a history here. He loves this country just as much as you and I."

"Then give him a little lesson in how to get along. That would be much better for all concerned. Now there. I've presented you with a reasonable plan of action. You convince Lun, and all will be well. I might even have a little something in it for you, so you can get out of working in a Chink laundry."

Doyle stood up. The goon put a hand on his shoulder to push him back down. Doyle hit it away. "Keep your hands off me!"

The goon made a fist.

"Easy, Clyde," Norton said. He stood up, walked around the desk, and faced Doyle. "You don't want to make Clyde angry, Mr. Lawrence."

"Are we through?"

"That all depends. You going to talk to Lun?"

"No. He makes his own decisions."

"But that's the problem. He hasn't."

"He has. He's refused you. Now leave him alone."

Doyle turned to leave. The goon was standing in front of the door. He wasn't going to move.

"You're not being reasonable, Mr. Lawrence."

"Tell your boy to move."

Norton sighed. "That chip. Too bad." Norton pushed a button

on a box that sat on his desk. "Looks like I need a little assistance in here," he said into a speaker.

In the silence that followed Doyle sensed the rising of raw power. Maybe that was what all life came down to after all. Who had the power and where they directed it.

The door behind the goon opened, and another large-framed man entered the room.

Doyle lost all breath.

The man was Thorn Fleming.

His face displayed a spectrum of emotion, from surprise to menace. Menace was where it settled.

"You look like you know this man," Norton said to Fleming.

"Yeah," Fleming answered. "I know this crumb." He smiled. "It'll be a pleasure to catch up on old times."

‖ 18 ‖

The director's name was Lieutenant Bert Hall. He insisted on being called by the full moniker. Not Mr. Hall or Bert. The only short-hand was Lieutenant, and he made that very plain to the assembled extras, which included Taylor Layne and Molly Pritchard as the new kids on the block.

Hall wore riding pants and boots, topped by a tunic with brass buttons. In one hand he held a riding crop, and in the other a mega-phone. His pencil-thin mustache reminded Zee of John Gilbert, who was causing women's hearts to stir on screens across the land.

Hall put the megaphone to his mouth and said in a high, reedy voice, "Listen, people! In just a moment an automobile letting loose at thirty miles per hour is going to come tearing down this strip of road."

The strip was Pico Boulevard near the town of Venice. This was the setting for a key sequence in the new Happy Sanders two-reeler, *Fly Boy*.

"In the automobile," the lieutenant went on, "will be Flora Smart, the leading lady. Only it will not be Flora herself but a stuntman dressed as Flora. You people are going to be citizens of the town, out for a Sunday stroll, when this shocking occurrence takes place. Now—"

"Excuse me," Zee said.

Hall snapped a look her way. "What? What? Who spoke?"

"I did." Zee raised her hand. "I was just wondering what the occurrence is."

"You *what*?"

"Well, I merely thought that if we are to give a reaction we ought to know exactly why so that our expressions might be perfectly suited to the occurrence. A mere speeding car is—"

"Who told you to think? You are an extra. You are not part of this crew. You are to stand and do what I say. Now—"

"But if we don't know—" Zee was stopped by Molly's sharp elbow applied directly to her ribs.

"That's it! I haven't got time for this! Get off my set!"

A stunned hush fell over the assembled extras. They looked at the ground as Zee began to stammer.

Molly jumped in. "Sir, please excuse my friend. She's a little excited about being here, that's all, and she is quite an excitable person already and I—"

"Enough! You and your friend are both fired! I want you out of here now! Let's get ready to roll!"

The lieutenant turned his back and began to stomp away. Zee thought her only chance at being a movie actress was leaving with him. She was about to dash after him when, from seemingly nowhere, the jovial presence of Happy Sanders flew into the little drama.

"Lieutenant," Happy said, "I am sure this little mistake can be cleared up. And I'm sure that Mr. Stroud, who personally placed these two young ladies into this picture, will be happy to hear that you have made such a generous decision."

Lieutenant Hall glared at the star, and Zee saw no love lost between them. But she instinctively knew who the real power was. It was Happy Sanders who had brought Stroud-General Studios to its position of prominence, Happy Sanders who filled the seats in the theaters, and not an ex-aviator who was employed by the studio to churn out two-reelers by the dozen.

Thus when the director's face softened into capitulation, Zee was not surprised. Hall waved his hand dismissively. "If you want them, you can have them. But don't let them talk to me again! Now let's get ready! Please!"

Happy Sanders turned to Zee and winked, then walked back to his chair, which was set up on the side of the road.

"That was a close one," Molly said. "What did you think you were doing?"

"It is called acting," Zee said. "I wanted to know what we're doing in this scene. Is that such a crime?"

"It is when you're just an extra. Now let's both be quiet and watch how movies are made."

Eventually Zee understood what the occurrence was that was supposed to be of such concern to the casual strollers along the road. A car was going to speed along in front of them. At the same time a plane would fly overhead. Happy Sanders was supposed to be flying the plane, but of course it would be a stunt double. From the plane would dangle a rope ladder. The leading lady, Flora Smart, was supposed to be in the back of the car. She was going to grab hold of the rope ladder and climb up to the plane. A stunt double would perform the trick.

In the movie, another extra explained to Zee, Happy Sanders played a man who dreamed of flying planes but who was only a janitor in the hangar. He shares his dreams with the daughter of the owner of several airplanes and even gets some lessons from a friendly pilot. When the girl, Flora, is kidnapped by a suitor, Happy takes it upon himself to give chase in a plane, which he steals from the yard. He drops the rope ladder and up she climbs. They fly off together, crashing into a barn, ending up in a haystack safe and sound.

It sounded so easy on paper. The filming was another matter.

On the first take the plane trailed too far behind. The car with the stuntman sped by while Zee and the other extras opened their mouths and feigned surprise. A solitary camera across the road caught their expressions.

A car with another camera in it followed the stunt car. But the timing was off and Lieutenant Hall ordered another take.

In fact, he ordered ten more takes, each time with a growing sense of frustration. Nothing went right. By the last two takes the timing was finally worked out, but then he had trouble with the stuntman, who looked more than a little ridiculous to Zee in a dress and wig.

A big argument broke out between Hall and the stuntman. Everyone could hear them shouting at each other. The director accused the stuntman of being a coward. The stuntman accused the director of being reckless. Then the stuntman tore off his wig, threw it to the ground, stomped on it with his shoe and stormed off.

The director tried to pull his own wig off, only it was his real hair that he tugged with all his might.

Zee seized the opportunity. She began crossing the road when Molly caught her and pulled her back.

"What are you doing?" Molly said.

"Don't worry."

"But I am worried!"

Zee patted Molly's cheek. Then she dashed across the road to Lieutenant Hall.

His face was flushed, and the reddish color deepened when he saw Zee in front of him. His cheeks puffed as if words swirled and fought within his mouth. Before he could explode, Zee said, "I can do it."

Now the lieutenant seemed too stunned for words.

Zee chimed, "I used to do things like this all the time back home. I always beat the boys in the rope climb, too. And you may have noticed that I am about the same size as Flora Smart. Let me try."

"Are you suggesting that I let you try to jump onto a plane? A girl?"

"What have you got to lose?"

"An extra! Have you considered that you might get seriously injured? Or worse?"

"What's worse? Losing an extra, or not finishing a film on schedule?"

The lieutenant looked as if he was thinking this over. Good. She had found his vulnerable spot—pleasing the studio.

Happy Sanders appeared, once again showing his perfect timing. "I'll vouch for her," he said. "I saw this girl take a fall like you wouldn't believe, and roll right out of it. She was born for this."

"Ha!" The director gave Zee a look from head to toe. "If anything happens, you bet you'll vouch."

Happy turned to Zee. "Are you sure you can do this?"

Zee wasn't sure at all, so naturally she said, "Of course."

‖ 19 ‖

You can do this, Zee Miller.

No. Not Zee. You are Taylor Layne, movie star.

Hardly. But in twenty minutes she had gone from nameless extra to nameless stuntwoman. She would be on camera! On screens.

If she survived.

"Now, girly," Lieutenant Hall said, "we are burning Mr. Stroud's money here. I want you to get this right the first time. The second you get to the rope ladder, you grab it and climb. Climb! Do you understand?"

"Climb."

Hall rubbed his face with his hand as if trying to rid it of a painful itch. "I'm going to regret this."

"No, sir," Zee said. "You won't be disappointed."

He regarded her for a moment. "You pull this off and I may get you a bonus."

"No," Zee said.

Hall's chin dropped.

"If I pull this off, cast me as the lead in the next Happy Sanders picture."

The man nearly keeled over. Zee stood her ground and smiled, as fetchingly as she could.

When the director recovered enough to speak, he said, "I give up! I absolutely surrender! Yes, I will give you a chance—"

"No. A guarantee. And a small part for my friend."

"Chalmers!" the lieutenant screamed. A ruddy-faced youth, the assistant director, rushed over as though to the scene of an accident.

"Yes, sir?"

"Get me a gun!"

"A gun?"

"Yes. I am going to kill myself."

"But, sir, no one has a gun that I know of."

Hall grabbed Chalmers's cap off his head and threw it at him. "Don't you know operatic satire!" He turned back to Zee. "All right!

Have it your way! But get on that ladder!"

She would get it on the first take. She pledged to Molly, to herself, and silently to the poor director, who was about to have a heart attack. *Just like back home. Grab and climb. A piece of cake.*

"This ain't no piece o' cake," the driver said. He was a friendly stuntman, Pete Dillard by name, dressed in the evening wear the character of the fiancé was supposed to be wearing. "I sure hope you ain't blowing smoke, 'cause that will not be very pleasant for any of us."

"No, Pete. No smoke. Maybe a little face powder."

He laughed. She was standing in the rear of the car, a three-seater specially decked with a hard bench in the back for Zee to stand on. There were two small wooden supports affixed to the bench that went about halfway up her calves.

"Once we're going good," Pete said, "you just look straight ahead. Don't look up. The ladder's going to dangle right in front of me and I'll be sure to get you to it. Watch you don't get your legs tangled in the braces. Any questions?"

Zee shook her head, but her nerves had all sorts of questions. They screamed their queries in bursts and pops. Zee tried to ignore them.

"All right, then. You get this take, and I will personally buy you and your friend the biggest steak dinner in Los Angeles. Deal?"

"Deal."

He put his hand out and she shook it. It felt rough and strong, and he held the grip and looked in her eyes, then winked his reassurance at her.

"Get ready," he said.

She was dressed now in the same costume her disgruntled predecessor had worn. The inside of the dress was held close to her legs with special garters the audience would never see. Part of the magic, she told herself.

The wind was starting up a little bit now. Zee reminded herself to be ready for it, to concentrate. To push away all thought except that of the rope ladder she was to grab.

Pete's cue to begin driving would be the appearance of the biplane flying at them from behind.

Lieutenant Hall screamed through his megaphone, "Ready!"

Pete started up the car, revved the engine. Zee looked down the road at the extras, lined up for their big moments. She thought she saw Molly waving.

For luck she waved back.

"Roll camera!" Hall barked.

Zee gave a quick look behind her. The crew in the camera car—a driver, a grip holding the tripod steady, and the cameraman—tensed for action.

Then from behind came the sound of the plane's engine. She looked back. It was approaching them.

Her heart did a flip.

"Here we go," Pete said. And the car started forward.

Zee almost fell out. *Terrific! You can't even stay in the car!*

She took a deep breath as the wind whipped her hair. Her eyes started watering from the wind's force. Clenching and unclenching her fists, she readied herself for action.

She'd have to get it on the first take. Have to! Hall was not going to give her a second crack at this.

The roar of the plane's engine overhead pulled her flesh into little bumps. She wished then that she could pray, that she had some faith that God was in His heaven and looking out for her.

But she was on her own.

The car picked up speed. Pete looked back at her, concerned.

"Just drive!" she cried.

He did.

The plane was now over them, then just ahead of them. Pete kept the car moving steady while gaining more speed to keep up with the plane.

In front of them a ladder unfurled from the plane.

This was it.

Zee's hands were wet, even in the cool air. She wiped them on her blouse.

The ladder was ten feet in front of her, nine . . .

Pete guided the car toward the ladder.

Zee put her hands in front of her.

Make it look real!

She took hold of the second to the last rung, and jumped.

Zee Miller, now known as Taylor Layne, was in the air. But she had caught the ladder too low. She was supposed to grab the fourth rung so she could put her feet on the ladder and start climbing.

Too late now. The plane began its ascent. She was holding her entire weight by her two hands. Her grip was not sure.

Hang on, hang on!

Her left hand slipped off the rung.

Zee looked down, saw the extras back on the road cheering and waving their arms.

She heard a voice from above. "Climb up!" It was the copilot.

Climb up? She'd be lucky if she survived at all.

Well, survive she would. She was in pictures! She wasn't going to blow it!

With all her strength she threw her leg up and managed to get her foot through the small square between the first and second rung. She thrust out with her leg just as her right hand lost its grip.

‖ 20 ‖

Doyle heard the man's voice as if it were coming from out of a tunnel. Distant, like an echo. Yet his mind told him the man was standing right next to him.

Doyle tried to throw a punch, to protect himself, but his arms would not move. That was when he realized he was on the ground. He smelled dirt and putrid water. He smelled blood.

The voice came again, more insistent this time. "Go on, you lousy drunk. Get out of here."

Struggling to open his eyes, Doyle realized his whole face was a mess of cuts and swollen skin. Yes, he was beginning to remember.

"I said get out of here. Come on. On your feet. I'd help you but I don't want to touch your lousy, stinking body."

It was night. That much Doyle could sense. "I. Need." Doyle could not utter another word.

"Ah, he talks like a drunk, too."

Was he talking to someone else?

Then the pain came. What had been a dull throb when he came to was now a million red-hot pokers jabbing him inside his skin. It was invisible hammers and claws having at him.

Through the slits that were his eyes, Doyle saw light. Someone with a lantern. Where was he?

"Come on, Mack," the voice said. "Help me drag this . . . oh no. Look at him."

Another voice, another man, said, "He's beaten to a bloody pulp."

"Go inside and call a doctor."

"At this hour?"

"Go on, do it!"

Doyle took a breath, too deeply. Shards of glass cut his insides. How much of him was broken?

"You just lie there, son. I own the store around front here. I don't like drunks, but something tells me you're not here because of a bad drunk and a fight. Somebody wanted to hurt you real bad, and that's what they did."

Real bad. Yes. Thorn Fleming and that other guy. Now it was all coming back to him. When he'd refused to do Norton's bidding, he got hit over the head with something heavy. It knocked him out for a time. Later, when he came to, he was in a car, too weak to do anything about it. He was like a sack of old laundry to the two big men.

They took him to some alley, pulled him out of the car, and while the one man held him, Thorn Fleming beat on him. What delight he must have taken. Doyle wondered if they thought they had killed him. If not, why did they let him live?

Doyle put a hand to his mouth. His lips were triple their normal size, cracked and lumpy. He stuck his index finger between them and felt loose teeth and gaps. He would look different after this, that was for certain.

"Get me up," he said, his voice thick.

"Now, you just stay there, lad. You're in no—"

"Get me up!"

The man helped Doyle to his feet. Remarkably, he could stand and walk, though the pain in his ribs took his breath away. They hadn't broken his legs. Fleming had concentrated on the upper body and face.

Doyle started out of the alley.

"Hey, wait for the doctor!"

Doyle ignored him. Mr. Lun. He was in trouble, if they hadn't gotten to him already.

The street lay fairly deserted this time of night. A late trolley rumbled past about a block away. Doyle made it to the corner and saw the street sign. Ninth and Broadway. He staggered from his injuries. How could he possibly get back to Lun's? No money for a cab, no way to get in touch.

He did need a doctor. But he needed to get to Lun first.

Doyle stumbled down Tenth Street, past a closed diner and a plain brick office building, the glass window of a clockmaker, finally stopping for breath near a gaudy red door in a shadowed archway. He was hunched over, as any attempt to straighten up brought pain in his mid-section.

He couldn't take another step. Chinatown could just as well be a thousand miles away. Now what?

"If your money's good, the drinks don't matter."

Doyle turned. The voice, a woman's voice, had come from the archway. At first he saw no one, but then a face appeared in the dim glow of a distant streetlamp. Doyle strove to open his puffy eyes and, through his vaporous vision, thought he saw a pretty girl. Her lips were red, and she had dark, bobbed hair.

"Did you hear me?" she said. "You can keep company, if you're able. Why don't you—"

"Help me."

She was near him now and he could smell sweet perfume.

"What happened to you?" she said, a small note of alarm in her voice.

"I need to get . . . home."

"You're blotto, mister, you—"

"No!" Doyle, despite the pain, straightened a bit.

The woman gasped. "Your face!"

"I have to get home. No money."

"Home?" she said skeptically. "You need a hospital."

"Please, front me for a cab. I have to get to Chinatown."

That brought an exasperated breath from the girl. "Me give *you* money? Ha. You ought to be in vaudeville."

So that was it. The first and last time he'd spoken to a woman of the evening had been in Denver, one night out on the edge of town when he was just looking for a cheap meal. He remembered his fascination. And temptation. His stomach won the fight that time.

Now it was no contest. "Please," he said. "I'm good for it. I'm army." He was reaching for anything that would give him credibility.

"Oh, are you, now? A doughboy?"

"Yes."

"I've heard that one before."

"I'll come back and give you the money tomorrow, I'm telling you."

"Now that's a load of piffle if I ever heard it."

"Honest."

"Con man! I suppose you think I'm just a hick waiting to be fleeced, huh? Better men than you have tried."

Useless. He should have figured. It was every man for himself. Or girl. He was all alone in the world, and he couldn't expect anything from anybody.

He'd try another block, another way. He started off again, not even knowing the direction he was heading, but he had to move. Move forward. Lun. Maybe he was dead.

At the next corner, wherever that was, Doyle had to stop and grab the lamppost. He'd maybe gone twelve, fifteen steps from where he'd met the prostitute. He was never going to make it anywhere close to Chinatown.

A sharp jab in his back. Jolts of fresh pain cracked through his body.

"All right, friend, state your business."

It was a cop.

"My, oh my, what happened to your face?" he said.

"Beat up," Doyle said.

"I'll say. What happened?"

"My business."

The cop grunted. "That's not the kind of business I'm asking you about. You heard of vagrancy?"

Doyle said nothing.

"What's your name?"

"I'm on my way home."

"That's not what I—"

"On my way home."

"And where might that be?"

"Chinatown."

"That's rich. I think maybe a night in the tank should give you time to think up a better one."

Doyle spoke in a wheeze. "You want to do some good, take me there. I'll show you."

"I don't like the way you talk."

"I suppose that's a crime, too."

"On my beat it is. You're comin' in—"

"Wait." It was the girl's voice.

"Evening, Nora."

"Hello, Officer Beck."

They knew each other? A fine kettle of fish this was.

"You don't want to be unkind to one of our returning boys."

"Him?"

"That's right. I've seen his medals."

Why was she doing this? At least it put a pause in the cop's plans for him, so Doyle clammed up.

"What happened to him?" the cop asked.

"I think he got into a political discussion with a Republican. Over Harding."

The cop snorted. "That's a good'un. Why'd you want to give your pal Beck the baloney?"

"Just trying to take a load off you," Nora said. "I'll see that this one gets home. Come by and see me sometime."

Officer Beck nodded. "Get him off my beat." With a twirl of his nightstick, he turned and walked away.

Doyle faced the girl. "Why?"

"I don't know," she said. "Maybe I felt like I needed to do a good deed. It helps balance the scales."

She left him at the lamppost, went half a block, and returned with a cab, horse drawn.

"I gave him fare to Chinatown," Nora explained. "Go get yourself fixed up."

He could hardly believe it. "Thank you."

"Go on, now."

"I'll be back with the money."

"I'd like to believe that, but I'm not gonna bet my silk stockings on it."

Those were the last words she spoke to him, even as she helped him into the cab.

He guided the driver to Lun's. The colored lights of Chinatown were a sharp contrast to the dull and dreary illumination of downtown Los Angeles. It was another world out here, complete unto itself, a world Doyle was glad to be in again.

Every step up the stairs proved to be a struggle in pain. His head felt light so that the narrow stairwell started to spin. He managed to get himself to Lun's door, holding himself upright with a hand on the doorjamb, and knocked.

No answer.

He knocked louder. "Mr. Lun! Are you in there?"

Nothing. With his open hand he slapped the door as hard as he could, over and over. He felt like he was sinking underwater.

A woman shouted from the door at the end of the corridor. She spoke in rapid Chinese. Even though he didn't understand the words, Doyle knew the meaning. *Shut up and let us sleep.*

"Please," he said to the woman. "Mr. Lun."

She took several steps toward him, chattering. She was wrapped in a plain robe, which she held on with one hand. With the other hand she gestured wildly at Doyle.

"Luns," he interrupted. He pointed at the door. "Luns!"

‖ 21 ‖

Zee's heart kicked in her throat as she waited outside the office of Sy Stroud himself. The antechamber alone would have been the largest single office Zee had ever set eyes on. It was done up in finely crafted oak and had a crystal chandelier for its illumination.

On one wall hung a single large portrait. Louise Townsend looked down, regal, as Marie Antoinette, the role that had made her a star.

"So this is the little girl that is causing such a problem, eh?"

"That's the one," Hall said.

Zee tried to clear her throat and ended up sounding like a steam drill. "But, Mr. Stroud, I did the stunt!"

"You speak when you're spoken to," Stroud said. He said it with a quiet authority, in a voice that commanded attention. Sy Stroud was not a large man, but he seemed to fill the room. His three-piece suit was crisp and sharp.

Stroud waved a hand at one of the studded leather chairs in front of his desk. Trembling, Zee sank into it, hoping to disappear.

The head of the studio sat on the corner of his desk and looked Zee up and down. Then he nodded. Was it approving or condemning? Zee had no idea.

"You don't think I hear things?" Stroud asked Zee.

"I beg your pardon?"

"You think I got where I am without I don't hear things?"

Zee blinked, trying to unscramble his meaning.

"Let me tell you, little girl, nothing in this town goes on without I hear about it. I know, you look at me, you think, Stroud! He's so big he can't hear everything. Maybe he's not so interested anymore in what goes on under his nose. But I know." He tapped the side of his nose. "I smell things, too. And you want to know what I smell?"

No, Zee thought. *I want to know how to get out of here.*

"I'll tell you," Stroud said. "I smell revolution. I smell anarchy. I smell the end of the happy family I have here. That's what Stroud-General Studios is—a big, happy family. So when one of my children talks rough, I hear about it. And I smell trouble."

Lieutenant Hall nodded slightly, a satisfied look on his face. Zee wanted to tear into him for betraying her like this. After what she'd done to save his movie!

"May I speak?" Zee said.

Stroud slapped his thighs and looked with consternation at Hall. "She's talking already and I'm not even finished yet."

Hall said, "That's what I'm saying."

"What is he saying?" Zee jumped up. She couldn't help herself. "This is unfair, Mr. Stroud!"

"Sit," Stroud commanded.

"I will not let this man tell you lies," Zee said. "I can tell you exactly what happened, and there are a lot of people who saw it."

"Young lady!" Stroud's bark sounded like a thunderclap. Zee shook. Stroud pointed to the chair, and Zee quietly sat down again. "You think Stroud is not fair to his family? You, you will get your chance. I want you first to listen, okey dokey?"

Okey dokey? "Yes, sir."

"That man there, he is called a director. He works for Stroud. I am Stroud. I own the joint. So when it comes to who does what, Stroud is the one who makes the decision." Stroud put his hand out about level with his face. "On the set, the director is next." Stroud moved his hand to the middle of his body. "Then maybe there is the star." The hand went below the waist.

Stroud got off his desk and squatted. He put his hand on the floor. "And right here are the actors. And you know what's below this floor, down under the dirt? It's the extras, little girl. The extras got no say on nothing."

The mogul stood up again. "Are you getting the picture?"

It was impossible to miss. Zee nodded.

"Now, what I'm hearing is that you made good on a stunt, but you were telling my director to put you in the next picture, as the leading lady yet."

"And he said yes."

Stroud's eyes widened as he brought his hand up to face level again. "Stroud makes that decision, remember?"

Zee dutifully nodded.

"So you're an actress, are you?"

"Yes, sir."

"You want to be in pictures, do you?"

"Yes, Mr. Stroud."

"You want to be the leading girl in the next Happy Sanders picture, eh?"

Zee swallowed, nodded again.

Stroud stretched a moment of silence. Finally he said, "Well, Stroud is not so interested."

Zee's heart dropped from her throat to her stomach. Her big mouth! Look what it got her.

"In fact, Stroud don't want you as an extra in his pictures!" He looked at the director. "Are you satisfied yet?"

Lieutenant Hall gave Stroud a curt nod.

"Okey dokey," Stroud said. "You can go."

Her head whirling, Zee started to stand up.

"Not you," Stroud said to her. "You stay right where you are. I got something to say to you, little girl."

‖ 22 ‖

Doyle woke up in a haze. An unpleasant smell revived him. On his back in a soft bed, he was strangely free of pain. In fact, his body felt somewhat numb. "Where am I?" he said.

"Home now." It was Mr. Lun's voice.

"What happened?"

"You beat up pretty bad. You get fixed now."

"Fixed? How?"

"Leave everything to wife."

Doyle turned his head and saw Mrs. Lun smiling widely and bowing. Doyle felt his bare chest. A strange plantlike thing was on top of him. His left cheek had some sort of thick bandage over it. He smelled spices.

"No touch," Mr. Lun said. "You lie still."

"What happened to you? The woman in the other apartment said something about a fire."

Mr. Lun looked down and shifted uncomfortably. "Yes."

"Yes what?"

"Fire at laundry. All gone."

Doyle balled his hands into fists. "I'm sorry I wasn't there to help you."

"You be quiet now."

"I know who's responsible."

Mr. Lun nodded slowly. "I know. Power too much. We go from this place."

"You can't leave." Doyle started to sit up, and when he did, the pain in his ribs returned. Mrs. Lun rushed over and gently pushed him back to the bed.

"We must go," Lun said. "Find new place, new city where people leave us alone."

"You love this city. This is your home."

"Nothing here. People bad."

"People are bad anywhere you go."

"Bad man here. Can't fight."

"No." Doyle sat up and waved Mrs. Lun away. "I am going to take care of it."

"Eh?"

"You get down," Mrs. Lun ordered.

Doyle ignored her. "Listen to me, Lun. I'm going to take care of business, you understand?"

Lun shook his head. "No, I see bad in your eyes."

"Then don't look."

Doyle finally let himself fall back on the bed. He'd give himself a couple of days to heal. A couple, no more, even if Mrs. Lun tried to get him to stay.

He wouldn't be staying with them any longer than that. He wouldn't be staying with anyone.

23

What could Sy Stroud possibly want to say to her now? Before stepping into his office she thought she'd secured an agreement to be the leading lady in the next Happy Sanders two-reeler. Now she wasn't even going to be an extra! Lieutenant Hall had stabbed her in the back. Maybe that was one of the rules of this game. Maybe she'd have to learn to play it better.

Alone now with Stroud, Zee fought back the urge to protest. That was what had gotten her into trouble in the first place. She was going to listen.

Stroud gave her a good looking over. "What's your name, little girl?"

"Taylor Layne," Zee said.

"Taylor Layne." Stroud seemed to taste the sound of it. "I like it. A little unusual. Like you."

"I'm sorry, Mr. Stroud, honest I am. All I wanted—"

"Stop with the talking already. It's trouble you think you're in? Let me tell you, when you're in trouble with Stroud, you'll know it. Now, it's not so bad. Only don't try my patience."

"I don't understand. Am I in trouble or not? You said I'm not even going to be an extra."

"You are telling me what I said? Not what I said. I said I don't want you as an extra—that's what I said. And I don't want you playing second fiddle to my Happy guy. I got other plans for you."

Zee shook her head in wonderment. What was going on?

Stroud took a briar pipe from a stand on his desk and began to fill the bowl with an awful-smelling tobacco from a gold can. Zee smiled politely as he lit the pipe.

"You think I don't see the daily film when it comes from the laboratory? You think I don't see you hanging by your leg from a ladder on a plane?"

"I'm beginning to think you see most everything that happens in all of Southern California."

"That's right, little girl." He paused and puffed a moment. "Only looking at you—you are not so little a girl, am I right?"

Zee had no idea how to respond.

"I make my fortune seeing what people will see on the screen. You are going to drive them crazy. You got the look of Pickford but with a little danger mixed in. Up close, I see something else in your face. I see trouble. You've been in trouble, am I right?"

Zee started to speak.

"You don't have to tell me. Stroud knows. Now, here's what I have to say. What you did in that car was sensational. Stupendous. I ain't seen nothing like it since Pearl White, and not even then. For a year I've been looking for the right girl to do a serial for us. *The Troubles of Tallulah.* I think you're the girl. No! I am Stroud! You *are* the girl!"

It took a moment for the thought to completely take hold in her mind. "You're saying you want me to be the star in a series of movies?"

"One reel. Think you can do that for me?"

"But Lieutenant Hall, he said—"

"Ah, don't give another thought to that washed-up aviator. He works for me, and not the other way around. I am going to want some tests made. We are going to do something with you. I don't know what yet, but when it happens, I'll know."

Zee couldn't stay seated any longer. She jumped to her feet, causing Stroud to move back a bit defensively. "Oh, thank you, Mr. Stroud. You won't regret this." She grabbed his hand and shook it violently.

"My arm is regretting it already," Stroud said.

"Oh, there is one thing."

"Eh? You are making with the terms now?"

"It's just that my friend, Molly, well, she is a talented actress, too, and she would be just wonderful working here. She's a hard worker—"

"Stop with the publicity already! If I told you there is no way I would take on another actress, would you walk out right now and be done with it?"

Zee swallowed hard but did not answer.

"I thought so," Stroud said. "But that tells me something. You know what you want. Okey dokey, I will give this girl friend of yours a look-see. That's all, you understand?"

"Thank you, Mr. Stroud! When do I report for work?"

"Let me get my no-good lawyers on the paper work. You can come in Monday."

"Monday it is." Breathless, Zee started for the door.

"Hey!"

Zee stopped, turned around.

"Aren't you interested in the money? You think Stroud doesn't pay?"

"Oh my goodness, I didn't even think—"

"You won't get very far in this business if you don't think about money. Stroud don't pay peanuts. You get a hundred clams a week to start."

One hundred dollars! Compared to Pickford and Chaplin, that really was peanuts. But compared to what she and Molly had ever made in their whole lives, it was the Colorado Lode.

"Deal!" Zee said.

"Deal?" Stroud threw up his hands. "She says it like she's a big wheel!"

‖ 24 ‖

Doyle looked at the revolver the man had placed on the counter. It was a .32 caliber, a pocket model. He wouldn't need anything bigger than that.

"Cartridges?" Doyle asked.

The gun merchant turned and pulled a box from his shelf and laid it next to the gun.

"I don't know," Doyle said.

"What don't you know?" The man seemed impatient now. It was late afternoon and he looked like he might want to close up the shop.

"I don't know what my preference is," Doyle said, even though he knew exactly what it was. It was the gun he had induced the man to place on the counter.

"You're wasting my time unless—"

The bell above the door jangled, and a bum walked in. He was bearded and dirty and shuffled like a drunk. Looking a bit frightened, he made his way past Doyle and the gun shop owner, and headed to the far wall of the store.

Doyle watched as the shop owner followed the bum's progress. He watched as the man's mouth opened slightly in disbelief. Doyle did not have to turn his head to know what was happening.

The bum was pulling boxes off a shelf and dropping them on the floor.

"Hey!" The store owner bolted from behind the counter and charged toward the bum, who calmly went about his business.

More boxes on the floor.

The store owner started screaming. Doyle calmly put the gun and box of bullets in his pocket and walked out of the store.

He turned, ran down an alley, and then blended into the hubbub of the next street. The plan had worked perfectly. Even though Doyle had to give the bum his last dollar, it was worth it.

Now it was just a matter of time before he used the gun on Jess Norton and Thorn Fleming.

‖ 25 ‖

The nun, elderly and brown-skinned, looked as if cured by the sun. She met Zee in the courtyard of the convent. Pepper trees created a canopy of green.

"I am Sister Mary Monica. I was told you wished to see me."

"I have something for you, Sister," Zee said. She took an envelope from her purse and gave it to the nun. It held half the money from her first Stroud-General paycheck.

"What is this?"

"A gift. For your work. It's not very much, but I want to help."

"That is very kind of you. How do you know of our work?"

Zee bit her lip. "Are the children at their studies?"

"Yes. Are you looking for a child?"

Yes, oh yes. "May I see them?"

The nun looked understanding but firm. "If you are looking for a child, you may return with your husband."

"Oh," Zee said quietly. "Yes . . . but may I not see them now?"

A troubled look crossed the nun's face.

"Please."

The nun glanced down at the envelope in her hands, then smiled. "In view of your generosity, I believe it would be acceptable for you to see the work you are supporting. Come along."

She led Zee across the courtyard, a sunny quadrant that included a rose garden. On the other side of the yard was a simple, squat building with curved red tiles on the roof.

"Our schoolhouse," Sister Mary explained. "The girls should be coming out in a moment."

The moment seemed endless to Zee.

Finally, the door of the school building opened, and a group of little girls, perhaps twenty in all, marched out. They were of all ages, the youngest of them appearing about six or seven years old.

Too old.

Desperate, Zee placed a hand on the nun's arm. "Is that all?"

"All?"

"The children, the children."

"Except for the young ones."

"Yes, the young ones. Where are they?"

"I believe Sister Martha has taken them for a walk."

"When will she be back? I must see . . ."

"What is it, my dear?"

Zee fought for control. "Please. May I?"

A look of profound understanding came into the nun's eyes. "I believe I understand. Come with me."

They went through a large wooden door in the adobe wall and came out on the other side. From here Zee could see the mountain range to the north that rimmed the valley. It was nothing like downtown with its cars and trains and concrete buildings. This seemed a setting open to life, rather than a restriction upon it.

The nun pointed. From the distance, another sister was coming toward them. Behind her, a trail of little ones, five or six of them. Could one of them be. . . ?

Zee felt light-headed.

She tried not to faint as the children's faces came close enough for her to make them out. There were two boys and four girls. Zee looked closely at the girls.

And her heart fell. There was nothing familiar about them.

Then, from behind Sister Martha, another little girl stepped into view.

There was no mistake. The girl was a miniature of Zee; in fact, she looked almost exactly like the photographs of Zee as a young girl. Hair, eyes, shape of the mouth. All the same.

Zee's heart expanded, straining against her chest. The little girl gave her a quick, shy look, and then grabbed a handful of Sister Martha's habit.

"Come along, girls," Sister Martha said. She began leading them toward the wooden door.

Zee almost cried out for her to stop. She wanted to run to the little girl, to embrace her.

"Are you quite well?" Sister Mary asked.

"What . . . is her name?"

The nun seemed to know exactly to whom she was referring. "We call her Isabel."

"How did she come to you?"

The nun took Zee's hand in her own and looked into her eyes. "Because of the love of a good woman, who sought the best for her child."

Tears came then, and Zee was powerless to stop them.

"Your daughter is in God's hands," the sister said.

"Oh, may I speak to her?"

"What has happened in the past is done. If you would do anything, you must pray."

"But—"

"It is for the best."

With a gentle pressure, Sister Mary led Zee around the walls, away from the inside.

‖ 26 ‖

There were four rows of tables with wooden benches, with each bench filled. Men on their last dime, denizens of the street, out of work and out of luck. Doyle felt right at home.

One last meal. He'd warm the belly, then take care of business. Norton and Thorn Fleming. And then turn the gun upward, under his chin. At least he'd know that his last act on earth was getting rid of two parasites. No, three. He'd have to include himself there.

Doyle moved to the counter where an older woman ladled out soup. Potato. He could smell it. Along with a chunk of bread and coffee. Doyle took the tray to the farthest corner of the room and found a place to eat alone. For about ten seconds.

"I thought I recognized you," a voice said.

Doyle looked up from his soup. The man standing there was indeed familiar—the socialist from the jail where Doyle had spent the night with a cracked head.

He sat down as if he'd found a long-lost friend. "Looks like your face got in the way of a Cossack."

In no mood for talk, Doyle only grunted.

"I'm glad, then, to run into you." The old man dipped his bread in the soup, took a bite, sending a trickle of potato liquid down his chin. "We need all the help we can get."

"Not interested."

"After all you been through?"

"You don't know anything."

"I know you didn't have that fancy scar on your cheek when I saw you in the clink. How'd you get it?"

"Pipe down, will you?"

"I'll not pipe down about revolution! We're ripe for it! The people know it, friend. We got Congress investigating all sorts of useless things, when the people really want 'em to investigate what five-cent cigars are really made of, you see my point?"

"No."

"Look around you! Outside on the street it's every man for himself. Downtown life is like a trip from the hospital to the morgue. We the people, man. We're going to make it happen."

Doyle took a sip of tepid coffee. "The only thing that's going to happen is everybody dies, and the pattern repeats itself."

The socialist was opening his mouth to answer when a man standing at the counter made an announcement. "We are very pleased to serve you tonight, gentlemen. We thank the good Lord for His bounty and that your stomachs may be filled."

"Ha," the socialist muttered.

Doyle, who had his back to the speaker, spooned some more soup.

"And as is our tradition we ask only that you give your attention for the next few moments to some words from our speaker."

The socialist shook his head. "Here it comes."

Doyle ignored him.

"Tonight it is our great privilege, and yours, I might add, that our speaker is one of the most eminent preachers in the world today. Frankly, men, I can think of many other things that should command his attention, so his appearance here tonight is indeed a privilege. He makes his home here and is the dean of the Bible Institute of Los Angeles, as well as the pastor of the Church of the Open Door. Gentlemen, I give you Dr. Reuben Archer Torrey."

Doyle turned around. Where had he heard those names before?

The man called Torrey held a black book in his hand. A Bible, no doubt. He had a crisp white beard and ample middle but seemed a fireplug of pent-up energy, ready to burst forth. His gray suit was three piece, perfectly tailored, and it matched his light gray eyes, which were striking, even from across the room.

"I thank Mr. Plummer for that introduction, but I will explain why I am here at the outset. I am here because the Lord told me to come here. It is as simple as that. I have something to say to you tonight but they are not my words. I am merely the messenger."

The socialist grunted. "He'll probably ask for a tip."

Torrey's voice was strong and firm. He spoke without hesitation. "I have a text tonight which I believe God has given me for this hour, a text that ought to startle every man in this room who has not accepted the gospel of Christ. You will find it in Hebrews, chapter two, verse three: 'How shall we escape if we neglect so great salvation?' I wish that that text would burn itself into the heart of every man here who is out of Christ. How shall I escape if I neglect so great salvation? I wish that every one of you who may go away from this place tonight without definitely having received Christ as Savior and Lord and Master would hear it ringing in your ears as you go down the street. 'How shall we escape if we neglect so great salvation?' I wish that every one who may lie down to sleep tonight without a definite assurance of being forgiven through the atoning blood of Jesus Christ and of acceptance before God in Him would hear it all through the night. 'How shall we escape if we neglect so great salvation?' "

Already the phrase was lingering in Doyle's mind.

"This is the part I hate," the socialist said to Doyle. "Having to listen to this claptrap in exchange for food."

But the words did not sound like claptrap to Doyle, for they were entirely different from the sermons he had heard all of his life from his parents' church. A series of sophisticates had filled that popular pulpit. From the age of eight onward, Doyle decided they were learned and erudite and yet lacked something he could not quite identify.

Now, listening to this man Torrey, he thought he knew what it was. He spoke as one firmly convinced that what he was saying was of the utmost importance.

Yet he was not like the fire and brimstone preachers Doyle had heard on occasion, as they blew through Zenith on various campaigns. Most of the time Doyle felt the raising of their voices in a theatrical manner was more rehearsed than felt.

Torrey, on the other hand, was impassioned but reasonable, his voice modulated but strong. As he spoke he occasionally hit at the air with his fist.

"My sermon is all in the text—the folly and guilt of neglecting the salvation that God the Father has sent through His Son and in His Son Jesus Christ.

"You notice I say not merely the folly but the guilt. There is many a man who thinks that perhaps it may be a foolish thing not to accept Christ, and admit the folly of it, but he has never realized the guilt of it. But I shall endeavor to show you tonight in the unfolding of this text that it is an egregiously foolish thing, an awful thing, to neglect this salvation."

Foolish? Awful? The words attached themselves to Doyle's mind like burrs in his socks.

"Amen, brother!" the socialist shouted with obvious derision.

"A revolution of the heart, brother," Torrey shot back, "which cannot be ignored! You cannot ignore the fact that God sent His Son, His only Son, down into the world to proclaim salvation. The great and infinitely holy God sent down His own Son to proclaim pardon to the vilest sinner. If you and I neglect this salvation, we are pouring contempt upon the Son of God, and upon the Father that sent Him.

"Furthermore, the greatness of this salvation is seen in the way in which it was purchased. This is a costly salvation. It was purchased by the shed blood, by the outpoured life of the incarnate Son of God."

"There will be blood in the revolution, parson!" the socialist said.

"Shut up," Doyle snapped. "Let the man speak."

"What's eating *you?*"

What indeed? Doyle was feeling uncomfortable, yet wanting to hear more. It was a strange, scary dichotomy in the brain that almost made him want to scream.

‖ 27 ‖

"Molly, we can't miss this!"

"Not you. Just me."

Zee grabbed her by the shoulders and shook her. "Molly Pritchard, wake up. This is John Raneau's home we are talking about. This is not any Hollywood party. This is *the* Hollywood party. And we are invited! Special guests of Mr. Happy Sanders himself! He's put in a credit at Mrs. Norris's dress shop. We can get new dresses, Mol. Free! We need to get going."

She was desperate to get going; she wanted to run to the party. She wanted anything that would help her to clear the memory of seeing her daughter for the last time. She wanted fun and noise and music. She wanted to drink champagne and maybe more. She wanted Molly to keep her company, and she didn't want to stop running until she was a star and nothing could hurt her again.

Molly sighed, moved to the window, and looked out at Bunker Hill.

Zee slid next to her and took her arm. "We're moving out of here the minute we get that first paycheck. Mol, we can't think of ourselves as normal people anymore. We're in the movies."

"You're in the movies. I'm along for the ride."

"But what a ride! Come along, Molly, we're a team."

"No." Molly turned to face her. "I don't feel that I'm part of the same world."

"When did this happen?"

Molly shrugged and sat on the one good chair in the room.

"Something's wrong with you, I know it." Zee pulled up the chair with the short leg. "Tell me what's eating you."

"It's nothing, really. I guess I'm seeing things a little differently, that's all."

"What things?"

"The movies. Wanting so much to be a success."

"It's within our grasp. What's so wrong with reaching out and getting it?"

When Molly did not immediately answer, Zee knew there was something deeper going on. She had always been able to read Molly, whose face was as open as a newspaper.

"Truth time," Zee said. "I want you to tell me exactly what happened to make you think this way."

"Think! That's exactly it. Maybe I'm thinking about it, really thinking about it."

"Okay, you don't need to get hot about it."

"I went to church yesterday, while you were at the studio."

"Church? On a Wednesday?"

"It was a lecture, actually. At the church downtown, with the open door, they call it. You remember that card the woman gave us in the square? That's the church."

"So they reeled one in, did they? You must have made them happy."

"Taylor, the lecture was on the lure of ambition, and I felt as if the speaker was directing it at me."

Zee laughed, to keep from feeling that her only friend in Los Angeles was taking a step, perhaps the first of many, away from their plans. "You want me to go speak to this fellow? Set him straight?"

Molly did not laugh.

"What's the matter with having a little fun? We can think about ambition tomorrow. Tonight, let's just enjoy ourselves."

Shaking her head, Molly said, "I am not at ease in that company. I don't drink, I don't—"

"Is that what your concern is? That we might go to a party and end up a couple of stewed tomatoes? When did you become such a schoolmarm?"

Molly's head snapped back. "That's not a nice thing to say."

"Then snap out of it! Come along."

"No, Taylor. Not tonight."

Zee moved toward the door. "Well then, I'm not going to let you ruin my evening. I'll just go without you."

"I want you to."

"A bit patronizing, don't you think?" Zee grabbed her coat and a nickel from the chipped cup that held trolley fare.

At the door Molly called to her, "Please be careful, Taylor."

Zee did not reply as she closed the door.

‖ 28 ‖

"The only blood that saves," the preacher Torrey continued, "is the blood of Christ. It is what makes this so *great* a salvation. The blood brings pardon for all our sins, deliverance from sin; it brings union with the Son of God in His resurrection life; it brings adoption into the family of God; it brings an inheritance incorruptible and undefiled that fadeth not away, laid up in store in heaven for us, who are kept by the power of God, through faith, unto a salvation ready to be revealed in the last time."

A mouthful, that was. The words filled Doyle's head and bounded around like fireworks set ablaze in a factory.

"When you think that God has put at our disposal in Jesus Christ all His wealth, and is ready to make us heirs of God and joint heirs with Jesus Christ, who can measure the guilt of neglecting and of turning a deaf ear to this wonderful salvation?"

"Cossack," the socialist muttered.

"But when the great King of Glory, the King of Kings and Lord of Lords, the great Eternal Son of God comes to you and me, in our filth and rags, and wants to take us out of our filth and rags of unrighteousness, and says, I want to adopt you into my family and make you an heir of God and a joint heir with Me, there are some of you men and women in this building tonight who, by your actions, are saying, Go away with your salvation, go away with your adoption into the family of God; I would rather have the crust of the world's pleasure and the rags of my sin than all the royal apparel of righteousness and glory which you offer me."

Suddenly Doyle wanted to leave. A flame was alight inside him and it made him squirm.

But it was the socialist who stood first. "We've heard enough from you, preacher!"

A few voices told the socialist to be quiet, but others offered half-hearted agreement.

"Not yet," Torrey said, not backing down an inch. Indeed, to Doyle, he resembled a boxer taking his stance.

"I do not want any man here to make the mistake of supposing there is any other way to salvation, other than the one name under heaven given among men whereby we must be saved. Salvation is in Christ, or it is no salvation at all."

"I say salvation is from the people!" The socialist raised his fist.

"So you are a preacher, too?"

"Why not? I have as much right as you."

"You offer a way of salvation?"

"Again, why not?"

"Suppose a man is in a burning building. If there were one way of escape by a fire escape, and another by a great broad stairway, he would have a perfect right to neglect the fire escape for the easier escape by the stairway. But if there was no way of escape but the fire escape, how great would be his folly in neglecting it! Men, you are in a burning building, in a doomed world. There is just one way of escape; that is by Christ. In Christ anyone can be saved. Out of Christ, no one shall be saved. By Christ, or not at all."

"Don't listen to him, men. The Bible is a book of confusion!" And with that, the socialist ran out the door.

Doyle stood to follow him, but Torrey went right on preaching.

"Men, you are in a burning building tonight, you are in a doomed world. But thank God, there is a way of escape, and one way only, in Christ Jesus. No one knows how long that way will be left open. I beg of you, do not neglect it, and then when it is too late lay hold on some rope of lame philosophy, and go a little way, and then let go and plunge, not six stories down, but on and on and on into the awful, unfathomable depths of despair. Men, turn to Christ tonight! 'How shall we escape if we neglect so great salvation?' "

Doyle realized that he was frozen in place, had not moved an inch toward the door. Torrey's words were wrapped around him like a chain.

"Come forward," Torrey said. "Come forward to receive Christ."

Doyle put his hand in his pocket, felt the gun. And for a fleeting moment he thought about giving it up, handing it to this preacher, and falling on his knees.

But the feeling passed. He charged to the door. As he did, he felt the concentrated look of the preacher on him, felt it as sure as if the sun were throwing heat on the back of his neck.

‖ 29 ‖

While the band played "Blue Moon" and "Look for the Silver Lining" and some hotsy-totsy new jazz that was all the rage, Zee wandered about, feeling a bit like a cactus in a flower garden. Even though she wore her stylish new navy blue silk dress, perfectly fitted and with hand-stitched embroidery, she was not yet a flower herself. Someday!

The mansion was a little girl's dream of a castle in a fairy tale, everything marble, polished wood, velvet ropes, and framed portraits—the largest being John Raneau on horseback. He looked like a cross between an Elizabethan king and a Southern outdoorsman.

And plants. Ferns and ficus everywhere, palms and other greenery. Why, it must take a full-time gardener just to see to the flora of the interior of the house!

It was behind one palm where Zee found a love seat that offered some respite from her adventures through the enormous home. And as she sat she wondered for the first time if she might someday own a mansion just like this one.

Why not? It was only money, and money followed fame, and if she made it to the screen she could well become famous. Look at what Douglas Fairbanks and Mary Pickford were doing with that huge home they called Pickfair. They were only movie stars after all.

Zee looked down and saw, partially hidden by a large palm frond, two feet pointing outward. It was one of the most familiar sights now in the world.

"Happy Sanders, come out of there."

The comedian laughed as he stumbled from behind the palm. He held a glass half filled with drink in one hand and, with the other, gestured in the manner of a bow.

"You caught me," he said.

"What were you doing?" Zee said, glad to see him but disconcerted by his obviously pie-eyed state.

"I was following you, my dear. Want you to have a little drink with me." A smile slipped up one side of his face as he held his near-empty glass aloft.

"No thanks, Hap. I'd better keep my wits about me."

"Aw, Taylor, I don't want to drink alone."

"Alone? There's got to be about a hundred people in this place."

"I don't mean that. I don't want to drink with all those phonus bolonuses. I want to drink with the woman I love." He staggered in place, closing and opening his eyes.

"Don't be silly. And you're drunk enough as it is."

"Only going to get drunker, my little silkworm." Happy took another drink.

"Why don't you stop?" Zee was concerned he would make a fool of himself in front of everyone.

"Why should I stop? Give me seventy-five good reasons."

Zee stood up. "You're funnier when you're sober." She reached for his glass, but he yanked it away.

"Ah, but the world is funnier to me when I'm drunk. Tell me, do you think I'm grotesque?"

"Oh, Hap."

"I'm in earnest, Taylor. I am not what anyone would call a good-looking man."

"You're beloved by millions of people. You bring them happiness and laughter."

"But the ladies don't love me, Taylor. Why couldn't I have looked like Valentino?"

"Because God made you to look like Happy Sanders." Funny, her mentioning God. It had just popped out. It was something her father used to say to her when she was very young. *"God made you that way,"* he'd say when commenting on some positive aspect in her character. But as she got older, and became less the apple of his eye, he had stopped saying such things.

"Leave God out of this, will you?" Happy Sanders drained the last of his drink. He waved at a servant and motioned for another. "I have enough enemies as it is."

"What enemies could you have?"

The sunny reflection of his moon face, his screen trademark, was suddenly gone. "You don't know what you're in for, do you?" he said.

"In for?"

"You're as innocent as a newborn puppy. Taylor, I wish I could spare you what is to come."

"What are you talking about, Hap? You're scaring me a little."

"Good!" Happy laughed. "I hope I scare you. Because you're going to find out what it's like to be a star. You're going to find out what they ask of you. Especially the women."

"Why can't I be different?" Zee said.

Happy wagged a finger at her. "Can't de bun." He blinked. "I mean, can't be *done*. It's the system, Zee. The power. The money. The glitter. Intoxicating, like the liquor." He held up his empty hand. "Where's my liquor?"

"Come on." Zee took his arm. "Let's go outside for some fresh air."

Happy jerked his arm away. "I'm not a child. And neither are you. They'll try to break you, Taylor. If you let 'em, they'll do it."

"I don't break easily," she said, surprised at the cool resolve in her voice.

Happy spun around, then fell into the love seat and put his head in his hands. "When I was a younger man I dreamed of playing leading roles on the Broadway stage. It's funny what an unspoiled mind thinks of itself. It dreams big dreams and torments you with large visions, a canvas as big as any screen in any movie house in the land. I wanted to be as respected as Lionel Barrymore. I knew I was not going to be the idol that Lionel's brother John is. But I thought that my acting ability, an ability I so desperately wanted and prayed for, would bring about that respect."

Zee sat next to him and said, "I have always believed that comedy is the hardest sort of acting to do. And you are one of the best, one of the funniest. When people talk of Chaplin and Chase and Arbuckle, they speak also of Happy Sanders."

"But there is no respect! Listen to me, Zee. They will try to put you in a box, in a prison, one from which you cannot escape."

"Prison?"

"Yes, like the lovely girl I once met named Theodosia Goodman. Ever heard of her?"

"No."

"But you have seen her. You know her as Theda Bara. The world knows her as 'The Vamp.' The very essence of evil!"

Indeed, Zee had seen nearly all of Theda Bara's movies, going back to her appearance in the film *A Fool There Was*, based on Kipling's poem "The Vampire." Bara's brooding dark looks and long hair captivated audiences.

"She was just a little girl from Cincinnati, Ohio," Happy continued, "and all she wanted to be was a romantic heroine. She finally got her chance after much heartache with her studio. Did you ever see her attempt at sweetness?"

"I don't remember."

"Not many people do. The film was *Kathleen Mavourneen,* and it was a complete failure. A flop! And it only served to lock the door on her prison cell. The same lock that is on mine. The same that will be on yours someday."

Zee couldn't help but see the irony. Here was a man with one of the most recognizable faces in the world, a man who made three million every year in salary, talking about being in prison.

The servant returned, handing Happy a glass with more amber liquid in it.

"Why don't you get out while the getting is good? Go back to

Hoboken or wherever it is you're from."

"Nebraska."

"Yes. Go back to the heartland, for they will hurt you here."

The cool wind through her body returned. "Perhaps I am not so easily hurt. Perhaps I'm not the good little girl Theda Bara once was, or you think that I am."

Happy looked at her with his rheumy eyes, like a man straining to gaze through a clouded window. "I would not want that to be true. I would not—"

Happy dropped his glass. It shattered on the marble floor. His head traced a small circle, and then he slumped over onto Zee with his full weight.

Another servant rushed over. "Is everything all right?"

"Is there an unused room where Mr. Sanders might sleep?" Zee asked.

"Do you mean, sleep it off?" the servant said.

"Yes."

"I suggest the library."

With the help of another servant they got Happy Sanders onto a divan in the library. Zee unbuttoned his shirt and took off his shoes and draped an afghan over him.

She had decided to leave the party when, as she stepped into the main hallway that led to the front door, she found herself face-to-face with the newest guests to arrive.

"Well, look who's done well for herself," Jess Norton said. He was decked out in a tuxedo with a gold watch chain and, with his white gloves and diamond stickpin, looking like the proverbial million bucks.

Louise Townsend, wearing a silver sparkling dress and large diamond necklace, held Jess Norton's arm. "Perhaps she is one of the servants, dear," she said.

Jess Norton seemed to be enjoying this little encounter between the two women. "Is that true, Miss Layne? I got a feeling you are a guest here."

"I was just on my way home," Zee said.

"So soon?" said Louise. "What a tragedy." Turning to Norton, she cooed, "Let's have a drink."

Norton's gaze did not move from Zee. "So, tell me what you've been up to since you left my place."

"I'm bored, Jess." Louise pulled at his arm.

"Relax, baby. I—"

Sy Stroud's voice broke through the hubbub. "There is my star!"

"Hello, darling." Louise brushed his cheek with her lips.

"I see you are getting to know the newest addition to the family, eh?"

Louise Townsend's eyes narrowed. "You have got to be joking, Sy."

"Now I'm Sy? No more Mr. Stroud?" The mogul threw his hands up in the air.

Louise ignored the gesture. "I said you must be joking."

"About movies Stroud does not joke. This girl here, she is Tallulah. She is going to get in lots of one-reel trouble."

"Well, this calls for a drink," Norton said. "And since it's my booze that's flowing, why not? Come on, Sy, let's serve the ladies."

The two men went off together, Norton putting his arm around Sy Stroud's shoulder like an old friend.

"You must be very proud of yourself," Louise said, sidling up close to Zee. "What did you do, and to whom?"

"I beg your pardon?"

"Come, come, we're big girls. You can tell me."

"There's nothing to tell. I did a stunt in a Happy Sanders picture and Mr. Stroud liked it."

"I'll just bet he did."

"I don't like your insinuations, Miss Townsend."

"Would you rather I come right out with it? All right. I can see it in your eyes. You'll stop at nothing to get what you want. We can understand each other a little, then. But I have already arrived. You have a long way to go."

"I know that."

Louise ran her fingers daintily over her diamond necklace. "I wonder how much you know." She paused, then leaned in to whisper, "Just know this. Don't ever try to come up behind me. I'll know just what to do."

Zee did not doubt Louise Townsend was in dead earnest. Zee said, "Good night," and swept past Louise toward the front entrance.

"Wait!" Sy Stroud caught her just as one of the servants was opening the large wooden door. "You're not leaving so soon?"

"Yes," Zee said.

"Without we have a drink first?"

"All the more for Miss Townsend," she said, and went out into the night.

She found herself in the middle of a bunch of autos, expensive and gleaming in the moonlight. She wondered which of them Norton and Louise Townsend had come in. Perhaps she could flatten their tires.

She began walking down the road, toward the Hollywood flatland. It would give her time to work off steam.

But she decided she didn't want to work it off. Louise Townsend wanted a fight, did she? All right, Zee would give her one.

‖ 30 ‖

From the street the place looked quiet, uninhabited. Every now and then a car or cab would drive up and people would get out. People dressed up for a night on the town. Overdressed for this section of Los Angeles.

They would knock on the door and a small window would open. Words were exchanged with someone. Then the door would open quickly and the couple disappear inside.

Doyle watched it all from the steps of the closed-up shop across the way. It was going on midnight, though Doyle hadn't kept track of time. He only kept track of the people.

And where they came out.

There was a side exit to the speakeasy. Doyle knew about it from working at Lun's. The burned-out laundry was boarded up next door to the gin joint. A scar on the city block.

Doyle fingered the gun in his pocket. He went over again, for the thousandth time, what he was going to do.

Norton's driver would bring the car around to the front. That was the pattern Doyle had noticed the last two nights. Thorn Fleming would enter the car first, and Norton, after some final instructions to the doorman, would join him.

Doyle saw himself approaching from the street side. As soon as Norton closed the door, Doyle would blast out the window and shoot all three occupants. He'd empty the gun, six shots. He'd reload and empty the gun again. Then he'd put one more bullet in the gun.

For himself.

Was he prepared to die?

He was not prepared to live in prison, so that answered the question. He was not prepared to live on the run. He was . . .

"How shall we escape if we neglect so great salvation?"

The words echoed in his mind, like the fire of a distant cannon. That preacher's voice.

He didn't want to think about that now. He shook his head and argued with himself. He was doing God a favor. *You hear that, God? If you're there, I am ridding this world of bad people, doesn't that count for something?*

"How shall we escape if we neglect so great salvation?"

I am helping the world; I am preventing a whole lot of trouble. There is nothing more to say, nothing more to live . . . There is nothing, nothing, nothing . . .

"How shall we escape if we neglect so great salvation?"

Why were these words going through him now? He saw the preacher in his mind's eye, remembered the certainty of the man. How could anybody be so sure of such things? He was an older man, maybe he knew something. Maybe not. Forget it. Concentrate. *It's late and you're tired and you're nervous because you are going to kill.*

Doyle took the gun out of his pocket and laid it on his lap.

"How shall we escape if we neglect so great salvation?"

Shut up. Ignore it. Think of something else.

Rusty.

No, don't think of Rusty. He will find out, Mother and Father will find out. It will get to them eventually.

What did that matter? They will be dust someday, too. Dust doesn't remember anything; it blows away and that's that.

"How shall we escape if we neglect so great salvation?"

He was going to go crazy now, that was it. Such a thing came with killing others, just a fact he would have to accept. Life was crazy, he was crazy, the world was crazy and people were better off dead.

What if he was wrong? What if the old preacher was right?

What if what if what if?

A man and woman, both of them laughing, staggered out of the doorway across the street. He was loud and uttering words that were barely coherent.

Doyle watched them as he would insects in a box. What would it matter if they were squashed right now? What difference would it make if they lived or died? They'd be better off dead. They just didn't know it yet.

He waited. Half an hour. An hour. Time lost all meaning. His hand grew hot around the gun.

A big black car pulled up in front of the place. A man got out of the passenger side. He wore a long black coat. He went to the door, knocked, waited.

A moment later the door opened and Thorn Fleming came out.

Doyle's heart pounded.

Fleming held the door for Jess Norton.

Now.

Doyle stood up. Jess Norton got in the car.

Now!

Doyle tried to move but couldn't. His feet and legs were frozen.

Fleming got in the car. Doyle had to go *now*.

The gun was in his hand. He couldn't move his hand.

"How shall we escape if we neglect so great salvation?"

Hellfire in his head, behind his eyes.

Let me let me let me! he screamed inside his brain.

‖ 31 ‖

"Now you scream! Louder! Reach for the gun, your hand trembling. More trembling! That's right. Then Black Bill takes a step toward you! You react. More reaction! That's right. Bill laughs and takes another step. You hold out the gun! Trembling! Pull the trigger! Nothing! The gun is jammed! He takes another step at you, full of menace. All hope is lost! Throw the gun at him! Cut!"

The filming came to an abrupt halt. Zee felt pleased with the results. She had followed the director's prompts to the letter.

The director, Forbes Franklin, was an industry veteran, having started as an assistant to D. W. Griffith. From there he had earned a reputation as a hard and fast worker, exactly the sort Sy Stroud liked.

They were on the set at Stroud-General Studios, which had been designed to look like a mountain cabin. Black Bill had kidnapped Tallulah and was holding her for ransom. But he underestimated her pluck. They always did! For pluck was the constant in all of the scripts Zee had read so far.

In this scene from the *Troubles of Tallulah*—*Tallulah in the Mountains*, the "girl of grit" managed to cut through her rope restraints in the cabin where Black Bill had her tied up to a chair. She did this by rubbing up and down against a single nail sticking out from the wall.

But just as she did, and was able to reach a gun Black Bill had left behind when he went out hunting for food, the villain came back. And that was the scene that wrapped.

"My dear Miss Layne," Franklin called out. "Approach me."

She did. "How about that, chief?"

"We must do it all again!"

Zee was shocked. "But why?"

"You're not *big* enough!"

"I beg your pardon?"

"Your face! Your eyes! Your very presence! You must be big, grand! That is how you must go about it. We are not shooting a parlor scene."

"I know, chief, but I assure you what I'm doing is *realistic*. The audience today is more sophisticated than when Pearl White was dodging bullets."

Forbes Franklin looked as if he'd been tweaked on the nose. "You are telling me about the audience? You are telling *me*? Just how long have you been in this business, Miss Layne?"

"I have been sneaking . . . going to the movies since I was a little girl back in Zenith, Nebraska. I'm not just an actress, I am part of the audience. And I know what I like."

"But—"

"Mr. Franklin, a new day is dawning in the movies, in acting. People want to think that what's happening up on that screen is real. Have you read about the Moscow Art Theater?"

"Moscow? What on earth—"

"That's right. Maestro Stanislavsky and the new school of realism. It's going to sweep over the theater world."

"You'll be sweeping the floors around here if you—"

"Just take a look, will you, at—"

"This is not Shakespeare we're doing here, Miss Layne."

"Please, sir."

"I haven't got time to argue. We shoot this scene again. Places."

The assistant director, who as usual was hovering at Franklin's left arm, shouted, "Places!"

The small crew began to scurry in readiness.

Disheartened, Zee didn't know what she would do when the camera started rolling. She'd look ridiculous, with the wide eyes and open mouth Franklin wanted. If she gave him that, no one would take her seriously as an actress. Like Pearl White, she'd be locked in a mold.

Edgar Dwan, the man who played Black Bill, edged over to Zee. "Just give the bloke what he wants." Dwan was a classically trained actor from England with a magnificent voice. No one, of course, would ever hear it on film.

"Mr. Dwan, don't you want this to be the best we can do?"

He laughed. "These are one-reel serials, my love. The groundlings do not care about the acting."

"But they must. If we make it real for them, so much the better."

"What they want is something *big*. They want to forget about being small. That's what most of them are. They are grinding out tired lives in the workaday world. We give them a few moments of forgetfulness. That's all. And if we do our jobs, we get paid. You don't have anything against getting paid, do you?"

"Places please!" the A.D. screamed. Zee moved to her place on the cabin set, where the props were being arranged once more by Pete Dillard, Stroud-General's best stunt coordinator, the one she'd met on *Fly Boy*. He was the one comforting, familiar member of the crew.

"Someday you'll be a director, Pete, and you'll direct a great picture and I'll be the star," she said.

"That sounds good," he said. "Meanwhile, go with your instincts."

"Huh?"

"I've been watching you. You have something in you that's just dying to burst out. Let it out."

"How?"

"You'll know. And when you do, it's going to be wonderful. Tell you what, I'll stand next to Franklin. I'll make sure he sees what I see."

"Clear the set!" Franklin shouted.

Pete gave Zee a pat on the chin and walked off.

Forbes Franklin leaned forward in his director's chair. "Now remember, Miss Layne. Big! Black Bill is going to come in that door and I want the people in the last row to see what that does to you. Understood?"

Zee nodded. Pete, standing as promised to Forbes's left, winked at her.

"Mark it," Franklin said.

The slateman placed the board in front of the camera. Zee closed her eyes, breathed in, and got as big as she possibly could inside her own body.

"Action!"

Zee looked at the cabin door. It opened. Black Bill stepped inside, his heavy fur coat dusty with corn-flake snow.

"Scream!" Franklin commanded.

Zee screamed as loudly as she could.

"That's it! Reach for the gun now. Tremble! More! Bigger!"

She reached for the gun.

"Bill takes another step!"

Zee held the gun up.

"That's right. He laughs!"

Edgar Dwan gave a hearty stage laugh, one worthy of Falstaff.

"You pull the trigger!"

Zee pulled the trigger.

"Nothing! Jammed! Now Bill takes another step! You react. Bigger! Throw the gun!"

Zee did not throw the gun. Instead she dropped it on the ground and charged Edgar Dwan, dove into the middle of his huge frame with her shoulder, and sent them both crashing to the floor.

Dwan hit with an *oomph* and look of utter shock on his face. Zee quickly stood and grabbed a wooden chair, raised it above her head.

A wide-eyed Dwan shouted, "Cut! Pleeaasse!"

"Cut!" Franklin shouted. His anger was palpable. Red of face, he jumped out of his chair and stormed onto the set. Zee gently put the chair down.

Franklin stopped in front of her and gestured with his fist, when suddenly Pete was between them.

"Sensational!" Pete said.

The director froze, looked back at him. "What?"

"That was one of the most realistic stunts I've ever seen!"

"I'm not a stuntman!" Dwan cried feebly as he slowly got to his feet.

"Sorry, Edgar," Zee said. "I don't know what came over me."

"It certainly wasn't acting! Oww!" He put a hand on his backside.

"Mr. Stroud will love this," Pete said. "You're a genius, Mr. Franklin."

"Eh?" the director looked befuddled.

"That was a master stroke, sir," Pete continued. "I've been on hundreds of sets and seen dozens of action bits. But this was the best one ever."

Forbes Franklin looked at Zee, at Dwan, at the crew, then back at Pete. "It wasn't half bad, was it?"

‖ 32 ‖

The flophouse had ten beds, five on each side of the room. Several men smelling of booze and dirt snored so loudly it vibrated Doyle's clothes.

But he barely heard them.

He lay on his back staring at the ceiling. In the dark it was just an expanse of nothingness. He heard his own voice in his head.

This is how it ends. You have no guts, no will, you have lost your humanity, so there is nothing, nothing, and this is the time to do it. Do it now and get it over with.

Doyle felt for the gun in his waistband. All it would take is a single bullet, and that would be it. Rest and peace and an end to trying to put things together, or to find justice in a world gone mad.

Rusty, I wish you didn't have to live. I wish you didn't have to find out what I've found out, that any beauty or truth you once thought existed is all a joke and was never really there. That's the thing no one ever tells you in school, they just want you to keep on going, keep on living, as if it all made sense.

But when you lose your will, when you can't even do the things you set out to do, then that's it.

Doyle removed the gun and held it, the weight of it substantial as he lay on his back. They would hear the shot and find his body lifeless on the bed, and they would shake their heads and say there goes another one, but another one who won't be missed, and I wonder where he came from anyway.

Nebraska. Old Omaha. Zee, where are you now?

He placed the barrel of the gun at his temple. It was cold to the touch, the finger of death.

‖ 33 ‖

Zee hadn't laughed this hard in a long time, and Pete had made it possible. He was a wonderful mimic, and as they sat in a booth in the Pacific Dining Car, one of Pete's favorite eateries, he did a spot-on imitation of Forbes Franklin. "It wasn't half bad, was it?"

She was laughing so hard she couldn't eat her dinner. Pete had treated Zee to the special, a sixty-five-cent sirloin with baked potato. He had the same.

Catching her breath, Zee said, "Thank you for saving me. I was sure I was going to be fired."

"You won't be fired. You're going all the way to the top."

"You're a good egg, Pete. I'm glad you're on my side."

"Of course I am. Why wouldn't I be?"

"Oh, lots of reasons. This is a hard business. A lot of rotten people around."

"Anyone in particular?"

Zee poked at her potato. "What do you know about Louise Townsend?"

"I thought so."

Zee looked at him. "You're not surprised though, are you?"

"You don't want to get into a fight with Louise Townsend. Not if you can help it."

"What if I can't help it?"

"Taylor, she is one of the most powerful stars in Hollywood. She's Stroud's favorite, and she's also got that rumrunner Norton on her side."

"Why doesn't Stroud tell her to stay away from Norton? It can't be good for the studio."

"On the contrary, it gives Louise some sort of allure that escapes me. I've seen her up close and watched her work. She'll do anything to stay where she is. She can hurt your career, Taylor."

"She's already going to do it. I think I've become the object of her vexations."

Pete turned silent for a while. A few other customers entered the PDC, an actual railcar the owners had converted into a diner. Zee had a sudden feeling that she didn't belong here, not anymore. She was better than this. Or soon would be.

Finally Pete said, "I just want you to know, Taylor, that you can count on me if you ever need anything." His voice shook a little as he said it.

"I meant it when I said you were a good egg, Pete."

"Is that all I am?"

Ah, so that was it. She suspected it but hadn't seen it coming so full on. She should have. "Pete, you're a swell guy, really—"

"But not in your league, huh?"

What should she say? He was not a movie star, and she intended to be a movie star. She had no time for men or love. She had tried that once, and look what had happened. Men, even good ones, could not be entirely trusted.

"Hey," Zee said, "you don't want to get mixed up with an actress. You know how dizzy we can be."

Pete nodded. "Dizzy people sometimes fall."

She knew that to be true, only it wouldn't be for her. If anyone was going to fall, it would be Louise Townsend.

"Remember this," Pete added. "If you fall, I'll be there to pick you up."

At that moment she wished she could love him. She took his hand and squeezed it, saying thank-you with her eyes.

A boy with an armful of newspapers entered the diner and began going booth to booth, offering his wares. Someday, she thought, she'd be in the papers, in glowing terms.

The boy came to their booth and asked if they'd like one.

"No thanks," Pete said.

Zee smiled at the kid, caught a glimpse of two words in bold print on the front page. And her breath left her.

The two words were *Happy Sanders.*

"Boy!" She ordered him back. "I'll take one."

The newsie handed her a paper and Pete gave him a nickel. "What is it, Taylor?"

Her eyes landed on the headlines.

Los Angeles Herald Examiner

Happy Sanders Arrested on Morals Charge!
Jolly Comedian Caught in Love Nest With 16-Year-Old
Mother of Victim Vows Legal Retribution

"Oh no," she murmured.

"What?" Pete said.

"Listen." Zee began to read.

"'In a scandal that is sure to rock Hollywood to its very foundations, Harold "Happy" Sanders, the beloved star of Krazy Komedies from Stroud-General Studios, was arrested last night on charges of lewd and lascivious conduct with an under-age girl. The debauch apparently took place in a motor-stop bungalow just inside county limits.

"'The identity of the minor is being withheld, but early reports indicate she is a girl from a Midwestern state who has come to Hollywood in search of an acting career. She was accompanied by her mother, who stated that she would make sure the arm of the law flexes every muscle in its punishment of Sanders.

"'A spokesman for Stroud-General Studios, Walter Lytell, released a statement which says, in part, "In America a man is presumed innocent until proven guilty. In Hollywood, too. But at Stroud-General we will not tolerate illegal or immoral behavior in our contract players."

"'Sanders is well known in Hollywood as a genial fellow, but also one prone to heavy drinking. The infamous "Hollywood party" that was the subject of a story in these pages last month reportedly figures prominently in the routine of the corpulent comedian.

"'Last night a party was held at the opulent mansion of Stroud-General Studios head, Sy Stroud. Several witnesses report having seen Sanders in a state of advanced intoxication. One witness, who has requested anonymity, says Sanders at one point was passed out and had to be assisted into a room to "sleep it off."

"'In recent months, voices of criticism of the motion picture industry have increased, primarily from the churches. In a sermon delivered last Sunday evening at the Church of the Open Door, Dr. R. A. Torrey stated, "The motion picture business as it exists today is beyond question a demoralizing institution. I know from personal conversations with movie people, some quite prominent, that it is exceedingly difficult for a young woman to reach any height in the movie profession without submitting to things that outrage every womanly instinct. I have known young men of lofty moral ideals who have chased the dream of becoming a movie actor, and it has been ruinous."

"'One can only speculate that such voices will rise in volume now with the arrest of Sanders.'"

When Zee finished, they sat in silence for a long time. She felt a sense of loss and sadness, and a kind of dread. As if something were out there waiting for her, some malevolent fate. If Happy Sanders could be caught in it, what chance did any of them have?

"You all right?" Pete asked.

"Dumbfounded."

"I've been around this town for a while. I could see this coming."

"Could you?" Zee snapped. "Then why didn't you stop it?"

"Who am I to talk to someone like Happy Sanders?"

Zee said nothing.

"Can I talk to you, Taylor?"

She shrugged.

"Be careful. There are lots of temptations."

"I can take care of myself."

"If you ever need anybody to help, I'll be there."

Zee forced a laugh. "Don't worry, kid."

But he looked worried.

‖ 34 ‖

"Wake up."

Doyle heard the voice through a haze of sleep.

"Wake up, I said." A foot kicked him in the side. "You know the rules; now you get yourself out."

Where was he? The smell of sweat and dirty clothes assaulted him. The flophouse. The super of the place, with his scraggly beard, stood over him.

"You brought a loaded gun in here," the super growled. "You fell asleep with it on your chest. It could have gone off when it hit the floor."

The gun. "Where is it?"

"Get out."

"Where's my gun?"

"You were gonna use it on yourself, weren't you?"

Doyle said nothing.

"And get my place all spattered with blood. If you want to kill yourself, do it outside. Here." He pulled the gun from his waistband and threw it on the bed next to Doyle. "I took out the bullets. Now I want you gone. And don't come back. I run a respectable place."

Doyle had to fight the urge to laugh. If this pit was respectable, what did that make him? Which was worse, the garbage or the rat in the garbage?

He picked up the gun and walked out, spilling into a white morning that blinded him. He realized it did not matter which direction he turned, or walked. It did not matter if he walked anywhere at all.

Failing at death, he now faced life again, which had remained unchanged. Some fate was keeping him from using the gun, this piece of iron in his hand, as if he were a puppet in the hands of a cosmic jokester.

Doyle looked into the bright sky. *Not so funny, is it? Maybe I'll pull a little joke. Pawn the gun. Get some money out of it. See how funny that would be. You laughing up there? Let's just see how funny that will be.*

‖ 35 ‖

The ranch was in a place called Beverly Hills, a recent city subdivision that was drawing a lot of movie stars and other wealthy Angelenos.

But to Zee, as she approached by car, the Happy Sanders ranch seemed more like a military compound. A private security guard stood his ground at the front gate and looked at Zee with steel-eyed resistance.

She pulled to a stop. "I'm a friend of Mr. Sanders."

"Yeah, you and eight thousand other people. Where's your autograph book?"

"I mean it." She stepped out of her Jordan and faced the man. "I'm Taylor Layne, from Stroud-General Studios."

The guard's face twitched as he studied her. "Sorry, but I got orders to keep out all the curious."

"I am not curious; I'm a friend. Please send word that I am here."

"Got no way to do that, ma'am."

"Then let me in."

"Can't do that, either."

She slapped her sides. "Then we're at an impasse, aren't we?"

"Looks that way."

A large black car pulled up to the gate, and a sharply dressed man with black hair and pencil mustache nodded at the guard. Immediately the guard began opening the gate.

Zee backed up a few steps.

The guard and the man in the black car conversed as the gate swung open.

Zee got in the Jordan and started it up. And at the precise moment the black car entered the grounds, Zee gunned her car right behind it.

She did not look back as she overtook the black car on the gravel road that led to the large home. Skidding to a stop, Zee jumped out of her car and ran to the front door. She didn't bother to knock.

Inside, she heard voices and followed them to a large room with a fireplace and mounted animal heads. Happy Sanders was quite the hunter, according to the press.

Four men in various states of agitation circled a seated Happy Sanders. One of the men was Walter Lytell. Zee did not know the other three.

They all looked at her.

"What are you doing here?" Lytell said.

"Taylor!" Happy, looking worn, his eyes heavy-lidded, put his hands up to her.

"We have work to do," one of the other men said.

"I came to see Happy," Zee said, going to him. She took his hands in hers.

Lytell sighed. "I'm sure we're all very touched, Miss Layne, but we are having a meeting here."

Just then the man from the black car entered the room. "What is this?" he said, his voice rich and smooth.

"Our boy has a visitor," Lytell said.

And Happy did look like a boy, Zee thought. A scared little boy.

"You are Taylor Layne," the new man said. "I am Harper Vaughn, attorney for Mr. Sanders. You can well understand how important it is that we get on with things."

"Sure," Zee said. "I just came to—"

"Please give me a moment with her," Happy pleaded.

"Look here," Lytell said, "we're going to save your hide but we haven't got all day to do it."

"One little moment," Happy said.

The lawyer, Vaughn, raised his hand magnanimously. He was tall, well dressed, thin-lipped. "Maybe it will help Happy relax a little. He looks like he needs it. Gentlemen, let's convene in the study."

One by one they filed out, Lytell giving a disapproving glance back.

"Thank God you've come," Happy said. "I was beginning to think I had no friends left at all."

"Surely you do."

He shook his head vigorously. "Rats from a sinking ship." He was sweating at the forehead even though it was relatively cool inside the house. He wore a white shirt with wet splotches under the arms. He was trembling.

"Listen," Zee said, "you're going to get out of this and come back better than ever."

"Never. I'm crucified. She said she was twenty!" His eyes were red and watery.

Zee knelt beside him. "We'll lick this thing, Hap."

He grabbed her arm, hurting her, but she didn't let it show. "Taylor, do you remember when I warned you about all this? Do you?"

"Yes, Hap."

"I wasn't drunk, and I wasn't joking. All right, maybe I was drunk. But I meant what I said. They'll take your soul; they'll take all you have to give. Look at me, I'm ruined." He let her go and put his head in his hands, sobbing.

Zee wrapped her arm around his shoulder. "None of that. We'll fight this together. We'll figure something out."

"I've got lawyers and PR men and accountants, and they all have funeral looks on their faces. There's nothing to be done."

"Hap—"

He snapped up and looked at her with wild eyes. "Nothing! Do you hear me? Get away while you can!"

"Hap, don't."

"Please!"

The lawyer burst into the room. "What is going on?"

"Nothing," Zee said. "Hap's a little upset, that's all."

"A little? He looks like he's about to faint. I think you should go."

Zee stood up. "I want to know what you're going to do for him."

Harper Vaughn set his jaw. "That's my job. I suggest you leave it to me."

"He needs—"

"I know what he needs. Now please, go."

She looked at Sanders, slumped in his chair so severely that he looked half his normal size. "Hap, if you want me to stay, I will."

He shook his head and waved a tired hand. "Go on, Taylor. Thank you for coming to see me. I won't forget it."

Nor would she forget his face as she left—haggard, lost, haunted. The look of a dead man.

‖ 36 ‖

So it was with great relief that Zee met Pete and Molly at the Owl, where they ordered ice cream sundaes and coffee, Pete's treat. He had another treat, too, signaled by the wide smile on his face.

"What is it?" Zee asked.

"You haven't seen the afternoon edition of the *Times*, have you?"

"What's happened?"

"Taylor Layne has happened. Look."

He placed the paper, folded to an inside page, in front of Zee.

Plucky Taylor Layne Captures Hearts as Tallulah
by Tamar Raines

The Troubles of Tallulah is the title of the new serial from *Stroud-General Studios*, now playing at the Bijou. If the first installment, Tallulah in the Mountains, *is any indication of what is to follow, we are quite sure Mr. Sy Stroud has another hit on his hands.*

Stroud's genius has always been the ability to spot a good actor or actress. Remember, Louise Townsend might have been left standing in a row of bathing-suited beauties had not Stroud seen something in her that warranted more attention. It seems he has done it again with newcomer Taylor Layne, whose spark and sparkle are sure to captivate a goodly number of motion picture patrons.

As Tallulah, a simple girl from the Midwest who finds trouble awaiting her every turn, Miss Layne does not fall into the vat of treacle such roles have brought out in lesser actresses in the past. She has the pluck of Pickford but adds to it a confidence and spark that makes her nigh unto irresistible.

We look forward to many more Tallulah adventures so long as Miss Layne is playing the title role.

Zee's heart was beating wildly when she finished. "The pluck of Pickford!"

"It's wonderful," Molly said.

Pete wagged his finger. "But Mr. Stroud is not going to like it."

Zee looked at him. "Why on earth not?"

"Because now he'll have to pay you more money."

The three of them broke into giddy laughter.

Tommy shook his head behind the counter. "I can hardly believe it. A movie star."

"Not exactly a star," Zee said.

"But not like them, either." Tommy nodded toward the other end of the counter. A couple—an unsmiling woman and a dirty man—sat silently sipping their coffee. Zee looked at them and shuddered. They were obviously citizens of the lower depths. How close had she come to becoming like them?

Now she was ascending like a Chinese rocket. Now she could buy food for herself, for Molly. And eat in classier joints.

Pete lifted his coffee cup. "To Taylor Layne."

Molly joined the toast.

"And to the new place Molly and I found to live," Zee said. "It's a real step up. Maybe now we'll hire ourselves a maid."

Molly flushed. "Now, don't go throwing away all your money."

"What good is it if we can't treat ourselves? Anyway, there's more to come."

"I know that to be true," Pete said. "You're going to be a great star, Taylor."

"You've been a chum," Zee said. She saw Pete's smile quiver just a bit at that. She knew he was falling in love with her, and her words were not exactly the ones he wanted to hear.

She wondered how she felt about Pete. He was decent and kind, and competent at what he did. He would always be a steady worker. He was certainly a good man to have on her side. When she'd had questions about set workings, he was always there to help, even standing between her and the director if need be.

But love? Could she love him? Since Desmond Nichols, her thoughts about men had been purely utilitarian. How they could be of service to get her to where she wanted to go.

She didn't want to treat Pete that way. But could she ever be fair to a man again?

"Let's go play somewhere, huh?" Zee said. "It's a beautiful Sunday in Los Angeles. Pete, fire up the flivver and take us to Santa Monica, what do you say?"

"The beach?"

"We'll play in the waves and laugh ourselves silly."

They all agreed. On the way out Zee cast a quick glance over her shoulder, one more look at the two poor souls hunched at the lunch counter. Did it make one bit of difference to their lives that she had done a small favor for them? Or were they the doomed, as she had almost—

She stopped. It couldn't be.

As if hypnotized she took a tentative step forward. Then another.

The poor, hopeless woman stood up, barely glancing at Zee, and walked out.

But it was the man Zee was fixated on. She looked more closely at his tattered coat, his dirty shoes, then back at his face. Surely not . . .

He turned his head and looked at her.

"Doyle," she whispered.

His eyes were sunken and dark. He seemed to have aged a decade. The mouth that had once spouted poetry to her with a sheepish grin was now downturned and thin-lipped. Under his days' growth of beard were purple marks, discoloration, scabs. Had he been cut or had some terrible accident? A jagged scar was etched across his left cheek. She tried not to look alarmed.

Doyle's mouth opened slightly as he stared back at her.

"Zee."

Her instinct was to enfold him in a hug, but something stopped her, something that seemed to say he shouldn't be touched.

"How good to see you," she said, only half believing it.

He made no answer. She noticed his hands shaking slightly.

"Hey, Taylor, let's go!" Pete was back inside, at the door.

"I'll be right there," Zee said, and gave him a look to indicate he should leave. Pete gave a curious look past her, shrugged, and went back out.

"Taylor?" he said.

"Guess what, Doyle? I'm in the movies. Taylor Layne is my screen name, and I'm signed with Stroud-General Studios."

He did not register surprise or congratulations. The news, in fact, seemed not to move him at all.

Then, softly, he said, "That's grand, Zee. It's what you always wanted."

"And what about you, Doyle? How long have you been in Los Angeles?"

"A few months, I think."

Zee sat on the stool next to him. This boy she had once known, maybe even loved, was now a man. But a man who was broken. "We must celebrate. I have friends outside, and we're going to the beach. Join us."

"Thanks, Zee. Or Taylor."

"For you, it's always Zee. What do you say?"

A wan smile played about his mouth, then faded. "I don't think so."

"Oh, come on, it will be fun. You look like you could use a little fun." The moment she said it she wished she hadn't.

"I must be a sight," he said.

"We simply must talk. We must. About the old times, Zenith High, the night you rescued me from the dance. Remember?"

"I remember."

Were his eyes tearing? Or rheumy? Maybe from drink? It was frightening. Had he been in the war?

"Then it's settled. Where are you living?"

"I'm . . . looking."

"Well, I know all sorts of places. I'll show you. Oh, Doyle, it is so good to see you. You don't know . . ."

"Good to see you, too, Zee. I'm very happy for you."

She felt that he was about to slip away. "Come along. We'll ride and have fun and—"

"Another time. I have some business to take care of."

That, she was certain, was a lie. Doyle had never lied to her before. Back in Zenith he seemed incapable of mendacity. This was not the same Doyle Lawrence.

But then again, she was not the same Zee Miller.

"Then let's meet later," Zee said. "When can you?"

Doyle looked into his coffee cup.

"I don't want to lose you," Zee said. "I've often thought of you."

Pete's car horn blared from the street.

"Here." Zee took a pencil and scrap of paper from her purse and jotted something on it. "Here is my address. Come see me."

Doyle looked at the paper.

"Promise me, Doyle. We'll catch up, we'll have fun. It will be so wonderful!"

"Good-bye, Zee."

She paused and put out her hand. He took it. "Oh, hang it all," she said, and threw her arms around him. He smelled like the city and decaying wood. She whispered, "Come see me."

He said nothing more as she walked out into a day of clouds.

‖ 37 ‖

Zee Miller.

And she had seen him like this. She had seen him for what he was, which was nothing. He was one of the lost of the city now, and a weak one at that. He didn't even have the courage to end his own life.

Now the past had come to mock him, to show him how far he had fallen. His past looked him in the face through the eyes of the girl he thought he loved once and maybe still did. Or maybe just the idea of her.

There was something different about her now. A worldliness that overshadowed the innocence they had once shared like a soda with two straws. It was the city. It did things to people, like it was doing things to him. And now he should just—

"Say, friend, can I stake you to a meal?"

Doyle looked up into an older gentleman's eyes, eyes friendly and warm.

"Thank you, but no."

"Please." The man took out a dollar bill and placed it on the counter. "I couldn't help seeing you talking to that pretty young lady. I'm sentimental that way. I like to watch young people when they talk. Please pardon me for butting in, but I've been down on my luck before, and I know what it's like."

"It's not necessary."

"Can I ask a question?"

"Sure."

"Were you one of our boys overseas?"

"What's it to you?" Doyle found himself clenching his fists.

The gentleman did not take offense. He slid onto the stool next to Doyle. "Don't worry about it. My son was over there. He's had a rough time, but he's starting to pull through. Please consider this a little way of saying thank you."

"Really, mister, I don't want it."

"Take it anyway." He clapped Doyle on the shoulder and walked out.

Doyle sat for a long moment, then picked up the dollar bill and ran his thumb over it. Paper. But it was what it represented that gave it value.

And man, being only flesh and bone, what did he represent?

Up until a few minutes ago Doyle would have said nothing. Now an act of kindness by a stranger was throwing all that out the window.

Don't believe it. It's just another turn of the wheel. The next turn will bring you back down again.

No, he told himself. *There is something to this. There's a reason you couldn't shoot Norton. There's a reason you couldn't shoot yourself. There's a reason Zee Miller saw you today. There has to be.*

There's a reason this man gave you a dollar.

Doyle held the dollar up before his eyes and looked at it with wonder. What could he do with this one dollar that would give him a reason for going on?

And, in an instant, he knew.

He knew that life came down to forks in the road. That either way made no sense to him, but there were two ways and one led to death, the other to something else. What the something else was he had no idea. But if he took the road of death, he could end up a sap, played for a fool by forces he knew nothing about.

And that was what he'd leave behind for the people who loved him—a sap. That was what Rusty and Gertie would think and they'd cry, as well as his father and mother and everyone who knew him, and Zee. They'd think about him and shake their heads sadly and want to banish the memory of him because it hurt to think about it.

He had a dollar and nothing else but the clothes on his back, and he had a choice.

He thought for a moment that he prayed, that he called out in a silent voice upward, but then he was on his feet and out of the diner and on the busy sidewalk. He walked and walked until he found a barber pole. He went into the shop, smelled the pomade and shaving soap, savoring it as if it were the smell of orange blossoms in the morning or the sea at sunset.

He had one dollar and a chair was open, and the smiling barber invited him to have a seat.

Sit, you fool, and get clean.

‖ 38 ‖

Pete was driving and gabbing away when Zee heard Molly ask, "Who were you talking to?"

"Hm?"

"Back at the diner. I saw you through the window. That man at the counter."

"Oh. Funny thing. Someone I knew back home."

Seeing Doyle that way tore at her. He was the best that Zenith had to offer. He was the one who was going to go farther than any of them. And now look at him.

"What is he doing out here?" Molly asked.

"Haven't the foggiest. I told him to come by sometime. But I don't think he will." She felt empty as she said it, as if she were looking at her reflection in a mirror that was far away. She couldn't quite see her own image, and yet that was all she could look at—herself, over and over.

We're different now, Doyle. Don't you wish we could go back and start all over again?

But that was no longer possible.

"You all right?" Molly said.

"Me? Never better. Come along, let's sing something. And make it loud."

‖ 39 ‖

Doyle, now clean-shaven, walked up the wooden stairs of the building on First Street, to the law office of Kathleen Shannon Fox. He wondered if he was crazy.

All night he'd felt as if a voice were telling him to come here. For what reason, he did not know. He only knew he had to be here.

He announced himself to a friendly woman at a desk in the outer office. "I have no appointment, but Mrs. Fox was my lawyer at one time. I wonder if I may see her for a moment."

The woman smiled. "I remember your name, Mr. Lawrence. One moment please." She picked up a handset and pressed a button. "Mr. Doyle Lawrence is here and would like to see you."

Presently Kit Shannon Fox appeared at the door to her office. "Mr. Lawrence, what a pleasant surprise. How are you getting along?"

A bit sheepishly, Doyle said, "To tell you the truth, I don't really know."

"Let's see if we can find out." She motioned for him to enter. "Rose, would you please bring in two coffees?"

Once more, Doyle sensed a power in this woman that he could not quite name. She was a handsome woman, to be sure, but did not bank on her looks. That alone made her a singular presence in Los Angeles where glamour was queen.

"I never thanked you sufficiently for representing me," Doyle said.

"Your look of relief was thanks enough."

"I . . ."

"Yes?"

"How did you come to be practicing law?"

She smiled. "That's rather a long story."

"Time is one thing I've got a lot of."

Mrs. Fox smiled. "My mother was defrauded by a lawyer when I was a girl and lost everything she owned. When she died, I vowed to help people like her. I studied law in a special program for women in New York and came to Los Angeles in 1903. California had only a few women admitted to the bar at that time. I planned to settle in and do estates and wills. I had no intention of practicing criminal law."

"What changed that?"

"Earl Rogers. Do you know the name?"

"Of course. My father talked about him. Said he used to be the best trial lawyer in the country."

Mrs. Fox nodded. "Imagine what the best trial lawyer must be like. Earl Rogers was even better. I literally bumped into him outside the courthouse one day and followed inside to watch him try a case. Later I went to work for him, and that's how I got my start. His office used to be just down the hall."

"Used to be?"

With a look of sadness, Mrs. Fox said, "Earl is in a sanitarium now. Alcohol has stolen his gifts. I try to see him and he rages against me, against his own children. I pray for him every day."

Rose came in with the coffee and placed the tray on Mrs. Fox's desk. She poured two cups and left.

"Does your husband practice law?" Doyle asked.

"I am a widow, Mr. Lawrence. My husband died in the war."

"I'm sorry."

"He was a flyer, with Eddie Rickenbacker. His name was Ted Fox. He was a great aviator."

She paused, her eyes reflecting an inner memory. She took a sip of coffee, then looked at Doyle.

"Now, Mr. Lawrence, how may I help you?"

"I felt I was supposed to talk to you for some reason," Doyle said. "The feeling wouldn't go away."

"What are you to talk to me about?"

"That's just it. I don't know."

"Are you in some sort of trouble?"

"I haven't broken any laws. Yet."

"Yet?"

"I have some unfinished business."

"Suppose you tell me about it?"

Doyle felt he could trust this woman. He felt it strongly, as if she were the only one in the world he could completely confide in. Again, he wondered what it was about her. It was strange and compelling. Maybe it was something in his conscience, what he had almost done.

"I almost shot a man," Doyle said. "Two men, in fact. These are men who deserve to die. They beat me up; they torched Mr. Lun's business. I want them dead."

Mrs. Fox waited, inviting him to continue.

"One of the men is Jess Norton, the bootlegger."

Mrs. Fox nodded. "He is well known in this town."

"Then you know he should be shot."

The lawyer took a sip of coffee, placed the cup down in its saucer. "The law says we are not the judges of who is to die."

"Forget the law," Doyle said, anger spilling out of him. "It's what's right and wrong."

"And how do we know what is right and what is wrong?"

"We just do," Doyle said quickly. He realized how weak that sounded.

"Ah, but we don't. We are in need of a code."

Doyle shook his head and chuckled.

"What is it, Mr. Lawrence?"

"You just reminded me of someone, an old man I rode the rails with. He said things like that, too. That without God anything was permissible."

"Sounds like a wise man."

"Maybe he was your father."

Mrs. Fox smiled. "My father was a preacher, and the wisest man I've ever known." She turned in her swivel chair and pulled a book from the shelf behind her. She put it down in front of Doyle. It had a black leather cover, the corners of which were old and frayed. "This is his Bible," Mrs. Fox said. "I've had it with me ever since his death."

Doyle picked it up, turned it in his hands. "Been a long time since I've had a Bible in my hands."

"Do you have one at home?"

"I don't have a home. I don't even have a room."

Mrs. Fox went to a bookshelf lined with legal tomes and took down a black leather-bound book. She handed it to Doyle. It was a new Bible. "A gift," she said.

Doyle ran his hand over the leather. Then he smelled it. The scent was fresh, clean and new. "Thank you." On the bottom of the back cover, in gold letters, was printed *Bible Institute of Los Angeles*.

"I've heard of this place," Doyle said.

"It's a great institution, which I have supported since its inception. The dean is Dr. R. A. Torrey."

Torrey. The man who preached at the soup kitchen.

"He wrote this." She handed him a pamphlet. "You might be interested."

Printed on the pamphlet was "Why I Believe the Bible to Be the Word of God by R. A. Torrey."

"I heard this man preach. I heard him the night I . . ."

"Yes?"

"Almost shot those two men."

"What stopped you?"

Doyle shook his head. "I don't know. I went out. I was ready. But then it was as if I couldn't move. I can't explain it."

Mrs. Fox regarded him carefully. "I think God has plans for you, Mr. Lawrence."

"Me?"

"What are your prospects?"

"Footloose and fancy-free, as they say. I have nothing." He suddenly held up the Bible. "Except this."

Mrs. Fox smiled. "I think that may be the reason you came here, Mr. Lawrence. Now about that room, I can arrange something."

Doyle shook his head. "I can't let you. You represented me once for no fee. I can't take any more charity."

"Who said anything about charity? Are you willing to work?"

Work? The word sounded wonderful to his ears. "Of course."

"Can you drive a car?"

"Sure." He hadn't driven for a long time but thought it must be like riding a bicycle.

"As I recall, you had a year at Princeton, is that right?"

"Yes."

"What was your course of study?"

"Ironically, I was planning to go into law."

"Why ironic? Perhaps that's another reason you are here. We can get to work on your little problem."

"Problem?"

"Norton."

‖ 40 ‖

"You look new!" Wong Lun said.

Doyle smiled. "Just a little touch-up."

"Come in, come in. Stay."

Shaking his head, Doyle stayed outside the door of Wong Lun's apartment. "I only came to tell you I'm going to take care of things for you. You're going to get the laundry back."

"No no." Wong Lun looked at the floor. "No more. Bad men too many."

"That's what I'm going to take care of, Mr. Lun."

"What do? Don't get in trouble!"

"I've already been in trouble. Knee-deep."

"Where you stay?"

"I got a little room downtown. It'll do."

"You need money?"

"I got a job."

"Do what?"

"A clerk, a runaround man. For Mrs. Fox."

"No laundry?" He seemed genuinely disappointed.

Doyle put his hand out and shook Lun's. "Thanks for everything, Mr. Lun. I won't forget you. You're getting back the laundry. You have to. Nobody cleans like Lun."

The little man beamed. "Right about that, my friend."

‖ 41 ‖

Doyle lay on his bed in the simple room he was able to rent on Olive Street. Compared to the flophouses he'd come to know so well, this was a step up into luxury. He had enough room to stretch out and an armoire for his meager possessions.

Which now included a new Bible.

He looked at it for a long moment, and also at the pamphlet Mrs.

Fox had given him. He opened it, curious about what this Torrey really believed and taught. There were as many Christian churches as there were orange trees, it seemed. What was Torrey's angle? If Mrs. Fox was in his camp, that was a solid recommendation.

The first paragraph was as direct as Torrey's voice:

> *Is the Bible the Word of God?*
>
> *If the Bible is the Word of God, the only trustworthy revelation from God himself, of himself, His purposes and His will, of man's beauty and destiny, of spiritual and eternal realities, then we have a starting point from which we can proceed to the conquest of the whole domain of religious truth.*
>
> *But if the Bible is not the Word of God, if it is the mere product of man's thinking, speculating, and guessing, not altogether trustworthy in regard to religious and eternal proof, then we are all "at sea," not knowing whither we are drifting, but we may be sure that we are not drifting toward any safe port.*

Doyle thought about that for a moment. His training in logic, honed over many a discussion with his father at the dinner table, told him Torrey was setting up a classic dilemma. And it was solid. If the Bible was the "only trustworthy" revelation from God, then certainly it was a starting point. But could that ever be proven?

> *I'm going to give you some of the reasons why I believe the Bible to be the Word of God. Not all the reasons. It would take volumes to do that. But I will give you reasons that will prove conclusive to any candid seeker after the truth, to anyone who desires to know the truth and is willing to obey it.*

A mighty claim indeed, Torrey! Doyle's mind was engaging him as if this were an intellectual boxing match. It felt good to be thinking deeply again.

> *I believe the Bible to be the Word of God first and foremost because of the testimony of Jesus Christ to that fact. Jesus Christ himself distinctly asserts that the Law of Moses is the Word of God, and that Scripture, meaning what we call the Old Testament, cannot be broken. If then we accept the authority of Jesus Christ, we must accept the Old Testament as the Word of God.*

Doyle sat up now and rested his back against the wall.

*But how about the New Testament? Turn to John 14:26 and
you will hear Jesus saying "The Comforter, which is the Holy Ghost,
whom the Father will send in my name, he shall teach you all
things and bring all things to your remembrance whatsoever I have
said unto you," thus setting the stamp of His authority not only
upon the apostolic teaching as given by the Holy Spirit but upon
the apostolic recollection of what He himself had taught.*

Doyle had never heard this line of argument before. The Bible had
always seemed the Good Book, with great principles for living. But
Torrey was saying that Jesus taught it was more than that, and that
Jesus had to be believed on this point if He was to be believed on any
other.

There was more. A lot more, all stuffed into a pamphlet that had
found its way from R. A. Torrey to Doyle Lawrence. He took it as a
challenge. There had to be a flaw in the reasoning somewhere.

He wouldn't look for it tonight. Tonight he would get a good
night's sleep. Because tomorrow he had to show Zee Miller of Zenith,
Nebraska, that he was not the hopeless stiff she'd seen in the Owl. And
he had to determine, once and for all, if she would figure in his life
once again.

‖ 42 ‖

Walter Lytell was large in the shoulders and neck and had a gravelly
voice. He might have made the perfect dock worker or heavyweight
boxer. Instead, he was the head of the publicity department at Stroud-
General Studios.

His current project was Taylor Layne, though as the trouble-
shooter for Stroud-General he had his hands in everything that concerned the reputation of the studio. Including Happy Sanders.

Zee sat impatiently in the chair as three makeup artists, two women
and a man, made circles around her. Using the tools of their trade—
pencils, pancake, daubs, sponges, creams—they worked on her face
according to Lytell's directions.

"Now if we darken the eyebrows and thin the lips, we get a little
Pola Negri going. Let's see that."

The artists hummed into service, wiping and painting, then standing back for Lytell to observe.

"May I see?" Zee asked.

"Not ready yet. No. Let's take the eyebrows up a little. Like Constance Talmadge."

The creams were applied, some of her face erased, and then more application. She could not see anything but Lytell's large head shaking.

"Now she looks like Wallace Reid," the male makeup artist said.

"Very funny," said Lytell.

"I don't want to look like Wallace Reid!" Zee protested.

"Leave it to me." Lytell put his hand under his chin. "What if we thickened the lips? What would we get?"

The makeup man said, "Constance Binney."

"Uh-huh. Or Colleen Moore."

"No, I think not. But if we curl the hair we get Elinor Fair." He laughed. "I'm a poet."

"Stick to the face," Lytell barked. "Give me Swanson lips."

Zee opened her mouth to say something but was immediately assaulted about the mouth. The artists did their work and smiled.

"Close," Lytell said. "But there's something missing. Some Bebe Daniels, maybe."

"Wait—" Zee said.

"Do you think you can do some Bebe Daniels?"

"I can do anything," said the makeup man. "All right, let's—"

"Hold it!" Zee sat up in the chair and threw off the makeup bib.

"What do you think you're doing?" Lytell snapped.

"I don't want to be anybody else, Mr. Lytell. I want to be Taylor Layne."

With a disgusted huff, Lytell said, "That's who we're creating here, in case you didn't know."

"What's wrong with what I am? Tallulah is a hit."

"Listen, dopey, Mr. Stroud wants to build on what he's got. That's what we do."

"I don't have any interest in being built on. I'm an actress, not a face. If Mr. Stroud wants to build me, tell him to put me in a full-length picture."

"Why don't we go all the way and let you take over the studio?"

Zee folded her arms. "And the first thing I'm going to do is find a new publicity man."

Lytell's face darkened into a burgundy not unlike the curtain at Grauman's Million Dollar Theatre. "Don't get too big for your bodice, missy. You're still just an employee."

"Yes, Mr. Lytell, one who is bringing money into the coffers of the man who employs us both."

Running his fingers through his hair, Lytell said, "Why do I get the feeling I'm gonna have a lot of sleepless nights worrying about you?"

"Because that's your job," Zee said with a lilt. "And making this studio more money is mine."

She believed that. It would come true; she would will it to come true. There was a sense of inevitability about it now.

"Say, Mr. Lytell."

"What is it now?"

"How is Happy doing?"

Lytell shrugged. "The papers are all over him, and the decency people are up in arms. How do you think he's doing?"

She could imagine. One scandal was all it took to kill a career. Without wife and family, Hap's only life was wrapped up in the movies.

So was hers.

That was why she ignored the small shudder of disquiet inside her. There would be no turning back.

‖ 43 ‖

"Hello, I'm Doyle Lawrence."

The girl at the door was rather pretty, in a fresh California sort of way. Not the painted-face kind of beauty popularized by the movies these days, but the comeliness of green fields and sunflowers. The house was nicely appointed, with ivy and wisteria on the outside and Spanish tile on the roof.

"Oh, hello. I'm Molly Pritchard. Taylor has told me about you. Won't you come in?"

"Is Zee —" Doyle stopped with a chuckle. "I don't know that I'll get used to this. Is Taylor at home?"

"She had to go to the studio. Mr. Stroud is having the publicity department prepare a big campaign for her. Can you believe it?"

Doyle shook his head. "It's been quite a climb for her."

"Would you like something to eat? I was going to prepare lunch."

A warm sense of welcoming flowed into him, something he hadn't felt in a long time. When he had come here he didn't know what he would feel. He supposed he just wanted to figure out once and for all what Zee Miller meant to him. Was it too late for there to be any meaning at all?

He had made the first, tentative steps back into the flow of humanity. He had a purpose now—to bring down Norton by force of law. But he was still unsure there was anything beyond that.

Suddenly, here was a friendly face and an invitation. It startled him with its plain, unvarnished kindliness.

"No," he said spontaneously, "I have another idea. How would you like to go on a picnic?"

"Picnic?"

"I've been holed up in dark places and diners and smoky rooms for too long. I want to breathe again."

Molly smiled, then looked at the floor, her cheeks reddening. "You have caught me by surprise. I don't know . . ."

"It looks to be a bright, sunny day. We could go up the road here and find a spot under a tree—"

"I'm sorry, but perhaps we should wait for Taylor."

Doyle looked at her, curious. "Did I offend you in some way?"

Her eyes widened. "Oh no, it's not that. Please don't think so. I was merely thinking, well, you are Taylor's friend, and I . . ."

"I see. You don't want to horn in on her territory, as they say."

Molly nodded shyly.

"Suppose you let me handle that angle. We have just met and we are going to be friends, and friends sometimes picnic, and have conversation, and live as if the world had fine things to offer. I need to know that it does right now, so what do you say?"

Slowly, Molly lifted her eyes to his. "I'll make us some sandwiches."

Fifteen minutes later they were in a Model T Ford, chugging up the canyon road.

"Nice lizzie," Molly said.

"It belongs to my employer." Doyle had to shout to be heard above the engine. "I'm working for a lawyer."

"Will you be a lawyer someday?"

He thought, *Yes*. Funny. He had not entertained any thoughts of pursuing the law again until she said that. Now it seemed almost natural, the likely next step in his reclamation.

"I just may, Miss Pritchard."

She paused. "Please, call me Molly."

"A pleasure. Call me Doyle."

They reached a spot high in the hills. It offered a breathtaking view of the entire Los Angeles basin—the city's business district to the east, orange groves in the middle, Hollywood to the west. They spread a blanket just off the road on a patch of wild grass.

Doyle watched as Molly set up the picnic. He wondered how she and Zee had ended up together. In some unnamed way she seemed Zee's opposite. She seemed someone firmly planted on the earth.

"Where do you hail from, Molly?"

"Sacramento. My parents own a farm."

"I take it you are an actress, like Taylor."

Molly laughed infectiously. "I thought I might try, but I know now that I don't have the talent that Taylor does. She is one of those who have something that cannot be learned."

"I think you would make a fine actress."

"You are a gentleman."

"Not yet," he said. "But I'm working on it. How did you and Zee end up together?"

"We met at a department store, applying for jobs. I was sitting by myself. Zee came in. You know, she comes in with a crowd even when she's alone."

Doyle nodded.

"She sat next to me and started talking, told me she was in Los Angeles to become a movie star. When I told her I wanted to be an actress, she said we ought to live together. And that's what we've done."

Doyle shook his head. "It must be an adventure."

"Oh yes. Taylor has a mind of her own, on everything from children to church."

"Does she go to church?"

Molly shook her head. "I've invited her."

"You attend?"

"The Church of the Open Door, on Hope Street. Dr. Torrey—"

"You're joking."

"Why should I joke about that?"

Doyle fell back on the blanket, looked at the sky, and laughed. "This man follows me. His name keeps turning up every time I turn around. I heard him speak once, and his words almost tormented me."

"Torment?"

"He spoke so persuasively, not like many men I've heard before."

"Would you come and listen to Dr. Torrey again?" She had a challenging half smile on her face.

"Church?"

"I think it would be nice to have some company."

Doyle plucked a blade of grass and put it in his mouth. "I'm not much of a churchgoer."

"You invited me on a picnic and here I am. How about returning the favor?"

He sat up and put his arms around his legs. "You don't by any chance sell insurance, do you?"

"Why no."

"Because you'd be very good at it." He looked at her and she smiled and blushed. "All right, Miss Pritchard. You're on. But only because I'm a gentleman and always return favors."

She extended her hand. "Then we have a deal."

He laughed. "Yes, insurance is definitely the game for you."

‖ 44 ‖

Zee was exhausted when she returned home. After her little run-in with Lytell, she had directed the makeup team herself. She had been made up, sketched, photographed, prodded, all the while working with the publicity man on her "official biography." No longer would she be a dull girl who had run away from Nebraska. She wanted to be the daughter of a French count who died in the war against the Germans.

Not a bad background, Lytell thought. Now all Zee would have to do is brush up on her high school French for interviews.

Tired as she was, the thought of going to another party gave her something to look forward to. So when she walked into the kitchen and saw Molly cooking, she swung her around. "Don't bother with that. We're going out tonight."

Wiping errant hair from her eyes, Molly said, "But I went to market and—"

"Silly, Doug and Mary will be there."

Molly squinted, confused.

"Pickford! Now we have just enough time for a bath. Come along."

"I don't think I will, Taylor."

"What is it, Mol? Just because you've started cooking? We can throw it out now. We have money enough to buy whatever we want."

"I know." Molly wiped her hands on her apron.

"Are you going to give me that same tired excuse about all the alcohol?"

"I don't like being around it."

"Who are you all of a sudden, Aimee Semple McPherson?" Zee stepped back and looked at Molly. There was no question some distance had grown between them in the last several weeks.

"I just don't feel comfortable around those people," Molly said.

"*Those* people? I'm one of those people. Are you not comfortable around me?"

Molly was silent.

"Why don't you come out with it?" Zee demanded. "Are you suddenly better than I am?"

"I never said that."

"You don't have to. Ever since you started sneaking off to church, you've been a wet blanket."

"That's mean."

"You haven't seen me mean, Molly. And you don't want to."

"No," Molly said. "That is something I hope never to see."

Zee forced a laugh. "Then let's go have fun together, just like we used to."

Looking at the floor, Molly didn't answer.

"What is it, Molly? Is there something you're not telling me?"

"Doyle Lawrence came to the house today."

The news inflamed Zee's annoyance. "Why didn't you tell me?"

"You were at the studio."

"Have you heard of the telephone?"

"Stop it, Taylor." Molly turned toward the stove.

"Where is he? What did he say?"

"He came to see you, and you weren't here. So . . ."

"So *what*?"

"We had a picnic."

Zee folded her arms. "Do tell. Where was this little tryst?"

"It was not a tryst, Taylor. He said it was a beautiful day and wanted to have a picnic, that's all. We went up the canyon a bit."

"How delightful. And when is he coming back to see me?"

"On Sunday. We are going to church."

Zee felt a prod, like the poking of an unwanted finger. "How very nice. Do you want some sort of medal?"

"Why don't you come with us?" Molly's face brightened a little too much.

"Ah, now I see. You and good old Doyle have hatched a little plot to reform Taylor Layne."

"No—"

"She's become wild, a denizen of Hollywood parties where the booze runs free and the girls run freer."

"Taylor, please, that's not true."

"I don't care what's true or not. Just leave me out of it."

Zee felt like a heel as she stormed out of the kitchen, part of her no longer caring. Another part cared deeply; another part wanted Doyle to want her again. For what purpose? Because that was the way it should be. He belonged to her, yes to her past, but it was *her past*, not Molly's, not anyone else's.

Oh, it was selfish and petulant, but that was what a person got to be when she became a movie star. Like Louise Townsend.

Like Taylor Layne.

‖ 45 ‖

John Raneau wore a thin mustache and had perfect white teeth, just like on-screen. Zee thought him even handsomer in the flesh. That she was next to him at all was like a dream.

Raneau was usually mentioned in the same breath as Valentino and John Gilbert. His last outing, with Louise Townsend, had set female hearts fluttering all over America. And now Zee Miller's was doing a flip-flop of its own.

"You are luminous, you know." Raneau offered Zee a cigarette from a gold case. She took it, to be hospitable. She had no idea how to smoke. She thought she could hold it, however, the way she'd seen sirens do it in the movies—sultry and mysterious.

Raneau lit it for her with his gold lighter, and she tried not to let the smoke go down her throat. It didn't work. She broke out into a cough.

John Raneau took her by the arm and led her through a door, into a library. "It wouldn't do to have one so luminous coughing like that."

"I'm . . . sorry." Zee's eyes were watering. "I don't know what's got into me."

With a laugh, Raneau said, "A Chesterfield got into you. You don't really smoke, do you?"

Zee looked at the cigarette in her fingers. "I'm afraid not."

"You'll get the hang of it." He took the cigarette from her and crushed it in an ashtray.

Raneau took her by the arm and led her to a settee. "Have you read Elinor Glyn?"

"Is that a book?"

"No, a writer."

Zee blushed but noted that Raneau had not smirked. Silently, she thanked him.

Raneau continued. "She writes romantic novels that are hugely popular, I'm told. Never read one myself. Can't stand 'em. I much prefer the real thing." He winked at her. "Madame Glyn wrote a piece in one of the magazines about sex appeal. She didn't call it that. She called it, simply, *It*."

"It?"

"That's right. That certain something that draws the opposite sex, and it is not something that can be acquired. One either has *It* or doesn't. Swanson has it. And Negri. And so, my dear, do you."

She was sure then that Raneau was going to kiss her. Should she let him? It would not hurt to have Raneau asking for her to be his leading lady. Yes, perhaps a kiss would be just the thing—

"We will continue this conversation later," Raneau said. "But as I am the host, shall we go back to the party?"

She remained on his arm as he played host, and suddenly it seemed all perfectly natural. He escorted her outside to dinner, which was served at a series of tables on Raneau's back lawn. The yard looked to Zee to be the size of Zenith High's football field. And on this field tonight were some of the most glittering stars in the Hollywood firmament.

Lon Chaney, the "Man of a Thousand Faces," conversed with Gloria Swanson, who in turn was seated beside Charlie Chaplin. Zee watched with amusement as Chaplin entertained the guest to his left by sticking dinner rolls on two forks and making them dance like legs with big shoes.

Zee gasped when she saw Rudolph Valentino enter the mix, with a mysterious young woman on his arm. Her gasp was not so much in seeing Valentino; it was the woman who took her breath away. John Raneau told her later it was a Swedish actress named Greta Gustafsson. "The word is she'll come over to Metro someday, but they'll change that last name. They're thinking of Grabo, or Garbo, or something like that."

She'll be a sensation, Zee thought, *if she can act.*

Naturally, Louise Townsend was in attendance, along with Jess Norton. But there was no Happy Sanders. His absence was the only damper on an otherwise exquisite evening.

Zee was seated between John Raneau and a writer from Stroud-General Studios named Blakely Eberhard. He was, in fact, the writer of the *Tallulah* serials. A former playwright from New York, he was near fifty, and Zee thought he must have been quite handsome in his youth. But the bags under his eyes evidenced his love of the bottle and general despair at taking easy money to write serials.

"I'm glad we are seated together," he told Zee. "Gives me a chance to fill you in on your next grand tale, cleverly entitled *Tallulah on the Trail*."

Zee smelled the liquor on his breath. "What kind of story this time?"

Eberhard shrugged. "Tallulah gets in trouble. Tallulah gets out of trouble. Art!"

"No, I mean what's the setting?"

"Who cares?"

"I do."

"That's your problem. This time you are out west. Cowboys. Indians. Tallulah. What more could they want, the great unwashed? I give it to them, but do they ever thank the writer? No!"

Zee laughed. "It sounds exactly the same as *Tallulah in the Mountains*."

Eberhard laughed. "Now you are learning, little one. There are rules in this game. The rules are quite simple and must be followed exactly. Righteousness must always be rewarded. Villainy must be punished, and rags are always royal raiment when worn for virtue's sake."

"But don't the people get tired of that? It's not like this reflects real life."

"It makes no difference that the theatergoers in real life know that the conditions in the motion pictures are often the reverse of their experience. Marry me."

Zee smiled. It was clear Eberhard had done some serious drinking. "Tomorrow. For now, tell me more about the rules. I want to know everything about the movies before I take them over."

Eberhard slipped a silver flask from his coat pocket and poured some liquid into his coffee cup. The writer sipped his brew, then said, "When spectators cross the threshold of the theater they must immediately throw aside all knowledge of existing facts learned through personal experiences, and take a ride on the magic movie carpet to the land of where-everything-is-as-it-should-be."

"What we have to give them," Zee agreed.

"Then there is the rule that every story must have love and romance in it. Without this no movie is considered complete and dire failure is promised the film which has failed to include copious love clutches in its action. Just try to complete the picture minus the cavortings of Cupid! The approved finale for all successful photoplays is a silhouette of the swain and his lady love in a beautiful clinch. That is what you and I are destined for, Taylor Layne. Don't fight it."

"But I will. What if I had a scenario in my mind for Tallulah?"

"Dear girl, what are you thinking of doing?"

"A little writing here and there, nothing much."

"Writing! There is no writing in pictures! Only reusing. Here are the plots. Number one: a young fellow gets thrown out of college. He is disowned by his father and under advice from Horace Greeley goes to Wyoming to show the cowboys how to ride horses. He saves the ranch man's beautiful daughter from the hands of Coyote Pete."

"Yes, I have seen that one."

"Number two: Casey of the Royal Mounted Police gets his man only to find the culprit is the brother of the girl he loves, thus setting up the very effective dilemma between love and duty. Both win.

"Number three: the society butterfly on a slumming trip meets the rough gangster and after five thousand feet of film reforms him just in time to fade out on a beautiful moonlight scene under a willow tree. I believe I made that one myself a couple of times."

"Are there any others?" Zee asked.

"Only one more. The one where the little girl, reared in an orphan asylum, runs away from the cruel keeper and after many trials and tribulations is reclaimed by her father who just returned from South Africa where he struck it rich."

"Yes, I do believe that covers it. But I want to give these something more."

"Don't try, my dear. Writers are not respected, and actors trying to become writers even less so! The audience out there doesn't think writers exist. They think the actors make it all up as they go along. I've done my part; now I must drink some more."

By this time white-gloved waiters were serving the meal, which consisted of Waldorf salad, Cornish game hen, champagne, and a mountain of strawberries and cream. The orchestra played as movie stars danced on the grass.

And Zee was part of it all. As she drank champagne and watched the carousel of luminaries, she knew she was in a state of bubbly alteration. The last vestiges of her past were falling from her like skin from a snake—no, like a cocoon when it becomes mere husk. Emerging was Taylor Layne, once and for all, and she would soon spread her beautiful wings over studios, theaters, and other—

"Having a lovely time?"

Louise Townsend stood unsteadily behind her, a drink in one hand and cigarette in the other. Her eyes were filled with a glassy malice, her lips curled.

"You look to be enjoying yourself," Zee said.

"I've earned that right. You?"

"I never thought that enjoyment had to be earned."

"Then it appears you have a lot to learn. And I'm perfectly happy to give you your first lesson."

Zee noticed that the lights were beginning to illuminate the yard in the encroaching darkness—candles, torches, and strings of lights hanging in trees. Flames reflected in Louise Townsend's eyes. "I'm always eager to learn when I can from you," Zee said. "You have had such long experience."

Louise cackled. "You have quite the clever mouth on you. Someday that is going to get you into trouble. So before that ever happens, let me tell you how to avoid trouble altogether. Do not ever cross over into my territory. That includes the areas of both motion pictures and men."

"I can assure you that I hope you and Mr. Norton will be very happy together."

Louise issued a puff of smoke from her mouth. It made Zee think of a dragon. "That takes care of the area of men. Remember also that you are a serial actress, and it would be best to stay where you will be happiest."

"That is up to Mr. Stroud, don't you think?"

"I know exactly what Mr. Stroud thinks, even before Mr. Stroud thinks it. I know, for example, that he has decided to make the greatest movie in the history of Stroud-General Studios, from Jane Austen's *Emma*. And he has decided who is to play that role. Mr. Stroud has a good eye."

"Congratulations."

"Spare me your patronizing platitudes, Miss Taylor Layne, if that is your real name, which I doubt it is. Stay out of my way. That's my message to you, dear." Louise threw back her drink and gave Zee one last glare before staggering away.

And as she did, Zee thought it was Louise Townsend who had better stay out of the path of Taylor Layne.

‖ 46 ‖

The Church of the Open Door was on the corner of Sixth and Hope streets in downtown Los Angeles. The magnificent auditorium—eight stories from floor to ceiling—had been dedicated to the Lord's work in the City of Los Angeles in 1915.

Conceived in the mind of R. A. Torrey, the church was to be strictly interdenominational. Torrey got the name from two passages of Scripture, explained in a framed document that hung in the church's lobby: *The first passage sets forth the truth that the whole object of the church is to present Christ to men as an open door for all who will enter. The second passage sets forth the truth that Christ has presented before our church an open door for service in reaching out to the unchurched of Los Angeles.*

Doyle and Molly read this as they entered the church Sunday morning. A good crowd streamed in as the chimes in the north tower played.

Immediately Doyle noted that he and Molly were not the best dressed people in attendance. He wore the one good suit he had, purchased only the week before on a loan from Mrs. Fox. Molly's dress was beige lace. The dress probably would have seemed mundane to Zee Miller, now Miss Taylor Layne. But to Doyle, Molly was as pretty as wild flowers on a spring day.

They took seats in the middle section. Soft organ music played as the people filed in.

"It's quite large, isn't it?" Molly said. "I'm afraid I've only been in small churches before."

"As have I."

"Were you raised in a good church?"

Doyle looked down. "It wasn't for me."

"And now?"

He looked at her. "Now there seems to be some hope."

She smiled.

Was there hope? The hymns they sang were certainly full of hope. Doyle felt on the verge of things, new things.

Torrey took to the podium. Once again, Doyle marveled. The man was not sawing the air with his hands, or shouting, or doing anything to try to create an emotional response.

But his clear, logical words were absolutely compelling.

And he was talking about the very hope Doyle had been contemplating. Doyle had heard people exclaim about some preacher or other that he seemed to be "speaking directly to me."

Doyle had never had such an experience. Until now.

"Before I came to believe on the Lord Jesus Christ," Torrey said, "I was one of the bluest men who ever lived. I would sit down by the hour and brood. That changed the day I really became a Christian, absolutely surrendered to God. I have had troubles. I have had losses. There have been times in my life when I have lost pretty much everything the world holds dear. I know what it is to have a wife and four children, and to lose everything of a financial kind I had in the world, and not know where the next meal was coming from. I was absolutely without resources, living from hand to mouth—from God's hand to my mouth. I have known what it is to be with a wife and child in a foreign country where they spoke a strange language, and for some reason or other supplies did not come, and I did not know anyone in the city well enough to turn to for help; but I did not worry. I knew it was all in God's hands, that it would all come out right somehow, and of course it did come out right."

Doyle bit his lower lip. He wanted to believe Torrey on this score, but how could he? It all seemed so fanciful. And yet Torrey spoke with absolute conviction.

"Now the question arises, what must I do to have this certainty and peace? I have told you what the Bible says about it. Believe on the unseen Christ Jesus. What does it mean to believe on Jesus Christ?"

Yes, thought Doyle, *what indeed?*

Torrey's next words came in a torrent. "There is no mystery at all about that. It simply means to put confidence in Jesus Christ to be what He claims to be and what He offers himself to be to us, to put confidence in Him as the One who died in our place, the One who bore our sins in His own body on the Cross, and to trust God to for-give us all our sins because Jesus Christ died in our place; to put con-fidence in Him as the One who was raised from the dead and who now has 'all power in heaven and on earth . . .'"

All power. The words reverberated in Doyle's head. Could it be true?

" . . . and therefore is able to keep us day by day and give us victory over sin, and to trust the risen Christ, putting our confidence in Him as our absolute Lord and Master, and therefore to surrender our thoughts and wills and lives entirely to His control . . ."

Surrender.

" . . . believing everything He says, even though every scholar on earth denies it, obeying everything He commands, whatever it may cost; and to put confidence in Him as our divine Lord, and confess Him as Lord before the world, and worship and adore Him. It is won-derful the joy that comes to him who thus believes on Jesus Christ. But one must really believe on Jesus Christ to have this joy."

One must really believe. Doyle felt a breaking within him.

No, hold on. Hold on. You are falling and you don't want to fall.

Torrey invited those who would surrender to Jesus Christ to walk forward and be received.

Doyle turned to Molly, said nothing. She seemed to read his face.

"I want to go," she said.

He felt then as he had felt that night on the street, that night of the gun, with Norton and Fleming waiting to be shot, and himself unable to move. Only this time it was not something outside of himself that held him back. It *was* himself.

Molly was standing now, hesitating, waiting for him.

He stayed in his chair, a sheet of flame arising within him, his hands gripping the seat like claws.

‖ 47 ‖

The moon shone gloriously bright, a silver promise in the sky above Hollywood. Raneau's Cadillac was as luxurious as some of the homes Zee had been in. She looked at the moon and stars and wondered again how the dream could be coming so true.

The smell of eucalyptus and sage and pepper trees filled the night air as Raneau sped the Caddie up a winding road, high into the hills. With the cover down, the wind blew her hair wildly and flooded her with thoughts of the possible.

Raneau seemed to know exactly where he wanted to settle the car, pointing its nose over a ridge. Lights sparkled below them like stars in the ground.

"Here we are," Raneau said, pulling the hand brake. "From up here you can see just about everything there is to see in Los Angeles."

Zee looked down, then at Raneau. "Why do I have the feeling you have been up here before, and not alone?"

"Ah, guilty. I cannot but tell the truth with you, Taylor. You have that effect on me."

"And why do I have the feeling you have said that before, to other girls?"

"By heaven you are a vixen. I should like to kiss you now."

He bent toward her, close enough so that she could smell the bourbon on his breath. She leaned back. "Why, John, if I let you, you'll think I'm fast. We hardly know each other."

Raneau stayed where he was. "I feel as if I've known you for years. That is part of your charm. Kiss me."

She put her hand up to stop him, catching his shoulder and pushing slightly. "Come now, John, do you want a scandal?"

"Scandal?"

"Everyone knows you and Louise Townsend are peas in a pod."

He sat back heavily. "That bat woman? I wouldn't want her cleaning my bathroom, let alone my pod."

Zee laughed. "It's in the papers, you know."

"It's all the publicity machine. Stroud loves to get stories planted. Good for business. But we all know Louise is in bed with Jess Norton. As you saw last night at the party, when she arrived on his arm."

"Why don't the papers play up that angle, then?"

"Because the papers are in bed with the studios. That's how the game is played, Taylor. They will lay off you, treat you like a queen, unless they smell blood."

"Blood?"

"Do you remember what they did to Bushman?"

Francis X. Bushman. Zee remembered that night so long ago in the park in Zenith, when Doyle Lawrence had teased her about wanting to kiss the movie star. Since that time, a scandal had broken out about Bushman and bigamy, and he hadn't been in pictures since.

"It's the church crowd," Raneau grumbled. "Always sticking their nose in. Puritans! Can't they let people have a little fun?"

"Fun," Zee said absently.

"Come on." Raneau took a silver flask from his pocket. "Let's have a little drink and then kiss."

"You impetuous boy, put that away."

"Why won't you kiss me, Taylor? Don't you realize you are in the position that a million American women would give their right arms for? You are in the moonlight with John Raneau!" He took a goodly drink from his flask.

Zee saw moonlight glint off the flask. In that moment she felt the spark of an idea. It was a thought unlike any she'd had before but was, like the drink in Raneau's flask, intoxicating. She thought of her father then, but quickly banished the image. She was far removed from her childhood now. A surge of empowerment went through her, setting her skin to tingling.

"A girl likes to be wooed, John."

"Eh?" He screwed the top back on the flask and slid it in his pocket.

"Wooed."

"Shall I get out and pick flowers? Tell you love poems? The *Rubaiyat of Omar Khayyam* maybe?"

"It's not poems I want, nor flowers."

"What then?"

"Sy Stroud."

Raneau sat in silent confusion.

Zee said, "You are the studio's biggest star, John."

"After Louise," he added bitterly.

"And that means you have influence with Mr. Stroud. He listens to you, because he must."

Raneau shook his head. "Stroud listens to no one. He keeps his own counsel."

"Yes, but his counsel is money. He cares little for anything else. You bring him money, John. Your movies are gold."

"Not *Santa Fe Trail.* I never should have made a Western."

"But your last teaming with Louise made her look even better."

"Bat woman!"

"Oh? Perhaps you can do the same for another actress."

Raneau eyed her long and hard. "Well, now. I see. Bravo! You have the killer instinct, Miss Taylor Layne."

She knew what he was talking about. "I don't know what you're talking about, John."

"You're no naïve farm girl from Nebraska. You know exactly what you want and how to get it. You'd like to use me to get you there. An exchange of favors." He paused. "But I am mad enough about you to take you up on it."

"John, you wound me."

"I don't think so. I think, however, you would inflict a wound on Louise Townsend. Tell me, does the movie *Emma* play upon your mind?"

Zee stiffened. "*Emma?* Movie?"

"You must work on your poker face, darling."

"It shows that much?"

"Like the moon above."

"Then let us not be false to each other, John. Yes, *Emma.* I would do anything for that part."

Raneau considered her thoughtfully. "I almost think you would. And I rather think you would like me to prevail upon Mr. Stroud to cast you in the role. Am I quite far off?"

Zee snapped a smile in place. "Let's not think of such things tonight. Let's drink in the moon."

The famous smile of John Raneau, the one that captivated hearts in theaters around the world, flashed in the muted silver glow of the evening. He leaned over to kiss her.

She let him. *This would be wonderful publicity for Taylor Layne! Where are the reporters when you need them?*

It was nearly three in the morning when they got back to Raneau's. It was deserted now, save for her car and one other parked near the front door.

Raneau pulled to a stop and turned to Zee. "Stay with me tonight."

"No, John."

"It's a big house; I'm all alone."

She patted his cheek. "You're a big boy, too. You'll get along."

"You know I'm crazy about you. Stay."

"John, I—"

"Please say yes."

Zee saw a dark form sit up in the other car. "Don't make him beg," a man's voice said.

Raneau stiffened. "Who is that?"

The form got out of the car and made his way toward them. Only when he was nearly upon them could Zee see who it was.

Blakely Eberhard held a bottle in one hand. His black tie flapped loosely from around his neck.

"Hello, Tallulah! Out for a little midnight spin with Hollywood royalty?"

"He's drunk," Raneau said.

"Very perceptive, John. I was drunk when I got here, drunk all night, and I intend to stay drunk for the foreseeable future."

"We'll take you home," Zee said.

Eberhard waved the bottle. "You think I can't drive just because I'm lubricated, tanked, stinko? Isn't the English language rich with euphe . . . eupho . . . words for drunk?"

Zee climbed out of Raneau's car and took Blakely's arm. "Come on, get in John's car. You need some sleep—"

He ripped his arm away and stumbled backward. "I'm already asleep! Sleepwalking, more like it. I've been a cadaver for years. I'm getting out before I end up like him."

"End up like who?" Raneau said.

"Oh? You haven't heard? That's right, you were out for a little joy ride when the party was breaking up. What a lovely party it was, John, until they threw a wet blanket over it."

"Tell me what on earth you're talking about, you sot."

Blakely snorted. "Everything was going swimmingly! I was watching some lovely young thing dance with Chaplin, and the champagne never ran out. It was a slice of paradise, old bean. And then someone had to go and spoil it all with a little announcement."

"Announcement?"

"Mr. Happy Sanders killed himself tonight. Took one of his own hunting rifles and did the job right."

All feeling left Zee. Night flooded her soul.

"Yes, sir, John, a real wet blanket on the party after that."

PART V

NIGHT FALLS

✦

We can recall when, in a majority of families, there was morning and evening prayer, and not a meal eaten until grace had been said. What has become of that old-fashioned family?

—Editorial comment, 1921

✦

Should the flapper, with her short skirts and cigarettes, her lack of corsets and her decidedly airy views about the insignificant importance of kissing, be suppressed as a menace to the nation's morals, or celebrated as its chief claim to art and beauty?

—Los Angeles Times, *June 3, 1921*

‖ 1 ‖

"You want to ruin my career, that's what it is!" Zee did not care if her voice could be heard throughout the studio. This dolt, this ignoramus, this poor excuse for a director was going to make her the laughingstock of the Saturday matinee crowd.

Forbes Franklin pulled at what was left of his hair and spoke through gritted teeth. "I am telling you what this scene requires for dramatic purposes."

"You would not know a dramatic purpose if it came up, sat in your lap, and shouted in your ear, *I am a dramatic purpose!*"

She was only vaguely aware of the other people on the crew shuffling their feet and looking down. She thought she saw Pete behind the camera staring directly at her.

"This is too much." Forbes Franklin threw his megaphone on the ground and stomped on it with a booted foot. "I cannot work like this!"

"Work?" Zee threw her hands in the air. "Is that what you call what you have been doing? You certainly had me fooled."

The director pointed a shaking finger at her face. "Don't think that you cannot be knocked off your high horse, missy."

Zee put her hands on her hips. "Who do you think people want to see when they plunk down their hard-earned nickels for the next Tallulah? Another Forbes Franklin picture? I know what people want. I know what they expect. They're going to see a great actress up there, not some cog in your machine. Now I suggest we get back to shooting a scene."

Franklin's face was growing redder by the second. "Look on the back of my chair. You know what it says? It says *Director*. That means this is my set and my crew."

"Oh yes? And any single one of them picked at random can do a better job than you!" She turned her head and saw Pete. "I think Pete Dillard should be directing this picture, and I'm going to tell Mr. Stroud so."

Franklin snapped a look at Pete. "We'll see about that." He kicked the remains of his megaphone and stormed off the set.

Zee counted this at least a minor victory for dramatic excellence. She took a deep breath, then smiled and winked at Pete. While the crew quietly walked away, she went to him and laughed. "How about that? You as my director! It was a bit of inspiration, don't you think?"

Pete did not smile.

"What's the matter?" Zee said. "Don't tell me you have some loyalty to that stuffy old windbag."

"That stuffy old windbag," said Pete, "has made you a star. He knows what he's doing. He's a veteran."

"I don't get it, Pete. I thought you were my pal."

"Well, if I'm your pal I should be able to talk to you plainly, right?"

"Sure. You have something on your mind?"

"You're on my mind." He hesitated, then found resolve. "I think you're becoming someone you don't need to be."

"A star?"

"I'm not talking about Taylor Layne the actress. It's possible to become a famous actress worshiped all over the world and still fail the test of being a decent human being. I don't want to see that happen to you."

Being scolded like this, by someone who was, after all, below her in the studio pecking order, did not sit well with her. Yet inside her a voice whispered that Pete was right. The only question was whether she wanted to hear it. "I'm perfectly capable of taking care of myself," she protested.

"You wanted to know what was on my mind, and that's it. If you don't want to listen, that's something else."

"Pete," she said softly, like a mother trying to calm a child, "it's been a long day—"

"It's still morning."

"Whatever the time. Franklin has gotten us all a little upset—"

"You're the one who's upset."

"So are you."

"Yeah, I am. What of it?"

This was a side of Pete she hadn't seen before. "Come on, pal, let's both forget this and—"

"Quit calling me *pal*. Is that all I am to you?"

So that was it. She should have seen it coming. Pete had fallen for her and she had chosen to ignore it. No matter. That was the way it had to be.

"Pete, I'm sorry." She put her hand on his arm. "I guess I haven't told you enough what a swell egg you are. Really."

"I don't want to be an *egg*. I want you, Taylor." He placed his hand on hers and looked her straight in the eye.

"Pete, I don't want you to think I'm ungrateful—"

"I don't need your gratitude!" He threw her hand away from him.

"You've got to understand. I'm just on the verge of breaking through, big."

"So?" He paused and studied her. "Oh, I get it now. You're moving into another part of the heavens. And I'm just a guy back on earth, helping a director run a camera."

"No, that's not—"

"Oh boy, what a dope I was. I should have seen this from the start."

"Please, Pete—"

"And don't do me any more favors in front of Franklin. I'm not going to step over him to direct anything that you're in. In fact, I'm going to ask to be transferred to another crew." He started to walk away.

"Hey, Pete, come back."

Her order was ignored. Suddenly she realized that it was the middle of the morning on what was supposed to be a busy day, and she was all alone on the set.

Loneliness was constant with her now. It seemed to have increased after Happy's death. That event had unnerved her in ways she was only now beginning to see, and flee from.

She would wait it out, this loneliness. She would wait it out and defeat it, the way she could defeat everything. She would go to the new house, the one she'd leased up in the hills. A house more fitting a rising star.

True, she would be alone there as well. Molly had chosen not to move up with her. Why she would want to stay in the modest apartment they shared was something of a mystery, though it was evident they had been drifting apart. Had been ever since she had started keeping company with Doyle Lawrence.

Doyle. Why was she thinking of him so much lately? She'd heard he was back on his feet, working for a lawyer. Solid citizen. Old Omaha.

At least he knows who he is, she thought. *But who am I? Who have I become?*

A longing like sunset, like the close of day, filled her then. Doyle. Maybe it was time to reclaim him again, and in doing so, reclaim something of herself.

‖ 2 ‖

The parlor was designed to give the impression of opulence, though Doyle could see the materials were of the cheapest variety. This was ostensibly a men's club. Los Angeles had several of them scattered around, from the exclusive California Club high on Bunker Hill to the more common establishments like this one on Eighth Street.

And all of them were now fronts for the illegal imbibing of liquor.

It was daylight hours, so naturally there was no drinking going on in the common area of the club. Doyle had heard that back rooms provided sanctuary for those who wanted to get to their drinking before nighttime. But that was not his concern at the moment.

A young man who looked like so many other young men of the city these days—nervously eager about the eyes, looking for the next moneymaking opportunity—met him in the foyer with an unfriendly gaze.

"Members only," he said sharply.

"I would like to see Mr. Handley, please."

"Mr. Handley doesn't see nobody without he makes an appointment."

"I'm making an appointment now."

The young man, who wore his hair parted in the middle in the old-fashioned style, stiffened. He was thin and looked like a scarecrow at attention. "You think you can get tough with me?"

Doyle sighed. "All I want is to talk to Mr. Handley for five minutes. After that, if he tells me to scram, I will. It's important what I have to say and maybe he would appreciate being told that I'm here. The name's Doyle Lawrence and this has to do with Jess Norton."

The mention of Norton's name did it. The scarecrow let down his pointy chin and said, "Wait here."

Doyle looked around, smelling the stale odor of last night's booze and sensing a certain heaviness of soul that permeated a joint like this. Los Angeles offered plenty of places to experience the same.

The young man returned and motioned for Doyle to follow. They went down a hallway until the scarecrow opened a door.

A squat bulldog of a man with a cigar planted in the side of his mouth stood up from behind a desk. "This better be important."

"That is up to you, Mr. Handley," Doyle said.

Handley took a perfunctory puff on his cigar as he stared at Doyle. He waved his arm, signaling the young man to leave.

When they were alone, Handley said, "What did you say your name was?"

"Lawrence."

"Never heard of you. How'd you get to me?"

"I'm good at asking questions."

"You good at getting your nose broke? 'Cause that's what asking questions can get you."

For a moment Doyle wondered if the man might take a swing at him. He certainly looked like he could have thrown more than a few punches in his day.

"What have you got to do with Norton?" Handley said.

"I have nothing to do with him yet. But with a little help I may have quite a bit to say about him later on."

Handley looked at him for a long time before answering. "You working for the police? The federals?"

"I am, but they don't know it yet."

"What is that supposed to mean?"

In the short time he had talked with Handley, Doyle thought he looked like a hard worker and straight shooter, even though he was engaged in an illegal trade. Doyle decided he could talk squarely.

"I know about Norton and how he runs things around here," Doyle said. "He's powerful but he's not liked. If he could be brought down, a lot of folks would be happy. But in order for that to happen, people are going to have to cooperate. I'm looking for those people. And when I find them I'll go to the district attorney."

Handley smiled derisively. "You think the D.A. is going to take an interest in this? He probably gets his rye delivered straight to his office by Norton himself."

"I believe I can convince Mr. Fallon to do his duty."

"How?"

"He's a politician, and he wants to be reelected to office. When enough people know what's going on, it won't look good for the D.A. to be sitting back and allowing the Volstead Act to be violated so freely in his city."

"What makes you so sure the people really care? From where I sit they like having their options open."

"I believe there is going to be a revival of spirit in this city," Doyle said. "What we need now is for a few brave men to stand up to people like Norton and get rid of his kind."

"You know that kind of talk can get you more than a poke in the nose, don't you? It can get you killed."

"Do you want to get rid of Norton?"

"I sell liquor here, in case you didn't know. Why should I cut my own throat?"

"Because Norton is cutting it for you. He's charging you and others outrageous prices, and forcing you to take his booze."

"It's true what you say, but that's business."

"It doesn't have to be."

Again, Handley studied Doyle. He removed the cigar from his mouth. "How do I know you don't work for Norton?"

"I guess you don't."

Handley stuck the cigar back in his maw and puffed a cloud. "I have to size men up all the time. And fast. Suppose I was to take an interest in your proposition, Mr. Lawrence. What then?"

"You agree to make a statement to the district attorney, and testify against Norton."

After a long pause, Handley said. "You have anybody else?"

"You would be the first."

"As long as I'm not the only one. Get back to me on that, Mr. Lawrence."

‖ 31 ‖

Doyle met Molly at the Owl Drug store for a hot dog lunch.

It was their regular Wednesday date. They even had a special table under the Palmolive advertisement. *For that schoolgirl complexion!* They ordered the same thing—hot dogs, Coca-Cola, and potato chips. Sometimes Doyle would come in early and read a law book, assigned to him by Kit Shannon Fox.

And every now and then he'd look at the Bible.

Since that night three months ago at the Church of the Open Door, when Molly had gone forward in response to the altar call, he felt like he was the most hesitant sinner in the city of Los Angeles. He was a man on a border, between two worlds. He wanted to believe as she did, but something held him back. He went to church with her, where Torrey preached a rugged Christianity—not a soft-sell variety that one could take or leave. But Doyle wasn't taking anything. Not yet. He had other challenges. Not just Norton. There was the matter of two women.

Molly was in love with him. He knew that. He knew also that he should love her in return. Maybe he did, even with the face of Zee Miller floating into his head every time he got near her.

"What fascinating area of the law are you on today?" Molly also seemed renewed. Since Zee had moved out into her home in the hills, Molly had started working days at Harriman's Department Store and studying nights at the Los Angeles Women's Stenographic School.

"Criminal law." Doyle held up his text. "How to deal with bad people without killing them yourself."

"Sounds civilized."

"That's me, a regular Dapper Dan."

Molly laughed. "You'll look dapper in front of a jury someday."

"I hope so. I—"

He stopped. A ragged man on crutches went by their table. He had one leg missing. Doyle couldn't help watching as the man made his way to the drugstore counter. When the counter boy, who was no more than eighteen or nineteen, came over to see what the man wanted, Doyle watched the conversation. The boy shook his head a couple of times. Then the man reached into his dirty coat pocket and pulled out a medal. Doyle could see clearly that it was a Purple Heart. The boy shook his head again.

"Excuse me, Molly." Doyle got up and moved to the counter.

"I can't do it," the boy was saying. "My boss said no more handouts."

The dirty man held the medal up in a quivering fist. "You can get something for this, a good something."

"Then why don't you try the pawnshop down the—"

Doyle said, "Give him what he wants."

The boy flinched. "My boss says I can't—"

"Never mind that. I'll stake him." Doyle looked at the man's face. It was as old as his own, no older. "What'll you have?"

"I'm not looking for a handout." The man held up the Purple Heart for Doyle to see.

"Put that back in your pocket. Let one soldier buy another soldier a meal."

The gripping desperation in the man's face gave way to a small beam of relief.

Doyle took out two dollar bills and laid them on the counter. "Give him a meal," he said to the boy. "And what's left put down as credit for next time."

The man reached slowly for Doyle's hand and shook it. He said not a word, indeed seemed as if he could not.

It was only when he got back to his table that Doyle realized he'd given away the money he was going to use for the meal he and Molly were eating.

"That was lovely," Molly said.

"Somebody did the same for me once. It's just something you do." He folded his hands and found that he was short of breath.

"What is it, Doyle?"

He took in a deep breath, fighting his pulse and nerve. He looked at Molly and knew he had to come clean.

"Sometimes," he said, "I wake up in the night screaming and I'm covered with sweat." He paused to see what her reaction would be. She was holding steady, looking at him. "I'm no different than a hundred thousand other guys. I don't know if I'll ever get over it."

"You will, Doyle."

"There's more." Doyle glanced over at the one-legged soldier at the counter. He was leaning over a sandwich and cup of coffee. Doyle looked back at Molly. "Sometimes I get filled with an anger that just washes over me. It scares me. I lose control. And I do things I wouldn't do if I was . . . normal."

He hadn't talked this way ever, not even before the war. The words became like blood from a wound, flowing and hot. "I had this friend, his name was Alvin, and he saved my life. But he lost his. I just couldn't understand, I can't understand, I don't know why it had to happen that way. I see him in my dreams. That's why I wake up screaming. I see him alive and I know what's about to happen and I want to stop it, I want to stop it in my dream but I can't."

He was still short of breath and realized he was shaking. Molly took his hand and he let her hold it. "I never want to hurt anyone, especially you."

"You'll never hurt me, Doyle." There were tears in her eyes.

He shook his head. "Some company I am. I take a girl out for a nice lunch and all of a sudden I get melodramatic on her."

"I don't mind."

He couldn't say anything for a moment. Then he forced a smile. "Will you mind when I tell you I don't have enough money to pay for lunch?"

"I'll take care of the bill."

"But—"

She squeezed his hand. "It's just something you do."

And in that moment, he did love her. Completely, without reservation.

"I'm going to see Zee," he said, and felt Molly's hand shake a little. "She has asked me to advise her on a matter."

"I see."

"I don't know what it is. She called Mrs. Fox's office."

"Then she needs you," Molly said. "Help her."

‖ 4 ‖

The home was on Argyle Avenue, high up in the Hollywood hills. It stood apart from its neighboring dwellings by way of a huge hedge that surrounded it like a battlement. A large iron gate kept intruders from access to the drive. Only today it stood open.

Doyle Lawrence was expected.

As Doyle guided the Model T Ford up the drive, paid for with an advance on his salary as Mrs. Fox's assistant, he could not help but feel the outsider. How far his childhood friend had come in the world's estimation. A large home with classic columns in the prewar style, white, surrounded with purple wisteria. The manicured lawn was, at once, beautiful and artificial. Part reality, part movie set. In Zenith, the lawns never looked *this* perfect. Not many things did.

Parked in front of the home was an elegant automobile that Doyle recognized from the numerous ads he'd seen for it—a Jordan Playboy. It was all the rage among the young women of Los Angeles. *The car for girls who want freedom,* the newspaper ads exclaimed.

Doyle shook his head, wondering how free Zee really was in all the encroaching splendor.

A maid answered the front door. She cast him a suspicious look. Doyle gave his name, and the maid's demeanor changed only a little. "Miss Layne is expecting you. This way."

She led him through the expansive home—the largest Doyle had been in here in the city—and out a pair of French doors. The back lawn was dominated with a swimming pool of fine tile and masonry.

Zee was reclining on a chaise longue, reading a script. She wore sunglasses and a soft white robe, looking every inch the movie star.

She jumped up with a smile, tossing her script down, came to him, kissed him on the cheek.

"How nice of you to come and see me, Doyle."

He nodded. "At your request."

"Yes, yes, forget that for now. It's good to see you! You're looking well. Los Angeles agrees with you."

"There are people in Los Angeles who have helped me."

"Isn't that grand? Let's have tea, shall we?"

"Whatever you like."

He sat on a wicker chair as Zee picked up a telephone. She waited a moment, then ordered that tea be served poolside. That done, she pulled a gold case from her robe pocket and opened it.

"Cigarette?" she offered.

"No thank you."

"I thought all you doughboys took up the habit." She picked up a small hand lighter from the table and lit the cigarette. Doyle could not help but note how she had changed. From the rambunctious girl he knew back home, the girl who climbed trees and reached toward a limitless sky, she was now a woman with sophistication. Or, rather, a woman trying her best to do all the sophisticated things. Zee's rise had been swift and she appeared to be grabbing every bit of it, savoring the flavor of her new life. But it did not become her. She seemed fragile inside a veneer of glamour, a crystal soul waiting to shatter if shaken too hard.

Zee blew a plume of smoke. "Do you approve of the house? I may buy it."

"It's very nice. Sort of a fortress."

"I have fans, Doyle, can you believe it? Fans!"

Doyle said nothing.

"You don't seem happy for me."

"Are you happy, Zee?"

She looked up at the sky as if searching for an answer. "Of course I'm happy. And you're going to make me happier."

And how, he wondered, could he do that?

The maid returned with tea on an ornate silver tray. "How do you take it, sir?"

"I have no idea," Doyle said.

Zee laughed. "Old Omaha! You are a fish out of water here, aren't you? Don't worry, it gets easier."

The maid, bemused by the whole thing, bowed and left.

"What is it you wanted to see me about, Zee?"

She sat back in on the chaise and took a long drag on her cigarette—posing, Doyle thought, for his benefit. "I was delighted to hear you have taken up the law. When I saw you in the drugstore that day, you did not look at all well. And now here you are, a lawyer!"

"Not yet. I have some years to go, working for Mrs. Fox. But someday."

"We will rise together."

He looked at her, unsure.

"What I mean, Doyle, is that I need a personal lawyer. I need someone to handle my affairs, someone I can trust. And I certainly can't think of anyone I trust more than you."

"But I'm not a lawyer—"

"Mere technicality. You can advise me, and look over things, and if it's something that needs a legal hand, give it to Mrs. Fox. Until you become full-fledged. Of course, you'll be paid a nice retainer."

Working for Zee Miller? He shifted in his chair.

Zee leaned forward. "The nice thing is we will simply have to spend more time together. Imagine that, will you? Here in Hollywood! The two of us, having a ball."

"Zee—"

"Do say yes, Doyle. You don't know how I've longed for some good old-fashioned company."

"Old Omaha?"

She waved at him. "Oh, we'll change that now. We'll come up with a new name for you."

"I don't think I'm the Hollywood type."

"You will be. It will be such fun!"

His chest clenched. He felt a drawing toward her but thought, at all costs, he could not let that happen. "Zee, I think you should know that I've been spending a good deal of time with Molly."

Zee stubbed out her cigarette in a porcelain ashtray. "I can't quite see you two together. No. Try as I might. But that's neither here nor there. Tonight we will talk business at *El Centro*. Have you been there? They have the loveliest—"

"I'm sorry, but I have a date with Molly."

"Why don't you break it?"

"I don't want to."

"Yes, you do."

Her eyes were cool and steady on him, not the eyes of the girl from Nebraska who had been brave and reckless and full of wonder. The wonder was gone, and the recklessness was of another type.

He stood. "I'm sorry, Zee."

"Don't go." She got to her feet and came to him, snatching off her sunglasses as she did. Her eyes, cerulean and wide under the blue California sky, locked on him. Then she threw her arms around his neck. She was shaking as she whispered, "You love me. You always have."

Doyle didn't move. He was on the edge of a cliff in the dark, not knowing which way to step, knowing only that the wrong direction would mean disaster. He could kiss her, and she would let him. She wanted him to. Did he want to? He had been seeing her face in dreams, despairing at times that he would ever really be free of her completely.

And then, like the light of the sun breaking through the gloom, another face came to him. Molly's.

Slowly, he took Zee's wrists in his hands and lowered her arms.

She snatched her arms away. "You're an idiot." She looked away.

"Maybe I am," Doyle said.

Zee sighed and brought her gaze back to him. "I'm sorry, Doyle, I didn't mean that. I—" She stopped, looking over Doyle's shoulder.

Doyle turned and saw a nattily dressed man approaching.

"Hello, John!" Zee snapped on a new face and a perky voice. "Come here and meet my childhood friend, Doyle Lawrence."

Raneau extended his hand. "Ah, another from the cornfields of Nebraska?"

"I was never very good at growing corn," Doyle said.

"No need," Raneau said. "This is Los Angeles. All the bounty of the earth is brought to us daily, ours for the taking. Would you mind if I had a word with Miss Layne?"

"I was just going." Doyle looked at Zee. She did not look back.

"Best to Molly," Zee said to the air.

⁐

"He seems a fine young man, Taylor," John Raneau said.

Zee felt a falling in her, like snow off a pine when the wind comes up. Cold. She willed herself to smile. "Let's not talk about other men. Let's talk about you."

Raneau shook his head admiringly. "You are a wonder. Even as I feel your manipulations I fall more in love with you. You are a danger-ous woman. My kind of woman."

He bent to kiss her. She offered him her cheek.

"Come now," Zee said, "I'm not so bad as all that. I want to have some fun. Where shall you take me?"

"There's a new restaurant opening tonight, Charlie Chaplin's joint. Shall I get us in?"

"Oh yes! That will be the tops. Reporters?"

"By the dozens."

"Let's! Now I have to go get something new and wonderful to wear. That's a full day of shopping." She patted his cheek. "Be a good boy and come back for me around seven." She started for the house.

"Taylor."

It was the note of dread in his voice that stopped her.

"Come and sit," he said, walking to her and taking her hand.

She pulled it away. "Something is the matter. Tell me. Right now."

Raneau took in a deep breath. "I thought you should hear this from me first."

"Hear *what*?"

"Mr. Stroud has decided to give the role of Emma to Louise."

The earth opened up beneath her feet, and the whole world began to spin faster. She put her hands to her head and then felt Raneau's arms holding her up.

"Come along," he said, guiding her to the chaise longue and sit-ting her down.

"It can't be," she muttered. "That part was mine. Stroud said it was."

"Now, look here, there will be other parts—"

"Not like Emma." A thick anger rose up within her. "I want that part." She stared at Raneau, but he was just a blur to her now. "And I mean to have it."

‖ 5 ‖

"Jess Norton?" the man said, voice quivering. "Don't know the man."

Doyle frowned. The man's name was Thadeus Koteki, and he was a Greek who owned a grocery store at the corner of Fourth and Olive, two doors down from one of Jess Norton's speakeasies. And if Doyle thought this was going to be easy, he now knew different.

"Of course you know who Jess Norton is."

"You hard of hearing?" Koteki's Greek accent was thick, and he pounded out each word as if it were hammer strikes.

"Naturally you're nervous about it."

"Nervous! Boy, that don't come half to what I am." Koteki lifted a crate of melons in two massive hands and set it atop a stack of three others.

Doyle said, "You know as well as I do that Norton and his muscle will keep taking protection money all over town. Until enough people stand up to him. Now I'm preparing a case—"

"You from the D.A.?"

"No."

"Then I got work." He moved toward the rear of his store. It was a half-enclosed market that stayed open late. The usual domestic help that shopped during the day had given way at this hour to a different clientele. A couple of young men in college sweaters were laughing and carrying on by the canned goods. Koteki cast them barely a glance, as if this sort of pattern were repeated night after night.

"Mr. Koteki, if we don't stop him now, it could mean worse trouble down the line."

Koteki whirled on him. "Listen, boy, I want no pipe dreams. I make my living, and I do what I got to to take care of my family."

"You're being bled. So are the merchants on this street."

"So? Blood makes the world go round, in case you don't notice."

Frustrated, Doyle followed Koteki to the very back of the store. "Mr. Koteki, if I were to promise you that you would not be alone, would you—"

The grocer put up his hand. "I'm busy, so why don't you—" He stopped suddenly.

Doyle turned around and saw the reason why.

Thorn Fleming shuffled toward them, his hands in the pockets of his coat.

"Now, ain't this a coincidence," Fleming said. "Did you know you have rats in your store, Koteki?"

Doyle looked deep into Fleming's eyes. They were empty caves, cold and concealing.

"Rats are bad for business." Fleming took another step. "You need somebody to get rid of the rats."

"I don't know this man," Koteki protested.

"No? You seemed to be talking pretty close when I came in."

"I was telling him to get out."

Fleming smiled. "You hear that, rat? I woulda thought you got the message the last time." He thrust one of his pocketed hands forward.

"You won't use that," Doyle said. "Not here. Norton wouldn't like it if one of his stooges went around bumping off citizens in public. No, it's the shadows for the likes of you, Fleming."

A chill hung in the air for a long moment. Fleming's eyes fidgeted. Behind them, Doyle sensed the brute's brain churning through options.

Self-survival won out. The large club of Jess Norton hanging over the attack dog Fleming was enough.

"We have unfinished business," Fleming said.

"You're finished now," Doyle said. "You just don't know it."

The big man forced a smile, but Doyle saw his cheeks twitch. Fleming looked at Koteki. "I'll be back tomorrow. We'll discuss business then." He turned and walked out, his frame knocking some cans off a shelf as he went.

Doyle noticed his hands were sweating. He rubbed them on his pants.

"I wouldn't want to be you," Koteki said. "Now get out of my store and don't come back."

‖ 6 ‖

"How like the prodigal doth she return."

Jess Norton sat behind his immaculate desk in his immaculate suit and smiled.

Zee smiled, too. She was going to match him tooth for tooth. "Quoting the Bible at me, Jess?"

"Shakespeare, my dear. *The Merchant of Venice*. Act two."

"Why, Jess Norton, you are an educated man. I never knew."

"You never asked. And you couldn't get away fast enough before you found out."

She was standing in front of him, having been shown into his office by that big gorilla he had working for him. What was his name again? Something to do with a flower. Thorn. That was it. He gave Zee the heebie-jeebies.

"Oh, let's not go back over old times." She went to the corner of his desk and sat on it, half turned to face him. She leaned forward so he could appreciate how her silk maroon dress accented the right places.

"Good to see you, Jess," she cooed. "How have you been?"

With his gloved hands, Norton fingered a gold watch fob hanging from the middle of his vest. "Can't complain. I'm breathing. And making a good living. Like you."

"It seems fortune has smiled upon both of us."

"Yes, I have followed your ascent with great interest. It warms my heart to know that you had your start in this town in my humble establishment. Gives a fellow a certain glow of satisfaction."

Zee couldn't tell if he was openly mocking her or trying to be charming. If she thought she could read what was going on behind his dark eyes she was mistaken. She should have known better. Jess Norton didn't get where he was in this city by being an open book.

"I certainly can't thank you enough," Zee said. "You did give me my start. I'll always be appreciative of that fact."

Jess Norton cocked his head. "My, what formal talk between friends. We are friends, aren't we, Taylor?"

"Of course. How silly of you to suggest otherwise."

"I wasn't suggesting any such thing. In fact, I hope we might get to be even better friends."

The office suddenly felt warm. But Zee wasn't going to let on. "And I know you have lots of good friends. Politicians and movie stars. Like Louise Townsend."

Norton smiled. "Why yes, Louise. A big star who is only going to get bigger. The role of Emma will be extolled around the world, won't it?"

"I should think," Zee said winsomely, "that Emma should go to a much younger actress. Wouldn't that fit the character better? Oh,

Louise was charming in her younger days. Now she has become a more mature actress, certainly able to handle parts that fit her stature. And a woman of thirty can play a number of roles."

Jess Norton's rollicking laugh filled the office. "You are a clever little girl, aren't you? You know as well as I do that Louise is on the downhill side of thirty-five. I can never quite figure out how far down. But you, my dear, are on the fresh side of twenty-two. Is it my faulty recollection, or is Emma about that age in the novel?"

"You're correct."

"Which invites a question. How is it that Sy Stroud missed such an obvious casting choice? With Taylor Layne making hay at the box office in such large bales with her *Tallulah* serials, and Louise Townsend having two disappointments in her immediate past, why do you suppose he should pick the wrong actress for the lead role?"

"Do you think he picked the wrong actress?"

"Do you?"

"Yes."

"At last the truth."

"What do you mean?"

"What I mean, dear one, is that ever since you walked into my humble quarters you have been acting, and not in a fashion that would inspire the movie critics."

"Come now, Jess. You're being harsh."

"I deal in reality. And the reality is that you have come to me because you desperately want the part of Emma and I'm your last hope to get it."

"Why, Jess—"

"No more acting. If you act I'm going to ask Mr. Fleming to come in here and escort you to the street."

He knew the game better than she. Well then, she would have to play harder. She breathed in deeply to calm herself.

"Despite your attempts to play Dr. Freud," Zee stated matter-of-factly, "I am neither desperate nor engaged in the theater arts. I came here to see you. I came to see you because I missed you. But if you would rather have me go . . ."

"Stay awhile. Will you have a drink with me?"

"Why not? Let's be gay. Just like old times."

Norton went to a cabinet, opened it, took down a bottle. He

poured amber liquid into two glasses and sprayed some seltzer after it. He handed her a glass, clinked it with his, and took a sip.

Zee did the same.

Jess Norton fixed his gaze on her. As always, he had something hidden behind his eyes. "If it were only in my power to grant you the role of Emma."

Zee tried to keep all signs of anxiousness from showing on her face.

"I'm a lover of fine art," Norton said. "The motion picture is coming into its own. A fine role like Emma should go to someone of the right age. Louise, star that she is, has been a bit erratic of late." He held up his glass and winked. "A bit too much of John Barley-corn."

"I would never cast aspersion on a great star like Louise Town-send."

"Oh no. Not you." He laughed. "But I have been known to do favors for friends. I always expect, however, that the favors will be returned. Doesn't that sound like good business sense?"

"Certainly, Jess. You've always had a good business head on your shoulders."

He put his drink on the table, hard. "Save your cheap patter for the Nebraska rubes. If I give something, I expect something in return. Is that understood?"

Zee swallowed, nodded.

"Good," Norton said. "Then you have a good business head, too. Don't you?"

Again she nodded, trying to keep her smile warm. But it was a cool wasteland inside her.

‖ 7 ‖

"What can I do for you, Mr. Lawrence?" District Attorney William "Bill" Fallon did not offer Doyle a chair. He was reputed to be a man who liked a good suit and fine cigars, and calculating political odds.

"I am assistant to Mrs. Kathleen Fox."

Fallon opened the humidor on his desk. "Mrs. Fox is a thorn in my side, has been for several years. However, if your aim is to learn the law, I cannot think of a better teacher. Cigar?"

"No thank you."

Fallon snipped the end of a cigar with a silver clipper, then struck a match. "Are you going to be a thorn in my side, too?"

"That remains to be seen."

Fallon scowled. "I repeat. What brings you to see me, Lawrence?"

"I've been making some inquiries regarding Jess Norton."

"Norton? That's quite a citizen about whom you've chosen to make . . . inquiries."

"Are you interested?"

Fallon squinted at him through a cloud of gray smoke. "Our office is quite familiar with Mr. Norton."

"Then why isn't he being prosecuted?"

"I beg your pardon?"

"He's a known bootlegger. He operates openly. My question is why he isn't being prosecuted."

"Excuse me, Mr. Lawrence, but I thought you said you were learning the law. Yet you suppose you can tell me what my job is?"

"No sir. Merely inquiring."

"Your tone did not suggest inquiry."

Doyle took a breath. "I'm sorry, Mr. Fallon. I am more than a little interested in the prosecution of Mr. Norton. We've met. It was not an amicable meeting."

Fallon motioned for Doyle to sit. "I'll tell you a few things, Lawrence, since you've taken the time to come up here. First, this office is well aware of Jess Norton and his activities. He is not the only criminal in Los Angeles, however. This city, with all of the growth in the last decade, has become a haven for all sorts of new criminal elements. The liquor trade is just one of them. We have bunco artists and bordellos and gambling. Every night it seems some other down-on-his-luck drifter finds his way into the city with an idea that this is the place that's going to be different. Do you have any idea about that?"

"A little. Not long ago I was one of those drifters."

"But did you commit a crime?"

"I spent a night in your jail."

"So have a lot of people, and still they come. But there is something that applies to all of them, Mr. Lawrence, no matter what station of life or what crime they may have committed. The presumption of innocence."

"Which can be overcome by proof beyond a reasonable doubt."

"It's proof that's the problem for fellows like Norton. They are insulated and smart."

"What about informers?"

"We had an informer once. You'll find him in the cemetery, under a marble marker."

"That's a risk I'm willing to take."

"But is it a risk witnesses are willing to take? What about that?"

"If I can provide them, will you prosecute?"

Fallon thought about it a moment, puffing his cigar like a sage. "I will promise you this, Lawrence. My door will always be open to you. And if I think we have enough to move on, I'll move. If I don't, I'll tell you directly."

"Fair enough."

"But don't have any illusions about my being able to protect you from Norton. On that score you're on your own. And I advise you to be very, very careful."

‖ 8 ‖

Sy Stroud paced his office like a caged tiger. Zee tried to keep up the appearance of complete innocence. She'd been ordered to Stroud's office the moment she drove on the lot. There was a tension in the air even at the studio gate. She saw it in the set jaw of the guard who delivered the message.

Stroud kept his hands behind his back, wiggling interlaced fingers. "You're some smart girl, you are."

"Thank you, Mr. Stroud, I always—"

"You don't know sarcasm when you hear it?"

"Whatever do you mean?" Zee used her little-girl voice.

"What I'm meaning is you can be too smart for your own ignorance, and that's maybe what you are." His face was pinkish, narrowed in a rosy scowl.

"If I've done anything to offend you, please let me know." Zee slipped casually into a chair and crossed her legs. Keep looking like all is well, she told herself.

Stroud stopped his pacing a moment and faced her. "Come now, you want to play the role of Emma or not?"

"Emma? Me?"

The studio boss slapped his sides and looked up in the air. "An actress yet! Why did I go into the movie business?" Stroud leaned against his desk. "Your friend came to see me. Paid me a little visit. Said it would be a very great favor to him to have you play this role, which incidentally I've promised to Louise Townsend. Ever hear of her?"

"Of course I—"

"Again it's the sarcasm. So you are getting your way. But it's a warning I'm giving." He pointed a stubby finger at her. "Don't fly too close to the sun. The wax on your wings will melt."

Zee put her hands in her lap, folded casually. "Mr. Stroud, please believe me when I tell you that I would never want anything to come between me and Stroud-General Studios. I am very grateful for every-thing you have done for me."

"I'm almost believing you. Don't worry. So long as people are pay-ing money to see you in my movies, I'm happy as a lark. But you watch your pretty little head now, understand?"

She nodded.

"The people you are playing with," Stroud continued, "they are not children." He shook his head and looked genuinely sad. He stood up and moved to the large window that looked out over his domain. "They come here, girls like you, looking to be in pictures. What some of them will do. They'd be better off staying home. Maybe that's what you should have done."

Zee stood and went to him. "Mr. Stroud, I won't let you down. I am going to make you a hit movie. I promise."

He looked at her. "Why didn't you come to me first? Why'd you get your friend to come here?"

"Would I have gotten the part?"

"Probably not. But I would have kept my good opinion of you."

"You'll have a better opinion when the movie comes out," Zee promised. "They'll be lining up to see it. I'm going to pack them in."

‖ 9 ‖

The day was clear enough to see the ocean all the way from Angeleno Heights. Doyle and Molly sat on a grassy hill, looking west. The red roof of the Arcadia Hotel and the gum trees along Ocean Avenue were plainly visible. White puffs of cloud drifted in a perfect blue sky.

The peaceful scene should have been re-created inside him, Doyle thought. There was every reason for it. But reason was little in evidence as he searched for the right words. He decided that directness was to be preferred.

"I saw Zee," he said.

Molly stiffened slightly. "Oh? And how is she?"

"Prosperous."

"I never thought it would turn out any other way."

He paused and studied her face and knew then how much he wanted Molly's happiness. "I don't want her to come between us."

"Do you think . . . she may?"

"I once asked her to marry me. I want you to know that."

Molly pulled at some grass but said nothing.

"I also want you to know that when I saw her, spoke to her, I knew that I was not in love with her. I thought I still might be. I needed to find that out. I found out."

Molly was silent, her breath melting into the breeze.

He took her hand, held it softly. "And now that you know, do you think we can go on as we are?"

"May I tell you something about Zee?" Molly said.

"Of course."

"There were times I wanted to strangle her."

Doyle laughed. He well understood.

"But she saw me through the tough times. When we had no money, when I was ready to give up and go back to Sacramento, she talked me out of it. She made me a stronger person. And, in a way, she kept me here so I could meet you."

"That's true."

"Zee will always be part of both our lives, but we have a new life now, together. And I want it."

Doyle drew her to him and she rested her head on his chest. The sky and ocean and everything in between filled him in that moment, and he thought for the first time since Alvin's death that the world finally did make sense and that God was in it.

‖ 10 ‖

The feeling of unease wouldn't go away. Zee tried to pass it off as the normal anxieties of the movie business, where every detail had to be cared for. But even as she did, she knew it was false. It was Doyle, the way he'd looked at her. Like he knew something about her she herself did not know.

She drove her Jordan fast up into the hills, the speed giving her some relief. The wind whipping through her hair gave both sound and sensation. She would use speed to do it, to keep clear of the doubts. She would never stop moving and they wouldn't be able to catch her.

Drive hard, drive fast.

She rounded the last curve on Argyle before her house. A black car was at the foot of the drive, blocking it. She screeched to a halt and gave a blast on the horn.

The big man, Fleming, got out. His look froze her. He meant business, and business would follow her if she tried to leave.

"Mr. Norton requests the pleasure of your company," he said. His voice was incongruous with the words, making them absurd and frightening.

"I am very tired. Please express my gratitude to Mr. Norton and—"

"He insists. Said you'd understand. I'll drive."

He drove. Without a word.

Jess Norton had dinner waiting in his private dining room at the Angel Club. For all the silver and candles and fine linen, they might have been at one of the finer restaurants in the city. The windowless room reminded Zee that they were not.

"I wanted us to have a little celebration together," Jess Norton said, raising a glass of champagne. "To your success in landing a role that will make you a big star."

"How thoughtful." Zee was determined to keep her tone light. She was not about to let Norton see that she was livid. That would only give him power over her. "But an invitation would have been even more thoughtful."

"What, didn't Mr. Fleming invite you?"

"Very funny."

"Come on, drink."

"I don't think so tonight. I'm quite tired."

"I insist." He waited for her to pick up her glass.

Zee kept her hands in her lap. "You can drink for both of us."

Norton paused, glared at her, then set his glass on the table. "I find your conduct a little odd, Miss Layne. In light of the fact that you have what you so intently wanted, and that a favor was done for you. That you would be so unsociable is a little surprising for the astute businesswoman I took you for."

"No less surprising than sending a gorilla to fetch me, as if I were some package?"

"But you are." Norton's eyes narrowed for a moment, before he set the glint back in them. "A lovely package."

She heard a commotion outside the door, just before it burst open.

Louise Townsend stood in the doorway, fighting a man in evening clothes who was clutching at her.

"I'm sorry, Mr. Norton—" the man said.

Louise slapped him. "Let go of me!"

"It's all right, Charley," Norton said. "Let her go."

Charley could not get away from Louise fast enough. She staggered into the room.

"Well, what a fine-looking couple. Stay here while I go and fetch my Kodak."

"You're drunk, Louise." Norton's voice was pure ice.

"That's a fine sentiment coming from you. You haven't seen me drunk yet. When I want to get drunk I will and then you will wish it was a hurricane that hit you."

"You'd better go."

"So now you are his favorite," Louise said. She began to laugh.

"Another addition to his stable. He's going to make you eat plenty of hay, dearie."

"Enough!" Norton slammed his hand on the table, rattling the china and silverware.

"You can't get away with this," Louise announced in a loud voice. "I don't care who you are, bootlegger and murderer. You'll see!" She walked unsteadily out the door.

Zee could see red roiling under Norton's skin. His jaw clenched. "Drunk," he said. "Stinking drunk."

Apparently the irony was lost on him. Here he was, the city's leading bootlegger, disapproving of public drunkenness.

"Let's not allow this unpleasantness to spoil our evening," Zee said. "Let's talk about—"

"Don't ever let that happen to you."

"Of course not, Jess. I'd—"

"And another thing."

She waited, her breath quickening.

But then Jess Norton's smile came back as if nothing had happened. "You're right. Let's enjoy our meal, shall we?"

Yes, enjoy a meal, and then get out. Keep the tone light, noncommittal. Skate lightly over the thin ice covering the poisoned water of Jess Norton. She could do it. She could do anything now. The world was hers for the taking, and not even Jess Norton was going to get in her way.

‖ 11 ‖

The building took up most of a city block on Hope Street. It was built with graceful arches and porticoes, and twin structures of thirteen stories each. On the side of the building, painted at the very top, were the words *Bible Institute*.

This was the place where Doyle would find Dr. R. A. Torrey. He simply had to see this man.

But the secretary, a gentle-looking but rock-solid woman, had a different idea. "Dr. Torrey is quite busy. It is his teaching day. Can you possibly come back tomorrow? We will—"

"Let the gentleman in." R. A. Torrey stood in his open doorway.

Rubbing his chin, Doyle entered Torrey's office, where he was offered a chair. Torrey's desk was neat and orderly. A Bible lay open in the middle of it. The preacher sat in his own chair and looked at him with his piercing eyes.

"How may I help you?"

Suddenly, Doyle was in search of words. "I don't know exactly."

"Are you in some sort of trouble?"

"No. I have a girl."

Torrey blinked. "What is your name, young man?"

"Doyle Lawrence. Let me try to explain. I have heard you preach, Dr. Torrey. I have read some of your writing. My girl, her name is Molly, came forward after one of your sermons to profess her faith. I have been reading and studying the Bible, but I can't seem to believe the way she does, and you do."

"Do you have any idea why you cannot so believe?"

Doyle thought a moment. "A book from God should be easy to understand, and the Bible I find difficult to understand."

"I believe the other way round. A book from God, a revelation of His mind and will and character, a book which comes from the infinite God to finite, fallible human beings *should* be difficult to understand. Were it not, I wouldn't trust it to be from an infinite God at all."

This was an entirely different view than Doyle had ever heard.

"The Bible has been attacked for centuries," Torrey continued, "and never more than today. Skeptics, men of science, philosophers, mockers, they are lining up as never before to take a shot at God's Word. Yet not one criticism has defeated the Bible in all that time. Even so, this fact is not enough."

"Enough for what?"

"For faith and fidelity to God's Word. Mr. Lawrence, may I relate to you something of my own experience?"

"Yes, please."

"When I was a young pastor, I went to Germany to study theology. I was particularly influenced by the new criticism of the Bible as taught there. It put me in a state of great bewilderment. I was troubled greatly. One day, walking from class, I came to the realization that the human mind can take any concept and find a way to cast doubt upon it. In that way any fact or belief will unravel. So how can we know anything?"

A very good question, Doyle thought, waiting anxiously for Torrey's answer.

"I brought this before God. I told him in prayer that from this time forward I would accept, by faith, that the Bible was His inerrant, infallible revelation. I would put it to the test. I can tell you one fact that followed. My ministry from that point on took on a power that in no way came from me, that cannot be explained in human terms. Everything that God has graciously done through me, from the hundreds of thousands of souls who responded to the Gospel over a worldwide preaching tour to the establishment of this great institute, has come as a result of this one step of faith."

Doyle pondered this for a moment. "I wish I had such faith."

Torrey spoke softly, but directly. "Faith is the gift of God, Mr. Lawrence, so you should go to Him for it."

"Don't I need faith to do that?"

"Faith the size of a mustard seed is all you need. Then, like the apostles, you can pray that your faith increase. But know this. Faith will not grow without obedience to Christ. Jesus said, 'I am the light of the world. He that followeth me shall not walk in darkness, but shall have the light of life.' The more closely we follow Him, the more our faith will grow. Are you willing to do that, Mr. Lawrence? Are you willing to put God to the test, and obey Him as a result?"

"I don't know!"

"Have you pledged your life and your future to God through Christ?"

"No."

"That is the beginning of all things."

A rock of doubt still sat within Doyle.

"Shall we look at the Bible together?" Torrey said. " 'For faith cometh by hearing, and hearing by the Word of God.' "

‖ 12 ‖

Los Angeles Times
September 15, 1921

Screen Beat
by Tamar Raines

"Hell hath no fury like a woman scorned," wrote the poet. Or was it a studio publicity man? In any event, last night at the Imperial, one could see the truth of the apothegm played out like the best scene in a movie drama.

Stroud-General Studios has decided to cast Taylor Layne, the plucky and popular heroine of the Tallulah *serials, in the plum role of Emma Woodhouse in that studio's upcoming production of the Jane Austen novel. Sure to be a huge hit, in the capable directorial hands of August Osterman, everyone in town (including this reporter) thought that the role would be going to Stroud-General's leading lady, lo these many years, Louise Townsend.*

In point of fact, a release from the studio's publicity department named Miss Townsend as the star, along with Stroud-General stalwart John Raneau. Leading us to ask, what happened?

We don't know. Is it that Miss Layne, in age and appearance, better fits the role of Emma? Miss Townsend, after all, has graduated to more mature roles of late. Could it be that Sy Stroud, studio head, sees greater box office potential in a rising star rather than a falling one? Box office receipts of the last two Townsend vehicles have been less than stellar.

What we do know is that Miss Townsend is not in the least pleased.

The plot, as they say, grows pregnant with portent. We shall keep our ear to the wires.

Zee put the paper down on the table by her pool and sipped her afternoon tea. Poor Louise. Zee almost felt sorry for her. Almost.

For how could she not delight in her current situation? Up here in the Hollywood hills, her dreams coming true?

Down below, the unglamourous workday was winding to a close.

The electric trollies were hauling working folks to Pasadena, San Gabriel, Alhambra, Whittier, and Artesia. Hill Street would be crowded with automobiles and streetcars, pedestrians and police. The hustle and bustle of a city trying to keep up with itself would be like the current of a fast river.

Doyle and Molly were in that river somewhere. For a moment she wondered about them, but only for a moment. They were of another world now. Life went on.

She picked up the paper again and turned to the funny pages. A little laugh would be nice. What were the Katzenjammer Kids up to?

Her maid appeared on the deck. "A young man outside the gate, Miss Layne. He insists on seeing you."

"Doyle Lawrence?"

"He gave his name as Mr. Dillard."

Pete. She had avoided him for weeks. She couldn't keep it up.

"Show him in."

He was dressed in a simple blue work shirt, like someone from the railroad tracks. Zee put a lilt in her voice as she welcomed him.

Pete didn't buy it. "I came to tell you good-bye," he said.

"Good-bye?"

"I'm going east. New York."

"Oh? How delightful. Whatever for?"

"They still make movies back there. I'm going to try to catch on."

"What's wrong with Stroud-General?"

"You."

She was taken aback completely. "Whatever do you mean by that?"

"It means I'm in love with you and can't stand to see what you're doing to yourself."

His directness hit her like a blow. "Oh, Pete, you're being stuffy."

"Am I? Good. Let's hear it for the stuffy people. Only I knew you when you were just trying to get a part in a Happy Sanders movie. What I saw then was a girl who was the brightest light I'd seen in my whole time here. Now I see that light dimming."

Now she was feeling assaulted, and anger started to flare. "Who cares what you think? I am doing quite well, thank you."

"No, you're not. Not when you've got Jess Norton around your neck."

"Norton!"

"There are no secrets in this town, Taylor. You're making a deal with the devil."

"I don't care to hear any more."

Pete put his cap on. "I just had to say my piece. Now I've said it. The rest is up to you."

"That's just the way I want it."

He nodded disdainfully. "I think you do. I'm sorry for you, Taylor."

"Get out, then! Go to New York! Go fall off the world, for all I care."

He began to walk away.

What have I done now? Idiot! Don't let him go!

She clenched her teeth against the thought.

No. No. No.

Zee bit her lower lip, and didn't move, until he was gone.

I don't need anyone. I will not let go of the dream! And I will handle the devil himself if I have to!

And then, without any inner warning, she wept.

❧

It was half past five when Molly came out of Harriman's Department Store.

"Doyle! What are you doing here?" She wore a black skirt and white shirtwaist, looking like the proper store clerk.

"I have to tell you, I have to tell you . . . ."

"Tell me what?"

The air seemed full of promise and peril, all at once, uncertainty and a thing more sure than any he had ever encountered. "I spoke at length with Dr. Torrey yesterday. I went to see him in his office. I had questions about the Bible. His answers made so much sense, more than I'd ever heard. When I walked out of his office, I had confessed the name of Jesus. I am to be baptized tomorrow."

Molly's face opened into a sunshine smile. "Doyle!"

"It's a jump off a cliff, isn't it?"

"He is there to catch you."

He looked down. "You know, Molly, I'm not a good man. I really don't think—"

"Oh, why don't you hush up?"

He looked at her, astonished.

"You have the good of Christ in you now, and that's where you start. You don't have to wonder anymore, be in doubt anymore, live in the past. You have a future now and it is assured. No more talk about being a bad man, all right?"

"If you say so."

"I do."

He nodded. And then she reached for his shirt and pulled him to her, and kissed him. Kissed him on the sidewalk in the midst of all the people and held the kiss. It was a little clumsy but altogether sublime.

When they parted, he was breathless. "Off a cliff indeed," he said.

13

"All right now, everybody settle down," the writer said. His name was Trebor Tate, and he was a longtime Stroud-General writer. He had written the scenario for *Emma*. Now he was trying to get the cast's attention for a read-through of the scenes.

They were gathered around a large table on a shooting stage, with coffee and sandwiches abundantly present before them. Zee munched happily, sitting next to John Raneau, the man who would play George Knightley in the Austen story.

She was, however, a bit confused as to why Tate was leading the discussion without the presence of the director, August Osterman. For one thing, the scenarist was usually the last man consulted after his work was done, even if he was a trusted writer. But certainly the director would be the one to make all of the major decisions regarding acting choices. But never mind. She was on the set of the film that would make her a worldwide sensation. Why should she complain about a writer? There were plenty of others who could do that.

Such as the distinguished English actor Herbert Morris, who would play the part of Mr. Woodhouse, Emma's father. He sat across the table smoking a cigarette and looking generally perturbed.

"I say, Tate," Morris said, "when will the real work begin? I daresay we want to get it right."

Some of the other cast members tittered.

"I will be addressing you for this first meeting," Tate said brusquely. He was a nervous man in his early forties. He rolled and unrolled the photoplay in his hands.

"Where is Osterman?" Morris demanded.

"My understanding is that he is in Mr. Stroud's office right now."

"Then why don't we move this meeting to Stroud's office?"

More laughter from the cast. Zee laughed, too, enjoying the camaraderie that was already developing on the set among the actors.

Tate ignored everyone and simply began to talk. "Now, Emma is the daughter of Mr. Woodhouse, and she is a clever, beautiful girl. She is—"

"Come now, Tate," Morris said. "We've all read the book. We have even read your script."

"I am merely trying to get us all together as I explain—"

"How you have improved on Jane Austen?"

Trebor Tate's cheeks started to take on a rosy glow.

"Come now, Herbert," Zee said. "Let's give him a chance, shall we?"

Morris swung around in his chair to face her. "I say, Miss Layne, whose side are you on? The proud fellowship of the Thespian, or the dull underworld of the writer?"

"I am on the side of this movie," Zee said. "So unless you have a scenario in your pocket, Herbert, what say we let Mr. Tate have his time?"

"Thank you, Miss Layne," Tate said; then he smirked at Morris. "Shall we—"

He was interrupted by the phone ringing on the conference table. He took the handset and listened, jotted some notes. When he finished, he stood up, as if he were going to make a speech. Or a eulogy.

"Ladies and gentlemen," Tate said, "I have some news."

Zee wondered what it could be. A new cast member perhaps? Someone borrowed from another studio? Or . . .

"Mr. Osterman has decided not to direct the picture," Tate explained.

"What!" said Morris. "He was the perfect man for the job. What on earth happened?"

"I am not at liberty to discuss Mr. Osterman's departure at this time," Tate said. "Besides, I don't know all the reasons myself. What I will tell you is that we have three strong candidates who are anxious to take over."

"I want to know their names," Zee said. "I will not work with just anyone."

"Now, now," Tate said, "no need to be concerned. The first is Mr. Walter Gates, who is under contract here."

"A hack!" Morris said.

"Please, hear me out. Another fine choice is Mr. J. James Haney, whose last picture was for Metro."

"Never heard of him!"

Zee patted Morris on the arm. "Herbert, let's postpone judgment."

"Judgment *Day* is more like it. Our acting souls are in jeopardy!"

Tate ignored him, plowing through with a pasted-on smile. "The last name is a very talented director from the New York stage." Tate turned to Zee. "In fact, Miss Layne, he came to Stroud-General Studios with the stated desire to work with you. He arranged a meeting with Mr. Stroud to tell him that he thinks you are the finest actress working in the motion pictures today."

"Well," Zee said with a flush of pride, "that's different. Who is this wonder-worker?"

"His name is Desmond Nichols."

"Never heard of him, either," Morris said. "Taylor, don't you think—" He stopped and clutched her arm. "What's the matter, Taylor? You're white as a ghost."

‖ 14 ‖

Zee practically charged Sy Stroud's receptionist.

"I must see him now," Zee demanded.

"He's in with Mr. Zukor, it's very important and—"

Zee did not wait. Before the startled receptionist could get out of her chair, Zee was in Mr. Stroud's office. A startled Stroud looked up. A rotund, balding man in rimless spectacles turned around in his chair. She recognized him as Adolph Zukor, head of Paramount Studios.

"I need to see you, Mr. Stroud," she said.

"You can see me now," Stroud said angrily, "and you can see I'm talking here. You can go out and wait—"

"This can't wait."

"Dirty laundry?" Zukor said. "Maybe you would like to come and work for me, Miss Layne."

Zee was silent.

Adolph Zukor stood up. "I will be going now. I think our business is complete. You know how to reach me, Miss Layne." He bowed and left the office.

Stroud was beside himself. "Since when do you think you can come in here like any Tom, Dick, or Henry? Eh? I own this studio, not you."

"Why did you hire some hack from Broadway?"

"You are questioning my judgment? I just put you in the role of a lifetime. And now you are coming here to question me about a director? We got a word for that. Chutzpah. That's what you got, lady."

"You don't understand. I can't work with him."

"He just got here. How do you know you can't work with him?"

"I have my reasons."

"Well, I got mine too. You can walk off this picture, if you like, but I'm telling you—"

"That's it, isn't it?"

"Eh?"

"You did this to get me to quit. You want me to quit. You want me to storm off and then you can put Louise back in without getting any blame for it."

"Young lady, your screw is loose. You are seeing things, hearing things. I think maybe you are going a little nutty."

"Well, I am not going to walk off this picture. You heard Mr. Zukor. There are people all over this town who would love to have me work for them."

Sy Stroud was silent, a smoldering silence. "Sit down and wait here." He paused until she sat, then walked out of his office for a moment. Zee tried to calm herself. Had she pushed too far, too hard?

Stroud returned, shaking his head. "What am I gonna do with you, huh? Little girl doesn't even know where Vine Street is, I take her and put her in *Tallulah*. Make her a star. What's she gonna be difficult for?"

"Mr. Stroud, it's not that—"

"Tut! Let me tell you a story. Ten years ago I'm buying a racehorse. Prettiest little filly you ever saw. But oh, what a temper! Could she get mad. I hired a jockey. Could he ride! But my filly, she still has that temper. What am I gonna do?

"I got two choices. I could take a horsewhip to the pretty little filly, or I could get the jockey to talk to her. So I put them in a stall, just the two of them, and told them to talk it over."

"What?"

"And what do you think happened? The jockey, he talked some sense into my little filly, and they became best friends. Won me a million dollars. You like that story?"

Zee cocked her head at him. "That was some *story*, Mr. Stroud."

"Stroud knows a good story." There was a knock at the door. It opened, and Desmond Nichols walked in.

"You wanted to see me?" he said.

Zee jumped to her feet. "What is this?"

"The jockey," Stroud said. "Who she doesn't want to work with." He pointed his finger at her. "Now I'm gonna go get a horsewhip. If you two can't work something out, I'll use it. Now, I will go have a cup of arsenic."

And with that, Stroud left his own office. Zee was unprepared for that. Her heart began to race. Alone with Desmond Nichols. She wondered what she would do if she had a gun.

"It's good to see you, Zee." Nichols took a step toward her.

"Stay there."

He stopped. "Come now, Zenobia Miller of Zenith, Nebraska. You've grown up. You're about to become a big star, just like I told you. Remember?"

"I remember some other things, too. Things that could get a man arrested and thrown into jail."

"You are being harsh."

"I am being harsh? What gall!" She was not going to tell him about their daughter. That was one secret she would take to her grave.

"Water under the bridge," Nichols said. "This is a chance for us to start all over again. You, the bright shining star. And I, the next great director."

"Not on my picture."

"Your picture? Is this your office? Are you running the studio?"

"Don't underestimate me, Desmond."

"Is that a threat?"

"I want you to take yourself out of consideration for *Emma*."

"That I am not inclined to do."

"I can make life very difficult for you here. I know people."

"People like Jess Norton?"

She was taken aback that he knew the name.

"I read the papers," Nichols said. "And I know a lot of people, too. Wouldn't it be interesting for them to find out about your sordid past?"

"You are the only sordid thing in my past."

"Precisely."

His eyes mocked her.

"What would people think about America's new sweetheart when they find out you dallied with men like . . . I shall let you fill in the blank."

"You monster, you—"

"If the papers ever got a hold of that, who knows what that would do to your budding career?"

"They would never believe it."

"Oh no? You remember what the papers did to the late Happy Sanders?"

"I'll let them know all about you, what you did to me."

"Your threats are unbecoming. Be smart. You don't want us both to go down together, do you?"

"You used me once, but now I'm the one who has influence around here. You're just some new director from New York."

"With two hit Broadway plays behind him. That means something, too."

"Get off this lot if you know what's good for you. In fact, leave town. I know people. People who you wouldn't like to meet."

He laughed, and it filled Zee with dread. "We're going to make great pictures together, you and I," he said.

"Never."

"And leave a great legacy for our child."

Zee froze in place.

"By the way," Nichols said, "do I have a daughter or a son?"

‖ 15 ‖

The train pulled into the Zenith station at half past four in the afternoon. Popping his head out the open window, Doyle watched the town approach, and it seemed to watch him back, welcoming him. How different from when he'd arrived the last time, after the war. Now it really did feel like home again.

Molly had been preparing nervously for the last ten miles, nearly breathless. He noticed his own heart beating faster than normal. To see his folks again when so much had changed. Would they notice the difference? He had amends to make, for the brooding presence he'd been the last time he was here. He wanted his father to be proud of him, and his brother to look up to him again. He wanted more than anything that they should warm to Molly, and she to them.

"There he is!"

Gertie's voice. Leaning farther out the window as the train slowed to a stop, Doyle saw his sister jumping on the platform and pointing to him. So much older she looked, in her light blue dress with collar and cuffs, and plaited brimmed hat.

But not as old as the young man with the red hair, standing tall and lean in a blue serge suit. Rusty was nineteen now and looked like his father as a young man.

And then his father and mother, dressed as if to meet a dignitary, with quiet, welcoming smiles.

Doyle waved, shouted, "Hello!" and turned back into the car.

"They're all here," he said.

"How do I look?" Molly smoothed her new, hand-tailored gray crepe de chine dress.

"You couldn't look better."

"I want them to like me, Doyle. Do you think they will?"

"They'll love you." He pulled her gently to her feet and kissed her. "You'll see."

When they stepped off the train it was his father who led the way with affection. He kissed Molly on the cheek and embraced her. The others followed suit, and Doyle reveled in the reception.

His mother had tears on her cheeks when she wrapped her arms around him. "I'm so happy," she said.

He held the embrace. "It's good to be home."

She stepped back, her hands on his shoulders, giving him a full look. Her smile faded a little when she silently traced his scar with her eyes.

"It's all right, Mama," Doyle said gently. "I'm whole again."

‖ 16 ‖

Not even the big man Fleming was going to keep Zee from talking to Jess Norton.

When they were alone in his office, Norton smiled and offered her a chair with a wave of his hand. He was holding a newspaper in his other hand as if it offered some timeless wisdom.

"Now, here's a story that's got me a little perturbed. Listen to this. 'There is much discussion as to the cause of the prevalent wave of brutal crimes.' You hear that? Wave of brutal crimes? That's libel, I would say."

"I haven't come here to talk about—"

Norton put his hand in the air to stop her. "One thing he says here is that abominable bootleg whiskey and homemade liquor promote insanity and crime. Insanity! Then he says crime is a disease, just like insanity, and our treatment of criminals and the insane is altogether wrong. Listen: 'No man can be perfectly sane or kind to his fellowmen when he has a foul colon, constipated bowel, congested liver, and gas pressure on the brain and nerve centers.'" He put the paper down a moment and looked at Zee. "You think I got gas pressure on the brain and nerve center?"

Zee was silent, waiting for him to finish.

Norton slammed his fist on the table. "Answer me!"

The small explosion caused Zee to jump in her seat. She fought for control. "I don't care to answer you," she said. "I want you to answer me."

For a long moment they looked into each other's eyes. Zee refused to allow herself to blink.

"That's what I always liked about you," Norton said finally. "Also what I don't like. You got that spark that makes for movie stars but makes life miserable for the people around you. I'm the kind of guy that doesn't like to be miserable. Now, suppose you tell me why you're here."

"I want to know what you have to do with Stroud-General Studios."

"That's my business. Why should I share that information with you?"

"Because I want to know."

"That's not good enough."

"Why not?"

"One thing you've got to understand about business. It's a give-and-take proposition. What have you ever done for me? You wanted the role of Emma. You got it. What did you give me back? Now you think you can come in here and throw your weight around, what there is of it, because you're going to be a big star?"

"I never intended to throw any weight around."

"Don't hand me that. You tried it the first night I saw you. And you've been trying ever since. Admit it."

"Jess, I never—"

"Admit it!"

His voice shocked her again. "All right. I'm sorry for barging in here like this."

Norton waited a moment, then smiled. "That's more like it. How about a drink?"

"I don't think so."

"Let's have a drink together. Get back on the right footing." He went to the small bar in his office and Zee let him go. She would have to go along with him if she was going to get what she wanted. He came back with two glasses, handed her one. He clinked them together and she took a sip. It was some sort of Scotch with soda, heavy on the Scotch.

"Now," Norton said as he took his chair behind the desk, "what is it that Jess Norton can do for Emma?"

"How much influence do you really have over Sy Stroud?"

"Let's just say Mr. Stroud and I have a mutually beneficial arrangement. He likes happy movie stars; I have ways to keep them happy. And I don't talk. For that Mr. Stroud listens to my advice every now and then."

"Did you have anything to do with changing the director?"

Norton shook his head. "I don't know anything about it. You have a new bird on the set?"

"Someone I don't care to work with."

"And you thought I might be able to pull some strings, huh?"

"Something like that."

Norton took a long drink. His eyes were shadowy, yet alive with a sinister glow. A panther's eyes. "I'm always willing to do a friend a favor."

Zee felt a rush of relief, but tinged with fear of the unknown. "Thank you, Jess. His name is Desmond Nichols and—"

"And in return you will do me a favor."

She waited.

"I would like the pleasure of your company tonight. A quiet dinner at my place."

She knew exactly what that meant.

"Why, Jess, how nice of you to invite me, but I have—"

"I'll expect you at eight."

"I'm sorry, but I have so much work to do before tomorrow."

"Don't play me for a fool. It wouldn't be wise."

She had to get out. Now. "Let's just call the whole thing off. I don't want your help."

"You've already got it."

Heart pounding, Zee said, "The price is too high."

"Don't think you can just walk out that door."

"That's exactly what I'm going to do."

She did, but with fear following.

‖ 17 ‖

It was good to have another meal in the homestead, one that was full of life and laughter and good talk. His father still lit up the after-dinner cigar, holding court over the family discussion. Doyle wanted Molly to get the full effect of the Lawrence family, and she was.

"Was only in Los Angeles once," Mr. Lawrence said, "and that was enough for me. People seemed a little too nervous out there. Is that where you're planning to set down your roots?"

"Yes, Dad. I'll continue my law studies with Mrs. Fox and stand for the bar."

Mr. Lawrence looked at Molly. "Think you can stand being married to a lawyer?"

"This one I can," she said.

"We're all insufferable at times," Mr. Lawrence insisted. "Nitpicking at this point or that. If he does that, give him a good swift kick."

"I'll keep that in mind, Mr. Lawrence."

"Tell us about Taylor Layne," Rusty piped. This drew a rebuking look from both Mr. and Mrs. Lawrence. Rusty's cheeks reddened. "I was only—"

"It's all right," Molly said. "I know all about Doyle and Zee. And yes, Taylor Layne is a real movie star."

"And to think she came from our town!" Gertie said. "What's she like?"

"There's still a lot of Zee in her," Doyle said. "Maybe more than ever. Say, what's become of her father?"

Mr. Lawrence frowned. "We heard that he stopped his preaching. Haven't heard much more."

"He's not seen much these days," Mrs. Lawrence said.

"He went loony," Gertie chimed, drawing a harrumph from her father. "Well, he has!"

"As you can see," Doyle said to Molly, "Gertie has inherited the famous Lawrence directness."

Mrs. Lawrence decided it was time to go through the family photographs, much to the chagrin of Rusty and Gertie. And Doyle, too, who at five years old had sported curls that would have made Little Lord Fauntleroy blush with shame.

⁂

"She's the cat's pajamas," Rusty said.

"I think so," said Doyle.

It was just like old times, sharing the room again, lying on their beds and talking as the moonlight streamed in through the window.

"When you're married and all, can I come out and stay with you in Los Angeles?"

"Stay?"

"I'm thinking of trying for the movies."

"Why would you do that? You've got a good job working for the bank. You're making five bucks a week, regular pay. Why would you throw that away for the screwy movies?"

"I don't want to work in a stuffy old bank all my life. I want to have adventures, like you."

"Believe me, you don't want to have the same adventures. Find yourself a good girl and settle down to a peaceful existence."

"What's it like, Los Angeles? They say it's got sun all the time and you can reach out your window and pick oranges if you want to."

"It's got sun and it's got darkness, just like any other place. A lot of the people out there seem to run as fast as they can so something chasing them can't catch up."

"Have you been to a gin mill yet?"

Doyle propped himself up on his side. "Where'd you hear about gin mills?"

"Come on, Doyle, I'm no rube. I read things. What are they like?"

The image of Jess Norton and Thorn Fleming befouled Doyle's mind. "They're run by no-goods, don't ever kid yourself. Guys who'd just as soon kill you as look at you. I'm going to put one of them out of business, for good."

"What're you gonna do? You gonna bump him off?"

"Calm down. I'm going to use the law."

"Ahh."

"Ahh yourself. Now let's say prayers and get some sleep."

"Prayers? We never used to say prayers."

"We do now, sport."

He got off the bed and knelt beside it, waiting for Rusty to do the same.

18

"All right, everyone!" Trebor Tate cheeped on the set. "Attention!"

Zee was already listening, arms folded, on the edge of her seat.

"Today is our first walk-through with our new director, Mr. Desmond Nichols! Let's welcome him, shall we?" Tate beat his hands together like hummingbird wings. The rest of the cast joined him in polite applause. Zee did not.

Nichols, dressed ostentatiously in riding breeches and boots like some Eric von Stroheim imitator, bowed. "Thank you all so much." He smiled and looked at Zee. "Thank you for your acceptance and willingness to work with me. I know we are going to become one big happy family."

He began to pace in front of the actors. "I have two shows currently running on Broadway, one starring Laurette Taylor."

"Impressive," Herbert Morris said.

"And I hope to do with *Emma* what I have done on Broadway, by creating a great big hit for us all to enjoy."

Some grunts and nods. Zee was only half aware of them. The other half of her was boiling. There was no way she would be able to do this. She sensed Desmond Nichols laughing at her inside himself. His posturing and jaunty smile sickened her.

"Now, down to business. I trust we have all familiarized ourselves with Mr. Tate's superb photoplay."

Tate smiled and nodded in gratitude.

Nichols opened his copy of the script. "Let us discuss the characterizations, shall we?"

The other actors reached for their copies. Zee remained motionless.

"First, our central character," Nichols said, "to be played by the lovely and talented Miss Taylor Layne."

"Bravo," Herbert Morris said.

Zee, ready to ignite, squeezed the arms of her chair.

"Emma is the daughter of Mr. Woodhouse, and sister to Isabella," Nichols said. "She is rich, she is clever, and she is a beauty. She can be quite caring, as with her father." He paused and once again looked at Zee. "Of course, she can be a snob, too. It is that aspect of the character that we shall explore. Quite interesting, and full of depth. Now, shall we move on to consider Mr. Woodhouse?"

"I don't think we shall." Zee practically leaped out of her chair. She heard Morris utter a disapproving grunt, but ignored him. "If you think that I am going to play Emma as a snob, you're sadly mistaken."

Stunned silence on the set. Trebor Tate was the first to break it. "Miss Layne, that is what the novel itself—"

"What do you have to say about it? It's the director's choice and he is not going to do it that way. Isn't that right, Mr. *Nichols*?" She drew out his name derisively.

"You have nothing to fear," Nichols said, smiling broadly. "You and I are going to do great work together."

"We shall do no work together until we agree on Emma's characterization."

Herbert Morris slapped the arms of his chair. "Stop being petulant, girl."

"Listen to your elders, Miss Layne," Nichols said.

The sound of his voice and the look of him, these were flame and fuse to her, and that was when she exploded. She let the rage have full force within her, and it was as if her body had a will of its own. She was aware of grabbing the chair and throwing it, and her screams. But it was almost like watching a performance.

And when the performance was over she thought, *You've really done it now.*

‖ 19 ‖

The next day was a tour of Zenith in Father's grand new Lincoln. With the top down, Mr. Lawrence gave Molly a running commentary about the history of the town, all the way back to frontier days. Then it was back to the house, where Mrs. Lawrence took Molly into the kitchen for a lesson in the domestic sciences.

With a couple of hours to himself, Doyle went for a walk to the other side of town, to the street where Zee Miller had lived. To the house where she had grown up.

Doyle paused outside the house. Its gray paint was now faded and the yard overgrown with weeds. The gate was falling off its hinges. Doyle let himself through carefully and approached the front door. The shades in all the windows were drawn.

Doyle's first knock was unanswered.

He tried again, heard a shuffling inside.

Then the door slowly opened.

Doyle tried not to let his face register shock. The Reverend Miller had aged twenty years. His eyes were heavy-lidded, his skin gaunt, his thinning hair entirely gray.

"Hello, Reverend Miller. I'm Doyle Lawrence."

The tired eyes looked at him closely. "Lawrence?"

"Yes, sir."

"Oh yes. It's been quite some time."

"Yes, sir."

"What is it . . . I may do for you?"

"I've been in Los Angeles, sir. I'm home for a visit." Doyle smelled the musty insides of the house. "Might I come in?"

Miller hesitated. "I'm not prepared to entertain at the moment."

"It's about your daughter."

Reverend Miller stiffened as if startled by an ominous noise. "My—" He stopped, looking unsteady on his feet.

Instinctively Doyle grabbed Miller's arm. "Come outside, get some air."

Miller offered no resistance. Doyle led him to a wooden chair on the porch. Miller slouched into it.

"Zenobia . . ." he muttered.

"She's in Los Angeles. She's gotten into the movies."

"Los Angeles? Movies?"

"Imagine that, huh? A Nebraska girl."

"You've spoken with her?" His eyes were anxious now, searching.

"Yes."

"How . . . is she?"

"She lives in a very nice house in Hollywood. I will give you the address. Maybe you'd like to write her. She looks well." Doyle battled for the right words, doubtful about her being at all well.

A long silence ensued. Doyle looked out toward the street, letting the man gather his thoughts. This must have been quite a shock to him after all this time. When he turned back he saw tears on Reverend Miller's cheeks.

"Oh, sir, I'm sorry . . ."

Miller put his hand on Doyle's arm. "Forgive me."

"No need."

"There is. I lost her. God forgive me."

And with no doubt whatsoever, Doyle said, "He has."

The words seemed to take Reverend Miller by surprise, as if unexpected coming from Doyle.

"I heard you preach once, Reverend Miller. I don't think you know that. I sat in the back of your church. I still remember clearly that you held the Bible in one hand and preached about Jesus dying and our need to be forgiven for our sins. I didn't like it then. But now I see it in a different light. And I know that you were being faithful to your calling and that God never stops forgiving His children."

With a heavy breath Reverend Miller said, "But I failed. I failed my daughter. I drove her away." He bowed his head and added, "If only I could see her one more time."

"Of course you can."

Miller shook his head. "She won't desire it."

"I'll arrange it."

"Can you?"

"I'll try, sir. I think I can convince her."

"I pray for her. I have ever since she left me. I pray that it will be well with her soul, that she would find her way back to her heavenly Father, even if her earthly father never sees her again."

"Yes," Doyle said. "It will be so. The Bible says, 'The fervent prayer of a righteous man availeth much.'"

A tiny spark of hope came to Reverend Miller's face. And it was that look Doyle kept with him as he returned home, taking the long route past the ironworks and railroad depot.

‖ 20 ‖

Zee was in a foul mood when she arrived at John Raneau's palatial home on Adams Street. There was a parking attendant taking cars, but she would not let anyone near her Jordan Playboy. She parked it where she pleased and marched into the festive atmosphere as if she were a queen looking for a retinue.

She was dressed in a royal blue chiffon velvet coat with fur collar and cuffs. With it she wore a hat of black panne velvet, the brim rolled jauntily up one side. It was an attention grabber, and that was, after all, why one attended such Hollywood soirees.

Zee immediately tossed her coat to a maid, revealing her silver dress with hem and tassels just below the knee. Then she grabbed a glass of champagne from a tray in the hands of a servant and immediately looked around at the faces.

She was greeted by various players, and she laughed and tossed her head back at all the hellos. She moved along to the beat of the music provided by the orchestra, floating through the party, wondering who she would be talking to for most of the evening.

It turned out to be Herbert Morris, not the one she would have guessed.

"And how is our star this evening?" Morris asked, taking her arm and guiding her to a less populated part of the home. They stopped in a grand hallway.

"Why shouldn't I be anything but lovely?" Zee said.

"Because there is trouble afoot."

"Trouble?" Zee said.

"And I fear there is more to come."

"Whatever do you mean, Herbert?"

Morris finished the champagne in his own glass, and Zee did the same with hers.

"Don't do it, my dear," he said.

"Do what?"

"Become a temperamental child actress. You'll last much longer if you comport yourself with grace and dignity, patience and respect. We are actors. Directors are paid to bring in a completed show, and we are the cattle that help him to do it. If you go along with directors, you will have more work, and more opportunity to shine."

Zee waved at another servant, also carrying a tray of champagne, and she and Morris replaced their empty glasses with those filled with fresh bubbly. For a flash of a moment Zee heard the voice of her father warning of the evils of drink. She shut it off by saying, "I know exactly how to shine."

Morris shook his head. "I was once in a production of *Antony and Cleopatra* with a young actress of exceeding promise. This was her first role of note, her big chance. She was difficult from the start. I found it hard to look her in the face, which made the love scenes a bit difficult. In any event, the show went on and the reviews were tepid. This actress blamed everyone but herself. No one wished to work with her after that. In this small world of theater where we toil, word travels fast. Bad news travels fastest. I don't want to see that happen to you."

"Can anyone ever really be free?" Zee said. "I mean, can an actress or an actor ever truly be unencumbered by charlatans?"

"An actor should not desire to be unencumbered. This is a collaborative art. We need the help of others. Don't be so foolish as to think you never need someone else's help."

"Help, help, help. Why does everyone think I need help? Am I some little nobody around here? I am the star of *Emma*!" She threw back her champagne. The bubbles burned her throat. She coughed a little of it onto her chin.

"Slow down," Morris said. "You don't want to be a sloppy drunk, whatever else stardom brings."

She was about to utter a rejoinder when a disturbing thought burst in her brain.

I am Louise Townsend.

Horrified, she found she was unable to say a word. And then she heard Jess Norton's voice behind her. "Sage advice from Mr. Morris."

Turning, she saw Norton standing there with a full glass of champagne in his hand.

Morris grunted noncommittally, and took the opportunity to slip away.

"You can thank me for rescuing you later," Norton said.

"Rescuing me?"

"You were making a fool of yourself with Morris. That's not smart."

"Would you rather I make a fool of myself with you?"

"Certainly. When will you try it?"

"Then give me something to drink." Zee practically grabbed the champagne from him and nearly drained it.

"You are in your cups, aren't you?"

"Why not? I want to forget all this."

"All what?"

She waved her arm. "I had the most dreadful time on the set today, no thanks to you."

Amused, Norton said, "I wasn't anywhere near the set, as I recall."

"Stop it, you know what I mean." Zee finished the champagne, her head starting to feel warm.

"You wanted some help with this director, wasn't that it? Did I not make it plain to you I would help?"

"Bosh." She put her hand to her head.

"Here, what's wrong?"

"Go away."

Norton took her arm and started walking her down the hall.

She tried to pull away, but he held her fast. "What do you think you're doing?"

"Stroud may show up. You want him to see you this way?"

"I don't care about Stroud. I don't care about you. Leave me alone."

"You're coming with me. You may not care about your career, but I do."

He tried to take the empty champagne flute from her. She threw it to the floor. It shattered.

"Still a stubborn fool," Norton said, pulling her along. Zee stumbled and nearly fell. Norton wouldn't allow it.

He pulled her into a dark room. Only light from the hall illuminated it. What she saw in the light was fuzzy, but it looked like a rack with several rifles mounted on one wall, and a stuffed head of some beast with horns above that. What sort of room was this?

The next thing she knew she was in a chair—thank goodness it was soft—and Norton was in front of her. She smelled his cologne.

"You sit here and sober up. I'm going to get you some coffee. You understand me?"

Sitting down made the dizziness more pronounced. She didn't know if she could move, even if she wanted to. She thought she would get sick for certain. "Yes," she muttered. "Coffee."

He left, closing the door, leaving her in pleasant darkness. She could hear the party going on in the main part of the house. Music and laughter and voices. Her stomach roiled and she stayed still, and silently pledged she would never drink again.

You were right about that, Papa. The evils of drink. I'm evil and I'm drunk and I deserve this.

So drunk . . .

Fool . . .

Jess . . . will I ever be rid of him?

She didn't know how long it was that her thoughts reeled around randomly; it might have been five minutes or an hour. Her head continued to swirl, faster and faster. She was blotted, all right, way beyond what she should have been.

Light streamed into the room.

"Jess?" Her voice was thick and tired. "Coffee . . ." No answer. The door closed, engulfing her in darkness once more. "I can't see you."

She felt his hands on her arms, lifting her.

"No, let me stay." She could barely manage the words now.

She was on her feet and fell against his chest. Now she really was dependent on him. How well he played his hand. Watched her drink, watched her get drunk, found a way to use it, to remind her how much he was in control of any situation.

She no longer had the will to resist him. When he lifted her head and put his mouth on hers, she let him. She gave into it.

And did not smell his cologne. The acrid scent was of soap and tobacco.

It was not Jess Norton kissing her.

With the little strength she had, she pushed away, knocking against a table. Then the man was at her again, grabbing her, forcing himself.

The world spun faster and she knew she was powerless, that she could not stop him.

"Don't fight it," the man said, and she recognized the voice.

Desmond Nichols pressed his mouth on hers, grunting like an animal.

‖ 21 ‖

"What's wrong, Doyle?"

Doyle and Molly stood on the corner of Main and Third, the hub of Zenith's downtown. It was their last week here and they had been enjoying a sunny morning walk.

"I'm sorry, what?"

"Where were you just then, the moon?"

No. He had been in Los Angeles, unable to keep his mind off the case he was trying to build against Jess Norton. Witnesses were hard to come by. Norton's reach was vast. There had to be a way to bring him down.

"I'm sorry," he said.

She kissed him.

"We'll cause a scandal," he said happily.

"I know."

Doyle looked around at the buildings, the streets. So much quieter and more modest than Los Angeles. No Jess Norton here.

"Molly, what would you say about living right here in Zenith?"

"Is that what you want?"

"I could join my father's firm. We could raise a family. It's not a bad place to have roots."

"You did well by it."

"And with the price of houses in Los Angeles. Four thousand for something halfway decent."

"Are you sure? Are you sure there aren't too many . . . memories?"

He took her by the shoulders and faced her. "Are you still thinking of Zee?"

She tried to hide it in her face, but he could read it there.

"Listen, Molly. You're the only woman for me. I can't make it any plainer than that. Except maybe by creating more scandal."

He brought her to him and kissed her.

They walked hand-in-hand down Main. *This is the feeling of pieces falling into place at last,* Doyle thought. God was yet mysterious, but since his confession of Jesus in Torrey's office that day, God had seemed to shower blessings. Molly, a sense of direction and hope. He was not about to let that go.

They stopped momentarily in front of the drugstore. The window sign had a smiling woman asserting that *Women who first are attracted to Holeproof Hosiery by its lustrous, sheer appearance are pleasantly surprised—wearing it—to find that its charming beauty is matched by unusually long service.*

Doyle picked up the morning edition of the *Zenith Herald.*

"What's the news?" Molly asked.

"Low harvest this year," Doyle said. "Oh, and a fire yesterday out at the old Tomlin place. And the new waterworks is pumping along nicely."

"How exciting."

He laughed as he turned the paper over. "If I didn't know you better, I would think you were being a bit—"

He froze, staring at the right-hand side of the page.

STUNNING HOLLYWOOD MURDER

Director Desmond Nichols Found Shot to Death at Home of Star, John Raneau
Taylor Layne Held as Suspect

Molly tugged his sleeve. "What is it?"

Doyle couldn't answer. His eyes swept over the story.

> *Taylor Layne, the star of the* Troubles of Tallulah *serials, has been arrested and charged with murdering director Desmond Nichols. The Hollywood murder allegedly took place last Saturday night at the home of film star John Raneau.*
>
> *The shocking crime is another in a series of scandalous news out of movie land. . . .*

"Doyle, please tell me what it is."

His voice distant and hollow, Doyle muttered, "It's Zee. She's been arrested for murder." He looked at her, saw the shock in her eyes. He held the paper up so she could read the story.

"We have to go back," she said.

"You mean that?"

"She'll need us. She'll need us badly."

‖ 22 ‖

Zee's head felt like a log that had been expertly split in two with an ax. The rest of her was in a whirling nightmare.

Harper Vaughn, her lawyer, sat with her in the cell. He was impeccably dressed, with a white carnation in the lapel of his coat. He smoked a cigarette, occasionally flicking ashes on the cell floor.

"Please try to concentrate," he said again. "I know it is quite traumatic for you, but I'm going to help you."

"Why am I still in here?"

"The judge is considering our bail motion. The D.A. is asking that it be a hundred thousand dollars. I argued that you should be released on your own recognizance. You are no threat to flee." He paused, puffed his cigarette, then added, "Are you?"

"Of course not. Has anyone come forward who knows what happened?"

"That's what we're trying to determine. Don't you remember anything about Saturday night?"

She rubbed her temples. "Somebody hit me in the head with a sledgehammer."

"You were passed out from alcohol when they found you."

"I didn't have that much to drink."

"The doctor who examined you thought otherwise."

"What of it? I didn't commit murder!"

"Of course, if you were drunk, that means you were not in the proper state of mind when you shot Nichols."

"I didn't shoot anybody! Can't you get that through your head?"

"If you don't know what happened, how can you be certain you didn't do the shooting?"

Fear swept through her. He was right. What if she did shoot Desmond Nichols?

"The last thing in my mind," she said, "is that Desmond was kissing me, pawing me. Then I couldn't breathe. Then I don't remember anything."

"You were in a room that held guns. Raneau is a gun collector. Perhaps you grabbed the murder weapon and shot him, in self-defense."

"But I didn't shoot!"

"The gun was found in your hand."

"How is that possible?" She tried to recreate the scene in her mind.

Harper Vaughn tossed his cigarette to the floor and crushed it with his shoe. "That is the question a jury will be asking, and we must find an answer."

What answer? None came to mind, only a bitter fact. Taylor Layne—who just a day ago was ready to pack the theaters for Sy Stroud, to ride *Emma* to the top of the movie world—was now suspected of murder.

Oh, Happy, you told me, you told me.

How had it happened? The descent, the taking away of it all?

Desmond Nichols, dead, shot. By her?

Why couldn't she remember?

And now her fate was no longer in her own hands, but in the briefcase of a lawyer, and in the publicity releases Lytell was sending out. These were not for her benefit, she knew. It was for Stroud, who was trying to protect his investment.

You thought you could do it on your own, didn't you, and now you can't do a thing! You could wind up in prison for the rest of your life. . . .

The thought shot her out of the cell, out of the dismal surroundings, back through time, back to Zenith, the warm sun of summer. She smelled the grass and heard the river. She was barefoot in the river, the water swooshing up her legs as she laughed. She was unconquerable.

If only she could go back, start over. Do things differently. Or was she destined to this end from the start?

Reprobate . . .

‖ 23 ‖

When they finally reached Los Angeles, Doyle and Molly took a cab directly to the First Street law office of Kit Shannon Fox. She was seeing a client to the door, a widow whose estate Mrs. Fox was putting in order.

"Welcome back, you two," she said. "I thought you weren't expected for another week."

"Taylor Layne," Doyle said. "She's been arrested. For murder."

"Yes, it's all over the papers."

"Her real name is Zee Miller. She's a friend. I knew her back home. Molly lived with her for a time, before the movies. Do you know if she's still in jail?"

"Bail was granted. Preliminary hearing is next."

Doyle shook his head. "I've been going nuts trying to figure this out," he said. "I don't see how Zee could have done this. It's not in her."

"I can only go on what I've read in the papers," Mrs. Fox said. "But there is a question about her mental state. Apparently she'd had a great deal to drink, and under the influence of alcohol anything is possible."

All too possible, Doyle thought. "Is there some way we can help her?"

"She has a lawyer, Harper Vaughn."

"Do you know him?"

Mrs. Fox nodded. "He's good. Works for the studios. Has gotten stars out of trouble before."

"I'll try to see her," Doyle said. "Convince her to have you represent her. Would you be willing?"

"She already has counsel, Doyle. That would be unethical."

"Isn't there anything we can do?"

Mrs. Fox thought a moment. "Present yourselves to Harper Vaughn as character witnesses. Maybe he can use you. It's certain she can use your friendship about now. The wolves in the press are out in force."

And the wolves were gathered outside Zee's home on Argyle when Doyle and Molly arrived. Doyle parked the Model T two blocks away, unable to get any closer, and the two walked up to the crowd of perhaps fifty people. A number of police at the gate gave the unmistakable signal that no one would be allowed to pass.

Doyle threaded through the assemblage, Molly close behind, listening to voices giggling and gossiping.

"Bet she's in there drinking up a storm."

"She's John Raneau's lover, you know."

"Isn't this terribly exciting?"

The first cop he came to was large enough to mistake for a wall.

"My name's Doyle Lawrence. I work for Kit Shannon Fox, the lawyer."

"So?"

"I'm a friend of Zee . . . Taylor Layne's. I want to offer my help."

The cop shook his head. "Sorry."

"Surely you can tell her I'm out here. With Molly Pritchard. Tell her that."

"I'm not a messenger service. Talk to her lawyer, Harper Vaughn."

"She will want to see me. Believe me—"

"Move along now. You want to stand around with the rest of these crazy people, that's your business. But twenty feet away from the gate."

"I'm not crazy—"

"Go on."

Doyle walked Molly to the edge of the crowd. "I need to get inside."

"But the police."

"Go back to Mrs. Fox's office. If I get arrested, arrange for bail."

"Arrested?"

He kissed her quickly. "Hurry." He ran up Argyle Avenue.

Zee's home backed up onto a hill, which scaled upward into a thick mass of eucalyptus trees and wild grass. By approaching from well up on the hillside, Doyle made his way to the rear of Zee's house. But the wall around the perimeter stood at eight feet or so. The question now was how to get over the wall.

There was but one possibility—a eucalyptus just outside the wall.

It would not be an easy climb, but if he could make it he'd be able to drop into the backyard.

He'd come this far, and so began his ascent. As he did he remembered that day in the park when Zee had climbed the tree. How exceedingly strange to be here now, climbing up a tree outside Zee's own backyard, the backyard of a movie star and possible murderer.

Doyle almost slipped off the wall when he recalled the admonition of his grandfather. *"Climb with your hands, not your feet."* He felt along with his hands, carefully testing grabbing areas before making a commitment. In this way he made it to the edge of the wall, still unseen. So far as he knew.

He rested a moment and looked through the foliage toward the house. He saw nothing. No one inside or out. Now was the time. He dropped into the yard with all the grace of a falling rock.

Slowly, so as not to draw attention, Doyle made his way to the house. A single orange tree stood in the middle of the yard, with a trunk that would hardly serve as a hiding place. He squatted behind it anyway, feeling foolish, but again unseen.

Now he could see through one of the French doors. A man in a suit passed by, talking to someone.

Doyle considered just knocking on the door. But if he did that, some underling might give him a rebuff. Maybe he should just walk right in. Surely Zee would want to see him.

Or so he hoped.

He stood and took his first tentative step past the orange tree.

"Hold it!"

Doyle knew, even before he turned, that it was a cop. This one was relatively young, but clearly anxious. Eyes excited, like he'd just captured the worst criminal in Los Angeles, he held a gun on Doyle. The gun shook in his hand.

"Don't move!" the cop said.

"It's not what you think." Doyle knew that sounded lame and wasn't surprised when the cop ordered him to walk out a side gate with his hands on his head.

❧

The jail cell where they took him looked like the same one he'd been tossed in his first day in Los Angeles. Then he'd been a hopeless derelict. Jail had seemed the natural place for him, a cage for a wounded animal. Whether he got out or not, lived or died, was of little concern to him. He was alone in the world.

How different it was now. Now he knew he was not alone.

They left him in the cell for nearly two hours, not letting him place a call to Mrs. Fox. Finally, a jailer showed up and unlocked his cell.

Doyle stood. "Am I being released?"

"Come with me and don't say a word."

He followed the guard up the stairs to the jail's main floor. They headed down another hall and stopped at a wooden door. The guard opened it and nodded for Doyle to go inside.

Where he saw District Attorney Fallon waiting for him.

"Mr. Lawrence, do you want to explain your bumbling about?"

What was Fallon doing here? "Am I being charged with a crime?"

"Don't tempt me."

"Am I free to go?"

"Not at the moment. I am aware of your friendship with Taylor Layne, but I advise you to keep your nose out of this case."

"Yes, I'm a friend, and that's why I went to see her. There's no crime in that."

"There may be."

"What are you getting at?"

"You have another friend in town, Jess Norton."

"What's Norton got to do with it?"

"He is mixed in with Taylor Layne somehow. And he's dangerous."

"You don't have to tell me how dangerous. That's why I'm trying to stop him."

"Stop trying."

"Why?"

"Because people are going to end up hurt."

"I'm not afraid of him."

"It's not you I'm concerned with. You went to see a potential witness, one Handley."

"Handley. He said he might be willing to testify against Norton. Said he would come to you."

"He never made it."

Doyle's jaw tightened. "Where is he?"

"They found him in his car on the old dirt road in the Cahuenga Pass. He had two bullets in his chest."

"Norton."

"We'll examine the bullets, but we won't find the gun. I am as certain as I am of anything that Norton was behind it. But that's not the kind of certainty that's evidence in a court of law. You follow?"

"Surely you can bring him in for questioning."

"We have in the past. He is one tough nut. Unless I have something to connect him, in some way—"

"We've got to find something."

"Not we, Lawrence. That's what I'm trying to tell you. Leave this alone, you hear me? I don't want to deal with more corpses than I have to."

‖ 24 ‖

Handley's murder consumed Doyle well into the night. His apartment seemed even smaller than it was, as concerns closed in upon him. Norton had raised the stakes significantly. Now what?

In light of Fallon's warning, would he simply have to sit back and wait for something to happen? Watch things unfold from the sidelines? No, not possible. He had to do *something*.

He tried to pray but his mind wandered. He opened his Bible at random, and his eyes fell upon the verse, *"And he cast down the pieces of silver in the temple, and departed, and went and hanged himself."*

No help there. He opened his window to let in some air, heard the sound of car horns on the street and shouts of a paperboy hawking a late edition of the *Examiner*.

And then a knock on his door. At this hour?

He hesitated. Another knock, louder this time. "Mr. Lawrence?"

Doyle said nothing.

"May I speak with you, sir?"

The voice sounded cold and phony. And that was when Doyle knew it was one of Norton's men.

Another knock.

Without another thought Doyle raced through the open window and out to the fire escape. The night was cold. Doyle scampered down the three stories and let the ladder lower him to the street.

Which way to go? Was there another man waiting for him out here? At least there were some people around, on the sidewalk, giving an eye to the man who had seen fit to escape a building that was not on fire.

Doyle headed uptown, walking fast.

"Doyle!"

He jumped. The voice came from a black sedan parked on the street. A woman's voice.

"Doyle, please."

Doyle looked in the window. Zee was inside, a black scarf flowing around her head.

"Zee, what are you doing here?"

"Get in."

"Was that your man up there?"

"My driver."

"He's probably still knocking on my door."

"Get in, Doyle. Please." She opened the door.

"Zee, I tried to see you."

"I know. That's why I've come." Her face was framed by the scarf, making her look like a frightened girl peeking out from behind a curtain. "Doyle, you don't believe I murdered him, do you?"

"Of course not. I know you never could have done that."

She shook her head. "Then you don't know me at all. Because I could have, Doyle. I'm capable of it. I can't remember what happened. I could have killed him. I hated him."

"But why?"

She closed her eyes. "Remember the day you left Zenith for college? I watched you go on the train."

"I know. I saw you."

"It changed me, I know it did. Your leaving took something out of me that I didn't fully understand. I ran away, to Omaha, where I met Desmond Nichols. I thought I was in love with him. He said we were to be married. We never were. He ran out on me. And I had a child."

Doyle's heart pounded as he searched for words that did not come.

Zee's driver put his face to the window, looking surprised to see Doyle sitting inside the sedan.

"Give us a few minutes," Zee said. The driver frowned and walked away.

"Doyle, listen to me. I have a daughter. Her name is Isabel. She's in a convent orphanage, in San Fernando. Oh, Doyle, she's a lovely girl . . ."

He took her hand. "You'll get through this. I'll help you; Molly will. Whatever it takes."

"Whatever it takes? Do you mean that?"

"Of course I do."

"Then marry Molly and take Isabel to be your own. And quickly."

"But you're her mother, you—"

"No, Doyle. I am not fit to be a mother. You know that. You know how selfish I am. And now I might go to prison. I cannot be a mother to a child, but Molly can. I want her to grow up with you as her father, Doyle. And with Molly as her mother." Tears in her eyes reflected the soft glow of the streetlight. "Do this for me. It's the one thing I can do, something right for a change. I haven't done something right for a long time. I'm lost, I'm . . ."

"Zee—"

"Tell me you'll do it." She squeezed his hand. "Tell me."

"All right."

She sighed with relief.

"And now I must tell you something," Doyle said. "And you must listen to me. The papers say you have been seen with Jess Norton, the bootlegger."

"Yes."

"You must steer clear of him, Zee."

"I know that."

"He may have murdered a man named Handley. I've been looking for witnesses to swear out a criminal complaint against him and Handley was one of them, and—"

"Doyle, it's you who must steer clear. I know what he's capable of."

"We both know him, then."

Zee let her head fall back against the seat. "It's all such a mess, isn't it? Not like when we were kids. Not like when we were dreaming together. All such a mess."

"I thought it was," he said. "A hopeless mess. But I don't believe that anymore."

She turned to look at him.

"Listen, Zee. I want to tell you something I didn't know before, didn't understand. About the mercy of God. The real meaning of it—"

"I'm glad for you, Doyle, that you've found religion."

"It's not that at all. Finding religion is not what I'm talking about. I'm talking about being the found one."

Zee looked out the car window. "My father used to say that there are those who are chosen by God and those who are rejected. The elect and the reprobate. And there's nothing you can do about it. I'm reprobate, Doyle. I always have been."

"Don't believe that. Jesus died for the sins of the whole world. Listen! 'Whosoever—*Whosoever*—shall call upon the name of the Lord shall be saved.'"

"I wonder what my father would say about that," Zee said.

"I've seen him."

Her eyes widened.

"Back in Zenith. I went there with Molly, to meet the family."

"You saw Papa?"

"Yes."

"How . . . is he?"

"Do you want the truth?"

"Will it hurt me?"

"Yes."

"I want the truth."

"He did not look well. He looked broken. When we spoke of you, he wept."

"Oh, Doyle . . ."

"Would you see him?"

"No." She looked at her hands. "I've caused him too much pain. I don't want him to see me like this."

"That is his wish."

"Then tell him . . ." She paused. "Ask him . . . to forgive me."

"Zee, you must—"

"Do not say anything else. Please . . ."

She fell toward him, onto his chest. Doyle wrapped his arms around her, enfolding her like a child, a lost child, scared and looking for home.

Home is not where you think it is, Zee. Not this city. Not the studio lot. Nowhere else but in the One who is looking for you.

Come home, Zee, and He will give you rest.

‖ 25 ‖

Los Angeles Times
November 7, 1921

PRELIMINARY HEARING IN TAYLOR LAYNE MURDER CASE BEGINS TODAY

County Sheriff to Have Extra Deputies on Hand in Anticipation of Large Crowd
by Don Ryan

The sensational murder accusation against Stroud-General Studios film star Taylor Layne moves to the preliminary hearing stage this morning at the criminal courthouse. A large crowd of the curious is expected to turn out, prompting County Sheriff Ray Higgins to order at least half a dozen more deputies to report to the courthouse for duty.

Miss Layne is accused of murdering director Desmond Nichols, who was to direct the upcoming Stroud-General picture *Emma*, in which Miss Layne was to play the title role.

At the hearing, District Attorney Bill Fallon must present enough evidence to convince Judge Matthew Overstreet to bind Miss Layne over for trial. Miss Layne is represented by Harper Vaughn, the noted trial magician who recently represented the late Harold "Happy" Sanders.

Throngs are expected to gather on the courthouse steps as . . .

Zee arrived in Harper Vaughn's auto, her heart pounding at the sight of the people clustered outside the courthouse.

"Courage," Vaughn said as he stopped by the curbing. "We will march in there like we own the place."

But Zee could not act and she knew it. She wore dark glasses and a floppy hat, like a criminal trying to avoid detection. Her legs felt like butter as she emerged from the auto and, holding Harper Vaughn's arm, began to ascend the stone steps of the Los Angeles County Courthouse.

A voice shouted, "There she is!"

Immediately the crowd began to move as one, a giant organism of flailing arms and twittering voices, surrounding her, pressing in.

Zee held Vaughn's arm as if it were a lifeline on the prow of a storm-tossed ship. The horde was a sea churning around her, threatening to swallow her up. Voices shouted at her from all sides.

"Taylor! I love you!"

"Say you didn't do it!"

"Why'd you kill him?"

"Murderess!"

"Sign my book!"

A passel of deputy sheriffs descended into the mass, dispersing the swarm with shouts and shoves.

Zee felt faint. Vaughn called a deputy over to take her other arm. Somehow she made it inside the courtroom, but it too was jammed with reporters and onlookers, vultures here to watch the prosecutor pick at her bones.

What a show, she thought bitterly. What a spectacle.

Taylor Layne had packed them in at last.

‖ 26 ‖

Doyle held Molly's hand as they alighted from the Ford, which puffed wisps of radiator steam into the morning air. The convent at San Fernando lay peaceful and bucolic, unlike the rough dirt roads they took to get here by car.

A brown-skinned nun welcomed them and showed them to an austere room, all brick and wood, functional and utilitarian, where they waited on a bench.

"Suddenly I'm nervous," Molly said. "As if it were the first day of school and I was the new child."

Doyle patted her hand. "I'll beat up any bullies that come your way."

"In a convent?"

He smiled. "Nuns are tough, so they say." He paused, then said, "Do you still want to do this? Take Zee's child as our own?"

Molly thought for a long moment. "I've had questions, certainly. But thinking about what Zee said to you, about her desperation, I see good coming from it."

"Tell me."

"Isabel needs a home, and we are going to have a home, and children. It will be good for her. And then I've thought if Zee gets through this trial, if she is set free, she can be part of Isabel's life. Being able to see her daughter grow up will give her a reason to live. A reason more than her desire to be a famous movie star. In that way, her daughter may lead her out of herself and toward something more important."

Doyle kissed her forehead. "You're an amazing woman, Molly."

She put her head on his shoulder and kept it there until an older nun entered the chamber. Her face reflected a good deal of time in the sun, and her wrinkles the wisdom of age. She smiled warmly as she sat on a stool.

"You have come to see about a child?" she said.

Doyle nodded. "We would like to adopt the little girl called Isabel."

Apparently surprised, the nun said, "May I ask how you know of this child?"

"Someone I trust has visited you and told us all about Isabel. She thought Isabel would be a perfect child for us."

"There is no such thing as a perfect child."

"But if we want her, what must we do?"

"It is not uncommon for young couples, desperate to start a family, to seek an adoption. We counsel them to wait and pray. And naturally we prefer that couples be of our faith."

"We are Christians."

"Protestant?"

Doyle nodded.

The sister leaned toward them conspiratorially. She whispered, "Personally, I don't think it matters to God so much. But don't tell anyone I said so."

"Never," Doyle promised.

"You both are very young. Perhaps this decision is being rushed? Perhaps you should meet the child first, and—"

"We know we want her. Please tell us what we must do."

With a wise and skeptical look, the nun said, "There is another reason for your desire, I sense."

Doyle sighed. "You are quite right, Sister. I'll level with you. This child was not born out of a marriage. I know the mother. She does not want Isabel growing up without a mother and father. This woman is in some trouble, and it would bring her great comfort to know that her child is being looked after by us."

"Comfort is a divine motive." The nun paused a moment. "I am Sister Mary Monica, and I received the child Isabel from her mother. She has visited here, and given gifts to our cause. I am glad that you seek her comfort."

"Then there is a chance?" Doyle asked.

"May I ask how long you have been married?"

Doyle shifted on the hard bench. "We are not married, as yet."

"Not married? But—"

"Oh, we fully intend to be."

Sister Mary shook her head slowly. "I am afraid I cannot hold out any assurances about Isabel, or any child to you. We require that a couple be married at least a year."

"But by that time she may have been taken by another couple."

"That is entirely possible, but as you can see—"

"What if we get married right away, Sister?"

"Still, a year of marriage is required."

Molly practically burst out with, "Sister, would it be too forward of me to ask that you pray about this? That we all pray, and seek God's will?"

The nun smiled and looked at Doyle. "Sensible girl." Then she added, "I will bring your case up with the Mother Superior. And we will all pray for God's will to be done."

‖ 27 ‖

William "Bill" Fallon was dressed in a gray three-piece suit with a black silk tie and pearl stickpin. His voice, Zee thought, would be perfect for a preacher or politician. Unfortunately, he was the district attorney, the chief prosecutor for the County of Los Angeles, and he had her in his sights.

"Your Honor," he said solemnly, "the People of the State of California would like to call Detective Patrick McGinty to the stand."

Judge Matthew Overstreet, a fiftyish jurist with bushy gray hair, nodded. "Detective McGinty, come forward to be sworn."

The detective was a serious-looking man, perhaps forty, dressed in a functional brown suit. His seriousness troubled Zee. Here was the first witness against her. He was real. And a policeman doing his duty. She shuddered anew at the realization that she was on trial for *murder*.

Fallon began his questioning by leaning against the rail of the empty jury box. "You are a detective with the Los Angeles Police Department, is that correct?"

"Yes, sir."

"How long have you been so employed?"

"Since 1916."

"Your father, Mike McGinty, was also a detective, was he not?"

"Yes, sir."

Fallon nodded. "A fine man, knew him well."

"Thank you."

What does this have to do with anything? Zee looked at her attorney. *Why doesn't he object?*

"In your time with the department," Fallon continued, "how many crime scenes have you been the lead detective on?"

"At least a hundred, maybe more."

"So you are an experienced detective, is that correct?"

"I would say so."

"On the night of September twenty-fourth, you received a call from headquarters. Please tell the court about that call."

McGinty turned toward the judge. "At approximately eleven-thirty-five in the evening, I was getting ready to turn in when I got a call that there'd been a killing in Hollywood. At one of those parties we've been reading about. I drove to the scene, the home of John Raneau, and was let in the house."

"Who let you in?"

"John Raneau."

"You recognized him?"

"Of course. Who wouldn't? But I asked him to identify himself anyway, which he did. I then asked him what happened."

"What did he tell you?"

Harper Vaughn stood. "Objection, Your Honor. Hearsay."

"I believe this is all foundational, Mr. Vaughn," said the judge. "The witness may answer."

McGinty continued. "He told me that there'd been a shooting, that someone was dead and that the bodies were upstairs. I asked him if two people were dead, and he said, 'One dead and one passed out.' I asked him if anyone had been in the room, and he said, 'No.'"

"What did you do next?"

"I entered the room."

"Was the door locked?"

"No."

"What did you see?"

"I saw two bodies lying on the floor, a man and a woman. I noticed that the woman was breathing. I determined that she was not injured but had passed out. She had a gun in her hand, a revolver. The man was dead. He had taken a bullet to the chest."

"Was the dead man subsequently identified for you?"

"Yes. Mr. Raneau identified him as Desmond Nichols."

"And the woman?"

McGinty nodded toward Zee. "The defendant, Miss Layne."

"Can you describe the room, Detective?"

"It appeared to be a gun room."

"Please explain."

"Well, the sort of room where a man displays his guns. It had rifles on the wall, a display case with some other types of handguns. That sort of thing."

Fallon strode to his counsel table and picked up a black-handled revolver with a tag dangling from the trigger guard. "I show you,

Detective, what I have marked People's Exhibit One for identification, and ask if you recognize it."

McGinty took the gun from Fallon, examined it, handed it back. "That is the weapon I removed from the room, the one found in Miss Layne's hand."

"Is that your name on the tag?"

"Yes. I tagged it and put it in the evidence lockup at the station. I brought it to your office yesterday and handed it over to you."

"What kind of gun is this?"

"A Colt revolver. Apparently one in a set of two. The other was in a display holder on a table."

"Thank you. No further questions."

The prosecutor returned to his counsel table. Harper Vaughn stood up. Zee watched his every move. He spoke without doubt or hesitation. "Detective McGinty, did you perform a test on the gun identified as People's Exhibit One?"

"I smelled the gun. It had been recently fired."

"Did you determine whether the bullet that killed Desmond Nichols was actually fired from the gun?"

McGinty smiled. "A ballistics test was conducted, and the bullet that killed Nichols definitely came from the revolver found in the defendant's hand."

"Do you have any documents to back that up?"

"I can produce the laboratory report if you like, Mr. Vaughn."

"Can you produce any other reports?"

The district attorney objected. "No other reports are necessary, Your Honor, so long as the one referred to by the witness is shown to be—"

"I am not asking for another ballistics report," Vaughn said. "I am asking the witness if there are any other laboratory reports related to anything else in that room."

After a pause and a nod from the judge, McGinty said, "Didn't need more lab work."

"Then your answer to my question is no?"

"Yes. I mean . . . yes, the answer is no. No other reports."

"Detective McGinty, you are aware of the latest findings in the field of gunshot investigation?"

"I know a thing or two."

"You know, for example, that gunpowder is discharged whenever a gun is fired?"

"Sure."

"And that residue issues from such a gunshot?"

With a slight squirm, McGinty said, "Yes."

Vaughn stopped his amiable tone and fired his next question like a verbal gunshot. "You did not test Miss Layne's hand for gunpowder residue, did you?"

Silence from the witness, then a furrowed brow. "It didn't seem necessary. She had the gun in her hand."

"You did not test her clothing for gunpowder residue either, correct?"

McGinty scowled. "She had the gun in her hand."

"Is your answer no?"

"No . . . I mean, yes. Yes, the answer's no. But I—"

"Then you have no way of knowing if Miss Layne ever fired that gun, do you?"

"I have my common sense."

"Fortunately," Vaughn said, looking at the judge, "that is not a legal category that is recognized in any court."

The gathered press broke into laughter. "No further questions," Vaughn said.

Zee was pleased as Vaughn sat down. But the pleasure lasted only a moment as she heard Fallon say, "Just a follow-up question, Your Honor."

"Proceed."

"Detective McGinty, was a fingerprint test performed on the gun marked People's Exhibit One?"

"Yes."

"And what was the result?"

"The prints on the gun matched the fingerprints of the defendant, which were taken when she was booked."

"Were there any other prints on the handle of the gun?"

"None."

"Nothing further."

Zee slumped in her seat, fighting sudden despair. Was it going to be like this all the time? Up and down? And the uncertainty of it all.

Will I ever know what happened in that room?

‖ 28 ‖

"May I be blunt?" the man named Lytell said.

"If I may speak bluntly as well," R. A. Torrey answered.

"Sure," Lytell said. "I like a plain-speaking man."

"You'll find that is what I am. Now, how may I help you?"

The movie man had made an appointment with Torrey but would not divulge the nature of the meeting. He said it was personal and important. He did offer that he worked for a movie studio in a very important position. Perhaps he was seeking spiritual guidance. Working at a movie studio, he would certainly need it.

Lytell smoothed his hair back with one hand. "Seems you've been coming down pretty hard on the movie business. Especially since one of our actresses, Taylor Layne, has been in the papers."

"That was not my intention, Mr. Lytell. My position on the motion picture business has long been a matter of record."

"You get out to the movies much, Reverend?"

"I don't get out to the movies at all."

"I find that very curious." But he looked as if he had anticipated this answer, and wasn't curious in the least. "Certainly as a holy man you want to know what is going on in the lives of your flock. And a lot of them go to the movies."

"I am not a holy man, just another sinner saved by grace. As for knowing my flock, I know people, I talk to people, I pray with people, I grieve with people. I've been alive a long time and I think I know something about people's lives. And I will tell you something you may not believe but which is absolutely true from my observation. I've never met a man or woman who frequents the theater or movie house who has not suffered harm in their spiritual lives."

"You tell them it's a sin to go to the movies?"

"No, I do not say that. I state what I believe, that indulging in things like card playing and the movies robs Christians of power."

"So you want to ban movies?"

"No, sir. I'm not legislating for the world. If it were in my power to pass a law that there should be no more gambling halls, no more theaters, no more movies, I would not pass it. I would not believe in it. I am simply trying to help Christians live lives pleasing to God."

"I think you're fighting a losing battle there, Reverend."

"The prospect of winning or losing is not how to choose a fight. Tell me, Mr. Lytell, are you a churchgoing man?"

Lytell shrugged. "Can't say that I am, Reverend."

"You have something against churches?"

"Going to church just isn't up my alley."

"Curious. Certainly, as a movie man, you'd like to know what's going on in the lives of people you make movies about. A lot of them go to church."

Lytell stood and put his hat on. "You make me nervous, Reverend."

"Then let me calm your nerves. Come hear me preach on Sunday."

"I'll get back to you on that." Lytell opened the door to the office and stalked out. That was when Torrey saw two young people, a man and woman, sitting in chairs in the reception room. He recognized the young man. "Hello again, Mr. Lawrence. What can I do for you?"

The couple stood and came forward. "We have come, Molly and I, to ask if you would do us the great honor of performing our marriage."

"Why, I would be delighted. Come in, won't you? When shall I calendar a date?"

"Can you do it now?"

"Now?"

The couple nodded eagerly.

"But the marriage license, the proper—"

The Lawrence lad took a paper from his coat pocket and held it up. "License."

"Come in, sit down," Torrey said to the anxious pair. "Marriage is not to be entered into lightly."

"We have been praying and reading Scripture," Lawrence said, "and feel this is right."

"You attend church together?"

"Right here, Dr. Torrey, at the Open Door."

"You are committed to serving the Lord in all things?"

The two nodded.

"You don't feel you are rushing this?"

"We are rushing, just as fast as we can," Lawrence said.

Torrey smiled. "All right. Let us pray together, the three of us. We will seek the Lord's wisdom, as promised in the book of James, the first chapter. If when we finish praying, we are all three in accord, I will perform the ceremony. But if we are not in accord, then we shall wait. Are we agreed on those terms?"

Lawrence looked at his fiancée, who nodded. "Agreed."

"Good," Torrey said. "Let us pray."

‖ 29 ‖

Next Fallon called Trebor Tate to the stand. He did not look at Zee as he walked past through the swinging gate of the bar. But his face was flushed as if he were nervous or excited—or angry.

After he was sworn in, Fallon asked, "Please tell the court where you are employed."

"I am a scenarist under contract to Stroud-General Studios."

"How long have you been so employed?"

"Since 1918."

"You are the writer for the motion picture *Emma*, to be filmed at Stroud-General, is that correct?"

"Yes, it is."

"That is the motion picture Desmond Nichols was to direct?"

"Yes."

"And who was cast in the role of Emma?"

Now Tate scowled at Zee. "Her. The defendant."

Fallon paused, and Zee could hear the scratching of pencils behind her. The reporters were going to be full up with material before this day was through.

"How would you describe the relationship between the defendant and the decedent, Mr. Nichols?"

"Very, very strained."

"Can you tell us why?"

"Objection," Vaughn said. "That calls for speculation by the witness. Have him testify to facts, not opinions."

"Sustained," the judge said.

"Mr. Tate, let's stick with the facts," Fallon said with a slight nod toward Vaughn. "Tell us what you observed that day, focusing only on the behavior of the defendant, Miss Layne."

"She was in a snit that day, let me tell you."

"Objection."

"Sustained." Judge Overstreet looked at Tate. "Facts, not opinions, sir."

"Well, it looked like a snit to me," Tate said, causing laughter in the courtroom.

The judge did not so much as smile. "Simply describe what Miss Layne did or said that caused you to think she was, as you say, in a snit."

Tate said, "She was short with everybody. Didn't smile, didn't say hello. She had her head down about something. But when Desmond Nichols came on the set, she started screaming."

"Screaming at whom?"

"Everybody. Me, the cameraman, the grips, but most of all, Mr. Nichols. It was pretty clear she had something against him."

"What makes you say that?"

"The way they looked at each other. It was like they had some history, you know? The way people seem to know each other?"

"What did she say, if you recall?"

"Oh, she said things like, 'You are not going to get your way on this. You are not going to run over me. Don't think you will.' Things of that nature. I thought she was going to throw something at him at one point."

"What was that?"

"I think it was a chair."

More laughter from the gallery.

"Was it your impression, Mr. Tate, that Miss Layne held a personal grudge against Desmond Nichols?"

"Objection," Vaughn said. "Calls for opinion and speculation."

"I'll allow the answer," the judge said.

Trebor Tate smiled. "Yes, indeed. A grudge. A big one."

"Thank you, Mr. Tate. No further questions."

Vaughn was on his feet in an instant. "Mr. Tate, you've worked at Stroud-General Studios since 1918, correct?"

"That's what I said."

"You've been on many sets in your capacity as scenarist, is that true?"

"Many, yes."

"You've worked with a lot of stars, haven't you?"

"Oh yes."

"You've seen a lot of things happen on sets, correct?"

"Certainly."

"Do you recall working with Louise Townsend on *The Red Queen*?"

"Of course. I wrote it."

"Were you present on the set the day Louise Townsend slapped the director?"

Trebor Tate looked stunned.

"Did you hear the question?" Vaughn said.

"I seem to recall that, yes."

"Seem to? That is not something one would soon forget, is it?"

"Yes, I recall it."

"And were you present on the set of *The High Hills*, also starring Miss Townsend?"

"I wrote that, too."

"At one point, didn't Miss Townsend scream at the director of that picture and refuse to work with him?"

"Yes."

"And was that director replaced?"

"Yes."

"Have you seen other instances of actors or actresses behaving in a loud, angry manner on the set?"

"A few times, sure. It can be a tense business."

"Tense, did you say?"

Tate nodded. "Like testifying in court."

Laughter again. But Vaughn remained unflappable. "Mr. Tate, on those occasions that you observed Louise Townsend in a, shall we say, *snit*, did you observe her murder anyone?"

"Not that I'm aware of."

"In fact, arguments on sets are quite common, aren't they?"

"I wouldn't say they're common, although it does happen. When you have creative people come together to make a motion picture, naturally tempers flare on occasion."

"In fact, you yourself have been known to be in a snit on the set, isn't that true?"

This time the district attorney objected to the phrase *in a snit*. The judge overruled him with a wave of the hand.

"Answer the question," Vaughn said.

"Never to the extent of jeopardizing a motion picture."

"Answer the question."

"What was the question again?"

"Mr. Tate, have you ever lost your temper on a set before?"

"Once or twice."

"Did you ever kill anyone because of it?"

"Of course not."

Some of the reporters snickered.

With that, Harper Vaughn sat down. "No further questions."

‖ 30 ‖

The Arcadia Hotel in Santa Monica was a favorite spot for visitors to Los Angeles, including presidents. A photograph in the lobby showed William Howard Taft in his white suit and straw skimmer standing by a palm tree outside the hotel. Taft obscured most of the tree.

Doyle and Molly paused to look at it. It was late afternoon on their wedding day. Torrey had married them at three. Mrs. Fox was their witness, after arranging their stay at the Arcadia—her wedding present.

"You see?" Doyle said. "We're in good company."

"Very impressive," Molly said.

"I promise you a real honeymoon once the dust settles."

Molly kissed Doyle's cheek. "Anywhere."

"Besides, it was right here in this hotel that one of the most famous cases of Mrs. Fox's career took place."

"Truly?"

"This was back in thirteen. She told me about it. There was a poker game going on at a room here, with a Southern boy named Johnny Creole and a gambler known as the Tennessee Sport, among some others, including a fellow named Pederson. Sometime in the early morning hours two gunshots were fired, and the Tennessee Sport was found dead on the floor. When the police came they arrested Johnny Creole, even though Pederson's fingerprints were on the gun. Apparently Pederson told a pretty good story."

"And Mrs. Fox represented Johnny Creole?"

"Everyone expected her to lose the case. Pederson testified that after Creole shot the Tennessee Sport he pointed the gun at him for a moment, then threw it to the floor. Pederson said he picked it up, and that's how his prints got on it.

"When Mrs. Fox cross-examined him, she asked him why Creole hadn't shot him, too. He said that Creole said the Sport had cheated him, but Pederson hadn't. Then Mrs. Fox asked him why he hadn't been afraid when the gun was being pointed at him, why he hadn't screamed or hit the floor. Pederson shrugged his shoulders and said he just hadn't.

"When it came time to sum up, Mrs. Fox seemed a little distracted in front of the jury. She was very quiet and subdued. But then she slowly went to the evidence table, picked up the murder weapon and proceeded to load it with six bullets she pulled from her pocket. She let out a yell and started brandishing the gun. People in the courtroom screamed. She pointed the gun at the prosecutor, who promptly dove under his table. The judge was even a little nervous and was ducking as he ordered Mrs. Fox to put the gun away.

"Mrs. Fox immediately apologized and said the demonstration was necessary to show how people naturally react when a loaded gun is pointed at them. She argued that Pederson's story didn't hold water. The jury acquitted Johnny Creole."

Molly laughed. "You're not going to be such a showman in court, are you?"

"Why not? Maybe some talent scout from the movie studios will see me, and I'll become a movie star. Would you like to be married to a movie star?"

"Movie stars are stuffy and insufferable."

Doyle felt the joy of the moment drain away.

"You were thinking of Taylor then, weren't you?" Molly said. "I was, too."

"The preliminary hearing began today." He put lightness back in his voice. "Let's not think of it, not tonight." He took her hand and led her to the elevator.

From the balcony of their room on the third floor, Doyle and Molly had a full view of the ocean and the orange fire of sunset. The sea breeze was bracing as Molly pressed close to Doyle. They listened to the waves in silence, and Doyle thought for a moment that all would be well. Everything would fall into place. God would see to it.

An ocean of feeling filled him at that moment. He reached down and lifted Molly into his arms. She put her arms around his neck.

He carried her inside.

‖ 31 ‖

The courtroom was once again filled to capacity. The papers, both the *Times* and the *Examiner*, splashed Zee's picture across their morning editions. Her face and that of Desmond Nichols, framed so they nearly overlapped.

Her curse.

At least this time an arrangement had been made to bring her into the courthouse through a back door. But when she entered the courtroom there was applause, which the bailiff promptly put a stop to.

Just before sitting in a chair she looked into the faces in the gallery. Each one was a unique rebuke. Each face had written on it her professional obituary.

Even the one that smiled at her and took her breath away.

Jess Norton had come to pay a visit to the hearing. He had on his white gloves and walking stick, with his big man, Fleming, sitting next to him.

He winked at her.

Sickened, more with fear than anything else, Zee practically fell into the seat. She felt Norton's look on her. It was actually a relief when Judge Overstreet gaveled the proceeding to order and Bill Fallon called what he said would be his last witness.

"The People call Syrus Stroud."

Voices erupted in the courtroom, buzzing with anticipation. Zee could hardly breathe. What did Sy Stroud have to say in the matter?

Judge Overstreet called for order as Sy Stroud marched in through the courtroom doors. He looked tired, angry, pugnacious as he stormed past Zee to the witness stand. When asked if he would swear to tell the truth, he gave a quick nod and said, "Stroud always tells the truth."

"Mr. Stroud," Fallon said, "you are the head of Stroud-General Studios, is that true?"

"This everybody knows."

"Please try to answer the questions directly," Judge Overstreet said.

Stroud shrugged. "Am I doing anything else?"

Overstreet sighed. "Continue, Mr. Fallon."

"How long have you been the head of Stroud-General, sir?"

"Since I started it with Arnie Goldman, that's how long. And that's 1911 I'm talking here. So you can figure for yourself."

"Mr. Stroud, I will be brief with you this morning, as I know you are a busy man."

Stroud grunted.

"You signed Taylor Layne, whose real name is Zenobia Miller, the defendant, to a contract, did you not?"

"I sign all my stars, and she was one of them."

"And what was the result of that signing?"

"Result? You have to ask? Another Stroud sensation. You've seen *Tallulah*, haven't you?"

"Let Mr. Fallon ask the questions," the judge said.

"Did you subsequently make a decision to place the defendant in the starring role of a picture called *Emma*?"

Stroud's eyes darkened. "Yeah. Another Stroud decision."

"You also sign directors?"

"Everybody. Nobody comes to work at my shop unless Stroud signs 'em. Why? Because I got an instinct. Can you argue with success?"

"You were responsible for signing the victim, Desmond Nichols, to direct a picture, is that correct?"

Stroud nodded. "He came to see me. From New York this fellow is. Got a couple hits. That's somebody you talk to. Instinct."

"Did you make a decision regarding his working on *Emma*?"

"Thought he might be a good choice to direct."

"What did the defendant think of that choice?"

Stroud scowled at Zee. "A fit she threw! In my office."

"Tell the court what happened."

"I'm having a meeting with Mr. Adolph Zukor, and Taylor busts in. Zukor leaves, and an earful I get from her about Nichols. So I get Nichols to come up and I tell them to work it out. I leave my own office so they can talk. But Stroud has a trick up his cuff."

"Please explain."

"I got a box for squawking. I leave it on. Outside I am listening to those two squawk."

A sick feeling passed through Zee.

"You were able, then, to hear the defendant and Desmond Nichols in conversation?"

"It was a slugfest, not a conversation."

"An argument?"

"With threats yet."

"Please tell the court what the defendant said that was threatening."

Harper Vaughn said, "Objection. Hearsay. Also, incompetent, irrelevant, and immaterial."

"Overruled," Judge Overstreet said.

"You may answer," Fallon said.

"She told Nichols that she would make him regret being here, and that he'd better leave town. Said if he didn't, she knew some people who could hurt him."

A ripple of stunned voices murmured across the courtroom. Overstreet pounded his gavel. To Zee it sounded like an executioner's ax striking wood.

"Did she say who those people were?"

Stroud looked out toward the audience, and Zee knew why. Jess Norton's name had indeed come up between her and Nichols. Would Stroud drag him into the case now?

"No," Stroud said quietly. "She just made it plain he better get out. That's all."

"No further questions," Fallon said.

Vaughn stood up. "No questions for this witness," he said.

Zee almost fell off her chair. "What are you *doing*?" she whispered.

"Be quiet," Vaughn said.

"But—"

"Just be quiet until I tell you to talk."

Bill Fallon waited for Sy Stroud to exit the courtroom, which he did with deliberate speed. "At this time, Your Honor, the prosecution rests."

Judge Overstreet nodded. "Mr. Vaughn, you may call your first witness."

"Your Honor," Vaughn said, "may I request an hour recess? Some information has come to my attention that I need to look into."

"One hour," Overstreet said, and gaveled the hearing into recess.

"What is this?" Zee said, anxiously touching Vaughn's arm.

"Be *quiet*," he said, "if you know what's good for you."

Vaughn led Zee out the back way and into his waiting car. He would not tell her where they were going, but it couldn't be far. Court would resume in one hour.

What would it matter anyway? The events of the preliminary hearing were too much to overcome. Zee was certain of that. She would be bound over for trial and then what? What jury was going to acquit her, especially when she had no recollection of what, exactly, happened?

The evidence presented would be enough to send her away to prison for a long time. She'd be past her prime when she got out, her film career dead.

Unless Vaughn had something to offer. But he wasn't saying a word. He drove in silence down Main Street, toward the end of the business district. He pulled into an alley and stopped by a stark metal door.

"In here," he said.

It was a dark, secretive place with no windows. A place of secrets. Vaughn knew exactly where he was going. Into a room with desk and chairs and little else.

"Now will you tell me what's going on?" Zee insisted.

Vaughn lit a cigarette. He did not offer one to Zee. "Patience. In a few moments you will make the most important decision of your life. Be ready."

"Ready for *what*?"

The lawyer said nothing, took a drag on his smoke.

Then the office door opened.

‖ 32 ‖

As Doyle drove the Model T back into town, he was troubled by the unanswered questions that lay in his path. *Their* path. Molly was part of his life now.

"Will you be happy living in a little apartment?" he asked. "It's only for a short time, till I start practicing law on my own."

"So long as we're together, any arrangement will do."

"And with Isabel?"

Molly looked at him. "Yes. God wants us to take her into our home."

"But does the Mother Superior want it?"

"She will."

Doyle turned down First Street and caught a glimpse of the copper-topped clock tower of the courthouse up the hill. Zee must be in there, he thought. And he said a silent prayer for her.

At his apartment, which was now a home, Doyle carried Molly over the threshold. "And I promised you a proper honeymoon. Mrs. Fox has offered us the use of her house at the beach. It's isolated, very romantic. We can start there, and work our way up the coast."

"Sounds romantic *and* nomadic."

Doyle set her down and she looked the place over. "Needs a woman's touch, I see. No time like the present."

As she set about what could be considered the rounds of the one-room apartment, Doyle looked over the mail. But he couldn't stop thinking about Zee. Maybe he should go up to the courthouse to see how things were with her. No, it would be impossible to get in. Half of Los Angeles was probably there already.

Someone knocked on the door. "Mr. Lawrence?" It was the voice of Norman Adler, the apartment super.

Doyle opened the door.

"Telegram came for you," Adler said, handing Doyle the paper. Adler was a nice old man who took good care of his charges. "Where you been?"

"Got married, Mr. Adler."

Adler peered in, then nodded approvingly. "Congratulations! I'm very happy for you, son. A good woman makes a man better, and couples always pay on time." He winked and left them.

Doyle opened the telegram. "It's from the convent," he said as Molly came alongside. "From Sister Mary. She wants us to come see her."

"When?"

"Today."

Molly took his arm. "Is it good news?"

Doyle looked at her. "It doesn't say."

⁂

Jess Norton and Sy Stroud walked in together. It was Norton who spoke first.

"A little rough in there today. How you holding up?"

Zee's throat clenched as she looked back and forth between her lawyer, Stroud, and Norton.

"Scared, that's how she's holding up," Stroud said.

"She should be." Norton slid into a chair. "She's in a deuce of a pickle."

"Do you mind telling me what this is all about?" Zee mustered all the moxie she could.

Harper Vaughn spoke. "There is no way that you can avoid going to trial, not with the evidence presented so far. Of course, you may be acquitted by a jury. Then again, you may not. In either case, a long trial will continue to hurt both you and Stroud-General Studios. It would be in the best interest of all if you could walk out of this courtroom today, a free woman."

"Of course it would," she said. "Are you saying it is possible?"

"It is."

She looked at the other men, searching for a clue. "How?"

"New evidence has come to my attention. If I present this evidence, it is likely that the judge will dismiss the case."

A sense of relief rushed into her. "Then do it!"

There was no immediate response.

"What are you waiting for?" she said.

"Some girl, huh?" Stroud muttered. "You better listen, missy."

"Let me have a moment with her," Norton said. "Taylor and I have an understanding."

Vaughn and Stroud left them alone, the door slamming with ominous finality.

With a lilt in her voice, Zee said, "Jess, whatever is going on?"

"Don't play any more of your girlish games. Just listen."

"But—"

"Don't talk. Sit down."

She lowered herself onto a hard chair.

"You have one chance, and one chance only," Norton said. "Consider carefully what that choice entails. You can be freed from this criminal charge, and emerge not as notorious but as something of a heroine. You will be bigger than ever. A star for the ages."

Zee shook her head and almost spoke, but instead heeded Norton's admonition to remain silent.

"If you do choose to be free, you will sign a new long-term contract with Stroud-General Studios. That's what Stroud wants. You are, after all, an investment. But you will also enter into a contract of a different sort. You will become my wife."

Her heart nearly burst out of her chest. She started to get up, but Norton pushed her back down.

"Don't move. You will belong to me, and I will now manage your future. Having a star for a wife will be good for business. But I don't want you to think that's all it is. Far from it. There continues to be something about you that I can't explain but don't want to end. I want us sealed in matrimony. It's the romantic in me. Do you understand so far?"

She hardly knew where to begin. "But how am I to be set free?"

"Leave that to Harper Vaughn. And me. You see, I am the only one in the world who knows what really happened in Raneau's gun room that night. And that is what is going to make you a free woman. If you agree to the terms I just described."

"You *know* what happened? How?"

"Because I saw it."

Now she wanted to stand but was riveted to the chair. "Why . . . why haven't you come forward?"

"No matter. It is entirely up to you whether I come forward now. If you agree, I testify. If you don't, you go to trial, and ruin."

"Did I do it, Jess? Did I kill him?"

"I'll do my talking in court. You want me to, don't you?"

What *did* she want? To survive, yes. To beat this thing, to go back to being in the movies. But—"How can you expect me to be your wife, knowing you have held this over me?"

Norton smiled. "Because you are one of the great actresses of our time. I have no doubt you will be up to the role."

That was the moment Zee Miller of Zenith, Nebraska, knew her life was not her own—and never would be again.

‖ 33 ‖

At two o'clock Harper Vaughn called Jess Norton to the stand. Even before Norton was up from his chair, Bill Fallon objected. "Your Honor! This man is a bootlegger, a criminal! I strongly object to his being allowed to testify."

"That is a slander," Harper Vaughn said. "Mr. Norton has not been convicted of any crime. If Mr. Fallon has proof of such, let him secure an indictment. Until then Mr. Norton is a competent witness."

Overstreet nodded. "I quite agree. Let the witness be sworn."

Norton took the oath. Harper Vaughn said, "Will you please tell the court about your line of work?"

"Sure." Norton looked at the judge. "I'm in the food and entertainment business, Your Honor."

Bill Fallon snorted loudly. Judge Overstreet's face remained stoic. And Zee just looked at Norton as if he were a bad dream.

Vaughn said, "And are you acquainted with the defendant?"

"Yes, I am. Miss Layne actually started her career in one of my nightclubs."

"On the evening of September twenty-fourth, did you have occasion to be present at a party at the home of actor John Raneau?"

"I was there."

"At that time, did you converse with the defendant?"

"I saw her there, yes. We talked a little."

"Tell us what transpired."

"I thought Miss Layne looked a little tired, so I suggested she take a rest. I walked her to a room in Raneau's house and sat her down. I told her to wait there while I went to get coffee for her."

"Did she resist?"

"Not at all."

"And then what?"

"I came back a little while later, maybe five minutes, and went into the room."

"What did you see?"

"I saw Desmond Nichols with his hands around Miss Layne's throat."

Vaughn paused. Reporters scribbled madly. Zee frantically searched her mind for any memory of that terrible night. Nothing. It was as if she had slept through the entire episode.

"Did it appear to you that Miss Layne was in mortal danger?"

"It was quite obvious."

"What did you do?"

"I was about to intervene when I saw Miss Layne reach behind her and pick something up. Then I heard a shot. Nichols fell back. And Miss Layne fainted. That's when I saw the gun in her hand."

"What did you do?"

"I found a servant and told him to tell Mr. Raneau to come to the room, but to leave my name out of it."

"Why did you not want your name mentioned?"

"For obvious reasons."

"Please explain."

Norton leaned back and looked coolly at the judge. "Your Honor, with men like Bill Fallon accusing me of all manner of things, I did not wish to get involved in matters of law. I didn't think there was any way Miss Layne could be charged with murder. But as I saw what was happening in court and the way the D.A. was twisting things, I couldn't in good conscience allow this proceeding to continue without the truth. That's why I have come forward now. I don't really care what happens to me, but I can't let an innocent woman get convicted."

Harper Vaughn paced to the center of the courtroom. "Is there any doubt or question in your mind, sir, that Miss Layne was in danger of being strangled to death by Desmond Nichols?"

"No doubt whatsoever."

With a theatrical turn, Vaughn returned to his table.

Bill Fallon threw his hands in the air. "I ask the court to disregard this man's testimony. It is tinged with suspicion, every bit of it."

Judge Overstreet scowled at the prosecutor. "Do you have an offer of proof, Mr. Fallon?"

Fallon uttered a reluctant, "No, Your Honor."

"Then I am not inclined to disregard this testimony. You may cross-examine."

Fallon wasted no time. "You were acquainted with the defendant before the shooting, were you not?"

"Yes," Norton said.

"In point of fact, you have a romantic interest in her, don't you?"

Norton shook his head. "Not in the least."

"You are trying to save her because you are in love with her, isn't that true?"

"Mr. Fallon, you are misinformed. My only interest is the truth."

"That would be for the first time in your life, wouldn't it?"

"Objection," Vaughn said.

"Sustained."

Fallon hardly paused for breath. "You saw the defendant shoot Mr. Nichols, correct?"

"In self-defense."

"That's not for you to decide. Answer the question. You saw Miss Layne shoot Mr. Nichols."

"As I've said."

"And your reaction was not to run to anyone's aid, but to run away."

"I had Mr. Raneau summoned."

"Very brave of you." Fallon turned to the judge. "I once again move that this man's testimony be stricken."

"Denied," Judge Overstreet said. "I will allow you to reopen your case to call a witness who can contradict any portion of this man's testimony. Do you have such a witness?"

The D.A. wearily shook his head.

"Mr. Vaughn, do you have any other witnesses?"

"The defense rests," Vaughn said.

"Then I will take this matter under advisement. Be back here in one hour."

‖ 34 ‖

Sister Mary Monica welcomed Doyle and Molly almost before they alighted from the Model T. She showed them into the same room in the convent where they had so recently pleaded for the adoption of Isabel.

"Thank you for coming," she said. "I have news."

Molly squeezed Doyle's hand so hard he almost yelped.

"Mother Superior and I went to prayer for your request," Sister Mary said. "Our reactions were the same."

"Favorable?" Doyle said.

Sister Mary nodded. "It was strong. It has never happened so before. We looked at each other and knew it was the voice of God. You two were in prayer, I know."

"Yes, Sister," Doyle said.

"Who are we to resist?" Sister Mary smiled. "But we are not, how do you say, irresponsible. After hearing from God, I decided to hear from your employer, Mrs. Fox."

"You spoke with her?"

"The telephone is a wonderful tool for our work. We have one, you know! I placed the call. And Mrs. Fox had very good things to say about you. You seem to be a responsible young man, working steadily, with a future in the law."

"I hope so," Doyle said.

"I must ask, are you ready to take on this responsibility now? Do you have the living arrangements for a little girl?"

"A small but adequate apartment."

"Ready for a little one," Molly said.

"More than ready," Doyle said, then blushed at his enthusiasm.

Sister Mary smiled. "Then I think there is just one more thing to do." She stood and went to the heavy door, opened it.

Another nun entered, holding the hand of a girl with blond hair who wore a simple brown dress and wary look.

Doyle could hardly believe it. The girl was the very image of Zee Miller.

"Meet Isabel," Sister Mary said.

∽◎∾

Judge Overstreet entered a courtroom filled with the tense anticipation only an impending verdict or ruling could bring. Zee fought hard not to appear nervous, but her blood was rushing through her head like a raging river.

Mercifully, Judge Overstreet got right to it.

"I have considered the evidence presented by the district attorney in this matter. It is up to me to determine if there is enough to justify a full trial on the charge of murder. I am the sole judge of the credibility of the evidence and the witnesses. I must consider whether the time and effort of a trial is warranted. Facts not in dispute are these: the accused shot the deceased with a handgun. The defendant and the victim knew each other, and there was some apparent tension between them. This alone, however, is not enough to sustain a charge of murder.

"We have the testimony of a witness to the shooting, Mr. Norton. He is the only witness to the incident in question. And he has stated unequivocally that the defendant appeared in mortal danger. The credibility of the witness was called into question by the prosecutor, but without any proof to back it up. Even if I were to throw out Mr. Norton's testimony entirely, that would not leave enough proof of murder to bind over the defendant.

"Therefore, I am dismissing the information filed against Zenobia Miller, also know as Taylor Layne. She is hereby discharged from further proceedings."

Pandemonium erupted in the courtroom as Zee buried her head in her hands and wept.

‖ 35 ‖

In the weeks following the stunning dismissal of murder charges against Taylor Layne, Los Angeles settled into a placid holiday season.

Thanksgiving came, and in the modest apartment of Doyle and Molly Lawrence, giving thanks took on a special significance.

Isabel Lawrence, nearly three years old, was the brightest light in their home. Too bright, sometimes, like the flame her mother had always been. Curious about everything, Isabel could also talk the proverbial blue streak with an amazing vocabulary for one so young. The Sisters had educated her well.

And it was everything Doyle and Molly could do to keep her from climbing around on everything from fire escape stairways to kitchen cabinets.

But the Sisters had taught her well, for she had manners at the dinner table and said "Please" and "Thank you" and "I beg your pardon."

For their Thanksgiving dinner Molly cooked her first turkey, and even if it was a little dry and a little black in places, it was for Doyle the greatest meal in the history of man's culinary pursuits.

It was at this meal that Isabel became a full-fledged member of the Lawrence family by making an announcement.

"I should like to live on the ocean," she said.

Doyle smiled. "Would you really?"

"Yes, sir." With great earnestness Isabel scooped up a spoonful of mashed potatoes and popped it into her mouth.

"Why the ocean?" Molly asked.

Isabel finished her bite before answering. "It is big and there are lots of fish to eat, and we can live on a boat."

"A boat would be rather small, wouldn't it?" Doyle said.

"But I am small."

"You're going to grow up."

Isabel gave great thought to this. "Then we shall get a big boat."

Doyle nodded, delighted with his daughter's problem-solving acuity and her apparent fearlessness about living on the sea. She was so much like Zee in more than just looks.

"Do you like the ocean?" Doyle asked.

"I have never seen it," Isabel said.

"You mean you never went on an outing to the sea?"

"No sir."

"Astounding. We must remedy that immediately! Molly, let's take Isabel to the seaside for a week."

Isabel's eyes widened. "May we?"

"I will see to it," Doyle said. "Mrs. Fox has a house at seaside, which she has offered for our use."

"I like Mrs. Fox," Isabel said.

"Then would you like to go to the ocean?"

"Oh, yes, sir!"

"Then we will," Doyle said. "But you must try to do something for us."

Isabel nodded eagerly.

"I would like it very much if you would call us Papa and Mama. Do you think you can do that?"

Isabel furrowed her brow and took on the question with all the seriousness of a potentate. "Yes. I shall do that. And we shall live on a boat."

Isabel practiced saying "Papa" and "Mama" continually for the rest of the meal and was a champion at it by the end.

After family prayers and putting Isabel to bed, Doyle sat down at the kitchen table with paper and pen.

Dear Zee:

I write to tell you that Isabel is happy with us, and we with her. You need not be worried about that. She is very bright and charming, like you. She has a good head on her shoulders and a desire to live "on the ocean." She has never seen the ocean, so we are planning to take her there. Mrs. Fox has a house on the beach at the crossing of Canyon Boulevard and the coast road. When we are there, I would like you to come for a visit.

I respect your wish that Isabel not know that you are her mother. That does not mean that you could not be like an aunt, a close family friend who will be able to watch her grow up. Would you consider that, Zee? I know that would make you happy. It would make us happy, too.

It seems that your best days are ahead, now that the bad trouble is behind you. You have been given a new start. The mercy of God is at work, and our little family would like to be part of that with you.

Tell us you will come to see us at the beach.

God bless you,

Doyle

Doyle prayed over the letter before folding it, then sealed it in an envelope.

"I'll take it to the postbox," Doyle told Molly.

"As long as you're out, we need eggs and milk for the morning," she said.

"It shall be so." He kissed her and went out into the cool of the evening. He dropped the letter in the box and then headed toward Koteki's Market. It would be a chance to give Koteki one more prompt. Though he'd been warned by Fallon to keep clear of the matter, Doyle wasn't giving up. He could not live comfortably in the same city with a man like Norton walking around free.

He thought of Wong Lun and the others like him who had suffered under Norton. It had to stop.

Thaddeus Koteki was not happy to see him. "You can buy here, but I don't want to hear you talk," he said.

"I just want to ask if you'll reconsider going to the D.A."

"I'm not going anywhere. You are. Out of my store."

The peace Doyle had walked in with was rapidly giving way to the old frustrations. He tried to tell himself to leave it all with God now, but that didn't work. He wanted to be the instrument of God on this one. Why wouldn't anybody join him?

He decided to wash his hands of Koteki and try another market. Let Koteki go down with Norton if that was what he wanted.

Doyle scolded himself as he turned up the street. *Some fine Christian you are turning out to be. Get the chip off your shoulder. . . .*

That was when someone grabbed him from behind and pulled him into an alley.

‖ 36 ‖

Zee looked at the diamond bracelet on her wrist and thought, *Shackles fit for a queen.*

"But, sweetheart, you haven't touched your food." Jess Norton's voice did not include holiday warmth. Rather, it held his characteristic mockery. They were in a private booth at the Imperial, one of the swankiest restaurants in Los Angeles. Away from inquiring eyes.

"I'm sorry," Zee muttered.

"We have so much to be thankful for. Let's see. You are back shooting *Emma* for Stroud, and the publicity is to die for, you'll pardon the expression. Do you realize you are a heroine to all sorts of women out there? And all the more dangerous and alluring to men?"

"I don't really care."

"Of course you do. You have come through the fire, stronger and better than ever. And now you are Mrs. Jess Norton."

Mrs. Jess Norton. The wedding, two days earlier, had been a sterile civil ceremony, presided over by a justice of the peace fifty miles outside the city limits.

I've received a life sentence, after all. Well deserved, Zenobia.

"How about a little champagne to celebrate our first week as man and wife." Norton pulled the bottle out of the ice bucket and prepared to pop the cork.

"Nothing for me."

"I beg your pardon?"

"No champagne." Zee looked him straight in the eye. "No wine, no hooch. Nothing."

"Don't tell me my wife has gone Temperance on me."

"That's what I'm telling you. So I would be glad if you would not speak of it again."

"Come, Taylor, our fun in life is just beginning."

"Not that way. I have consented to be your wife. I will stick to the deal. But I will live the way I choose. I will continue to live in my own house. And I will not join you in your drinking. Ever. Is that understood?"

Norton laughed as he poured himself champagne. "I have a strong-tempered woman, but she drives me wild. I give her a toast."

He raised his glass as if at a wedding.

Or a wake.

❧

Thorn Fleming held Doyle against the brick wall, his massive hands full of Doyle's coat.

"Told you to stay away from Koteki, pard." His breath was stale onions and beer, his face as ugly as ever.

With all the force he could muster, Doyle shot his arms up and out, breaking Fleming's hold. But that allowed Fleming to plow a fist into Doyle's stomach. It felt like it went through his body to the spine.

Doyle fell to his knees, wheezing for air.

"Now, look at you," Fleming said. "If only wife and baby could see you now. You're just like any other bum on the street."

Wife and baby? He knows. . . .

"But wife and baby are gonna be widow and orphan, you get my meaning? This is the last warning."

Sucking air, Doyle didn't move.

"L.A. ain't the place for your family. You got a week to pack and get gone." Fleming grabbed Doyle by the hair and lifted him to his feet. He held Doyle's head still. "You understand, pard?"

"Or you'll do what? Put two slugs in me like you did Handley?"

In the split second that Fleming's eyes blinked with a dullard's confusion, Doyle jammed his knee into Fleming's most vulnerable spot. Beer stink issued from the big man's mouth in a burst. Doyle gave him an uppercut, snapping his head back.

Doyle knew he didn't have much time. Fleming would recover quickly, and was probably packing a gun. He threw an arm around Fleming's neck and pulled him into a headlock.

Fleming stood up straight, then spun around, taking Doyle with him like a tail on a kite. Doyle pulled harder, choking Fleming's air passage. Fleming flailed and backed Doyle into the wall with massive force. Doyle kept his grip, full of a fury that would protect his family at any cost.

Once more Fleming tried to dislodge Doyle against the wall, but his effort was weaker.

The big man stopped flailing and fell to one knee.

Doyle did not relent.

And then it was Doyle holding up the limp body of Thorn Fleming.

Doyle let him drop to the ground. Then he went into Fleming's pockets, finding a billfold, a gun, and a mean-looking blackjack. He put the revolver and blackjack in his own pocket.

He then ran all the way back home, bursting through the door.

Molly squealed. "What on earth?"

"Listen to me. Get Isabel. Get some things together."

"Doyle—"

"We haven't got much time. We're going to Mrs. Fox's house tonight."

‖ 37 ‖

The next day's filming was spectacular, in Zee's humble opinion. She brought passion and frustration and verve to Emma Woodhouse. Maybe it was true what they said about great art—it sprang from great personal tragedy.

If that was the test, she was going to be a monumentally successful actress.

They knocked off at four and Zee went straight home. Longing for a warm bath and a house full of peace and quiet, Zee kicked off her shoes, took the day's mail from the maid and sent her home. Tonight it would be just her and warm milk, a good book and sleep. And no Jess Norton, who thankfully had some "business" to attend to. She was determined to enjoy a night alone.

She arranged the davenport with pillows and a blanket, and settled in. The studio had forwarded a package of fan mail to her. *Tallulah* was still popular, but Zee knew *Emma* would be a movie for the ages.

She put the package aside and turned next to a letter from Doyle. She opened it with eager anticipation. It was his first communication with her since his telegram about Isabel. As she read the letter she was filled with a mix of elation and dread. That Isabel was happy brought tears of joy to her eyes. And Doyle wanted Zee to join them at the beach! The prospect of seeing Isabel with Doyle and Molly—that was what frightened her. Would it be a good thing for Isabel? Would it be selfish of Zee to see her? What would it do to Molly?

Oh, she could think about that later. What mattered was that Isabel was with the two best people she knew in the world, and she would grow up safe and secure.

Zee put her hands behind her head and just lay there for a long time, smiling.

When she went back to the mail she saw a thick brown envelope with a return address in Zenith. The name, however, was unfamiliar to her. A woman named Fredericks.

She quickly opened it, finding a one-page letter and another sealed envelope.

> *Dear Miss Miller:*
> *I am writing with the unhappy news of your father's death.*

Zee sat bolt upright, her body trembling.

> *He died peacefully, with a few members of the church gathered around him. I was there, and found the enclosed letter in his study. The letter was not posted but is addressed to you. I thought you should have it as quickly as possible.*
> *The funeral arrangements are being made, and we hope that you will be able to come. . . .*

Zee couldn't finish the rest. She felt cold and weak, all vibrancy draining out of her. Her hands shook as she held her father's letter. She did not open it at once, fearing what she would find.

Finally she ran her nail along the seam and took out the letter, written in her father's recognizable hand.

> *My dearest Zenobia—*
> *It has taken me some days to gather the courage to write you. I do not want to bring any more grief to you than I have already. I know that I was not a model father, and for that I am truly sorry. I only hope you believe that I did what I thought was best for you. In that I failed, and I ask you to forgive me.*
> *The news of your troubles has come to Zenith, and if I thought I might be of some help to you, I would come to Los Angeles. But I dare not come lest I cause greater turmoil.*
> *I was visited by your old acquaintance, Doyle Lawrence. A fine young man. He is your friend, and should you need someone to confide in he will stand you in good stead.*
> *If you feel you can answer this letter, it would gladden my heart. I long to see you one more time, but I shall not force the issue. No matter what your response, know that I have never ceased praying for you, and shall not so long as I draw breath.*

Zee closed her eyes against her weeping. *Oh, Papa, Papa . . . I want to talk to you! So many things I shouldn't have done, things I should have said to you. You need to know . . .*

But there would be no more words, no more knowing. She wept until her body could produce no more tears. She drifted off into a fitful sleep.

And dreamed of Isabel.

In the dream they were walking hand-in-hand through the back lot of Stroud-General Studios. People kept looking at them and remarking what a lovely little girl Isabel was.

Zee would say, "This is my daughter!" and smile, and the people would all smile back.

Happy Sanders was in the dream, beaming at her and nodding his approval.

Hap!

And then Zee and Isabel walked onto a shooting stage, only inside it was not a set at all. It was Zenith.

Zenith in the summer when a soft wind was a comfort and a band was playing in the park.

Zenith, and her father was there.

Papa.

And Isabel ran into his arms. He lifted her high, his granddaughter, and held her to his chest.

He looked at Zee and said, "You've done well."

Zee dreamed of Isabel and Zenith and her father. She asked God if she could stay.

A violent shaking woke her.

"Get up." Jess Norton looked down on her like a vulture.

"What. . . ?"

"On your feet."

He pulled her off the davenport. Her eyes were sore and her head light. "Jess, what is it?" She saw Fleming looming in the foyer.

"Your boyfriend, Lawrence. Where is he?"

She shook her head, trying to clear it. "I don't know."

He grabbed her arm, hard. Pain shot up to her shoulder. "You're holding out on me. You always hold out on me. It used to amuse me, now it doesn't. I want to know where he is."

Zee yanked her arm away. "I don't know and wouldn't tell you if I did."

He slapped her, knocking her back to the sofa. Her cheek was on fire. He pulled her up again. She was a rag doll in his hands.

"This is business. He knows too much about me, and he's probably yakked about it with you. We need to have a little talk with him, Mr. Fleming and I. Now where will I find him?"

He was going to hit her again. She didn't care. She was not going to utter another word in his presence.

When she didn't answer him he threw her to the floor, her head hitting the tiles with a bone-jarring thud. She felt a trickle of blood issue from her nose.

Norton jerked her up, turned her to face him. "Answer me!"

Zee spit in his face.

He shook his head, put his hands up to wipe the spit off. Zee broke from him and ran for the back door.

"Get her back here!" Norton shouted.

It was a labor to get one foot in front of the other, but Zee pushed herself. She heard the heavy steps of Thorn Fleming pounding after her.

Get to the door! Get out and scream!

But who would hear? Who would respond in time?

She made it to the hardwood of the hallway, slipping as she tried to turn a corner. Her shoulder slammed into the sharp edge where two walls met.

She saw Fleming not ten feet behind. He was incredibly fast for a big man.

If she made it to the back door she'd have to unlock it first. No time. Fleming would be on her in an instant.

Zee turned right into the kitchen.

The first thing within her reach was a breadboard. Without a thought she picked it up. As soon as Fleming appeared in the doorway she threw the board at him with all her strength. It hit Fleming in the chest. He stumbled back.

But only stumbled. And she couldn't keep throwing things at him forever.

The meat cleaver might do it. She grabbed it off the chopping block, readied it.

Fleming bared his teeth. "You don't wanna do that, Miss Layne."

"Get back." She held the cleaver higher.

The big man shook his head. "I don't wanna hurt you more than a little bit, Miss Layne. I might get mad if you give me trouble."

Come closer and I'll give you trouble.

Fleming began to circle around the chopping block that separated them. He kept his eyes fixed on hers, looking ready to move if she tried to cut him like a side of beef. And that was all he was, beef that served its master, Jess Norton.

She took a tentative step backward, examining her dwindling options. She could make a lunge and hope the blade found its mark. Or she could turn and run out the other kitchen entrance and make her stand somewhere else in the house.

Fleming, still watching her, picked up a skillet and held it like a shield.

And smiled.

She knew then she would have to kill him. Whatever it took, that was what she had to do. And what a nice new scandal that would make.

Fleming took another step forward, ready to fend off any blow. "Put it down," he said. "There's a good girl."

She gripped the handle tightly. Her hand was sweating. She drew back, ready to strike. *Go for the legs first.*

Her arms snapped back, almost ripped out of their sockets. Norton! He had her from behind. Fleming shot forward, grabbing her wrist and squeezing it so hard she thought the bones would crack. The cleaver fell from her hand.

"Should've just slipped her some champagne," Fleming muttered. "She's too much trouble."

"Shut up," Norton spat.

Slipped her some champagne?

She was dragged back to the living room and thrown onto the davenport where Fleming held her in his clutches.

Slipped her some champagne . . . Her head was throbbing, but thoughts were becoming clear. "You knocked me out that night," she said.

Norton said nothing, his arms folded across his chest.

"The champagne. You drugged the champagne. I didn't shoot Nichols, did I?"

Norton shook his head.

"You shot him. Your gloves . . . no fingerprints. The gun room.

You had it all planned. You made it look like I did it. All this just to control me?"

"You thought you could walk out on me, remember? You needed to know that I always get what I want in the end." For a split second he looked pleased with himself. Then his face soured again. "You also need to know what happens when people cross me. Let's go."

She tried to move, but Fleming had his bear-trap hands on her arms, and that was where they stayed until he forced her into the back of Norton's car.

‖ 38 ‖

Mrs. Fox's beach house was a quaint Craftsman design, keeping its natural wood color. It had two bedrooms, yet Isabel wanted to sleep with Doyle and Molly. Doyle consented. Isabel seemed to sense something was wrong, and it was only natural that she did not want to sleep alone.

Molly sang until Isabel drifted off to sleep, her breath soft and rhythmic. And for a moment Doyle forgot all about the troubles in the city. He had a wife and child, and was complete.

"Doyle?"

"Hm?"

"Will we stay here?"

"For a couple of days or so, until I figure what to do next. I'll go see Fallon with Mrs. Fox, tell him what's happened. Mrs. Fox won't let Fallon off the hook. They'll have to bring in Norton and Fleming. With a little persuasion, they may get Fleming to talk. If Fallon has any backbone, that is. If he doesn't, I'll go to the papers with the whole story and force Fallon to act."

"When do you think it will end?"

Doyle reached over their daughter and stroked Molly's cheek. "Soon."

When he heard both wife and daughter sleeping, Doyle slipped out of bed. Wrapping a blanket around himself, he stepped outside and stood on the deck, gazing at the ocean. A silver streak of moonlight painted the waters. Doyle recalled the words of Scripture, *"The heavens declare the glory of God; and the firmament sheweth his handiwork."*

He paused, listening to the waves. Listening, he realized in an instant, for something more. The voice of God. But how would he know it if it came?

That was when he began to sense an inner prompt—a still, small uttering, as real as the chill in the air.

‖ 39 ‖

Up through the canyon they went, Thorn Fleming driving, Norton sitting with Zee in the back, watching her. They were going to do it to her up there, at the top, kill her and then throw her body down the gorge. Maybe make it look like an accident. Wasn't that the way they did it in the movies?

She looked out the window and saw the moon. And for the first time since she was a girl she thought heaven might be real.

Oh, Papa, I'm sorry.

Oh, God, help me. I'm sorry, I'm sorry.

A panoply of pictures flashed through her mind, all at once, a kaleidoscope of memory. Sunny days. Zenith. Wading in the river as a child, looking at the sky, wondering what life was like in the big old world.

Doyle in the park. Climbing a tree. Wanting him to kiss her.

At least she hadn't talked. She hadn't told him where Doyle was. If only she could stay alive long enough to warn him, to get him to take Molly and Isabel out of Los Angeles for good.

God help me . . .

"Don't do it, Jess," she said.

"Do what?"

"Kill me."

"You're shaking like a leaf. Or a fly caught in a web."

"I'm not going to beg you."

He shrugged. "My own wife doesn't have to beg me for anything."

Zee's voice shook. "I thought I was clever. I don't think that anymore."

"You'll be cured of cleverness soon enough."

"What are you talking about?"

Norton looked forward. "She wants to know what we're talking about, Thorn. Should we tell her?"

Fleming shrugged his shoulders.

"You're going to see firsthand what happens to people who try to do me wrong," Norton said.

See? See what?

The canyon. Where were they taking her? Toward the ocean . . .

Toward Doyle!

But how could they?

Isabel. Molly.

How could they know?

"Yeah," Norton said, reading her face. "Your boyfriend." He took a piece of paper out of his pocket. She could barely see it by the car's interior lights. "Found this at your house."

He handed it to her. It was Doyle's letter, the one inviting her to the beach house.

No, God, no.

"You can't," Zee said, her voice a thin reed.

"You have to see for yourself. I'm going to make you see it."

Frozen by fear, Zee couldn't move.

Oh, God, Isabel. Doyle. Molly. God! Jesus, I'm sorry. Oh, Jesus, save them.

What could she do?

Norton carried a gun. In his coat pocket. She knew that.

She had to get it.

No time for thinking, for pausing, for anything but stopping Jess Norton. She'd shoot him if she had to. Yes, shoot them both. Nothing else mattered. Protecting Doyle and Molly and Isabel, that was the only thing.

She saw Norton eyeing her with a malignant stare.

‖ 40 ‖

Doyle pulled the blanket tighter around his shoulders. God was telling him to pray for Zee Miller.

She was in trouble. That she had escaped a criminal indictment was not the end of her unrest. Her soul was in jeopardy and under bondage.

Yes, he had to pray.

Just last Sunday Torrey had preached on prayer, and told of praying for years for his brother's conversion. Even when his brother seemed to stray further and further from any hope, Torrey prayed on.

Doyle recalled Torrey's strong, resonant voice as he finished the account.

"After fifteen years of praying, never missing a single day, one morning God said to me as I knelt: I have heard your prayer. You need not pray anymore; your brother is going to be converted.

"Within two weeks he was in my home, shut in with sickness, which made it impossible for him to leave my home for weeks. Then the day he left he accepted Christ.

"Oh, men and women, pray through! Do not just begin to pray and pray a little while and throw up your hands and quit; but pray and pray and pray until God bends the heavens and comes down!"

Doyle prayed aloud for the salvation of Zee Miller.

‖ 41 ‖

The car's head lamps illuminated the dark canyon road. Fleming had slowed his speed, being careful on the turns.

Giving Zee a chance to pick her moment.

But even as she considered going for the gun, Norton pulled the weapon himself. "You look nervous," he said. "Worse, you look desperate. Don't think I won't use this on you."

Her entire world imploded, falling in on itself, covering over all hope. She didn't care what happened to her now.

Isabel. Doyle. Molly.

"Jess, stop the car. Let's talk this through."

"No talk."

"Please—"

"Shut up! I don't want to hear your voice. If you shut up I might go easier on you. See, my dear, I want us to be happy. What you'll see you'll remember for the rest of your days. And since a wife cannot testify against her husband, it will all be our little secret. We can go on just as before."

The car moved on, relentlessly.

Zee's skin crawled over her bones with the tingle of fear and powerlessness. She couldn't let this happen. She could make one desperate play for the gun, but if Norton shot her that would be the end of it.

Yet she couldn't just sit here and let him continue on toward Isabel, Doyle, and Molly.

Oh, God, help me.

Then she knew.

She could do one other thing.

Dear God . . .

She jumped up. Her head hit the ragtop. She saw Norton jerk in surprise.

He raised the gun as she dove over the seat and grabbed the wheel in the hands of Thorn Fleming.

She heard the gunfire and felt something like a hot fist in her back. She kept both hands on the wheel, flopped over onto the front seat, and turned the wheel with all her might.

Thorn Fleming fought back.

The car lurched. Claws of pain gripped Zee's spine. She pulled her legs up under her, pushed off the seat. She drove her shoulder into Thorn Fleming's face.

She heard him groan as his head snapped back. In that quick moment she saw Norton in the dim glow of the interior lights, his eyes wide and vicious and, now, frightened. She knew then he was just like any other man behind the bluster.

With all her available strength and leverage, Zee jerked the wheel hard left. The moment she did, she knew she had her victory.

The car listed, held for a moment, then rolled and rolled, as she was tossed like a stone inside the car. Faster and faster the car went, her body jerking, helpless, her mind whipping back in time, reliving when she'd jumped into a barrel and rumbled down a hill, thrilled, scared, hurting.

Her head smashed against metal and flesh, neck cracking, and she heard an animalistic grunt and the crunch of car against rock, the jarring of all her senses.

Save me, Jesus . . .

Rolling, crashing. Faster, faster, then . . . weightlessness, as if the car were flying, and she knew final impact was a split second away . . .

Isabel . . .

‖ 42 ‖

Doyle held Isabel's hand as they dug their toes in the wet sand. Fog shrouded the beach this morning. The water was cold. But Isabel squealed with delight when the brine swept over her feet and ankles, swirled, then sucked back toward the ocean.

Doyle breathed in deeply. There was something life-giving about the sea, as if it were the pulse of God keeping the world alive. Now Isabel was feeling the beat of God's heart in her feet, in her body shivering and basking in the ebb and flow.

The foamy water *shushed* up again and Isabel laughed. How much she seemed like her mother, open and embracing and full of wonder. Doyle decided he would write a poem that afternoon. He would settle in the chair on the deck and for a moment put away all troubled thoughts. He would remember what it felt like back in Zenith, to try to write something pulled out of the deep mines of the soul. He would write a poem for Isabel.

He heard Molly's voice calling from the house. "Come on, baby," Doyle said, lifting Isabel to him. Her dark blond hair smelled like ocean and kelp. She kissed his cheek. It was the first kiss she had ever given him.

He held her close as he approached the house. The fog had thickened, creating the eerie sensation that the house was the only inhabited place in the world. Then he saw Molly, and a man standing next to her. It was McGinty, the detective who had testified at Zee's trial.

Cold gripped Doyle. It intensified when he saw the look of concern on Molly's face.

"It's about Zee," she said.

Doyle handed Isabel to Molly. "What is it, Detective?"

McGinty said, "You sure you want the girl to hear this?"

Molly nodded and started toward the house with Isabel. "Let's make some hot cocoa, shall we?"

When they were alone, Doyle said, "What is it?"

McGinty looked at the ground. "Miss Layne. She's dead."

"Dead?"

"She was found in a car at the bottom of the canyon, about a mile from here. She was inside with Jess Norton and one of his men."

"Which one?"

"Fleming. Something else you should know." McGinty paused. "She had a bullet in her back."

Doyle's head felt light.

"Looks like Norton shot her. His gun was in the car. It had been fired once."

"But why?"

"In the car box we found an incendiary device."

Doyle tried to form coherent thoughts.

"Here's what I think," McGinty said. "Norton was coming here to finish you off. I think Miss Layne was trying to stop 'em, made a ruckus, got shot, and in the confusion the car went over."

The world grew silent around Doyle. Without another word he began walking toward the ocean. McGinty must have understood, for he didn't call him back. Doyle strode into the fog, to the water's edge, numb.

He knelt in the sand. Ocean waters lapped around his legs, yet he felt no cold, no wet, felt nothing but the insatiable maw of grief swallowing him whole.

‖ 43 ‖

Los Angeles Times
December 3, 1921

Hundreds Turn Out for Taylor Layne Funeral
by Tamar Raines

The funeral of Taylor Layne drew hundreds of onlookers to

the Hollywood Cemetery on Santa Monica Avenue yesterday. Film fans gaped and gawked at the line of cars carrying movie stars and other luminaries onto the grounds. Several policemen tried to keep things orderly. Only one man was arrested when he tried to break into the chapel. He was screaming "I love you, Tallulah!" as the police threw him into the back of a paddy wagon and drove off.

In attendance were some of the brightest lights in the Hollywood firmament. Among the mourners were John Raneau, Louise Townsend, Mabel Normand, Buster Keaton, and Mary Pickford. The eulogy was delivered by Sy Stroud, head of Stroud-General Studios, where Taylor Layne came to stardom.

"When I first laid eyes on Taylor Layne," Mr. Stroud commented, "I knew she was something special. Stroud can pick 'em, they always say. That's just what I did. But now, all too soon, we must say farewell. . . ."

⟋℮⟍

Doyle awoke in darkness. He heard the waves outside, reminding him that he was with his family at Mrs. Fox's beach house. Sleep was not going to return easily; he was now completely awake and alert because of the dream.

Molly slept soundly beside him. He slipped out of bed and made his way through the house and into the bedroom Isabel now occupied. Her soft exhalations were peaceful, comforting. He could stay here all night, breathing in harmony with her.

He went to the front room and gazed out the window. The sky was black, the moon obscured by clouds. He knew the moon was there, even without the light. He knew it as surely as he knew the truth of what the dream had told him.

Doyle shivered in the cool of the room, remembering the cold of the day before, at the cemetery with Molly. A policeman had denied them entrance to the funeral. They were not on the approved list for what turned out to be just another Sy Stroud illusion. It didn't matter in the end. Doyle knew Zee was not there. A fantasy named Taylor Layne was in her place.

Doyle knew where Zee was.

"Doyle?"

Molly came to the window and huddled close to him. "Is anything wrong?"

"No, darling. Nothing wrong. Go back to bed."

"Can't you sleep?"

"I had a dream. A vivid, amazing dream."

"Tell me."

He put his arm around her. "It was Zee. I saw her standing in the most beautiful place. Trees and flowers and sky, but not like we see them. They had color and life and . . . it's more than I can describe. Paradise is what it was. It was all bathed in a light that was also alive. And Zee was there in the middle of it, happy. She didn't say anything, but she looked at me and I knew she was telling me everything was perfect. And then . . . Alvin was there. He was there and he was look-ing at me with that old grin of his, and he was telling me the same thing, that he was perfect and happy. I was filled up with the light, and I thought I might cry out because of the joy. And then I woke up." He took a breath. "I've never had a dream so real, Molly. It seemed more than a dream. Does that sound crazy?"

"No," Molly said. "God has used dreams before, hasn't He? And I've had a peace about Zee. I can't explain it, but there's never been a moment of doubt with me that she is at rest with God."

Doyle pulled Molly into a full embrace, feeling her warmth. He kissed her softly, and she went back to bed. Doyle stayed. He knew he wouldn't be sleeping this night. He settled into a soft wing-back chair, pulled a blanket over himself, and looked out the window. He could hear the ocean undulating in shadow, majestic and mysterious, like God himself. The sea could soothe or rage, nurture life or take it. No man could possibly know every mystery that roiled in the watery uni-verse, just as no man could know God completely.

But a man could know God's mercy for himself, and touch a frac-tion of infinite love, just as he could experience waves crashing against rocks on a coastline in California and know a power that simultane-ously buffeted a million unseen points around the world.

Doyle watched the sky for a long time. His communion with God was as real as the sound of the waters and the spread of the heavens.

Then a portion of cloud opened up. Doyle saw stars, a sparkling surge of them. They stood out brightly against the black of night, and Doyle could not help smiling. He could picture Zee right there, barefoot and dancing, cheering on Alvin Beaker as he poked holes in that divine blanket.

EPILOGUE

HOME

✦

It may be well for those who are prone to lose perspective in the teeming present-day maze, to pause occasionally and take inventory of this marvelous age and nation in which one lives. . . . The American citizen of today is living in a greater nation and civilization than is written of in all history. He has but to use the seed of ambition that lies in every breast, since it is possible for him to reach any position which that ambition might create.

—Shaban Bey, January 11, 1925

|| 1 ||

**From the Desk of
Dr. R. A. Torrey**

August 3, 1925

My Dear Edith—

Your mother and I were delighted to receive your letter, and to hear about your good experience at Wheaton College. It is a great joy to me to have a daughter who is faithfully teaching the Bible to a new generation.

You ask if I miss my teaching duties at BIOLA. I will always look back fondly on my tenure there. But since my retirement from the Church of the Open Door last year, I have been busier than ever teaching the Word of God wherever the Lord leads! Just last month we finished a wonderful evangelistic campaign in Asheville, and saw many souls come to Christ.

I am now sixty-nine years old. The Lord has seen fit to allow me to continue to preach and teach His Word. So far from missing anything, I am filled with anticipation at what the Lord will accomplish in the time I have remaining on Earth.

Write again as soon as you are able. Remember that the time is not far away when the Lord himself shall descend from heaven with a shout, with the voice of the archangel, and with the trump of God; and the dead in Christ shall rise first; then we that are alive and remain shall be caught up together with them in the clouds, to meet the Lord in the air; and so shall we ever be with the Lord.

Affectionately your father,
R. A. Torrey

‖ 2 ‖

Zenith Herald
September 4, 1925

Offices of Lawrence & Lawrence Open on Third Street
Father and Son Join Forces for the Practice of Law

Wallace Edgar Lawrence looked every bit the proud father yesterday as he welcomed his son, Doyle, into his law practice as full partner. Mr. Lawrence the elder will continue to concentrate on land use, estate planning, and corporate matters. The younger Lawrence has not announced a specialty, but judging by his recent cases he seems most interested in the criminal law. His latest victory was the acquittal of Roland Stiles, a vagrant accused of robbery.

It was during the defense of Stiles that Doyle Lawrence exhibited a flair for the dramatic when he brandished a pistol in the courtroom, sending the district attorney scurrying under his table . . .

‖ 3 ‖

Zenith Central Park was beginning to come alive with activity. The band in the shell would soon be striking up the last concert of the summer.

The entire Lawrence clan spread themselves out on three blankets, along with a big basket of chicken, potato salad, and cheesecake in the middle.

Doyle lay on his side, a piece of grass in his mouth, happily watching his family prepare to stuff themselves.

Molly helped his mother prepare the feast, setting out china and silverware and cups for the lemonade. His father sat in a canvas chair, smoking a cigar and humming "Stars and Stripes Forever." Doyle had never seen his father happier, except perhaps on the day Doyle came back to Zenith with Molly and Isabel in tow, to settle down for good.

Rusty, now twenty-three, was off throwing a football with some of his friends. With his shirt sleeves rolled up he looked like Red Grange himself, ready to zigzag through a field of defenders.

And then there was Gertie, a beautiful young woman of nineteen, happily playing aunt to Isabel, now six and a half. The two of them had their shoes off and Isabel squealed with delight as they ran around on the cool grass.

"Look at 'em," Doyle's father remarked. "Makes me almost feel young again."

"You're still young, Dad," Doyle said. "And you've got a lot of law to practice yet."

"*We* do. I have to keep an eye on you, you know."

Doyle laughed and sat up. "What do you think of all this, Dad? Having a whole new family around you, a grandchild."

Mr. Lawrence was contemplative for a long moment. "I won a case in the United States Supreme Court once."

"Yes. *Shirk v. Griggs.*"

"Back in '07. What a marvelous moment for a lawyer. To walk into that chamber, with all the tradition. To stand in awe as the justices come out to take their places. I hardly remember a word I said. But one thing I'll never forget. At the close of my argument, Justice Oliver Wendell Holmes himself looked down at me from behind that big white mustache and said, 'Well done.' I tell you, I about busted all the buttons on my suit. It was the proudest moment of my life. But you know what? It doesn't hold a candle to what I feel right now."

He put out his hand. Doyle took it, exchanging a strong grip.

"I'm happy you're here, son," his father said. "Happy you've come home."

Gertie suddenly appeared in front of them. She was shaking her head and pointing. "Doyle, come."

"What is it?"

"That daughter of yours. She's up a tree!"

Doyle got to his feet and looked where Gertie pointed. Indeed, Isabel was halfway up a tree. Doyle's mind surged with remembrance. It was the same tree Zee Miller had once climbed, years ago when they were together in the park. The tree he'd fallen out of right under her nose.

"What are you going to do?" Gertie asked.

"Nothing."

"Nothing? But what if she falls?"

"She's not going to fall."

Isabel's voice sang down from the tree. "Papa! Mama! Look!"

Molly rushed to Doyle's side. "Do you think she'll be all right?"

Doyle put his arm around his wife. "I know she will."

"Look!" Isabel Lawrence chirped, and reached toward the sky.

AUTHOR'S NOTE

One of the joys of researching this novel was learning more about the life and work of R. A. Torrey. At the time my son was a student at Biola University, in an academic program named for Torrey. But I knew little about him, because little exists. There is one small biography of Torrey in print, Roger Martin's *R. A. Torrey: Apostle of Certainty*. I did manage to find a 1929 profile of Torrey (who died in 1928). This was *Reuben Archer Torrey: The Man, His Message* by Robert Harkness.

I am indebted to the doctoral dissertation of Dr. Kermit Staggers, *Reuben A. Torrey: American Fundamentalist 1856–1928*, for much of the background material on the life and education of Torrey. I also owe great thanks to Wayne D. Weber, Reference Archivist at the Billy Graham Center, Wheaton College, who allowed me access to their archives, which houses a treasure trove of Torrey papers and letters.

My research convinced me that R. A. Torrey is one of American Christianity's great figures. He has been somewhat overshadowed in history by D. L. Moody, Billy Sunday, and Billy Graham. Yet Torrey had evangelistic results that surpassed even Moody's, and his legacy (which continues through Biola University in California) is of inestimable value to the kingdom.

A few comments, therefore, are in order.

Torrey was born on January 28, 1856, into an upper middle-class family in Hoboken, New Jersey. He excelled in his academic studies and was accepted to Yale College at the age of fourteen. The college advised him to wait another year. Torrey eventually became the youngest graduate in the history of Yale.

At Yale, Torrey continued to excel in his studies, receiving a world-class education. As a freshman he studied the Greek classics as well as algebra, geometry, and trigonometry. He was particularly skilled at languages, getting top marks in Greek and Latin.

Torrey desired to become a lawyer. His mother, however, entertained another dream. After Torrey was born she dedicated him to the service of God and never stopped praying that he would become a minister.

His mother's prayers were answered in dramatic fashion.

During his junior year at Yale, Torrey suffered from a severe bout of depression. It got so bad that one night he seriously considered taking his own life. He was very close to finding the means for doing so when he suddenly stopped, dropped to his knees, and called out to God. "In my awful despair," he would say later, "I lifted my heart to God, and I told God that if He would take the burden off my heart, I would preach the gospel, though previously the whole ambition of my life was to be a lawyer."

God removed the burden immediately, and Torrey's life changed forever. After graduating from college he entered Yale Seminary, where for three years he studied Greek, Hebrew, church history, biblical theology, sacred rhetoric, and homiletics, among other courses. He was getting a classic, intellectual seminary education, one that might have seen him entering academia.

But then he encountered Dwight Lyman Moody.

In 1878, Moody, by now a world-famous evangelist, came to New Haven for a revival series. Torrey and some of his Yale classmates decided to check out this curious preacher, who had no formal theological training. But instead of remaining skeptical, Torrey and his friends were captured by Moody's preaching, caught up in the admonition to go out and win people to the Lord. That very night Torrey witnessed to a young lady and won his first convert to Christ.

He worked in the inquiry room at Moody's meetings for the next six weeks. It changed the whole course of his ministry.

Eventually, Moody called on Torrey to help him establish the Bible Institute of Chicago (later renamed Moody Bible Institute). Moody appreciated Torrey's intellectual and pedagogical gifts, and the two became a powerful force in what would later become the Bible Institute movement, a network of over a hundred such institutes that established the fundamentals of the Christian faith in the twentieth century.

After Moody's death in 1899, Torrey began a world evangelism tour that resulted in tens of thousands of conversions. He also continued to preach and teach at Bible conferences in America.

In 1911, Torrey accepted the deanship of the Bible Institute of Los Angeles. This would result in a Bible training program for laypeople that made a huge impact for the kingdom of God. In addition, he became the pastor of a new church, which he named the Church of the Open

Door. He served there from 1915 to 1924.

Torrey had five children, one of whom, Elizabeth, died at nine years of age. Despite his stern appearance, he was by all accounts a warm and fun-loving father. He took time for his children and wrote letters to them throughout his life.

In November of 1917, he wrote to his daughter, Edith. Edith, who would serve as a Bible teacher at Wheaton College from 1924 to 1958, had written her father with concerns about the war and what it would mean for America. Torrey wrote back and said, in part:

> *That times are getting very dark we know, but that the Bible has taught us to expect, and has also taught us that in such times as these instead of being filled with fear or anxiety or worry we should lift up our heads because our redemption draweth nigh. It is true that men's hearts are failing them for fear and for looking after those things that are coming on the earth, but all this simply indicates that the glorious day is coming when the Son of man shall return, and the darker the night the nearer the dawn (Luke 21:26–28), and so instead of growing sad we grow jubilant.*
>
> *The war does not cause me any anxious thought. I have little doubt that a good many people will lose most of their property, and that quite a few will lose friends. As to the property, if we are really Christians, our affections are not set on these things, and if we really mean what we have taught and said we believed through the years it would not disturb us at all if everything was swept away. Our affections and our thoughts are set upon things above (Col. 3:1–4). We are not looking at the things which are seen, but the things which are not seen. As to the loss of friends, if they really are Christians what is there to worry about? They simply depart to be with Christ, which is very far better (Phil. 1:23).*

Torrey, ever the teacher, almost always included Bible citations in his letters. A former student of Torrey's, Dr. William Evans, who was himself a noted preacher, had this to say about the great teacher. It is a perfect summation of the man and his mission:

> "He often reminded me of Saul of Tarsus—cultured in the classics of the Greeks, dominated by the Hebrew passion for religion, and commandeered by the Roman dream of world domination, who laid all these at the feet of his divine Master and humbly became Paul, the bondslave of Jesus Christ."

ACKNOWLEDGMENTS

My heartfelt thanks to Gary and Carol Johnson of Bethany House for their confidence in me, and in this project; and to Dave Horton and Luke Hinrichs, my editors, for their insight and support over the long course of the writing.

As always, my wife, Cindy, was the initial reader of the manuscript and gave me her usual trenchant advice. On my smart days, I took it.

A HEROINE WITH A HEART FOR JUSTICE

Following fast on the beloved SHANNON SAGA, Kit Shannon returns for more dramatic law cases, more romance, and more early 1900's Los Angeles history.

Engaged to a man who may be more than he appears, and faced with some of the toughest cases of her life, Kit now must struggle to preserve her fight for justice against those who would stop her.

THE TRIALS OF KIT SHANNON
by James Scott Bell

A Greater Glory
A Higher Justice
A Certain Truth

❖ BETHANYHOUSE